Art by BluebirdDesign.
Text set in Baskerville

Published by Blue Rune Publications
Copyright © 2020 by Gregory Scherzinger
Artwork Copyright © 2020 by BluebirdArt

ISBN: 9781732468474

First Edition

Available on the web:
Powell's Books, Barnes & Noble, Amazon, et.al.

for the Muses

THE
DECK
OF THE
NUMINON

a fantasy novel by
GJScherzinger

The Dragons Teeth
Cabin
The Stands
Bridash
Granite Mountains
Emerald River
Ceniago
Camelback Mountains
Black Gate
Vale of the Houri
Sultan
Assai desert

Venarrion Forest

an Steppes

Tenigra

ashkara

The Jinals

Chained
Lakes

Deneles

Sabrasco

Maeki

Empire

Madajar
Jungles

nian

◈ i ◈

Soft ambers of flickering light played gently across the taut brown felted covering of the broad escritoire. Three candles, held in the grasp of a torchiere, created a shimmering halo that hovered protectively over the oaken desk, casting the remaining chamber into deep, dark shadow. Seated in a high-backed chair and partially obscured by the close light, a hooded figure maintained an elegant carriage, serenely composed as a small box was contemplated, a casing expertly carved and oiled by the ages. Runes and sigils inlaid along its edges spoke of origins centuries ago, in a language known to few, written with the marks and tailings of the necromancers.

The figure turned the box; hands guiding it in a slow, ritual revolution, fingers gliding over the expertly carved braid that graced its flanks, then across the acorns carved into both long edges, an exhibit viewed with reverence and reflection. Satisfied, or the obeisance accomplished, a well-manicured fingertip slid over one of the acorns, pressuring the opposite within the same moment. A slight click could be heard, damped quickly within the stony dimness of the chamber.

Despite its antiquity, the lid released smoothly, revealing inset hinges of white gold. The box was placed carefully on the escritoire and opened completely. A folded parchment lay tucked within the lid. Once released of its pocket, the crisp paper furled open like an insect's wings, stiffly finding new bounds as it was laid on the baize desktop. A circlet of faded ink expressed its borders, a knot of lifeless scrawls written long ago.

Lined with soft velvet the sanguine color of old wine, the box was divided into two equal parts. One half contained a small leather-bound book; the other, a deck of cards. Both were extracted from their nests and placed on the desk, the box reverently set to one side. A long moment was spent as the solitary figure contemplated the items in the flickering light. At length, the book was opened, its pages as fine and thin as an eremite's psalter, the edges stained with a trace of burgundy and tipped with gold. Framed by a knotted border, only the title graced the front page, scripted by a wide quill with ink the color of cinnabar.

'Numinon'.

A trick of the candlelight caused the dotted *'i'* to flicker like a small flame on the paper. The following page was blank, a thin vellum that lay like a ghost over the first script. With a light touch, it was drawn aside and the opening line uncovered. Written in an ancient form of Jimalian by a practiced hand, the long flourishes above and below the fluid script made the ink appear to move under the trembling amber candlelight.

'If you fear the wolf, leave the wood.'

The page was turned impatiently, snapped across to reveal the next. Centered in the page, a knotted circular pattern similar to the carved edges of the box, curled and shaped under the flickering candles, forming into cursives written in the same ornate style.

'One burning candle reveals all.'

The cowled figure rose and, cupping the flames carefully, puffed two of the candles to extinction before settling back comfortably into the cushions of the chair. As though driven by some capricious gust, the Numinon turned the page of its own volition, revealing a page of simple script without embellishment.

Review the nature of the cards.
All may find a place in the augury as fortunes allow.

The deck was carefully fanned across the parchment. Under the wavering light of the single candle, the old lacquers attained an indelible and brilliant gloss, the colorful inks polished and glowing with a fresh glaze. Minors and Royals of the four suits: Quills, Cups, Roses, and Swords, were revealed in the spread, the more impenetrable mysteries of the Major Arcana appearing to gaze back with questioning intent as the Seer's eyes passed over them.

The Book eased over one page, scripting instructions to return the cards to their stack. The Seer's motion was swift, the cards slid expertly together and turned face down. Another clean page turned in the Book. With the waffling glow from the weak candlelight casting its lumens upon it, a tracing began to emerge from the center, laying across the thin paper like amber smoke.

In the privacy of thought,
state your goal.
Intention is felt in all the Realms.

Your qualities will be known and expectations
unfold from this point.
Begin.

The moment of intent became apparent as the Book flipped its pages again, deep within the volume. A vaporous trail of fresh inks shifted and searched from the knotted border into the empty page, as a pattern was left within the meandering wake. Long box shapes evolved, shifting into four. Small, precise text named the placeholders, four cards marking the *Caer Ri*, the Castles of the Kings.

As the book revealed its instructions, the lifeless inks of the parchment arena began to glow, as though fired from beneath. A braided knot was revealed from the dead inks at its edge, running its eternal course around the perimeter marked by brands at the corners and cardinal points. '*Numinon*' flared to life at the center with fresh, hot ink and tracings began to scatter across the arena, sketching a map with the fire. With burning clarity, the outlines of the Western Kingdoms began to fill in, marking the populations and treasures of the land.

When the locations on the Arena were in place, the knotted patterns in the margins of the Book snaked out, writhing into the fluid Jimalian script.

Choose the mark

The cowled figure briefly studied the page, the Castles *Perilous, Pinnacle, Tower,* and *Destiny* identified by their ancient names. A decision had clearly been made in advance as little time elapsed before the symbol marking '*Pinnacle*' was chosen with a touch of a finger. The back face of the stacked Deck began wavering with feathered delicacy under the candlelight,

Chapter 1

Thin clouds scudded past the full moon, their dark shadows galloping like ghostly messengers across the silver-lit landscape. One vaporous puff, it's dried currents livid in the moonlight, drifted through the lofty granites of the mountains and into the vales of the Upper Stands, a floating curiosity that meandered and wove as though searching the ground for an elusive scent. A gust, driven by a higher wind, laid the simmering cloud low, where it came to wrap itself around a tall spire of rock like a mantle, refusing to dissipate in its passing. The greyed light of the moon remained in its vapours, despite the shadows of night, glowing like snow as it sank among the stone and stubborn trees that clung to the granite monolith among the Dragon's Teeth.

Aptly named, the Teeth were comprised of pinnacles and spires of stubborn rock thrusting up from the rounded meadows and dales of the plateau called the Upper Stands; castoff remnants of the high peaks of the Granite Mountains which towered above them. The fractured spires, gnarled pines clinging to their flanks, girded the Western edges of the range before merging into the tall cliffs that braced the Black Gate far to the South.

The moon-filtered light of the vagrant cloud continued to settle like a suffocating shroud around the rocky spire, curling and gathering at the base as though the hem of a tunic. Vague lightnings shuddered outward as the cloud lay like a heavy weight, forcing the rock to grind into shape, creaking and rumbling with the effort.

Like a beast seeking to free itself from its bonds, the goliath burst from its shimmering cocoon, violently casting aside the cloud and shaking the ground in vast tremors that cracked and shattered across the plateau of the Stands. Violent airs crackled around the shifting avatar of stone as it twisted, its head forming with the rolling thunder of grinding rock, a cavernous stare from its cave-like eyes directed towards the darkening, western horizon.

Tearing free from the screes and bracing shoulders of rock, the colossus shifted its view southward and began a laborious plodding, splintering trees and shaking the ground as it shattered all in its path. Gaping ravines were crushed into the cliffs guarding the upper plateau as the monstrosity gouged its way down to the lower lands. The giant continued its relentless, trembling march in a straight line towards the steep gorge that guarded the Stands, the fortress of the Black Gate. The quilted valley of the Emerald River lay before it, a tapestry sewn thick with farm and field, strewn with hamlets connected with the weaving threads of roads.

The city of Ceniago sprouted like graceful reeds along the banks of the Emerald River, nestled between the canyon of the Black Gate and the fertile plains of the Lower Stands. The Eve of Baltine was nigh and the trading city was festive and full with those celebrating the fertile traditions of Spring. The lords and gentry had long ago arrived from the Citadel of Bridash, bringing their offices and government with them.

The first hint of the destruction that followed came as distant rumbles, which revelers confused with other festivities, far more raucous than their own. As the trembling increased, many of the celebrants sought decks and balconies to see which party could be causing such a violent display.

Confusion and laughter peppered the Spring air, jokes of failed fireworks and military ineptitude accompanied new toasts and another round of drinks. The fractured thuds that had some of the drunker revelers clinging to walls and door frames, began to dampen enthusiasm as they craned to see the bombastic sights that must surely be tied to the trembling approach.

The goliath loomed out of the moonlit night, a magnificent moving wave of stone that refused to crest. The ancient walls of Ceniago had not stood as defense for generations. Only a few policing soldiers loitered along the battlements and if a spear was cast, it was never noted. The old walls proved incidental to the giant. The ground-shaking impact of its huge feet preceded it as the stones of the city wall began grinding. Mortars dissolved to coarse dust as the mortices were crushed, sending sections crumbling to the ground, the heavy blocked stones crushing all beneath.

Stone and timber were rent apart, the guards fleeing for some improbable shelter. Destruction lay in scattered rips and tears as the behemoth crossed the outer city, shops and homes at the mercy of the crumpling impact of the giant's colossal feet or the sweep of its churning stone arms as it cleared its path.

Swaying chandeliers and cracking marble finally shattered the celebrations of the large galas in the city's trade center, laughter and music replaced by the shouts and clamor of disarray. The approach of the stone behemoth through the narrow lanes came unseen by most, an incomprehensible barrage of thunderous explosions and collapsing dins, until the merciless giant loomed overtop, ghostly lit by the waxing moon. Each stride was another devastation, crushing those too frozen in their terror to run.

The richer palaces favored by the Lords and Traders lay close to the water, enjoying expansive views offered by the crested banks of the Emerald River where it approached the neck of the gorge. Many of those who had crowded the parapets and towers to observe the destruction, were fed into the wreckage as their platforms collapsed from the seismic convulsions that accompanied every laborious step of the giant. The tapestried affairs of the nobles turned into a disarray of lost souls looking for escape, yet with no clear notion of where to run. Panic preceded the chaos that marked the passing ruin by the granite leviathan, the monied estates and towers crushed with the same nonchalance as the poorer, eastern walls. State Guards and soldiers ran in hurried packs to stations too late for their help, or within the shades of the next destructive footfall.

Bright conflagrations flashed into existence as braziers were dashed to the ground and warming fires were blown apart in explosions of timber and stone. The giant made no more attempt at destruction than to clear its path, a resolute march that continued to the narrow flats that lay at the open-

direction, capping the spine of the Granite Mountains that nudged against her meadow.

Again, her mind conjured up images of the demon and the conflict that had drawn them together. The dwindling tremors had the same monstrous feel. Something dire had occurred and Cerra cast out a mental plea, hoping he would hear.

'Yutan.'

She had not felt his presence for over a day, though it was not unusual for him to leave for days, even weeks on end. He had a different notion of time and his nature was ever locked to the mysteries of the elements that created him. No answering thought nor shimmering appearance marked his return. The wild turmoil of her sudden waking had diminished along with the subsiding tremors and she steeled herself to clean the mess up by the door. Her cup. The other crash had been a comfrey jar. She pictured the steps she would have to take and those she would have to avoid, as she felt her way back inside.

Cerra's first stop was the kitchen table to snatch up her sticks, long round dowels of etched metal fashioned like eating pikes, crafted by the Oskaran smithy, Luskin. She made a fist of her red hair and jammed them in, securing the curly thick mop that was forever fighting for its own way. She had just dug her brushwhisk from the closet when she heard the wobble of the leather flap that covered one of the kitchen window panes. Quick, light thuds marked the descent of her cat to the floor and the light pad of his feet was evidence of his approach.

"There you are, Kamir." Cerra felt him bump as he pushed his head against her ankle. He offered an irritated yowl in reply.

"That ruckus out there … it wasn't you was it?" Kamir pushed against her ankle again with a low mewl that ended in an inquiring tone.

"No. I *don't* know … and I have no idea of the time, either; I'm not as awake as you. Now, mind yourself, I've got to clean up."

The presence of her cat was a calming influence. In ironic absurdity, the only thing darker than her vision was the sleek, coal black fur of Kamir, yet she had no problem painting the picture of a miniature panther in her mind. "Dark as the devil's ink," had been one description of him after he had appeared as a wee kitten at her doorstep years ago. It was her guess he had jumped from a potter's wagon while they had camped at the lake. He quickly became her constant companion and more than once Cerra had relied upon him to guide her. She didn't need his help at the moment and gently pushed him aside as she knelt to sweep up the shards of her cup, dropping them into a bin. She felt the floor for dampness and was glad that it had been empty.

Picking up her brushwhisk and bin, she negotiated her way to the spot by the pantry where her comfrey jar had fallen. She had lived in this cabin by the small lakes for over a decade and every inch of it was as familiar to her as her own skin. She let her hands run lightly over the shelves to make sure no other pots or containers were poised to fall and deftly pushed a couple back into their correct rows. She was glad that it had only been one of the comfrey jars to fall, for it was easily made fresh. The Agrimoni paste would have been another story; those flowers were difficult to find.

quarter, came to stand with Katarin.

"Bersan. Go back to your farmers and gather them for their arms. Don't muddy the waters." Pryan didn't like Derst. For a member of the aristocracy, the older man had a disturbing affinity for the plain folk, one he couldn't understand. Plain folk were not the elite for a reason and were best regarded as interchangeable parts to be used at the behest of those monied and fit to rule. It irked him that the man dressed as plain as the folk he espoused.

"Everyone needs to 'take a stand'."

Bersan ignored the self-satisfied smirk that Pryan flashed to punctuate what he saw as his clever stamp on the issue. "I believe the Gate can be well defended without the mobilization of more troops, especially since we don't know that Abbysin was behind the attack. It could have been ..."

"Who?! Could have been who?!" Pryan blustered as though he alone had arrived at the only conclusion and was waiting for the rest of the assembly to catch up. "The 'what it was' doesn't matter ... idiots! You just have to think to come to the right opinion."

"I'll leave you to your brilliant conclusion," Bersan continued amicably. "I merely came to get Katarin's opinion on our military organization. I'm glad to have gathered yours as well."

"I've heard her opinion. Women don't really have a head for these matters, so you're welcome to it." Pryan responded while looking at neither, searching instead for someone more likely to share his view on the matter. He found a mark and raised his voice to be heard over the slurry of heated conversations filling the reception hall.

"Hey there, Rudani, I've come up with a rallying cry." Pryan gave off an excited wave before leaning back to the Duke, as though sharing a confidence. "Rudani has more to invest than words. Westre, you'd do well to do the same."

"I have good command of my purse as you should know," returned Lord Sevekin with a snarl, further evidence of his brooding temper. "However, I am curious what he intends. He had property damages too."

Bersan was ready to object, for many people had been sorely damaged by the events as well, but it was apparent Pryan had found willing support from Sevekin and they strode off without further acknowledgment. Katarin gave Bersan's elbow a grateful squeeze.

"Thank you, Bersan. I believe that man could wear me out just by walking in the room and I'm fatigued already. It worries me too, that his bluster is shared by a good many. Even Westre, though he is admittedly an easy lead."

"No matter the issue, there will be those who would rather gather in empty words to fill their heads, than solid advice that requires thought. When they look for a mouthpiece, they find the biggest mouth. *Heh* ... Pryan is no more than a cushion that bears the mark of the last person to use it." Bersan chuckled. "Primare Histon called all together, yet he's not claimed the floor. And may not, if I'm any judge, until the parties have exhausted their arguments in tidy groups. We'll no doubt hear Denalo's rallying cry again. He's likely already had someone commissioned to make it into a banner for his manor. 'Banner for the manor.' Remember where you heard that first." Bersan did a subdued and passable mimic of the pompous lord with a wink of his eye.

"He seems to have a knack for self-promotion," responded Katarin with a dry laugh. "Ignore him for the moment and have one of these breadbites. The meeting, should Histon decide, is best served if your appetite isn't distracted."

"I've been talking mostly with Ser Holder." Bersan took one of the small appetizers and plopped it in his mouth. "Delicious. I wish I had more appetite ... oh yes, about Ser Holder ... as the Commander of the Standish forces, his voice is the one I'm most interested in. Here, I see his Captain of the Gate at his side ... leave the trays to the servants for a moment ... I'm curious to hear his thoughts."

Durst motioned to a liveried servant to gather in the polished brass tray and Katarin snatched up a glass of wine on a near sideboard to join Bersan, who diplomatically steered her to Wellim Holder, the Standish Commander. As the armies of the Stands were militia, there were few Regulars, those men that made military matters their occupation. Holder had been the Commander for the last three Councils, a span of eighteen years, during which only one threat had been raised. The relatively recent spectre of the Gates still preyed upon the minds of many, inexplicable forces that threatened the pastoral confines of the isolated Stands. Rather than being the center of a lot of questioning by the Lords in attendance, Holder remained apart in tight conversation with three subordinate officers who executed a short, formal bow to Katarin as they approached.

"Lady Moors, Ser Derst. Have you come to offer your military advice? We've heard naught else from the rest of the

Lords. The Primare is waiting for a consensus from the room, though I would like to share my opinions first." Dressed in his field uniform, a fitted grey tunic with leather embellishments and rank, Holder cut a bold figure.

"Exactly. And I for one would like to hear your strategy before it is shaken apart by those warriors who fight their battles from their stuffed chairs." Bersan had the demeanor of an over-taxed tutor, with more knowledge than patience for the pupil. "Lady Moors is particularly interested as Ceniago is obviously the most directly affected from any assault."

"As we already have been." Katarin gave a slight nod of acknowledgment to the Commander, a courtesy of his rank; though shorter, she carried the weight of her responsibilities with obvious grace. "Your expertise is essential…. and so, I am more than curious to understand your intentions, before we hear the solutions of many."

Holder sketched another short bow, a nod that appreciated Katarin's inquiry. "Lady Moors. There are always those championing war, aren't there? … especially those that have never held a sword in battle. I intend to advocate a more diplomatic approach."

"Diplomacy doesn't suit the mood of these Councils at the moment."

The commander rolled his eyes to the side with a snort. "It is easy to shoot arrows into the air. I prefer a solid target."

"What matter of diplomacy?" Bersan tapped his chin as though puzzling out a difficult problem.

"The best that I know of," replied Holder. "A mission to advertise one directive while accomplishing another."

"You mean a spy in the midst?" Katarin sounded amused, taking a sip of her wine. "Ambassadors are always suspect, are they not?"

"Of course. For your ears only, I've already sent an agent to Abbysin to negotiate a meeting as a Council with them is inevitable. I have it on Captain Ferriman's recommendation that he knows someone who may not arouse suspicions, some-one not known in the diplomatic circles." Holder motioned to one of the officers, a handsome man with chiseled features and a well-groomed shag of coarse dark hair that was steeling to grey. "This will not be part of any official presentation I will give today though. I prefer to play my cards close until I know who my enemy is, rather than just the cut of his sword."

"Of course, Ser Holder." Bersan leaned in close, "Whom do you have in mind."

Captain Ferriman offered the information at a terse nod from the Commander. "A remarkable woman, one who sees and hears better than most."

"I see….," Katarin was glad to hear that subtlety was more on the Commander's mind than the rattling of swords. "Then I suggest you employ her swiftly, as the hawks in the room will be screaming for chickens the more they see fit to rouse public opinion against fowl. The destruction of The Gate and rav-agement of Ceniago has given them a lot of fuel."

Chapter 4

Haviana whisked quietly down the marbled hall, the only sound the faint rustle of her white linen tunic. She gathered it close about her and quickened her pace, an effortless trot that was near silent in her slippered feet. Haviana's look was as exotic as befitted her name. Her mother was a Pernian native and her father ... her father remained unclear about his origins, even to her, though his exceptional height and auburn hair spoke of other worlds. She had inherited a wild mix of both parents. Rather than her mother's straight raven locks, her hair was the color of raw cinnamon. She wore it layered close, accenting the nut-brown skin that showed her mother's native heritage, save that it was dotted with tiny freckled spots that definitely marked her a child of her father. Her body, not overly tall, was slender with graceful limbs and her hazel eyes gave her the look of a young fledgling hawk.

The summons by the Sybelline Mother was troubling and as Haviana neared the chambers she tried to analyze whatever transgression had caused it. She had already attained the knotted cincture of the Ranifore by exceeding the entry exam requirements, bypassing the slim ranks of the novices, though she would not see her scapular for months yet, nor the Tertiary veil for another year.

She was too new to the Sybelline enclave to be of any

notice, even so. She was not given to antics and whispers as were the other young students. Instead she found her refuge in scrolls and books, for even the driest was an adventure of words and ideas. Although books and lessons constantly absorbed her attention, she missed nothing about her, observing even the most minute details in her curiosity. Which made the summons to the abbess' quarters at the hour of the Nones even more of a surprise, delivered in a sealed missive not an hour ago by one of the Sisters. The messenger, a scribe by the ranking colors on her scapular, neither introduced herself nor commented, merely departed without as much as a raised eyebrow.

Surely an infraction would be the only reason for such a call? Despite wracking her brain for mistakes, Haviana still had nothing to consider by the time she reached the apartments and offices of the Sybelline Abbess.

She was surprised to see the same Sister that had delivered the note. However, this time instead of silence, Haviana was greeted warmly as though a Sybelline of rank and status and shown directly into the abbess' inner apartments, a study off her sleeping chambers and overlooking the river. The open airs made the young girl relax a little, the skies a constant that drew her.

The Mother Abbess looked up with a warm smile that further set Haviana at ease. No one prepared to deliver reprimands would be so disarming. She waited until the attending Sister left the chambers before speaking, giving Haviana a moment to quickly scan the room. Rather than the neat and orderly apartments she anticipated, the Abbess' offices were

strewn with oddities, most accompanied by notes and references. One item, a silvered ball about the size of a grapefruit,
seemed the object of greatest interest, judging by the calipers
and measuring devices nearby. The orb had a mesmerizing
quality and she found herself studying it, intensely.

"It's quite handy at discovering direction … and distance.
A remarkable tool when one has many horizons to travel." The
Abbess' voice broke her concentration. " … please, sit down."

Haviana caught the gesture and quickly moved to sit in the
chair next the Abbess' desk, a little embarrassed that she had
been caught in her inspections. The Abbess showed no sign of
annoyance, instead seemed quite amiable as she shuffled a few
papers and turned them upside down to one side.

"If you were anywhere else besides within the walls of the
Sybelline enclave, I'd have you call me Susinna, for I am not
one for ceremony. I know your mother … and father … very
well. I would not be sitting here were it not for them. You should
know it is not for what I owe them that they hold my respect,
but for the people they have proven themselves to be. They are
fearless souls … *heh heh* … and I enjoy them even more for their
sharper wits."

Susinna looked carefully at the young woman, gauging her
reactions as she spoke. The calm and accepting posture told
her that Haviana was entirely comfortable with her upbring-
ing. She did not expect an answer and continued. "You show
every sign of being their offspring … undeniably smart and
eager to learn." Susinna's smile drooped, a measure of sadness
crossing her face. "Therefore, it pains me to send you away."

Haviana's stomach seemed to drop deeply, leaving her

feeling void, her skin momentarily an empty shell. "I've done nothing wr …" She barely had a plea formed on her lips when the abbess continued.

"Oh. Well, I didn't say that quite right, did I? I meant that I have an errand for you, Haviana. I'm afraid it will interrupt your schooling."

"An errand." There was no questioning in her voice as Haviana felt her senses tingle, a sudden burst of relief and attention spiked by immediate curiosity.

"Maybe you should think of it more as a 'mission'." Susinna countered. "It will involve some discretion. And tact."

"I've never been known for tact. Aren't there other Sisters more qualified than I?" Haviana knew it was a bold question. She would not be here by happenstance. The Mother Abbess gave no clue that she had heard the question.

"They call you Havi, do they not?"

"Yes."

"You've adopted the Gyrfalcon. A most marvelous bird. It's attention to detail and ferocity suits you well." Susinna looked out towards her balcony mulling over her next words. "So unlike your parents … yet we are all our own people, are we not?"

"Yes."

The Abbess turned back to face Haviana. "You asked if I had more qualified Sisters to, *er,* send … on this errand."

"Mission."

"*heh.* Mission. I'm glad you're taking this seriously from the start." Susinna gave the young woman another appraisal. Young or not, she had a strong disposition, further advanced in her training and abilities than her years. She had her parents to thank. "Yes, there are more qualified candidates. I have very strong misgivings about sending you at all, yet to do nothing is worse. The fact is, I can't send anyone … important."

"You want someone who won't attract attention." Havi stated, following the Abbess' trail of logic.

"In a manner of speaking, yes. And, for reasons I'll explain, one not in position to directly affect the proceedings." The young girl was intent, her sharp hazel eyes already absorbing information. "Some years ago, there was a purge within the order … your mother may have mentioned it?" A glance was enough to see that the young girl was well-versed in her mother's history. "As it happened, a number of Sisters went missing, many dead, sadly. But for the grace of the fates, your mother could have been one of them. Some artifacts also turned up missing during that unfortunate time. Without divulging the entire list, I will speak of one …" The Abbess drew a card from underneath the small stack of old parchments and turned it face up on the desk. " … the Deck of the Numinon."

Haviana remained silent, waiting for the Abbess to continue and noting details of the exposed card with a glance, the lacquered figure an ancient goddess by her reckoning.

"This is one of the cards … *Azinnan* … the *High Priestess.* The Deck … a story in itself … was commissioned long ago by one of my predecessors. A fortune telling deck by its nature … but also a creator of fortunes. It was devised by a mage who lived for a time deep within the mountains of the far Jimals. By all accounts, he was quite a powerful one and the Abbess had a long affair with this vizier in the course of her Office.

The Sybellines are known for the power of their Oracles. It is part of who we are, no? The spirit that dwells in the deck is the result of their collaboration."

She passed the card over to Haviana, who took it carefully, as though handling a relic. The novitiate turned the card over, the old lacquered paint appearing to glitter with life and power when the light chanced to glance over it a certain way. The figure of the High Priestess was seated on a lotus flower as a throne. Bees decorated the hems of her robes and on her head lay a crown of crescent moons. Havi's eyes sharpened with a raptor's intensity, examining both sides as Susinna continued.

"The High Priestess represented the Abbess who had the deck formed, though by lot, the onus belongs to her heirs as well. It is considered the most powerful card in the deck, which is saying a lot. She had the good sense to remove this card and hold it separately, so it could not be used against her." Susinna retrieved the card and studied the face of it for a moment while she spoke, as if addressing the High Priestess of the Deck.

"*One* of the cards. There are seventy-six more and many of them quite dangerous in the wrong hands. Of course, in malignant hands, even a minor character can become a deadly one." She turned her attention back to the young novitiate. "Make no mistake. It is a live thing … that deck … as are all things conceived by majics, dark majics most of all. For decades the cards have been kept hidden … and apparently forgotten … until recently. Each Card tells a story and embodies a trait … every symbol drawn has a meaning. Because I am tied by my Office to *Azinnan*, it is my fate to be linked to its voice and it is telling me some activity has enlivened the Deck … and with dire consequences. I want you to locate it."

Haviana's mind raced. This was more than an errand, more than a trip to the market or extra studies. The mantle of implicit trust fell over her, a heavier weight than she expected. She could easily defer, citing her youth and uncertainties. She enjoyed the classes and schooling, even some of the novices that shared quarters with her. She had a multitude of questions clamoring for attention, though one jumped to the forefront as she replied with only a moment's hesitation.

"Where should I begin?"

Susinna allowed a reluctant smile to cross her features. "*Heh* … it's difficult for me to tell where you get your impetuousness from. Either parent would qualify. Note well, everything I say is in utmost confidence." A quick glance indicated the young girl would hold her secrets, her hazel eyes sharp and bright with purpose. "Use of the cards draws players from among us. You should know that from now on, as far as the deck is concerned, you have drawn a card, though I can't tell you what it is. I simply don't know. As the cards are cast, yours will come up at some point. It will be a minor card in any event and not one likely to be a threat to the user." Susinna lifted the High Priestess card again with a bemused look on her face. "You begin to see the nature of my dilemma. It is an irony that, as my card is removed from the deck, I am prevented from acting directly. And so … you are my messenger."

The Abbess set down the card and turned the top sheet of paper, a thick vellum yellowed with age. Four women were sketched out, each as different as the seasons, a unique defining mark denoting their House.

"These are drawings I found within our archives of the original notes that were made, ones the vizier likely followed in creating the Deck. These are the Queens of the four suits … Quills, Cups, Roses, Swords … rulers of their suits as only Queens allow. There are no Kings as a gambler's deck would have, but instead are represented by the Castles of the Kings, the Caer-Ri, which are the embodiment of the People that live within. The creator of the deck recognized that the populace can wield great power. The other Royal cards are Princesses, Princes and Knights, strong and powerful, yet no match for the power the Queen can place on events. I am not a gambler by nature, but I would place my bets on one of those being the mark, the likely avatar for who controls the deck … I don't know which. Any less of an agent would surely be destroyed by the power of the Deck and I fear the consequences in any event."

Susinna tapped the upper left of the four drawings. " *'Nuith'* … the *Queen of the Quills*. *Nuith* is one of the eternal ones and considered the strongest of the four. She is certain to be involved. Her avatar is either very powerful or simply well-chosen. It is my belief that if you can locate the woman involved, the Deck will not be far away."

"I'll start at once."

Susinna was glad to see that despite her words, there was no young girl eagerness in Haviana's demeanor, just an earnest anticipation of what must be done to prepare obviously running through her mind.

"Good, for that is my intention. It is well you can take flight, as few of our Sisters can. As a messenger, speed can be of essence ... a little of the reason you settled in my mind for the effort. I think you inherited your father's luck too. I may be counting on that a little bit too. Do you know your geography? *Ummm* ... some travel is involved."

Haviana nodded.

"Then study a route that will take you to the far West," Susinna finally noticed a blink of surprise from the young girl. "... yes, there is quite a distance to consider ... through the Jimals to the Abbysin. Perhaps even to the Stands themselves. I daresay you'll be gone for a while. For the record, I'll have it known that you're fostering with the Amindar Prioress. Should either Xavier or Yaxkin ... your parents ... ask, I'll let them know the facts. They have my complete confidence as few others have."

Haviana felt a thrilling surge. Traveling such a distance meant the lofty airs and currents, a freedom not allowed since she had been knotted with the Ranifore's belt. It would take days. She could feel herself soaring already.

"How will I know ... her ... the Queen?"

Susinna smiled at the young woman's obvious enthusiasm and appreciated the control she exhibited as well. "You have become a card in play. While not an important one, it is inevitable that your paths will cross. In any event, the Queen will not be someone of a common nature, sure to be treated with great deference. It will be a test of your ability as a Seeress, a Sybelline, to determine your mark."

Chapter 5

Cerra woke when he moved, an effortless shift away from her to a space in the hall. She shifted her head with a pleasant stretch, giving her a moment to allow the glow of him to center in the darkness of her vision. She could feel the heat from his body on the bedding, a delicious warmth she wanted to absorb on her bare skin. It felt nearly as delectable as his attentions during the night.

"A rider approaches." Yutan spoke in his customary soft monotone. His low voice was a soothing balm, a fitting counter to her bright tones.

"How far? *Hah* ... knowing you, whoever it is just left Ceniago. Oh, and good morning." Yawning and smiling, Cerra pushed herself to sit against the headboard, brushing hair and sleep from her waking face.

"The Wagon Turns." Yutan continued to stand, staring outward. The spot he referred to was about an hour's ride away towards Scott's Mill, a longer route used by traders and merchants, which bypassed the shorter and rockier horse path. From there, anyone traveling north would pass by Cerra's cottage.

"Then I have still have time for breakfast." Cerra stretched languidly as she continued to revel in Yutan's heat and was reluctant to get up. "You often warn me when they leave the

Mill and I have half a day to wonder who it is. And ... like as not ... it's no visitor for me."

"You have time for breakfast," Yutan agreed. He never wasted words, which pleased Cerra as she had plenty to waste. " ... and kafi."

"Good. You know what's important." In spite of his laconic nature, little stresses emerged as humor and Cerra was quick to recognize their dry roots. "As you're already up, you can start the pot."

"As you wish."

Cerra watched the glow of his form leave her vision when he turned into the kitchen. Kafi would be ready in moments. Yutan would compress a pebble to heat within his fist and drop it in the water. Even as she thought of his process, she heard the quick burst of steam. She flipped the covers back, accompanied by the disgruntled mewl of Kamir.

"Oh, there you are. I thought you were outside already."

She left the black cat to find his way out of the linens as she reached for her robe, hung on its customary hook by the bedstead. There wasn't a sound from Kamir, so he must be curling his way back to sleep. Yutan's image came back into view as she padded into the kitchen. She buried herself within the glow of his arms.

"*mmm*. I should be tired-er... *mmph* ... more tired than I am."

Yutan turned within her embrace and draped his arm over her shoulder to keep her close.

"Then, there is no need for the kafi."

"Hush you." Cerra murmured as she burrowed in tighter,

punching lightly into his chest. "Those are fighting words. You've taken on armies; but never a redheaded girl with a kafi craving."

"I have been warned."

"Yes, you have. You should know, people that don't drink kafi are likely to die before their noon meal. It's medicine, I'm only playing it safe."

Yutan gave her a final soft nuzzle then turned her toward the nook table. "I'll watch the path."

"I'll watch my kafi." Cerra sat with satisfied relief and heard a cup set down with a positioning slide in front of her.

Though it had been a few years since he had been freed of his curse, Yutan still remained wary of the human culture he was once again part of. As much as the townsfolk of Aleston knew, Cerra still lived her solitary existence in the cabin a half days ride away; though a few of her women friends had remarked on her renewed vitality. To explain Yutan, the demon, was more than she could account for and so his existence remained a secret, an arrangement that suited them both. She watched him leave, enjoying the argent essence of him within her blindness for as long as possible. He would not go far. He favored the impassiveness of the earth and the fluidity of water so he would often stand as a cairn of stone, unnoticed by the trail, or simply dissolve in one of the small nearby lakes. As the years had passed, she came to feel the nature of his transformations by their sounds and the smell of the air. There was no mistaking the crunches and rumbling which announced his shift into the hard granites that were rife among the Dragon's Teeth of the Upper Stands.

Cerra sipped on her kafi, pausing awhile to revel in the heated glow of the morning sun as it lay against the window panes. Like her warm bed, it was apparent there wouldn't be enough time to enjoy the luxury of the moment. Rather than cook a rich breakfast, she decided on a quick assembly of goat cheese, cut basil, with a soft egg laid over a toasted slice of soured dough bread. The bread had a hard crust that she enjoyed most, gifted to her by Annee, the weaver, when she had ridden to town two days past. She could never get the trick of making loaves like those Annee was able to produce.

She had just placed her dish into the sink, vowing to wash it with the lunchware, when the thoughts of Yutan gave her pause.

'This one approaches. The cabin path near the lake. One of the warriors.'

Cerra knew he had little regard for those who bear arms and viewed them all with distrust. The rider was on the trail to her cabin. She would have a visitor after all. She was still in her robe and she snorted to herself as she considered having Yutan stall him. *'That wouldn't do at all'.*

She felt in her closet for a light cotton tunic, for it would be warm today, with an apron to drape over the top. Tamara, who made her clothes, was careful to use a variety of colors that would blend well and accent Cerra's wild red hair, no matter their application. She had no care for the color of her garments, it was the texture of the fabric that was of paramount importance to her sensitive fingers. By the weave she recognized the apron with a nicely beaded fringe, a slight bit dressier than she would normally wear but it wasn't that often she had visitors. She had just tossed them on over her head and belted everything with one of Annee's knit straps, when Yutan interrupted her musings again, his voice intoning within her consciousness. At times she felt wrapped in the very nature of his being, his connection to the elements so strong.

'Ware the gate.'

'I'm fine, you lovely thing. I have you to watch over me. I never fear.'

Her thought burst with smiles as she gathered the mass of her red hair and stuffed her long metal pins into the roll. The thin, scribed rods were one of her most treasured possessions. Her life had once depended on that simple variant of eating sticks and, since then, she appreciated that they had not let her hair down either. She reached for another cup and poured some kafi into it. A tray sat on the left shelf at thigh level and she slid it up to the counter, grateful she still had a few fairly fresh biscuits left. If the visitor turned out to be disagreeable, she could just eat the treats herself. Cerra added butter and jam to the tray before touching her way down the short hall to the front door. The soft pad of Kamir's paws was heard pacing behind her and she was greeted by the clops of the horse and clink of harness as soon as she opened the door.

The rider pulled up when he saw the red-haired woman step out onto the porch. She was much like he remembered her, part of his past, time and people measured more in tours of duty than years. Whisking from beyond her feet like a magical extension of her shadow, a black cat trotted out and poised itself at the head of the stairs, intent on the visitor as though passing judgement.

This was a simple woman on the face of it, though he had seen the scope of her power. He watched her carefully set down a tray and felt a small shiver pass through him. It was a placid scene yet conveyed an arena poised for danger, as though marksmen were sighting him in ambush from the sharp rise of mountains that loomed at the base of the small lakes. Even the cairn of boulders that guarded the trail seemed to have eyes on him. It may be a spurious thought, yet he felt on his guard. Even with all his years, he knew little of women, even less of the blind and nothing of the worlds that controlled the wild majics of sorcery. At the moment, the cottage, nestling in meadows between two small lakes, seemed a very satisfying alternative to the barracks and scattered family life of a soldier.

Despite the wild, untamed nature of her red hair, the short woman added a certain peace to the scene, dressed in a plain wheat-colored shift with a maroon scapular over the top, which sparkled with amber beads at the fringe. The simple garb was tied with an olive sash that accented the pleasant roundness of her figure. He could see her looking out in his direction. He remembered their past meeting. Blind or not, she seemed to miss nothing. Artis Ferriman rocked himself smoothly from the saddle.

"Good woman. I've come to seek your assistance."

Cerra heard the man speak and thought of Yutan's cautioning. She barely knew anyone who soldiered at all, save one. Although previously they had only exchanged a few words, this voice had the same stoic resonance.

"Captain! What a pleasant surprise," she called out. "Please join me on the porch. It is a long ride from … well, a long ride from anywhere, so rest yourself."

Ferriman started a little, not expecting to be recognized at all. He had another misgiving about her hidden arts; however, the brightness of her welcome left him feeling much as he had long ago, willing to forego his qualms.

"Once again, you surprise me. You know who I am."

"I have trouble with faces…. but I rarely forget a good voice."

Her response made him smile. He tried his best to match her self-deprecating humor as he flipped the reins over a bar mullioned between two posts near the gate.

"Those who remember my face best are likely those who would sooner forget it."

"All save your family, I'm sure. They must be missing you now." Cerra could hear the steady walk of the captain's approach. She also sensed Yutan's concern and put it aside.

'We should find out why he is here, don't you think?' She set herself down in the chair, still shaded by the gabled cover of the porch. "Please, have a seat."

The sound of his footsteps crunched to a stop short of the three steps he would take to gain the porch.

"You are the one they call Cerra … of the Meadows."

"Indeed."

"I am Artis Ferriman. Captain of the Gate."

"Ar-tis Ferri-man." Cerra repeated the name as though savoring a new taste. "I'm glad at last to know your name."

"You left before our introductions were complete."

"I suppose I did." Cerra smiled. Given the wild nature of her exit, she might have rather enjoyed conversation with him instead. She was certain to have caused a great deal of bewilderment. "It's time we caught up, then. I don't have many guests ... other than a neighbor or two. I'm glad I have some biscuits to share. And kafi."

Once again, the captain was taken by the engaging enthusiasm of the blind woman. She gazed at him with warm brown eyes that appeared directed at his heart, instead of the normal darting attention eyes pass on.

"The kafi is a gift to be sure." Artis stepped onto the porch and shed himself of his riding cloak, dropping it on the railing before settling himself into the wooden chair. A small comfort after a long ride.

"You're right to reserve judgement on the biscuits, though this time they've turned out rather well, I think. I can scorch things if I'm not careful."

"I imagine you take a great deal of care with everything," Artis observed. "By the looks of them, the biscuits didn't suffer. I didn't come here to ... "

"Of course, not ... but the morning is much too pleasant to take to business first." Cerra took a bite and continued as she smacked her lips clear. "I think I'll find your company far more interesting. I know nothing of you save you guard the gates to our home. You must have a remarkable story."

Artis chuckled softly. He had tales aplenty and not all of them savory, nor worth telling. There were more than a few that he'd soon forget. "It's one I've grown into. I imagine your story might be more remarkable. The incident at the Gates ..."

"*tut tut* ... you're too close to business, I think. In a moment

… tell me … how did you come to be a soldier? You weren't born one and I doubt you rose to be Captain by dint of a wealthy family. I hear the voice of some experience." Cerra took a sip of her kafi, smiling out in the direction of the lake, her eyes sparkling. Artis couldn't help but wonder what she saw.

Cerra had the glow of Yutan within her sight, standing like a beacon in the night. Unbidden, a satisfying connection extended between them. The demon was listening too. There was intrigue in the air and Cerra was eager to get to the reason for the Captain's visit, though everything she felt was based on what she could piece together in her mind's eye. The man's view of his own history would help her paint the picture.

"We in the Stands have not been one for war. Not many soldiers … and you are right, I did not come from a wealthy family." Artis thought of the small croft he grew up on with six others to compete for their mother's attention. The home he was so eager to leave. "I signed on as a trainee in an Abbysin mercenary company. I had a notion to travel."

"I must say, I found that notion odd at one time." Cerra thought of how, before her long journey, even a trip to nearby Aleston was a taxing adventure. "You surely have seen some marvelous sights."

"Other than the camps and barracks … those I gladly keep to myself … yes there are some incredible sights to see, though I must admit, there is little better country than the Stands in which we live."

"Tell me of one place … I love a good story … and then I'll be most eager to entertain your business."

"One place." Ferriman had seen much over the years, easily digested and distilled into his memory. Yet, there was a place that still haunted him for its ancient beauty, a jungle kingdom which lay on the edge of uncharted lands and myths. "Maybe the most remarkable is the land furthest from here … Rejana. I was a mercenary for many years … for the Traders. I was sent there as the posting for my first command. It was new territory for the Trader's as well, so my office seemed to carry more weight. Imagine, if you will, a grand city overrun with jungle, so ancient the buildings have become one with the trees. It was hot there. *Heh* … it would rain daily in the afternoon, for about an hour or so … the same time every day, as if ordered. Rejana was memorable for both its antiquity and the distance away from home."

Ferriman didn't want to delve into the difficulties he faced doing the bidding of the Traders who immediately began subjugating the local population. He was quick to relinquish his command to another lieutenant eager to advance his career when the opportunity arose. He sought to bury his restlessness in more active arenas and surviving the various conflicts bore its own burdens. Successful in battle, with the innate ability to lead, he drew more alarming assignments and commands, while his taste for the Traders and their subjugating wars first left him cynical, then bitter.

Ultimately, he discharged his position in the high ranks of their Guardsmen with short notice. He had come to know nothing except arms and with it, the conflicts of others. If he was to continue to be all he knew, a soldier, then he'd only continue to fight for his native soil.

"It took a long time to work my way back. But my homeland is where I belong. As strange as the sights I've seen throughout the world, there have been none stranger … or more curious … than those I've experienced here in the Stands." Ferriman smeared a little jam on a piece of biscuit and took a bite. "These biscuits are just fine, so you know."

"And you're curious about me. It's been awhile."

"You must admit, you left me much to be curious about. The tales surrounding the Gates haven't lost any embellishments in the years since."

"I suppose not. We've heard the tales, even up here." Cerra's crooked smile left Ferriman convinced that the woman was fully aware of what transformations had taken place at the Gate. What would she think if she could view the monument that had replaced the one of the Ancient King. It certainly seemed to embody her welcoming nature. He let the matter rest for the moment, not sure how much he truly wanted to know. Her black cat hopped onto his lap as if ready to inspect him. Ferriman couldn't help but stroke down its sleek back.

"Your cat … he also seems to be intent on discovering more about me."

"Ahh, Kamir. If he's found your lap, it's a good sign. He can be very standoffish with strangers."

"Kamir? An odd name."

Cerra giggled, as though having to admit some questionable antic of her youth. "I confess I gave the naming little thought. He was a kitten and when I said *'come here, come here'.*" She patted her thigh in memory. "Well, he trotted right over, so I decided that was that. I spell it 'K.a.m.i.r' … more princely don't you think?. He really is a most remarkable cat."

"He has found himself immortalized as well. Perhaps rightfully so." Ferriman pressed. "Personally, I see the transformation at the Gate as a good one. Many said the old King looked far too stern. I found you … not long afterwards. What good is a command of soldiers if they cannot work as scouts? In all of the Stands, there was likely only one blind woman with hair as remarkable as yours."

"The woman who gives me a combing in town says the very thing." Cerra snorted, welcoming the diversion. She gave her tangle a brush back. "She also shears the sheep."

Ferriman waited a moment before replying, watching her smiling face. She was clearly at ease and enjoying herself. "You are in skillful hands then. In any event, I am grateful, whatever powers were employed at the Gate, for the restoration. Your mark has been left in the world."

Cerra tried to hide her smile behind her cup and took a sip of kafi. At the time, much to her astonishment, the rumors and tales that reached her ears told of the immense monolithic carving at the Gates as having been restored as a woman, with unbound hair and a cat at her feet. She had chided Yutan severely, objections that fell on deaf ears. It still amused him.

'See? The repercussions yet remain.' She knew she would not get a response. She took another tack to deflect the Captain from the subject, hoping to know more about his quest. "You speak of the city of Rejana … the Black Gate … sights I shall not see, except through the eyes of others."

"Your opinions may be less clouded because of it," Artis observed, dryly. The jade eyes of the black cat intent on his features spurred the next question. "What is it then, that you see? What creates your 'vision' of the world?'"

Cerra settled back in her chair with a rueful smile, taking another sip as she pondered his question. As if on cue, Kamir jumped back to her lap. She had heard him hop from the Captain's chair and was anticipating that he would curl up on her before long.

"Everything counts, dear Captain."

"Please, call me Artis."

"If you insist, Artis, though if the occasion arises, your ... are they called squads? ... if that occurs, then I should most certainly address you by your title." Cerra paused to let out a little laugh. "I am sincerely glad to be far from the world of armies. My only war is with the buttercups in one corner of the strawberry patch. I fight back mostly by imagining their flowers to be a gruesome brown, though everyone tells me they are the most brilliant yellow, as their name implies. But that is not my inspiration as you can guess. I have not always been blind. I was seven ..."

Remembering the world of sight had long since been a refuge of distress to Cerra. Now it was an invaluable resource, the fanciful palette from which she drew the pictures in her mind. The senses that remained to her had become far more acute. Smells and temperatures, textures and tastes, all lent their colors to the mixture as she painted the scenes that evolved before her. Since her experiences with Yutan, her senses had sharpened even more. Witnessing the black severity of the Void had enlivened her perceptions even more, as though in retaliation. She stroked Kamir and sipped at her kafi while she tried to make sense of the fanciful scenes that she could create, to visualize the world in such a way that the Captain could appreciate. It was a question that had not been asked of her and she found some contentment in her explanations. She felt her world insular and childlike, a place only she could see. The rest of the world she could only sense, strange events or sounds could raise the most extravagant images.

"So, you see, Artis, what my eyes can't see, my mind creates. It is a malleable structure, to be sure, though I manage some very good accuracies in my mind's paintings. I am able to fare well in the small little corner of the world that I know. I cannot afford to be lax, rest assured. Tell me. You are here alone and not accompanied by an aide as befits your rank. Your sword must be secured with your horse, for I cannot imagine you would be without it. I hear no creak of leather or plate to indicate you are wearing the accoutrements of an officer. Instead I smell wool and cotton … your shirt must be fresh this morning, for it still has the scent of drying on a line. You likely stayed at Maree Nels' hostel in Scott's Mill, I should think … *heh* … and had her breakfast as well, or you'd be here earlier. She's a lovely woman. As I put it all together, I'd say you're here on some official business, yet not willing to have that known. At last I'm done rambling." Cerra added with a mischievous smile. "Now you can divulge your mission."

Artis well-remembered her accuracies at their last meeting. Once again, she had measured him precisely and it reminded him why she was vital to his mission. She lived in a world he would never understand and a domain like hers, was now threatening his.

"I wish some of my scouts were as observant. The woman, *er*, Miss Nels, indeed keeps a fine hostel. You also keenly surmised the nature of my business. I do not wish to draw attention, maybe because I am not sure of the wisdom of what I do. Usually I am more decisive but there has been a threat to the Stands that I do not understand. Powers were unleashed not long ago that I had witnessed but twice before … the second time was in your presence. I hope you can help me understand."

Cerra thought of the cataclysms that had roused her weeks before, the shuddering earth and the warnings of Yutan. News arriving since that night from Ceniago had an echoing familiarity to it. The Gates had once again fallen to wild majics. Except this time, the demon, Yutan, was not involved.

"Oh yes. A terrible night. I remember. As it happened, the tremors began not far from here." A sudden look of concern washed over her face. "Understand, I had no part in whatever that was."

Artis turned to look at her. "Of course not." He wanted to give her the honest appraisal his face would show, then realized again that dealing with her would be very different than others within his command. He turned back to the view of the lake and mountains that the woman seemed to enjoy so much. "If I thought that, I would be here in a much more official capacity. That is not my intent."

"Then a favor, I imagine. If I refuse, there is no recording your failure. If you succeed, you have a significant prize."

"A tool, more accurately." Artis knew she was leading him to his request and rather enjoyed her intuitions. "A prize is for victory and I won't feel anything close to 'victorious', until this riddle is solved. A tool, however, is something to be valued for its usefulness and kept ready, even if there is no job to do."

Cerra thought of her gardening trowels that she fought to keep clean and free from grit and smiled with her observation. "Some tools work quite well even when they're tired and a bit rusty."

"And less likely to be coveted or stolen." Artis turned to look at her, knowing she could sense his attention. "A tool that someone might overlook. An agent."

"Ho!" Cerra nearly spilt her kafi and Kamir sat up in her lap, alert at the sudden disturbance. "An agent?! I can barely manage outside my own house. An agent for disaster, I should think." she concluded with a chuckle, not entirely sure she wanted to encourage the Captain's notion.

She stalled with the thought, stroking Kamir's back, who returned to his curled nap, content. Cerra felt emanations from Yutan. Of course, he had been listening. She sensed the same element of surprise and curiosity. *'I know. It is the resemblance to your own being that makes me wonder.'* She let the thought travel to Yutan and turned her head slightly to the Captain.

"But I hear you're serious and no one rides this far to tell a joke, not even the potterman, though he tells a good one."

"The only mystery more obscure than you is the one facing me now. You command powers …"

"Please, Captain. I command nothing. I am what you see, a woman and nothing more." Cerra shook her head with a rueful smile as if accepting some inner reprimand. There was an uncertainty surrounding the moment, as if her life was about to change. "There are many times that I'm not sure if I've lost a horse or found a rope. I know you want to hear more than that and I'm at a loss to explain. I will admit some connection to the elements; but they are their own and not to be bidden by me nor the affairs of men. To ask more of what I know or feel would confound the both of us. Truly, I have no power."

Ferriman munched thoughtfully on another bite of biscuit. He doubted he'd get any more of an admission than that. Power circulated in the small vale that held the woman's cottage, yet she remained pleasantly unaffected and charming. "May the link, if that is as it is, serve you well, serve us all well. I have had another opportunity to observe you and you reinforce my first impression. If you'll forgive me, madam …"

"Oh, please, call me Cerra."

"If you like. Maybe it's a habit of command, familiarity has no place in the courts or the battlefield."

"I have to point out that I'm not under your command, nor in the courts. Yet. So, I'm hardly worth a grand title." Cerra had no illusions about her place in upper society and it showed in the purse of her lips. She brightened immediately as a new idea presented itself. "Besides, those without titles are seldom given as much attention. Anyway, if there is some difficulty, familiarity may make the difference and 'Cerra' may be the only name allowed in time."

"Cerra, then." Artis smiled. "You possess two of the most demanding traits of a good agent: discretion … and competence. I don't have to add you are a good listener."

"That I do … well." Cerra gazed out to the spot where Yutan stood, statue-like. "I'm listening now while you speak, to the airs around me. The waterfalls seem muted and the heat of the sun comes and goes. Clouds are backing up against the mountains. They won't bring rain, there isn't enough moisture in the air, though enough to frizz out my hair another breath or two. What I hear most of all is my home. I am reluctant to leave it."

'I would leave here to know.'

Yutan's thought didn't surprise Cerra and her immediate response was agreement and understanding. Even so, a tension gripped her stomach. Change. She could feel its subtle hand prodding her. She knew what the Captain's response would be. The long pause, accompanied with a sip of his coffee, had an air of necessity captured within it.

"It is your home that I wish to protect." Artis followed her gaze to the lake where the monolith of stone guarded the path. He reflected for a moment on the extraordinary sorcery employed against the ravaged gate, before continuing, "I am fighting the unknown. You are the only 'unknown' that I feel is on my side. I don't know what to do with you as an agent, or even where to place you. But I must put you in the field … somewhere … or I'll find out nothing."

'A dangerous place to be.'

Cerra echoed the demon's words aloud. Ferriman gave no answer, absorbing the serene nature of the meadow while allowing the blind woman to stir her notions into some sort of decision. Behind her thoughtful pose, Cerra was overrun with the demon's thoughts, finding herself encouraging his intent curiosity.

'This is the work of the vizier. My creator.' Yutan was torn, a link

to his past exposed like a raw nerve. *'A part of me, no matter how the sorcery appears. The earth shuddered with the agony of the device. I must discover the source ... the taste of it still lingers.'*

Cerra felt her heart both sink and quicken at her decision. There was no truly safe place. She had learned much about herself enduring the trials surrounding Yutan's release. She inhaled, breathing in the memory of that daring venture.

'You have become my life. You asked for my help before,' she reminded Yutan gently. *'Now it appears I have two looking for assistance ... three if you count the land.'*

'There is nothing without the earth.' Yutan's reply was fierce. *'No harm will befall you.'*

'Not even a demon can make that claim.' There was both humor and surety mixed within her thought and she felt agreement between them. *'I do not want to leave my comforts but the fates have guided this man here. These are dire events and I hesitate to ignore them. I think to do nothing would haunt me. We must try ... together.'*

Ferriman's mind had wandered back to the mysteries confronting him, revisiting the alternatives that had wormed through his head since he had decided on this uncertain course of action. He knew he had nothing other than what chance assistance the mysterious blind woman could offer. The placid lake and meadow created a sylvan atmosphere of ease and contentment that many would be loathe to leave behind, as safe and comfortable as the cat curled on the blind woman's lap. Caught up in his doubts, her answer came sooner than he expected.

"My dear Captain ... Artis. I'll be your agent. But you must do this for me ..." Cerra turned and reached out, placing her hand upon his arm with remarkable accuracy. "… Take a room again with Maree Nels. She'll enjoy your company … and you, hers. Give me three days and I shall be at her door."

The red-haired woman had the most complicit smile, as though there were no anxieties involved with the decision. Her bright face, as she sat with her kafi and biscuits and dozing cat nestled in her lap, lightened his spirit somewhat, yet Ferriman knew better. He had seen the same bravado from many a soldier who believed he had taken on one mission too many but was game, nonetheless. Ferriman covered her hand, which turned with subtlety to give his a squeeze, a gesture that conveyed remarkable reassurance.

"Three days."

PERILOUS

CAER RI ZE

© Bluebird 2020

◈ ii ◈

One burning candle damped all but the arena of parchment in darkness. Within the stone chamber, a figure sat bent in concentration, intent on the portents that lay measured in its glowing marks. The contemplation was measured by the slow accumulation of dripping wax from the candle, a bright, liquid drool, quickly cooling opaque as another dribble lay atop.

A card, the castle identified as *'Perilous'*, one of the four *Caer Ri*, lay upon the arena, its position drawn in a map by simmering brown inks that marked the parchment like the singe of a hot brand. The wax in the lone candle could patiently accumulate until the remainder pooled and choked what was left of the wick, leaving the flame to gutter and die. The Book of the Numinon exacted the same amount of patience, for when the candle was extinguished, so too the reading. One of its pages lay open, bathed in the soft, fluttering, amber light, a simple inquiry emblazoned on the vellum.

'Are you sure?'

Two circles wavered below the script, their glistening centers lined with obscure marks representing the choice to be made. The motion, when it came, was tentative and unsure, yet in the final stroke of the fingertip, a decision was made: Castle *Perilous* was marked.

The crisp, translucent pages of the Book fanned over with thin snicks as it settled to another page. The Elementals again came into view, intricate outlines depicting the faces of the *Enûma Eleiš*. Their names were captured in the inked frames; the fires of *Ddraig och*, the airs of *Simargh* and the waters of *Marid*, were represented in fresh brown inks. The image of *Gigant Cawr*, the Stone Giant was scarcely detectable, the pattern of its design worn and old, spent of life.

As before, the book required a choice to be made, the invitation delivered by glistening, fresh inks that reflected the wavering glow of the candle, alive with majics. The decision was long in coming, the candle inching down along its accumulation of wax. The Numinon lay patient for the moment that finally came, the gryphon-like *Simargh* chosen by the touch of a fingertip.

The Book shuffled its pages in the instant, a few leaves flicking over to reveal the full image of the Elemental Wraith of the Air.

Without the benefit of a shuffle, the top card was drawn from the deck and turned onto the parchment arena where its placement was obvious, positioned within the arcane circle where its mark on the map sizzled with fresh ink, laying crossways over Castle *Perilous*.

Simargh was exposed with all of its richly lacquered colors, a Gryphon split in its depiction. The edge touching the top of the circle showed the beast gathered in white smoke while the inverse counterpart was wreathed in dark smoky tendrils. The wavering candlelight reflected heavily on the wings as though giving the phantasm motion on the stiff face of the card.

Given the sideways position of the card, the cowled figure returned attention again to the Numinon, which had illuminated the page describing the elemental creature.

Simargh represents the unpredictable in life.
An unexpected change which will be favourable,
may not seem that way at first.
With the element of Air,
change is about to happen and soon.

Hunching over the old Jimalian script, cribbed in a fine hand below the etched image, the Seer's fingertip traced the wording further, moving slowly, mindful of the translations, as the text described traits and expectations, until they lingered on one spot, as though reading the entry twice.

'When negative, there will be a current of events that
are not in your favour, a downward spin in the airs
changing fortunes significantly, seemingly for the worst.
Circumstances arising outside of control, renders the
unwary helpless and powerless. A run of difficult
circumstances may also be a result of poor decisions.... '

Neither up nor down, the answer revealed nothing and the Book was shut with a brief show of pique. It responded by spreading itself open again with a flurry of rifling paper until it lay on an empty page, words forming of their own accord.

"Draw your Avatar".

The top card was drawn and the *Queen of Roses* was laid within the mark that came to life, fanned by a brief fire within the arena. The box was positioned at the top of the arena as though in command of all below. The card depicting the powerful Queen was richly drawn, depicting a figure of stark beauty in a rose-pink gown, cloaked in ermine and standing in the centre of a grove of barren trees, spring cornflowers at her feet. In her left hand she held a staff, tipped with an unopened crystal bloom. The golden trim of her rose-emblazoned shield glowed under the candlelight as if drawing rich heat from the flame.

The response of the cowled figure was silent, a simple tap of a fingertip to the parchment sufficed; the Book shuffled to the page of the Court Cards with the depiction of the *Queen of Roses*, a powerful card of the Royal Suits. The flowing script was again traced by the fingertip, mindful of the words. The page turned to reveal more associations, expressing the positives of the card.

> *"Her advantage is being able to work through difficulties*
> *intellectually to a regal standard.*
> *Her staff speaks of her pointed actions, clear, sharp and*
> *incisive, gilded with attractive promise as shown by the*
> *lustrous rosebud at its head.*
> *She is the most beautiful of the Royals, drawing influence*
> *to her with an irresistible force. It is her logic that makes*
> *her an invincible ally, though alone, the weakest of the*
> *Queens in the Heraldry."*

Other pleasant and magnanimous traits were cited for the bearing of the Queen. The last sentences painted the lesser, reversed traits associated with the card. The Seer paused, the ink seemed unnecessarily thick and striking. The review was brief, fingers skimming the script until coming to rest on the final words, which lay apart as an admonition:

> *"The Queen of the Roses has the ability to be overly*

*critical, cold, judgmental and cynical. Allowing emotion
and old obsessions or internal identities to get in the way
of clear judgement. Past hurts can distort her intuitive
psychic qualities, leaving her unable to find her own
identity as too lost in another's influence. She deals with
that which involves the mind, not the heart.
Can also be vengeful, temperamental, shallow and cruel."*

As the reader traced progress to the end, a caveat began
to scroll underneath the summary, another paragraph etching
itself in the same fluid hand.

*'This card can also promote overcoming old fears and
patterns, ridding the self of them.
Bring them to the surface and conquer them,
although it will be a difficult lesson.'*

The parchment arena began to glow, the inks wavering
and glowing in the candlelight as if gathering in the ambers of
its fire. One final notation appeared, given import by its lack
of ornamental serifs.

*'The Card will remain in play for
the remainder of Events.
Select a card at random to reveal your support.'*

With a light sweep of the hand, the deck was laid in an
arch, the wavering feathers of the card back beckoning in the
light. A corner of one card in the center of the fan jutted further than the rest, the omen sought, and the *10 of Roses* was
drawn and turned to study.

Centered in the knotted borders of the card, ten roses gathered like a rich bouquet, buoyed by mystic coins in a formation
known to have power in the Arcana. The coins floated in dark

waters and goldfins lurking beneath caught the candlelight with their scales so that they appeared to swim with life.

A powerful card, especially when matched to the ruling suit of the Queen. The Numinon flipped its thin pages to reveal the card's quality. Given the alliance, the Seer read carefully.

The 10 of Roses provides good luck attending material affairs, favor & popularity. Regard a general period of improvement in all aspects of the endeavour. It oversees settlements and financial gifts. Good luck as well as good management in financial affairs, for the 10 involves financial security after hard work and planning. This gain can be at the expense of others without penalty for the reward, symbolized by the flourishing Roses, is clear.

Wealth creates power with its generation.

There was more to read, though the augury was well received as acceptance was achieved when the card was placed on its mark in the Arena, set in fresh inks next to the Queen. With the ally in place, the Book shuffled to the front, where warnings and messages were displayed.

Complete the divination
as the matter of consequence is determined.

Dutifully, the deck was gathered and stacked and the top card drawn. Hesitation, like a capture of breath, held the card before being turned and laid down in the glowing Eastern mark of the Arena, well outside the conflict identified by the map upon it. The *3 of Quills* was revealed again, a bird of prey in flight through the stone portal, '*Messenger*' written in script within the bottom of the frame.

No move was made to read the import of the minor card,

instead a chuff of relief sounded from the Seer as the grimoire flipped its pages towards the beginning, shuffled by an unfelt breeze. A page exposed itself for a brief moment, written like a document or deed, with seals of office accompanying the official writing.

Defacto, saɪni 'daɪi

It is Done.

Chapter 6

Four scrolls. For the Abbess, the number seemed both inadequate and too substantial, the answer to the dilemma of the cards lying somewhere in their records. Four missing oracles of the Sybelline, forgotten in the years following the purge as new issues and revelations came to the fore.

Susinna reviewed the records, hoping to find a clue as to the identity of the one holding the dangerous deck. That all may be dead, was a real possibility. What made these four scrolls of interest, were the capabilities of the Sisters that were unaccounted for. The Oracles of the Sybelline were shape-shifters, each given to talents inherent in their chosen beast. There were some adepts comfortable with two or more changeling personas, though they were few. Most had only one animal within their identity, and all too many of the oracles chose safe and docile avatars for their talents. The common house cat was deemed suitable enough for them, content with their scholarly pursuits.

For Susinna, she had found the Springorn gazelle admirably suited for her personality, a communal soul with grace, agility, and alert intelligence. Since she had held the reins of Abbess, there had been little opportunity to exercise her animal spirit, though it remained ingrained in her very being.

Susinna sighed, the personality involved with the deck would hardly be associated with such cooperative beasts as gazelles or house cats, so she had searched among the missing for those who harbored more aggressive talents. She had no choice but to conduct the inquiry herself, spending long hours in the archives with only vague ideas and hunches to guide her search. Those had slowly been narrowed to the four scrolls that sat unfurled on her desk.

Four missing oracles of note, all of them at one time powerful in their stations. Camdin the Boar, Linara the Spider, Sylvena the Bear, and Majenko the Jeweled Asp. While she couldn't be sure, one of them may yet live, possessing the type of aggressive personality likely to attempt to wield the dangerous cards of the Numinon. All of them had been known to her, for she had fashioned the amulets for many of her Sisters. In spite of her parameters, two of the possibilities seemed unlikely. Camdin was as stubborn and fierce as her chosen beast, equally unpredictable, though she had never known her to be dishonest or spiteful. Years of isolation could change one and Susinna was reluctant to put the scroll aside. Sylvena possessed many of the same headstrong traits, though seemed even more doubtful to cause strife, for Sylvena had thrived in her periods of solitude and was not one given to the trappings of power.

The two remaining scrolls gave Susinna the most pause. Linara was as cold and calculating as her chosen avatar, the long-legged Yellow Lantern spider, and one to cast her webs with patience. Majenko was the fiercest of the lot and the only male in the narrow range of alternatives. Male Sybellines were a rarity, chosen mainly for breeding potential and given power to match their mates. It was their aggressive male nature that too often reverted to their animal selves, leaving insanity and death as their only reprieves. The Jeweled Asp, for which Majenko was known, was especially dangerous, a mere drop of its lethal poison meant sure death within the hour, as the body slowly forgot how to breathe. He had gone missing even before the purge, though there was no accurate accounting for the disappearance of the Deck. Would that this was as simple as using the Book of Ways to locate the renegade oracle, or even the Orb that measured residual majic of spells. It had been her use of the Orb that gave her the indications she needed to send the young and inexperienced Haviana to the West.

Susinna spared a moment to consider her choice in Haviana. The Gyrfalcon that the girl had adopted was admirably suited for observation and quick decisions. She would have to rely on the girl's fierce nature to see her mission through. She picked up the Empress card, noting with irony that her power had been pulled from the deck. Haviana, would have to be her strength.

Haviana felt like walking, time spent more for the reflection of her humanity than crossing any appreciable distance while lost in the wild of the Gyrfalcon. The morning had lost its coolness and here in the mountains, the heat of the day would be long in coming. She gathered her shawl about her shoulders, a feathery length of light wool, white with tufts of cinnamon in its weave. Her fingers touched the amulet about her neck, her link to herself while she embraced the spirit of the Gyrfalcon.

She was well beyond the tangled rainforests of her youth, whose soaring trees provided roosts and food for the other great birds of prey that lived there. Here in the high mountains, far west of Lumenaria, it was the earth that soared into the heavens, ragged, lofty chains of rocky peaks separating the fertile valleys scooped between them. She reveled in the change. Swirling winds and sheer cliffs provided powerful updrafts and currents to propel her forward as she flew, the power of changeling she had inherited from both her parents. They favored the mighty cats, though her father had first bonded by accident to the timid n'Ori, a beast fashioned as though a fox had wings. She was eternally grateful to her father, for it was he who had taken her on a first flight when she was but a toddling child.

It was flight, especially that of the majestic white and cinnamon Gyrfalcons of the great forest, which had captivated her since that moment and not long afterwards, she had found her power in the great raptors.

So many times, she had thought it would be easier to remain as the bird, courting far fewer cares and concerns. There was clarity in those moments when she flew, the only thought was observation, the only goal was prey. Without the link of the amulet, it would be difficult to find her way back. She was still young, in her sixteenth year, though her parents said it didn't get any easier to ignore the draw of the beast. Yet, they had found themselves at ease with it and let their experience be her guide. The sharp-eyed, decisive traits of the bird had become her own.

She was in a vale between two cragged ridges, permanently capped with snow, another new experience she would have to explore when she felt she could afford to tarry. The further she removed herself from the safe confines of the Sybelline cloister, the more urgent her mission seemed to be. There was no information or guidance and she wondered if she was already hopelessly behind the course of events.

The Abbess had directed her to the mountainous region of the Jimals. Havi had deduced, even before the interview was over, that the round instrument on Susinna's desk had somehow provided the clues. Now that she was airborne and away from the familiarity of her native lands, it was the thin bones in her ears as she flew that gave her direction, orienting herself with the pulses that stretched between the earthly poles. Now as she walked, collecting her thoughts, it was the westward sun that reassured her.

The road she happened on was well-groomed and maintained, an obvious caravanner's route. The highest mountains of the Jimals still lay ahead, looming in the distance and lit with close radiance by the morning sun. Like the frequencies of the earth that guided her while she flew, the illustration of the Queen of Quills that the Abbess had shown her drew her on like a mariner's lodestone. There was nothing defined in her search, just a notion that would not escape her sharp eyes when it was there to be seen, like the slight movement of a mouse in the field.

Havi's sharp ears caught a trace of rolling sound from

behind her, a distant hint of riders. Relaxed and satisfied with her position, she looked about, feeling the essences of the land and judging the loft of the air. She smiled. She would cross many leagues before she set down again. She spread her arms, unfurling the shawl gathered about her shoulders and leapt, confident the winds would take her.

Chapter 7

Shifting airs began to gather over the grassy steppes of the Alatian plains. Sparklets of light glittered as the overcast fogs were squeezed of their thin moisture. The shimmering beads, caught between vapor and droplet, grazed the motes of grit layered close to the ground and ignited them with the charge of their passing. A flutter of scaled wings dotted the light, a tiny Gryphon snapping for air, a fleck among the similar nipping motes of dust. Another bead of charged vapor glittered to life, caught up in the flutter of its predecessor. The djinns were too meager to have a voice, merely puffs of air sent among other insignificant glints of dew. Small zephyrs rose in paltry circles of dust, evaporating into quivering life as the motes discovered their affinities, forming a pinch of cloud, a mirror of its parts.

More wisps of vaporous dust curled into the air, meshing with the others, a waving aggregate of tiny Gryphons, imaging a larger self in the murmuration of its flight. The twisting flock beat the air into more vagrant puffs as it gathered speed over the land, gaining size as it sought altitude, hungry for the space of air necessary to sustain it. The cloud dipped and turned, the whispering rustle of wings building in intensity as the uncounted zephyrs gathered into a coherent fusion, a colossal Gryphon of squalling dust and light, which nipped and snarled in unified intent. The air was filtered as the apparition swept through it, with more subtle impurities added to its flight, snapping reflections of the larger form.

The emanation, an accumulation of countless motes in mindful unison, coasted along with vagrant flaps, lifting the phantasm with soaring grace, wingtips swirling in cyclonic fervors that trailed to vapors. Tall grasses whipped and bowed in shuddering prayer as the ghostly Gryphon scudded over them, the path of its flight leading to the sharp and majestic mountains of the Jimals.

A biting wind pulled at Barist's cloak, unseasonably cold for the time of the year. He was glad to have grabbed it before he gained the watch. The night before had been warm enough that it was forgotten and unneeded. Now, in the dingy hour before sunrise, the sudden, frigid gust had an odd pressure and sense of purpose that caused him to stifle a yawn. There was no color in the wee hours, even with the moon hanging low over the horizon to the west. The bright red cloak of the Watch seemed a lifeless grey, as chill as the night. He drew it closer about him.

Watch duties in Safrasco were considered honorable posts, as the fortress had no enemies to press its walls in the years since Abbysin had folded the Jimal kingdoms within their sovereignty. The entrance to the marbled city was fronted by three ancient watch towers, renowned for their stout but graceful rendering, constructed in the old years of the warring satraps. The morticed stone and adjoining battlements were granites of steeled blue and rich, rusted browns, unearthed from a forgotten quarry high in the mountains. Gold leaf and cobalt trimmed the most ornate trappings and embellishments. Labradorite and onyx fascia were a lasting testament to the rich satrapies that commissioned them. Carved into the columns and lintels were a myriad of scenes depicting mythical beasts and arcane creations involved in heroic dances with the gods that surrounded them. Slender pillars lined the bastions, which were shaded with sculpted roofs. The same elegant pillars held up the domes topping the watchtowers, ornate with sculpted and painted patterns that swirled to their crests, rounder and more bulbous than the newer, sleeker towers that loomed behind.

Tonight, Barist had drawn the favored westernmost post, the tower with a commanding view of the royal palace, its towering presence framed by the steep, tree lined mountains which formed the northern pass. From his vantage he could observe the caravan route traveling North along the lake. The flat reflection of the lower Chain lake defined the western horizon, with the road leading to Saamed laying just beyond his vantage. Barist glanced across to the next tower, which overlooked the southwestern approach. Squinting into the dark, he could just make out the shadow of Reese Moge, a strange, gaunt man who preferred the dark watches and had the look of a ghoul. Just out of sight, was the tallest and southernmost tower, manned by the large, officious Lidsey Garma, another one who preferred the night watch. He drew the South watch tonight, though Barist would lay odds that he would be dozing.

From the South tower, one relayed messages with a lamp frame across the wide vale to the twin fortress of Saamed, which guarded the central pass. Built in the same golden age, it echoed Safrasco's graceful towers and ancient fortifications. Spear and helmet were no longer required of the watch, just a pair of eyes and a modicum of vigilance would keep his position secure. Garma had his own affairs and his sleeping habits were none of his concern. Barist lobbied for as many of the day watches as he could. The women of the markets were easy quarry for his proud swagger and regular employment, the red cloak his proud claim to officialdom. Though, at the moment, he would be satisfied just to have his shift done early, given the sharp wind that gathered in the air.

A sudden gust sent reflecting ripples flashing across the lake surface like a warning. Barist imagined the fisherfolk up the northeast shore might not be out in the morning, wisely tucked safely in their berths should the weather continue to brew. The blustering wind picked rapaciously at the trees that rimmed its shores, tearing away fresh leaves and late blossoms. Not a curious person by nature, there was an ill flavor to the draught, which kept his attention directed outward to the western horizon.

Another shift of wind blew along the walls, a passing rush that emerged like the sigh of a banshee expelled from the buttressed stone. Barist squinted, a drift of sand borne on the sharp blast stinging his cheeks. Without averting his gaze, he held a palm up to protect his face. A storm cloud appeared to approach the lake, blown by the western gusts. Silhouetted by the sinking moon, it seemed to be moving like a living thing, the vagaries of the heavens shaping it like a clawed lion, the vaporous fringes of the storm sweeping like the wings of a giant bird. For a moment it held him transfixed, the head of a lion appearing to roar defiance as the cloud changed shape. He shook his head. Only tired eyes had such feverish visions, yet he rubbed at them as if to erase the vision. Another look revealed glittering shafts of moonlight penetrating the tempest as it boiled over the lake. That momentary glance had Barist thinking the storm might be breaking up; then the immense downward beat of its vaporous wings brought the horror into focus with sudden acceleration. Spectral lightnings sheeted within the cloud, most brilliant in the fore, blazing like the eyes and gaping jaws of a fearsome beast.

Barist's blood ran cold, unsure of his sight and even the nature of the alarm. He shot a glance across to the next tower to see if Moge was seeing the same wild apparition. The spare man was caught in a rapturous gaze, his eyes locked on the western sky as well. Barist turned back in time to see the wings of the massive cloud swipe downward with another billowing stroke, hurtling the storm forward with abrupt turbulence that blocked his sight. Barist fell back with the gust, raising his forearm to shield himself from the tearing wind. The rope for the alarm hung close. He could hear the heavy bell vibrating its tone under the sudden onslaught, as though begging to be rung. His eyes still didn't comprehend the approach of the murderous storm. It gusted at the wall, a demon Gryphon, yawning open the lightning maw of its devastation.

Barist couldn't reach the bell pull. Terror transfixed him

as the thunderous, snapping cloud shattered itself against the guard towers of Safrasco, the infinitesimal nips of legion blights of air shredding flesh and stone in a passing instant.

The turbulence slammed into the ancient towers, the countless motes of its entirety snapping with the same mindless hunger. Rock, mortar, bone and sinew all ground to dust as the voracity consumed them. The expulsion of the impact sent hot, roiling glooms flowing like waves into the streets, the remains of the towers caught within its terrifying, dark embrace. Choking clouds billowed through the avenues and alleys in the aftermath, blanketing the entire city with the powdered remains.

The multitudes of the demonic clones lost the glimmer of their animation with the impact, their life consumed with their appetite, the tiny carapaces of their existence coasting away as particles of suffocating air, settling around the towers like so much dust.

A pall of lifeless haze hung over Safrasco as the sun rose, much as thin smokes from an old fire. The remnants of the watchtowers punctured the gloom like the stumps of dead, broken teeth. Fine dust powdered the streets and lanes, a flour of soul and stone forever mixed in its grit.

Chapter 8

Calling together the Jimalian council, at least those that could be raised on short notice, was an effort reluctantly managed by the Ducesin Linarest. It was not easy to gather the elite, along with their opinions and demands, from the expanses of the three great rift valleys that cut between the towering mountains of the Jimals. The twin cities of Safrasco and Saamed had the advantage of being the Jimalian centers of trade. Heated by the great desert and plains to the west and cooled by the expansive lakes, the graceful, marbled cities were an ever-temperate and welcome resort to the elite; most notably, the Ducet and Ducesin of Marsena, as the centermost valley was known, the titular rulers of all the Jimals. Their summer palace, reached by an ornate causeway, grasped a thrust of rock rising from the lake.. The regal compound was an elegant and imposing fortress to a city resplendent with graceful arches and exquisitely turned minarets. Its golden topped towers and balconies, trimmed in malachite and lapis lazuli, loomed high over the manicured parks edging the lower lake.

A wealthy population of lesser mayors and landowners throughout the Jimals maintained holdings or agents within this vital link to the North. The marbled city lay adjacent to the lucrative caravan route known as the Pernian Trek, an artery that followed the great Marsena valley and led to the Eastern Empires of the Perns and beyond to the Trader States. The next pass into the Upper Jimals, lay five days ride to the east along the Trek, even without the burden of cargo or caravan. That was until recently, when the Northern passes under the vigilant eye of the watchtowers became blocked by the strange catastrophe. White dust still coated the streets of Safrasco, the dissipated remains of the grand old watchtowers, driven into cornered piles like drifted snow. At the gateway, mounds of the powdered stone lay like dunes blocking the route north. The detour was one not favored by many traders because of the added distance, though with diligence and a labor pool derived from the stocks and gaols, the way was proposed to be cleared in another week.

Makiel Ma'Gilrie could think of nothing else but the necessary repairs even as Andigar, the Tenigran mayor, rambled on about the changes that must be made to the Abbysin relations. Ma'Gilrie considered that, for anyone who had ears to listen, Andigar's words smacked of gaining favorable circumstances rather than solving problems, for somehow his end remarks always insisted on a lost profit or missed opportunity. In spite of his overt complaints, in the week following the calamitous disaster surrounding the towers, Andigar had been maneuvering with the caravanneers to carve out advantageous rates and exclusive passages.

Makiel did not trust the Tenigran mayor. Slender and well-groomed, his dark hair sleeked back by expensive sheens, Andigar had ever been out for himself and that much was in evidence now, as the mayor spoke of tightening security. He was scheming, Makiel was sure of it, though he waited for a long pause in the mayor's delivery before trying to make his point.

"My dear Mayor. I think you overstate the problem and the effort it will take to restore trade through Tenigra. And by that, I mean the entire northern Jimals." Makiel held his fingers out, much like a tutor making a point. His expression indicated that any coherent answer at all would be surprising. "Safrasco will be fine, so my concern is for the north. I shouldn't have to point out that we are all of a kingdom; when one of us suffers, ultimately we all do."

"Of course, you're right." Andigar thought the older mayor naïve and slow to take advantage of many opportunities. Bespectacled, with a balding pate, he even looked like the tutor he once was, given title by the old Duce, obviously in a moment of senility. "But is trade our immediate concern? You … *we* … have suffered a grievous attack by the Abbysins …"

"We don't know it was the Abbysins. I've said before …" Makiel was interrupted by a hand gently laid to his shoulder, the Ducesin Linarest inserting herself between the two officials. Her constant servant, the deaf-mute Steban Mallbre stood respectfully back, his cold eyes watching all in the room.

"Of course, it was the Abbysins. Who else could it be?" Linarest spoke with the calm assurance of one used to command, even though she often stood in the shadow of her more effusive husband.

"I'm sure I don't know." Makiel bowed politely. "Nor does anyone else. Can any one witness bear credibility as to what they saw? No. All the more reason to study the situation."

"You conveniently forget the assault on the Stands... three, was it four years ago?" Andigar spoke to Makiel, nodded graciously to the Ducesin, thus acknowledging her acumen. "It wasn't that long ago, is my point ... The Abbysins had armies marshaled at the gates ... *pfft!* ... I don't have to tell you the stories that circulated after that affair."

"A lot of wild speculation ..." Makiel felt he was losing any hope of audience or agreement. The thought of calling up an army was more than his scholarly discipline could bear. "We gain nothing by ..."

"They've done it again and who else? By the latest accounts ... you've heard them ... the Gates have shut again, by as strange a means as the attack on our venerable watchtowers. It's more than plain to see that the Abbysins are back to their warlike ways and using curses and sorcerers to do their bidding."

"Even more wild speculation." Makiel looked over his wired lenses. "When you hear something that makes any sense, then we can direct our energies. To abjectly accuse ..."

"And you want to know why?" Andigar didn't want to hear the lesson and gave Ma'Gilrie no chance to offer another. "Trade. That's why. When has it been otherwise? Even though we fly under the banner of the Abbysins, they seek to take in as much as possible and give as little back to us on the fringes."

"Yet you somehow plan to use the current disaster to the watchtowers of Safrasco to enhance your own coffers at the expense of the Northern Jimals. You look to increase your advantage with the trade guilds, while making a point to restrict it at our border."

"The lord Mayor no doubt has added expenses to bear." The Ducesin came smoothly to Andigar's defense and let no one breach the argument, motioning instead to a portly figure, cloaked in regal maroon and huddled with two wizened old men, equally resplendent in their finely woven robes. "Oh, husband, give the treasurers a rest from your concerns. Our lord Mayors would like to hear your views. As would I." Linarest bowed her head slightly in obvious deference to the Ducet. "I've heard the arguments before but I confess to not being able to air them as well as your gracious self."

Risherade Mirbek was well-fed. No volume of robes could diminish his portly figure, which he exhibited proudly as a token of his regency. "The people don't want to see a dog-hungry king," was his favorite saying. Ma'Gilrie added silently to the dictum in that, *'a king shouldn't want to see 'dog-hungry people',* as Mirbek pushed his way to Linarest's side.

"Views? Not a matter of views. What is there to view? The remains of the Safrasco watchtowers? I've assembled the warlords from all three of the Jimal states, that's my view. Hrmmph. I can see Abbysin from here. A particularly nice view."

In spite of Mirbek's dire words, Ma'Gilrie couldn't help but note that Risherade was fair gleaming once his practiced bombast was over.

"You prepare for war, Sire." Ma'Gilrie's eyes widened, shock and concern evident. "I thought the purpose of the gathering here was to discuss … learn what we can … yet it appears the decision has been made. I must say that there is nothing to indicate … "

"My lord Mayor. There is everything to indicate." Risherade grinned at him, a self-satisfied smirk that let the Mayor know he was being humored. Ma'Gilrie inwardly bristled but kept his demeanor concerned as Risherade continued, "Why the Abbysin themselves are known to be war-like and employ wizardry. The Gates at the Stands … my case entirely."

"Lord Andigar was quick to point out the same, but … "

"He has obviously thought on it more than you." Risherade was jovial, clapping Ma'Gilrie on the back as if wanting the old mayor to join him in a round of drinks. "There are other concerns, my good Mayor. Take an occasional look outside your own city walls."

Ma'Gilrie felt deflated. At present, by the futility of his arguments. There was sure to be even more exasperation later, caused by the sure drain on the resources of the Jimals. It was not a land prepared to make war. He took a quick glance over to the treasury officials that Risherade had been talking with. They were in discussion with another of their kind. By the look on their faces, no troubling issues were being discussed. On the contrary. Perhaps the Ducesin had catered the affair too well.

"I must urge restraint, Highness, until we know more. It is the right thing to do."

"And wait until the next strike? Every master of war will tell you that to wait while your enemy plots is, to invite defeat." Risherade looked around proudly at his assessment, while Andigar and Linarest beamed their support.

Ma'Gilrie, in spite of all of his studies, had never heard of any such maxim and he had studied the journals and tactics of famous conflicts and generals. He opened his mouth to respond but had no ready argument for the nonsense. Regardless, Risherade would have given him no chance, his round cheeks as merry as a reveler on Midwinter's Eve.

"Within a fortnight, troops will be mustered at the borders, a tremendous wall, the best of the Jimals. Abbysin will think twice before attacking again."

Ma'Gilrie groaned aloud. The Ducet read the lapse as agreement, while the Mayor further anticipated the depletion of Safrasco resources. For the moment, Ma'Gilrie had tuned out the Ducet's rebuttal, catching what he knew he would hear anyway.

"We are fortunate that the Lower Jimal routes remain open to trade and revenues in Andigar's capable hands." Risherade turned to the Lord as if seeing him in a newer, more profound light. "There are bigger issues at stake and I believe him. Glad the Jimals have his forward thinking."

The Mayor was determined to make his point. If troops were indeed being mobilized, he would not allow Safrasco to be shorted and drained in the process. "The passes of Safrasco shall be opened before long. If there is to be a presence of troop and manpower, it would be a tremendous help if they were available in clearing the debris."

"Nonsense." Risherade gave the Mayor a simpering smile, as if regarding a childish request. "Armies are not at the ready while sweeping dust."

The Ducesin smiled with her accustomed charm. "My dear Mayor. You worry far too much. Surely you see the strength now … the Jimals are united in effort. This is a tragic event, true, but it plays to our advantage, coming at a most propi-

tious time. I think the yoke of Abbysin rule has been felt long
enough by their levies and restrictions. We look to your guidance to make sure Safrasco does its part."

She turned to Andigar as though sharing a secret between
them. Ma'Gilrie marked their silent exchange. The Ducesin's
views on taxes were well-known, quick to collect and tight to
extend. Ma'Gilrie had nothing left in him at the moment. A
quick glance about the assembly found no allies. In spite of
the willing talk of arms, whatever alliances were being discussed had less do with war and much to do with advantage.
He could see it in their faces as they talked.

Even the inscrutable Steban Mallbre, the Ducesin's aide,
showed traces of satisfaction. Deaf and mute, he stood on the
fringes of the room like a slender reed at the pond's edge, thin
as if food refused to transfer its vitality. Ma'Gilrie was careful
not to catch Mallbre's notice, who analyzed everything in his
sight with a passionless regard. Mallbre remained intent on
the Ducesin and any who might approach her. He may be deaf
and mute but his joyless eyes missed nothing. The Ducet was
puffed up in the moment, the call to arms a victory already
won. Any further arguments would be dust before the wind.
Ma'Gilrie nodded to the Ducesin.

"I shall keep accounts."

Chapter 9

Forges were rarely quiet in the Armorer's Guild, even in the most placid of times. Abbysin arms were prized throughout the many kingdoms; from the far Isles of Arghana to the Trader States in the East. The curved blades favored by the Sevilinians were forged here, as well as the Pernian swords known for their whistling strikes. Mercenary divisions traveled the continents and their outfitters had no allegiance, save the quality of their tools.

Chenli sat on a veranda behind the forge, an inner courtyard that once belonged to his father, Chen Foragge and now worked by his uncle's son, Patan Foragge. Chenli was particularly proud of this forge, where the great mechanisms that powered the trebuchets were cast. Though cousin, Patan Foragge long ago filled the role of brother, a relation Chenli lacked, yet it wasn't brotherhood that held them in tight union, merely the profits of their endeavours. The Foragge sons were the Masters of the Armorer's Guild and owned many of the most dedicated forges.

Legions of journeymen and apprentices drifted into the Guild Quarter of Abbysin like grains of sand and, if sifted out, would provide an army. A guildsman must not only be able to make the tool but wield it, a fact that Chenli considered paramount for anyone who would man his forges.

"If they don't know how it is used, how can they make it right?"

Patan could see the validity of the argument, yet didn't agree with his cousin, one of the very few who could take that liberty.

"I know what you mean but you don't have to be a scribe to read a book. I need craftsmen, not warriors."

"A book won't save your life."

Patan could argue that as well but let it pass, wanting Chenli to reach his point. The older man didn't often leave the halls of power, preferring to pull his reins within the private secrecy of his quarters.

Jord the Younger, privately known as 'the Cheerful', a sobriquet often attributed to one given to madness, maintained his own courts as Emperor and issued whimsical and extravagant edicts when they occurred to him. Chenli kept himself close by, quartered within the center of the Chancellery, a five-sided edifice that dominated the Rule, the center of Abbysin government. Each face offered a different entry, given the nature of its business: Trade, Diplomacy, Accounts, Judgements and Guardianship. Regardless of the outer facade, all doors eventually led to his chambers, protected by his private guards. Chenli sat in the center like a receiver of stolen goods, plucking information and issuing far more subtle edicts. The merchants and moguls of the Abbysin knew where the real influence dwelt and it wasn't within the scepter held by the cheerful Jord. In marked contrast to the Emperor, Chenli wore a permanent sneer, even when off his guard as he was now, in the familiar privacy of the Guild family holding.

"A book doesn't command the price of Abbysin steel, though they'll likely last longer in the minds of men. That is not my concern, nor yours. We have no argument either way." Patan tapped out his pipe against the stonework framing an empty firepit. "You didn't leave your burrow to discuss the Guild. For that you'd have summoned me to the Rule and likely wouldn't even feed me for the effort." Patan added with a slight taunt. He motioned to a plate of spitted kebabs, still warm from roasting near the forge. "Granted, your offices have lousy kitchens … here you can rest easier … a little fresh lamb. There's some Standish ale too."

"You eat better on this side of the Strait. The royals like their food dressed as fancily as their offspring. All gravy and little meat." Chenli snarled, looking disgusted with the idea of hospitality but was quick to snatch up a kebab. "It is exactly the Guild that I am here to discuss. A question of loyalty."

"We are loyal to our customers, as always. Please don't expect anything else." In spite of Chenli's irritation, Patan looked bored, too familiar with the Chancellor's bluster. "What's festering under your armor?"

"So long as the Guild serves the needs of Abbysin first, we have no argument. Both borders are faced with threats … the Stands, and now the Jimals. I'm sure you've heard." Chenli sheared off another bite of his kebab.

"Of course. An hour after you unless I missed my guess. And so?" Patan had his own sources of information, many serving his cousin as well. It's only fitting they should share their intelligence to the Chancellor first.

"Then you know that they accuse us of the attacks. Abbysin!

Anyone would have to have arses flat as salt biscuits to believe that. I've been forced to mobilize, on two fronts."

"Good for business." Patan poured a measure of ale into two cups and handed one to the Chancellor, who took it with his customary grimace.

"Of course, it is. The Jimals are still part of our empire. As long as the tithes come in, let them shake their swords as much as they like. I'll shake a few swords back at them and feel good about doing so. It's a showy investment and doesn't cost all that much for the effort." Chenli's eyes narrowed as he took a gulp of ale and shifted his thought. "The Stands. Now there is a ripe fruit, ready to pluck. Their vaunted Gate is no more. I have my best forces there, those damn Paladon Crussars, even that mercenary cavalry of all Cherros horse… they're expensive, so you know I'm serious." he growled. "You likely already aware of all of that … I'm telling you now in any event."

"By now, Constance Alewife at the One-Eyed Snake Inn knows … and from there, the rest of Abbysin." The sailor's slang for a gossip elicited a mordant crease of a smile from the Chancellor. Patan figured it must be the ale, which brought him to a better topic of discussion. "It is interesting that you mention the Stands. I have a large order to fill … from the Stands. Arms, mostly swords, spears and the like. It comes at the request of some, 'Lord Pryan'. Claims to be one of the wealthiest men in the Stands. This ale we're drinking was sent as a gift, by the way."

"Never heard of him. What of it?" Chenli had the cautious look of a skeptic who has already decided any news would be unfit to hear.

"I'll fill it, of course. I just wanted you to know the Guild is in a position to sell to an immediate adversary. Not our best goods … Thymsen swords, I don't know why armorer's like those things except that they look good on parade. I'll include the pikes that were due to the Gold Coast with the lot. They've not fully paid for the last order."

"*Hmmph*. Traders hold on to their coin until the marrow is gone. How is this Standish lord paying?"

"If I am to believe the messages … and I'm reading between the lines … I'd say he intends to pay with uncut stones. He's not clear. He says the price is no object."

"Gold. And weighed proper. He can pack the jewels up his arse next to his other worthless stones."

"My thought as well, though I had the scribe phrase it with more thoughtful terms. I've already relayed them by messenger."

"Well think on this, cousin. While this 'conflict' is keeping our Guilds busy, I want to know who … *who* is churning this up? It reeks of wizardry and the last poor bastard I heard of that attempted such devilry is still cast in stone at the top of his tower. I checked, of course. He's still there, so I doubt it was him."

Chenli wasn't quite convinced as Patan could plainly tell. Wizards played in different realms. All the more reason to keep their kind in check. He waved his hand as if to dismiss the whole thing, goading his cousin to explain further. "Again. Why do you care? Our borders are secure and our forges busy."

"You should leave the West Quarters more often. This rich

food is giving you gas and that remark stinks of it. I don't care that it *is* to our advantage. I can ride that horse. I *do* care that I have no idea who is pulling the strings."

"And you need an unofficial inquiry." Patan sat back, the Chancellor finally getting to the point.

"Officially, I'll get the same obsequious line of well-wishers with the same half-baked rumors. Put all together they don't make enough for a meal." Chenli took another snap at his kebab to make his point. "I need something I can chew on until I can decide which side this wizardry is favoring and given the swamp at court, I'd rather not use my own network. For that I have you."

"You fear someone in our own court?"

"I've ruled out Jord … ever paddling with one oar. His half-circles don't concern me. Someone will benefit. I want to make sure that it is us."

"I'm sure you'll have no objections to employing one of the Hashini."

"You can use a *naschgirl* so long you get answers. It doesn't matter to me." Chenli lost his customary snarl for a moment as he looked around. "Do you have more of this ale?"

"Not here. But I'll send the rest of the barrel around to you." Patan gazed at his cup, the nut-brown beverage prized within the empire. "It also occurs to me where a good place might be to put my ears to the ground."

Chapter 10

Beyond the cooling influence of the plateau, Cerra could feel the changes in heat and humidity that characterized the Lower Stands. As she rode in silence, she considered the journey a substantial step beyond her safe routine. She enjoyed her comforts and the surety of her daily life, tools necessary to cope with a sightless world. Nevertheless, she could feel those anxieties sharpening her senses, forcing her to assimilate everything new into an ordered mental compartment, labeled much like the herbs in her closet.

As with the last journey taken beyond the safe cocoon of her meadows, there was the guiding light of the demon to lead her forward. Together, their resolve had been strengthened by the knowledge of the second sorcerous attack, this time on the watchtowers of Safrasco.

'It has his stench, the vizier's work again.'

His taciturn presence gave her courage and was merely a thought away should she need him.

It was the well-meaning Captain who gave her the most aggravation. Since she had arrived in Scott's Mill to accept his charge, he had been most solicitous to her every need, catering overmuch to her blindness. She felt that if she allowed him to fend for her as much as he considered necessary, she'd fall into useless repair. He was also used to command and having his biding done, without question. She smiled as she rocked within Sugar's sure steps, stroking the sleek fur of Kamir, wedged in her lap over the crown of the saddle. That had been the first test of their relationship, when she arrived at Maree Nels' hostel in Scott's Mill.

"You brought your cat?"

"He brought himself. I had nothing to say in the matter." Cerra chuckled, working to sidestep the irritation in the Captain's voice.

"This is a mission, not a trip to the market."

He seemed short-tempered and impatient because of the presence of the cat. Perhaps he had spent too much time idling while he waited for her, Cerra considered. Even so, she had her own flash of annoyance with the Captain's attitude. Though a mostly silent companion, Kamir was a reliable shadow and a constant she found comforting the further she left her cabin behind. His vocal prompts had often given her sure direction.

"If I am your agent, it is as *I* am … not as someone else. Get a real agent, if that is what you want. Kamir is a better companion than most." She softened her tone. "*Heh* … he certainly helps me keep light on my feet. You can believe me when I say I can see the world much better because of him."

Ferriman looked again at the black cat, who gazed at him for a moment with regal intelligence before leaning back to lick at its shoulder, as would any cat. He still had no suggestion as to the woman's apparent powers and thought it best not to press. The trip would provide plenty of opportunity to discover the blind woman's temperament and strengths. A small crease of a smile crossed his face. There was a confident fire in her response. She would not be so easily cowed. He relented his tone, anxious to return to Bridash without issue.

"Forgive me, then. I'll concede that remarkable times called for remarkable solutions." Ferriman tried to match her tone. "A cat. I won't make an official entry to the roles; though I'll note that you are providing your own horse."

"Sugar." Cerra added firmly.

"Sugar." Ferriman considered it an apt name. A sturdy, dark bay mare with flecked patterns of white dotted on its rump and chest.

"I was going to name her Kafi, but she's so sweet." Cerra smiled at him and the brief confrontation was forgotten.

Cerra gently acquiesced to the Captain's solicitous behavior, as Ferriman seemed uncomfortable enough as it was, as though unused to feminine company. Yutan mostly carried himself behind them, preferring the vaporous companionship of clouds or raveling in the dusts and breezes. He was solicitous in his own way, once shouldering ominous thunderheads aside to ensure that her passage was pleasant and dry. She rarely saw his form, spread thin in the airs but his thoughts touched her constantly, giving her much reason to smile.

She could feel the curiosity driving him, much like the Captain, as well as an almost apologetic tone for creating her involvement. It was an attitude that had grown within the intuitive and quiet Yutan, who had become more used to his human qualities over the past two years. Ferriman noticed the occasional pleasant closures of her eyes and inward smiles, clearly communing with some inner voice. Once again, he eyed the cat that lay content over the saddle.

When they reached the Standwall, the line of cliffs that girded the flanks of the upper plateau, Cerra asked to stop at the overlook marking the top of the Falling Rocks cut.

"I've been here once before," she remarked, sitting comfortably in the saddle. "I want to take in the view again. There is seating near the top, if I remember correctly."

"You do." Ferriman obliged, guiding them over to a wayside, well-used by those just completing the long ascent. Beyond them, the wagon route carved its way down the face of the cliffs in well-hewn cuts and arching buttresses, one of only three passes gaining access to this upper plateau. The blind woman's horse pulled up correctly as though by some unseen hand. Ferriman eyed her cat as he dismounted. It made a quick leap from the saddle as if anxious to gain the ground, only to saunter over to the rock wall that guarded the wayside from the cliff and jump up the waist high abutment with ease, tucking its tail carefully as it settled to look at the view. Cerra dismounted and started to reach for her cane, tucked beneath the wing of her saddle.

"Take my arm instead." Ferriman offered.

"Gladly." She smiled broadly and accepted his elbow as he led her the few steps from the horses to the wall, stone set in low arches by masons generations ago. She closed her eyes in pleasure as she let the wind wash over her. The gusts fluttered and pulled at the heavy curls of her hair and she pulled the bulk of it close to her neck as she inhaled deeply. Cerra allowed the open air beyond her to fill with sound and scent. Ferriman looked out over the familiar sight, unsure how he would view it as a non-sighted man. He was mixed with both curiosity and the desire to further test the blind woman's acumen.

"Beg your pardon ... Cerra ... I can't help but ask ... what are you looking at? ... what 'view' are you taking in?'"

"No pardon needed, Captain. I daresay hardly anyone asks what I see. It's easy to assume I see nothing at all. I don't. I'm sure a moonless night has more features to recommend it. What I have are my memories from childhood and they paint scenes for me. They are surely fanciful, not at all like the real thing, it just helps my mind reach out and give me a sense of place."

"And here ... what do you see?"

"*Ahhh* ... one of my favorite imaginations is seeing from the air, and the cliff allows everything to be spread open in front of me, like a bird in flight." Cerra suddenly thought of another cliff on the flanks of the Granite mountains, one that had not been as kind, she pushed the memory away and continued.

"It can be breathtaking to be sure, the sheer amount of space in front of you. I sense the lower plateau as being flatter, the flavor and sound of the wind is from a long way away and not buffeted such as it is by the mountains or the Dragon's Teeth near my home. Much of it, I imagine, is in pasture and under the plow ... I can smell the grasses, even traces of sheep. Surely there must be the dark shades of hedgerows and roads to be seen. So now it is a quilt and someone has done a delightful bricbrac in fresh greens and some colorful accents ... I told you it was fanciful. In this light, even the Emerald river must be apparent, glinting silver by the light. That's as I have it pictured. Scents and sounds work a little like paint for my imagination."

If Ferriman had asked an artist to describe the scene, he could hardly have done it better. "A fairly accurate description."

"I see as well at night. ... *heh* ... as long as I maintain enough insight to imagine when I've gone too far ... I'll do well enough." Cerra added with a laugh, making Ferriman chuckle.

"I have a lot of help," Cerra continued after a moment, looking out over the panorama before her. The images she fancied were blued in patches by the presence of the demon, who had layered himself among the clouds. "Stories from the vagrant ragabag men and potters add to my world view, even beyond the Stands, though I understand they can be given to exaggeration."

"Less than those that rule." Ferriman observed drily. "You know the Trader language then? It is normally the domain of the courts. Certainly, common to the alchemies."

"Oh yes. I have my teacher to thank for that. It's because of the herbs, really ... she wanted me to learn because she didn't want language to be a further barrier. I have found it most handy. I sew my labels with their runes as they are easy for my fingers to read. I know a smattering of Abbysin, though I wonder if I can learn any more. I think my head is already too full as it is."

Yet again, Ferriman looked at the cat who was observing the space beyond the low wall like a hawk in high airs. The young woman was exhibiting traits he'd find remarkable in any agent; yet, despite her easy charm and lack of pretension, there was an aura of power that seemed to wrestle about her.

She exhibited a force he couldn't identify, such as a gust of wind that sometimes seemed to run before her or a tumble of airs that weighed heavy but didn't quite threaten rain.

The feeling remained for the rest of the journey, an easy two days ride to Bridash, the ruling capital of the Stands with a convenient array of inns along the way to satisfy their needs. The plateau of the Upper Stands lay like a horseshoe, open to the Black Gate far beyond. The Emerald river cut deep into the top of its arch, where the city of Bridash, an ancient name denoting *'the bridge'*, began its existence. The city grew to span the river along the edge of the Upper Stands, where its green waters emptied over the cliffs in a thunderous cascade. A similar construction was built below the falls, uniting the fertile banks of the Lower Stands. It was the largesse and vision of past kings and the boldness of their architects that conspired to unite the two, as they came to knit together over the ages, becoming a fortress mounted on the magnificent cliffs and poised like a graceful sentinel overlooking the broad expanse of Standish lands.

Cerra had long heard of the ancient center of kingship. Beyond its reach, within the deep mountains to the north, lay the old monasteries of the Greycloaks, centers of learning for many who professed to the arts of the alchemies and sacred geometries. She was glad to have Captain Ferriman describe the city to her as they neared. The sound of the falls and the industry of the population competed, leaving a drone in her ears that took a while to get used to.

"I forget how noisy cities can be. I remember the first time I was truly in such a place ... Abbysin. To me it felt like a bees' hive. This feels the same, though this hive sits within the same wall as the water." Cerra turned slightly, a crooked smile on her face. "Do those that live here have rocks in their ears for the water to wash over? It must be so to be a part of the falls every day." Far from a complaint, Cerra felt rejuvenated by the power she felt emanating from in front of her. The Captain assured her they had but an hour's ride ahead of them before reaching the gates of Lower Bridash.

"I shall be glad for the journey's end, though I still have little notion of my purpose." Cerra let out a brief snicker. "The road through your diplomats and royalty will involve far more twists and turns and I won't have my horse to guide me."

"I am counting on you to be … as you say, 'who you are'." Ferriman encouraged. "You already listen well and don't reveal all that you know. There is little I can prepare you for otherwise."

Cerra gazed out toward the city, which felt like it loomed in front of her even from the distance that remained. Yutan, her demon, had gathered over the city, leaving a sparkling cast of argent within her dark sight. She felt herself reach out to him.

'It's good to know you're close by. Though they're as human as I am, I'm going among those I truly don't understand … the rulers of men.'

'They are not to be trusted.' The demon's answer was immediate and forceful.

Cerra understood his prejudice. To him, men of power considered only their own gain. She didn't have enough experience to argue his claim, though she feared he might be right.

'They are to be learned from … I can try at least. I think I must.'

She felt she was reassuring herself as much as Yutan.

'I am here. I rest.' He would not say more.

She wondered, as she often did, how taxing it might be for Yutan to hold different elements. He never admitted to exhaustion. Cerra leaned over to the Captain. "I hear the rumble of rain."

Ferriman had heard nothing, though in the instant she spoke, a growl of thunder was heard from the clouds gathering over the city. The gray skirts that formed under the clouds proved the rains were falling on Bridash. He noticed the beatific smile on Cerra's face. She did not reveal all that she knew. He wondered if the sword he was intending to wield might have two edges equally sharp. There was little else to do except maintain his direction. A warrior who intends to live doesn't think of getting cut.

◈ iii ◈

Castle *Tower* lay face up on the sepia map, blazoned in the darkened arena by scorched inks that had been laid upon the creased parchment. In the flickering candlelight, the lacquered skies surrounding the spiraling castle, seemed fired by sunset. The seated figure contemplated the implied augury of fire from the hidden depths of the draping cowl. The card remained the object of intense scrutiny and the vivid colors seemed to flare under the attention. The seer's deliberation wavered with the candlelight, decisions scrolling in and flashing away as designs were considered. Writings and sigils that lay hidden within the parchments' borders, fluctuated in intensity as they waited for a choice to be made. One line in the Book caught the seer's attention, a last note in the decision.

> *When applied correctly, the Dragon denotes a swift,*
> *sudden and strong action taken. Creativity and luxuriance,*
> *blooms and flourishes in its passing. Strongest in the*
> *Summer and in the North quadrant.*

The Numinon released its instructions when the touch of a finger was laid upon its pages. The chosen card was drawn from the top, as though waiting all along for release and placed within the sizzling mark that formed across Castle *Tower*.

Ddraig och was exposed, a coiled dragon given life by the element of Fire. The card appeared to burn, created from the same tortured paints that glimmered life from the candlelight. The sideways position gave no clue to its power. A quick glance at the inverse quality revealed the omens of mistake.

> *In the Inverse, there is no virtuous goal to focus on and the*
> *Dragon becomes aggressive and cruel.*

The hands clasped together again in contemplation, while the figure waited for the ensuing move; the Book involved in its own arcane strategies. The parchment arena wavered in the light of the one candle, the edges of the circular markings moving as though seeking an alignment of worlds and stars.

With a flip of onionskin paper, the Book laid its instruction on the ensuing page.

> *'For the Counter … Draw any card'.*

With a wave of the hand, the figure slid the pile aside, fanning the cards, face down in a small arc to the side of the arena. The figure weighed the unknown choices. Then, decisively the choice was made and *Briah, the Knight of Swords*, was revealed and placed on its fresh mark within the arena next to the crossed fates of *Enûma Eleiš* and *Caer Ri*.

A tense sigh broke the silence, a cold breath in the still room. The Numinon opened to the card referenced with a thin shuffle of pages.

> *The Knight of Swords flies through the air on his winged*
> *steed, his sword pointed over a mariner's compass that*
> *entails the sky, indicating the clarity of his direction.*
> *He is the only one of the Knights to be shown without*
> *armor, such is the strength of his purpose.*
> *Instead, his surcoat is tailored,*
> *a loose cape depicting his freedom,*

with the badges of many realms blazoned
on the trappings of his steed.

The Seer relaxed as the material was read. Although one with power and adept, the Knight was not one of the major arcana. The script in the book detailed the Knight as a champion of a just and creative life, yet the descriptors also revealed a force tarnished by the soils of conflict. Still, his suit matched that of the *Caer Ri*, an alliance of strength.

The cards were gathered and ready to be placed within the carved box when the pages of the book shuffled heavily, revealing another instruction.

The Knight is entangled. Place the top card.

As the Book waited for a response, a fresh mark appeared on the parchment almost as an afterthought, smoky tracings extending from the Lone Sword. The move was impatient, the card drawn with a snap, though it was laid down with far more consideration and reverence, for one of the Major Arcana was revealed, a card unbound by the laws and rulings of the Suits.

Abaddon. The Demon.

Chapter 11

Campfires dotted the low hills that spread out beyond the Emerald river. Freed from the confines of the Black Gate, the river widened and arced south to the Sultan Sea, leaving a thin, fertile slash that knifed across the Assai desert. It was the biting cold of the wind born of the stark desert night that gave rise to the numerous fires found in the pits and barrels of the army camp. The Spring days were already sweltering, the conflicted nature of the nearby desert making it either too hot or too cold for the comfort of all, save those hardiest of souls.

The encampment lay scattered among the scrub trees that pocked the higher ground above the river. Beyond the collected bunching of the gathered army, the shattered remains of the Gate could be seen within the shadows of the narrow gorge that guarded the entrance to the Stands. The flatter plains that bordered the gates had easily held the armies of the Abbysin in the past and twice those armies had been decimated. Paterus, the Abbysin commander, had looked upon the flats with the same superstitious regard and held his forces back from the reach of the river, well beyond the arrows and curses of the ruined Gate.

Starrel Thot was glad to have his command, the Patterned Horse, set further behind in the rougher hills. He also had the thankless task of Second Hand to the Commander. As a mid-officer and aide-de-camp, there was no glory in the commission, nor extra mark of silver in his pay, merely a badge proclaiming the bearer of official news, which was generally regarded as bad. His face was rarely welcomed, especially among the lower infantry troops, who were constantly being censured for their slovenly habits. It was too early for his next slate of rounds, which would occur before the next watch was set. Until then, he sought the refuge of his own company of Cherros Dragoons.

The famed horsemen of the Steppes disdained the use of armor as employed by the cavalry, instead preferring to slash in with lightning speed on horseback and attack on foot, saving their mounts for a swift retreat. Their skin was browned by centuries inhabiting the plains and the Cherros horsemen retained their traditional dress of woven robes that mimicked the grasses of the prairies, their straight black hair bound or hooded with the same cloth. They had put aside the conventional paints of their naming clans, instead adopting only the black and white slashes of the warrior across their cheeks. Normally their belts and headwraps would be colorful, sporting individual embellishments commonly bestowed by wives and mothers. Instead, as a mark of their sacrifice and autonomy, the belts were of uniform brown leather with cord-braided laces denoting rank. Bone fragments decorated their saddle fringes, tallies of battles fought, though the Cherros insisted that only one tally counted, that the saddle was occupied.

The horse lines lay behind him as Starrel lingered on a

stump outside his tent, holding a steaming cup of broth. His First Horse, Narya Thot, handed him a gristled knot of sinew. Narya was a much younger man, yet carried himself with the practiced air of a veteran.

"Better for potency," Narya observed. "A good night for a fire."

Starrel absently put the dried meat into the cup. It would be surprisingly succulent in a few minutes. Until then, he was content to sip at the broth, warding the sudden chill of the evening. One small fire was enough for his company, well used to the chills of the night steppes. The Abbysins were less hardy and the past few nights had seen far more than the normal cookfires to tend. The sparse, brittle trees that stippled the low hills were quickly being stripped of their lower branches and the smell of dung rose from the smoke.

"If the Spring night doesn't break before long, those bombard battailes will be forced to torch their trebuchets and bows." Starrel observed drily.

"The wood will run out, and the dung too, before our orders come. We are of no use here, a surgeon's knife at the hands of a blacksmith, who, by the looks of it, has been a busy tailor for the well-dressed army." Narya chuckled with the slur directed at the heavy armor worn by most of the soldiers and infantry.

Starrel recognized the truth in that but said nothing. As Second Hand, he was not given to offering his opinions on the tactics employed by the Commanders, merely passing on orders to be obeyed. Narya knew the other wouldn't talk without provocation and kept on.

"Is there word on our disposition? The Cherros led the first command here. Since then, we have been moved further back as the siege engines and foot soldiers arrived."

"No. And there will likely be no word. Besides, we are better off on the fringes, we still get paid, so that complaint can be put to rest. The Abbysin are not under our feet and we are one step closer to our mother plains."

Starrel was content for the moment, idle between his calls to duty. The broth was still warm and that was enough. Still, he felt his lieutenant's frustration. The Cherros were not accustomed to biding their time in useless endeavours. He knew Narya well enough to know that he would not repeat any confidences.

"The command has its orders; Paterus can do nothing except obey them." Starrel shrugged as he took a bite of the softened meat and let the juices collect in his mouth before swallowing. "Say nothing to the men, but have them pay particular attention to their gear. It is my intuition … we'll be sent to the East. Dispatches came with this morning's messenger. The bones of war shake in the Jimals. It is a better field for our Dragoons than the lands within the Black Gate."

Starrel didn't like the thought of a protracted battle within the Stands. Once beyond the Gate, there was but one way out, by retreat. A smart General might easily trap any army that dared enter. There was no tactical advantage to be gained, though he kept his views to himself. A Cherros thought differently than the military minds of the Abbysin. The Dragoons were prized mercenary troops, merciless and efficient and therefore expensive. Their losses were tallied and charged and would not be wasted in a fruitless endeavour.

"We will be ready. There is no need for extra attention to our tackle. What Cherros would let it be less than perfect?"

"Even so. Men get lazy when they are inactive. Say nothing in particular, just keep them ready to ride at a moment's notice."

"Of course."

Crackling snaps drew their attention down to the flatter ground, where clustered campfires dotted the foot-soldier's billets like dandelions in a field. One of them had flared into a scrub pine which began to torch, spitting red and gold sparks as fire bloomed in the thin, oiled needles and pitchy bark. Heated airs eddied around the sudden wildfire, like a dust djinn over the sands, sending flames in gaseous whips that urged the other cookfires into similar fiery caprices.

Starrel shot a glance to the banners marking the Commander's pavilion. Crimson and orange licks of fire flickered from their cook fires like snake's tongues, reaching to taste the incendiary flavor of the nearby pines. "Douse the fires … and assemble the Dragoons. Now!"

Narya had seen the sudden burst of flame from the footsoldier's camp and responded without acknowledgment or salute, shouting directions to the farriers and armorers as he ran to his tent. Starrel started for the command pavilion when another explosive crackle shattered a pine, dropping a crooked split of the tree in front of his path with a shower of sparks and a gout of flame.

Fire continued to swirl, the campfires all pressed by some unseen fuel. Soldiers were dropping their dinner bowls and cards, looking towards tents and possessions or stumbling away from the dried grasses surrounding the camps. The dervishes of flame began to merge, as more crackling pines and low campfires threw blazing scales of crimson and gold into the air. Starrel stood frozen for a moment as he watched the fires coalesce into a gaseous mold.

Sheets of flame spread like ragged claws as the center winds grew in tempest, the funnel forming a fiery snout with baleful eyes scorching hot above its flaming maw. Each lick of flame fluttered into the swirling center to form wavering triangles of dragon-like teeth, scything scales and monstrous claws, raging as it gained fuel. Fire began to dance throughout the scrub pine as his eyes took in the inferno, lashing out in hot vapors like a creature of terrifying myth, etched in the air with burning inks.

The mass of flame wrenched around, its calamitous eyes passing across his form as it turned, spurring Starrel into action. He bolted for the Commander's tent as trailing fires from the sorcerous beast whipped like a spiked tail against the siege engines staged beyond the camps. Wood and pitch combined with the impact to explode in phosphorus brilliance.

Officers were ineffectually shouting orders at each other and their confused messengers, as Starrel neared the Commander's pavilion. Suddenly, a crackling wind caused him to instinctively duck. Talons of fire, trailing acid smoke, surged overhead and sliced through the tent like burning knives, the fiery rip of rending canvas overlaid by the screams of those within. The pavilion bloomed in conflagration. Starrel shuddered to a stop and bolted back towards the Painted Horse lines without hesitation. Chaos was charging through the foot soldier and heavy horse encampments. Heat washed past him in waves, pushing him as he raced up a short hummock to the Cherros lines. He saw the horses freed of their hobbles and saddled, though most of the men were racing about, gathering belongings and setting packs. There were no commands to relay and the curse of the Gates ... it could be nothing else ... was an enemy for which he had no weapons nor commission to fight.

"Mount and ride! Now!" Starrel shouted as he ran towards a lean roan that held the end position of the picket. His Second tossed the reins and they bounded onto their mounts in unison as others reached the horse lines.

"South. Reach the sands!"

Starrel spurred forward through the whirling smokes of the camp, which seemed to burst with scalding heat as they passed. He pounded up the low rise, racing his horse past the divide of trees where he wheeled to a stop at the crest of the hill, waving the rest of the troop towards the sandy benches beyond the reach of both river and trees.

Behind, the mass of flame was rising majestically from the mad capers of fire that raged throughout the encampment, drawing in the air with violent gusts. Starrel's dark hair whipped at his face as he gazed upon the raging crimsons and golds of the apparition beginning to rise with ponderous sinuations of its blazing tail, lifting in shreds with the crackling smoke of the burning ground. A hideous blazing maw snarled, while fiery claws grasped at the gases for flight, growing larger and lofting ever higher in their ethers. In the fireglow he could see clusters of soldiers racing towards the river, too few considering the numbers that had been amassed.

Starrel froze as the dragon's burning gaze passed over the encampment. There was no escaping its violent wrath should it advance upon his troop. He fought to still his breath as the spectre's eyes were drawn beyond them, the fiery enchantment beginning to shear away from the torched remains of the army and towards the Black Gate. Its sinuous flight pulsed the air like the rush of heated bellows, leaving a trail of cindered debris and smoking soots which further blackened the night as it swept in the direction of the Stands.

Once past the cloak of the scrub pines, Narya turned, jerking his horse to a halt at Starrel's side. "What is it that I'm seeing?" Narya was a solid fighter in battle but his eyes looked as wide and wild as a raw recruit seeing a blooded sword for the first time.

Starrel had the same level of disbelief, though he had the advantage of years to add ice to his veins. He watched the shredding flames of the dragon diminish as it gained distance away from them, the sinuous curves of it's serpentine flight finally disappearing beyond the protective screen of the nearby Granite Mountains.

"The curse of the Gate ... is what you're seeing. I've seen it before and well enough."

Once the fiery apparition had wormed into the night, little more than scattered, angry fires and pandemonium rose from the remains of the encampment. There was an army to salvage, though he had little hope for the Commander. A new one would take his place. Starrel made his decision ... a new adjutant would be best to parlay whatever orders were next.

"A count." Starrel stared at the destruction, requesting the number of his troops as though taking stock after a battle.

"Two missing. Phlanel and Denem. We have their horses, though."

"Good. The curse has voided our contract here. East to Safrasco. We'll make a new accounting there." Starrel finally turned to face his Second, relieved for the moment to take his eyes away from the destruction. His face softened for a moment as though anticipating rest. "We can stop among our people on the way."

Chapter 12

Dignitaries lined the stonelaid entrance to the assembly hall, dressed in their robes and badges of state. Slender columns of snowy marble held back a lattice of stained glass, brilliant windows framed by graceful arches that rose majestically to fall back into the center, tied by a sparkling chandelier. Beneath the candelabrum stood a graceful statue of a woman carved from the same pure white marble, beckoning with placid eyes to all that would enter. Inana, the Standish symbol of justice and equality, was posed with her hands held palms up, a symbolic bridge of birds arched between them. The drone and chatter of conversations were muted by the chancel airs of the hall, which tinted and flitted like iridescent jungle birds, as light was cast through the colored prisms of the tall windows.

Cerra had a hard time feeling the extent of the hall as she was led in on the arm of Captain Ferriman. She had supposed she would be introduced piecemeal to the society of Bridash, as fate would allow. That notion had been dashed quickly, for shortly after they had arrived at the halls of upper Bridash, she was escorted immediately to her guest of state apartments and fitted for a gown.

"I assure you, this isn't necessary." she had complained, feeling more irritated at getting swept from one place to another than she was for the undue attention. It would take days to assess her surroundings, being turned and directed faster than she could paint the locations in her mind.

"In society, appearances are everything," Ferriman replied in a flat tone, stating nothing more than a simple fact. "The assembly this evening is to discuss defenses. However, there is no occasion in Bridash that doesn't warrant pomp and ceremony … one of the Lords … Lady Moors, actually … requested the dress. You'll get well fed, if nothing else. A proper presentation assures that everyone will know who you are from the beginning. It is better than emerging in pieces, which is certain to inspire an assortment of rumors and innuendos. There will be enough of those as it is."

"I'll try to be a proper guest." Cerra wasn't entirely convinced and held her arms up as a young woman draped cloth over her shoulders. She still wore the comfortable linen and felted wool of her riding clothes. She felt them much more appropriate. "What are they putting on me?"

"If you please, madam … silk and worsted wool from almanas," answered the woman fitting the cloth and making notes. "A splendid green, like the dark of the forests, piped in maroon which will complement the same color in the underskirt. There will be a cream-colored tatting around your neckline and framing the cut of the waist."

"I'm sorry that your artistry is wasted on whatever appraisal I can offer, it does feel lovely though. Who are you?"

"Ashtree Mazin. I'm still a student seamer. My artistry, as you say, won't be wasted by you. Oh no, not at all. It's the eyes of the other women that are sure to notice. These colors, I've long sought to marry and none of them have had the courage, nor the red hair to accent the look. You have the shape to drape it well, so I think you're the perfect subject."

"Ashtree. A favor if you please." Cerra traced the seams of the gown on either side of her hips to see if they were placed right. "Can you make a little cut in the seams on both sides ... and add two small pockets? I can feel by the folds that they won't be noticed. They are such a help."

"Why ... of course." The young seamstress sounded both curious and amused by the idea. "I certainly have enough end pieces to make them and it'll only take a moment. Now let me help you shrug that off. I'll have it seamed fitting and proper before you can finish your tea cakes."

Cerra felt like she was modeling the gown and not herself, an awkward notion as she was urged forward a step by the gracious Captain. A puffed and important voice announcing their arrival into the official gathering.

"Captain Artis Ferriman of the Southern Guard ... and ... Lady Cerra ... of the ... Meadows ... " Her surname was pronounced quaintly, as though presenting something pleasantly homespun at a debutante's ball. Though she couldn't see them, she could feel the eyes upon her as they stepped forward to enter the hall. The space of the gallery caused her unfocused gaze to drift upward, above the heads of those already in attendance. Although she couldn't see their critical looks, she could hear their assessments well enough; a hubbub of whispered notes about the quality and color of her dress, the handsome groomed Captain of the Guard, the wild flaming red hair, even the pleasant nature of her figure, all of which garnered comment. The most hushed remarks were directed at Kamir, who placidly scanned the room at ankle level as he padded quietly at her side.

"Her cat ... it's black ... an omen surely. How does she get it to stay with her?"

"She's blind, poor thing."

"Her walking stick ... she carries it like a queen. Where's she from?"

"I don't think I want to talk with her. What could I say? Ask her who made the dress."

Cerra felt curiously equal to the task, escorted by the respected Captain. She leaned in a little closer to Ferriman's arm as she bespoke him, still gazing with a beaming smile in the direction of the glittering glass windows that left flecks of warmth on her cheeks.

"You're right. I've created an image in an instant, haven't I?" She chuckled softly. "The audience knows a little bit about me now. Not where I'm from exactly, but certainly how I see the world."

Ferriman gave her arm an encouraging squeeze as they walked forward to be presented to the Basileus d'Cyning, titular ruler of the Independent Stands, who was holding court beneath the gaze of the statue. Ferriman stopped with an official click to his heels, "Highness."

Ferriman gave a quick bow, "I present Cerra Meadows to your offices."

"Lady ... Meadows. You grace the court with your presence." She could hear the age in his voice, a controlled articulation honeyed by years of diplomacy. She had always wondered what the voice of a king would sound like.

"I feel ennobled by the experience," she replied truthfully, whilst doing her best to curtsy; though the motion became little more than a bow of her head as she tried, unsuccessfully, to find the edges of her skirt for a proper sweep. She could feel the power inherent in the room, the quiet speech in sepulcher airs. "I am at your pleasure."

She heard a satisfied *'humph'* from the Cyning as Captain Ferriman filled in the introduction. "She is here as an observer, and my guest. She may offer some insight to the issues that currently face us at the Gate."

"I see."

Cerra could feel the Cyning's scrutiny and felt as proper and formal as her dress. She quelled her natural responses of jest, adding another bow to divert her eyes to the side. Oddly, she felt she listened better if she didn't look at whomever was speaking. The change in the Cyning's voice indicated he was addressing his next words to Captain Ferriman.

"What kind of insights might those be, Captain?"

"She was witness to the restoration of the Gates, these few years past."

Cerra felt the ruler's gaze return and the change in the timbre of his voice marked his attention on her, while still speaking to the Captain.

Basileus regarded the short, pleasant woman who stood in front of him. Though her gaze was often misdirected, she captured her poise with a steady, sincere smile and her walking stick, crowned with an intricately carved pine cone, gave the impression of royal intent. The enormity of the collapse and the equally cataclysmic restoration of the Gates, had created quite a stir of speculation. Guards and caravaners alike had treated the new guardian with reverence. The colossus that had been destroyed by terrifying majics had been resculpted by majics just as inexplicable. A woman with wild hair, a staff and a cat at her feet had replaced the sword, buckler and crown of the ancient king. He eyed her semblance more intently.

"And tell me … Cerra … what did you see?" His voice lowered with genuine curiosity, in part concerning her blindness but also a personal interest in gaining insight on an event that had puzzled many.

Already she felt as though she was swept up in the private currents of the court, as it was clear the Regent thought she had information of a secret nature. "Sadly, I saw nothing. But … I did feel the integrity of our land being restored. It was all I was given to witness."

"Of course. And the sorceries … for that's what they were … what had you to do with them?"

Cerra thought carefully before answering. Yutan was best a mystery unrevealed, for there was no tale that would encompass him.

"I am as you see me, your lordship. I may be dressed for your courts, though I am truly a woman content with her lot." She closed her lids briefly, as though in self-reflection, an attempt to divert the discussion back to herself. "I have learned much about myself in the past few years. In not seeing, I have come to trust nature and perhaps speak for it again. The gods know I have no majics nor spells to play with. The nature of … the world … will sometimes reveal itself to me. It was the spirit of restoration that brought me to the Gate that day. I truly hope to be of service to you as an observer and assist as I can."

"A blind observer. Leave it to the military mind to arrive at that conclusion." The voice came from Cerra's left, blustery, yet anaemic. A new presence had intruded, lofting in with a wave of importance and now the voice was directed at her, drawn with barely contained sarcasm. "Why do you suppose you're here?"

Cerra felt immediately insulted but held her composure. She pictured someone weak, even as she calmed herself from showing a flush in her cheeks. "I can't guess the motives of the military … ser …"

"Pryan … Denalo Pryan."

"Ser Pryan. … well, as I said … I can't guess the motives of Generals, though I would imagine that if the general is victorious, he likely made many calculations inside his head, long before the battle was fought." She did her best to smile in his direction. Strangely, an odd crinkle appeared in her dark sight, which she attributed to her imagination trying to paint an image of him, a flat and lacquered image of two faces regarding both directions. The fanciful image seemed appropriate. "The general who loses likely did not think it through first. Ser … Pryan … it is a singular experience to meet you. I envy those whom you've not yet met."

"Of course. My pleasure too," he replied, using a condescending tone Cerra had no problem hearing, as if the company would be less for his absence. She was glad to hear his exiting pronouncement. "I'll leave you to the military minds. But before I do, you want to know of motives? I'll tell you. They're either for profits or influence, ... something generals don't have a head for."

"There is more to service than profits, Pryan. You've not been here long enough to fully grasp that." Basileus Cyning had bristled at the interruption, though had held his displeasure in order to observe how the blind woman would respond to the Lord's posturing. He allowed himself a broad smile when he heard the blind woman's clever rebuttals. Captain Ferriman had a hard look about him, an unreadable soldier at his post as Pryan blustered on, confident of his position as a matter of birthright.

"While other Lords have been shuffling about ... or having the blind lead the blind as is apparent, I've had success in strengthening our position, further barring any attack by the Abbysins."

"I appreciate your concern, Lord ... Pryan." Basileus sounded thoughtful, though Cerra could easily hear the irritation in the Regent's reply, disguising it with a slight laugh. She was not sure she would have the same resolve, but took note of Artis Ferriman's silent tact and kept her thoughts and retorts to herself. Basileus made his own dismissal of Lord Pryan clear.

"Your remarks will be central to our discussions to be certain. Thank you, Ser."

Pryan harrumphed in apparent victory and nodded away, satisfied. The very air seemed to relax with his passing. As

Regent of the Stands, Cyning had his own misgivings about the motives of the military mind, as well as the unclear ambitions of the woman that stood benignly in front of him. There was clearly more to her than a blind peasant woman, yet her sincerity was genuine, a rare commodity in court. Basileus broke the rare protocol of proffering a hand, but did so to assure Cerra with his gentle grip. Speaking directly to her, his voice was fatherly.

"In spite of the Lord's short view, I'll be interested in hearing what advice you might have to share, Lady Meadows."

"Of course, Lordship."

Titles came odd to Cerra's lips, though she managed without noticeable hesitation. Releasing her hand, she heard him turn to the side, the rustle of clothes indicating that others, aides or advisors, had come to his audience. She was clearly being dismissed. She curtsied again, much better this time as she swept the gown correctly, which added to her smile as the Regent surely missed her effort. Ferriman, thankfully lead her to the fringes of the hall.

"Welcome to the Standish Court." Artis commented with a dry grin. "I think you met the worst of it straight away."

Cerra exhaled audibly, as though she could finally breathe normally, scrunching her face into a rakish grin. "As fat as butter, that one. I think I like him better unmet. *Hmmphh.* Court feels like swimming when there are sharks in the water. There aren't any where I live, of course, but I imagine it's ok to do so, except when they feed. *Heya* … speaking of which, you did say there would be food? That distraction will aid my observations. If I stay in one place for a few moments, I can assess the room and I should be able to dive right back in. It's only a touch more formal than a dance in Marrinight's loft. I'll be just fine."

"You may have to swim before you're ready, as those of interest will find you. Two approach now, the Baronies of Moors and Westre. The commander general is looking in my direction, so I imagine he would have words. Can I get you anything first?"

"A drink, Captain, if you please. Send some water with lemon or a little watered wine." Cerra leaned closer to him. "Your General certainly takes first call. I think I'll be fine in avoiding the sharks. I wouldn't mind sitting for a few minutes, so you'll probably find me in a chair when you return … if there is one."

"There are … and …" Ferriman raised his voice to a comradely level by way of introduction, " … may I introduce the Lady Moors of Ceniago and Sir Westre, who represents baronies gracing the Upper Stands." He touched her shoulder with an aside. "I'll see about your drink."

"Thank you, Captain." Cerra could feel the presence of the two royals, the light scents of Lady Moors foremost as the taller Westre loomed slightly behind. She was glad that it was the Lady who spoke first.

"How lovely to meet you. And please, call me Katarin. I get 'Ladied' enough and I would know you better." Katarin's voice was aristocratic and clear, yet warm and inviting as she traced the back of her hand down the tailored sleeve of Cerra's gown. "I see the dressmaker has caught your features well. I'll commend her."

Cerra had no doubt about her genuine interest. Despite the urge for familiarity, Cerra sketched a small curtsy, nodding her head with a smile. "This is a lovely dress, milady Katarin, or so they claim. It feels so to me. I've never had anything quite so nice. I'm truly grateful." Cerra placed her hand on Katarin's arm, adding a quiet, sisterly note with a grin. "It has pockets."

Katarin chuckled, liking the young woman immediately, her impish smile warm and welcoming. Despite her blindness, she had the most remarkable brown eyes, lit with an inner light. Katarin turned to Sevekin. "Lord Westre ... this is our guest, Cerra of the Meadows."

Cerra held out her hand and Westre gave it an uncertain shake.

"It's my pleasure to meet you too, Ser Westre. Captain Ferriman says that your holdings are of the Upper Stands, which I am very glad to call my home. Are Aleston and Scotts Mill in your domain?"

"Aleston? No ... thankfully, my lands are much closer to Bridash." By Westre's remark it was clear he thought Aleston was beyond hope and culture, stuck in the hinterlands. He was not speaking to her either, his voice trailed as if he were looking about the room. "If you'll excuse me, ladies, I need to direct my attention to other matters."

He didn't wait for a response, though both Cerra and Lady Katarin acknowledged his departure. A waiting servant took the opportunity to deliver a silver goblet of sparkling water with a wedge of lemon.

"Could you set it down ... next to a chair?" Cerra turned

to Katarin with a smile. "And could you set me down next to it? Sitting for a moment or two will help me get my bearings and enjoy the drink."

"Of course. There are settees just over here, not ten steps away, just beyond the atrium near the balcony." Katarin directed the servant to place the goblet and took Cerra's elbow with a sisterly hug. "I'll join you for a few moments. The men will talk on at length before a woman's voice will get through. I can save myself the breath and get to know you a bit too."

"Most everyone seems gathered in the center, so I imagine we'll be out of the way." Cerra was grateful to sit and to have the diversion. At first, the nearby talk had evoked renewed curiosity about her, along with a few furtive remarks, though it had soon drifted back to more immediate concerns. Katarin felt like a friendly beacon in uncertain surroundings.

"Have you always lived in Aleston?" asked Katarin. "Your red hair is very unusual, hardly seen outside the Arenish Isles."

"I don't know where I was born. But I remember my mother … when I still had my sight. I was very young." The question raised a memory that didn't surface often: her mother, freckled cheeks and milky skin, her long red hair glowing in the candlelight, bending over to tuck her in. They had just been to the fair and she had been exhilarated by the day. Cerra's eyes were alive with pleasure and her mother had never seemed more beautiful, bending over to tuck her in to her bedding. "Yes. My red hair must be from her." Cerra snickered, smoothing at her plaited hair, a feat she'd rarely attempted herself. "I think I got the unruliness from the weather. By all accounts, we may be in for a spell of no rain."

"*heh heh*. I can see it's a handful!" Katarin leaned in close and brushed at one of Cerra's wayward curls. "I'll tell you a secret, I wish mine had half its curl. My hair would hang straight as a die were it not for my curl setters."

"Oh my! … Curl setters would languish with me. Hair is the biggest reminder I have that I can't control everything." Cerra sighed with an impish grin. "I just sleep on it and wait for what's next."

Katarin patted Cerra's hand. "We all have reminders … of what we can't or can control. It doesn't seem like much, most of the time." A small sigh escaped her lips, "*Heh* … someone asked me how you keep your cat so close."

"Oh, that's easy!" Cerra laughed. "I'm a warm cushion that moves. He likes his comforts."

"Will you be in Bridash for long?"

"I hope not, really. As I mention comfort, I absolutely love the familiarity of my home. I'm only here at the Captain's behest, so it depends on him." Cerra mused with a wry look, then tried to brighten her comment, not wanting to discount the Bridash hospitality. "However, I'm sure if I spent some time here, I'd likely enjoy it very much."

"The Captain has engaged you as an advisor, I understand."

"Yes. That's how he's employed me, though he's a very knowledgeable man, so I imagine I have little advice to offer." Cerra leaned in a little, sharing a confidence. "Actually, I feel more a participant in a game where I don't know the rules."

"At the moment, I doubt anyone here knows the rules, nor

the game. Your advice will be as appropriate as anyone else's. And I'll likely look to you myself for suggestions, for most here have offered solutions to a problem they don't understand." Katarin patted Cerra's hand. " And ... at the moment, I must go and listen to them. Will you join us? Basileus is giving me an annoyed look."

"Oh, if you please, allow me sit for a moment. It's easier for me to judge the room."

"Of course." Katarin gave Cerra's hand another squeeze. "We'll talk more."

Moments after Katarin left her side, Kamir hopped into her lap, a slight mewl as he leapt, her only warning. She was glad she didn't have her drink in hand.

"*Oof* ... where have you been?" The black cat curled into immediate repose. "Yes, these functions can tire."

She slid her walking staff next to the bench, picked up the goblet of lemoned water and took a grateful sip. Absently stroking Kamir's sleek fur, she caught morsels of talk within the hall. The conversations were as varied as food laid at a feast. The even tones of Ferriman in discussion with his commander were easy to discern and now that she was familiar with the voice of Moors and Westre, she was able to trace the waves of their conversations through the low rumbling babble of the gathered officials. Cerra could only guess at the cabals and factions that wove their net within the government of the Stands.

'*I sense danger.*' Yutan's warning tone broke into her thoughts. '*Are you threatened?*'

'*Oh no. I'm enjoying myself. I think. Your company is preferred, though. Maybe afterwards ...*' Cerra knew he would catch her playful drift. *'Now, I'm trying to listen and there are a lot of people talking.'*

Yutan held his reply, a sense of watchful concern remained, which made her smile at his protective nature.

It didn't surprise her that the spindly voice of Pryan, filtered through the din of conversations within the great hall. She had only met him moments ago and would be glad to undo the memory. There weren't many people that she felt instant dislike for and now, the result of some malevolent twist, his reedy and insubstantial tones rang in her ears as unwelcome as a mosquito. In spite of her distaste for him, she found herself drifting back to what he was saying. It was the inclusion of Westre in the hushed conversation that centered her attention. The two Lords must only be twenty or so paces away, standing near one of the pillars. She took another sip of her lemon water and gazed out to the room, away from their conversation, yet much more in tune with her ears.

"What else is there to do except mount some sort of campaign?" Pryan paused for a moment and his voice changed, a little lower as though dabbling in intrigue and thick with arrogant smugness. Cerra strained to hold onto the thread of the conversation, barely catching Pryan's next words. "I did the right thing. The smart thing. I have procured a contract for arms and if you were of a mind, you'll invest too. Already there are those who advocate war. The attack on the Gates was an affront. Call it what you will, there is opportunity here, if you ask me. And act fast about it."

"I think it might be sound..." Westre sounded uncertain, as though he had already committed, yet needed more convincing to bolster his resolve.

"Of course, it is. Arms are like ale. They will always make money. I intend to take advantage, even foment opinion in favor of the war if need be. In war there are winners and losers. The winners are those who profit. I'm a winner, you can bet on that. And … I have other backers. You are in the best company." Pryan added with a more secretive boast. Cerra could well imagine him looking around with suspicious eyes.

"War isn't a popular choice with the population," Westre was warming, his voice betraying that he didn't share the opinion of the masses.

"*Bah!* Who cares? Who among them has the coin to pay for their opinions … let them squawk for their talk is cheap. I tell you, conflict is inevitable. There is nothing wrong with taking advantage. While those muttonheads-in-arms employ blind advisors to see them through … *har har har* … in no time at all, they'll see the value of my swords. It is your Landholders that should be of interest. Have you talked to them?"

"Most of them hold their assets close." Westre grunted, as though he was making an old and tired argument, then his interest level changed. "But you make a point. You say you have a reliable source? We can't afford to wait on shipping."

"Ever practical. Of course, I know the best people."

Cerra smirked in spite of herself as she eavesdropped. Pryan sounded like a fishmonger who had just sold the fusty remains of his sketchy catch, and not a moment too soon. "All the best. No one knows them better than I."

"Abbysins, naturally."

"Who else? They have the best pikes. Not everyone knows

that. And does it matter if it is the Abbysins? Further, I'll tell you a secret. The Jimals … swimming in riches. I said I know the best people, did I not? For our part we put up a modest … not too small mind you, this is serious business … say a reasonable investment that will yield quick returns. Get a few of those fat Lords you mentioned to loosen their purses. They won't be sorry. I'm telling you, the Jimalian assets will guarantee your investment. Besides, if we wait for the Standish army to fortify themselves, we shall be in our cups, sucking on pap, and learning how to salute their damnable Emperor. Think on it … but not too long, mind you. Hind teat never gets much."

"I'd feel stronger about this if your payments for the duchy were current." Westre lowered his voice with an edge, touching on a topic that was obviously stale between them. Lord Pryan was quick to interject with assurances. Cerra could well imagine him clapping the reluctant Westre on the back, even as he led him into a fetid marsh. She didn't dare turn in their direction but brushed back her hair, for they were talking close and the general murmur of the gathering was getting harder to filter out.

"That's the nature of this investment. As you can see, I've devoted my resources … to the protection of the Stands, mind you. I'm sure you won't regret waiting for the payoff." Pryan's voice wavered, as though looking about and, for a change, apparently not wanting to attract an audience. " … *er* … *humph* … I must go … an important meeting … important meeting. Send me your answer tomorrow. The order is already being negotiated. You won't regret it."

Cerra felt an odd chill, the distaste of such unprincipled

humanity so unfamiliar to her palate. The papery image of a lord with two faces infected her vision once again as she switched her gaze towards the pair.

She lost Westre's reply as she tried to sort out Pryan's last words. What meeting could be more important than the one he was attending? There was likely none, she considered drily, hearing the self-absorbed lord hustle away with a stream of hasty goodbyes trailing in his wake. More likely avoiding his creditors …

The approach of Captain Ferriman interrupted her thoughts, the distinctive tread of his step tapping the floor decisively with a long and easy stride. His voice was a welcome one.

"Forgive me for my absence. The Commander General had more questions than I anticipated. Not the least of which, was you."

"I'm glad I wasn't there to overhear. I hate being the topic of discussion in more than one circle."

Cerra looked at him as she grabbed her walking cane and stood. She had an odd twinkle in her eyes, like a fishwife targeted on a bit of gossip.

"I assume you've heard something." Ferriman let her steady against his arm. She looked about, taking one last sip of her drink before she set it down.

"I have found that many people think that if you can't see, you're unable to hear as well. I'm a little disheartened to hear some of what passes for conversations in the halls of power, though I really should know better. Living in the remoteness of the Dragon's Teeth keeps me blessedly naïve."

"And maybe, more objective."

Cerra didn't get a chance to relay the content of her eavesdropping, as Yutan's voice came to her mind in sharp alarm.

'A beast approaches. Ill sorcery! It bears down from above.'

Cerra startled back with questioning notions that were drowned out by the ferocity of the demon's thought.

'I will protect you.'

She clasped Ferriman's arm, speaking low and anxious, weighted by the intensity of Yutan's sudden alarm. "Captain. I fear danger! I think you should alert the watch."

Ferriman followed her unfocused gaze as she stared out beyond the balcony to an oddly glowing smudge that lay in the skies to the south, obvious concern written on her face. He had learned long ago that it is better to act on a warning and chance a false alarm, than to ignore one and risk calamity. He snapped for his aide who arrived at his side with quick efficiency.

"Have the watch stand to immediately. Every station. Go."

The aide left without a word, intent on his orders, while Ferriman laid a hand to Cerra's shoulder. "I know better than to think you play me on. I mean to alert the gathering, though I don't know what I'm going to tell them. Wait here."

The Captain left her near the settee but his concern about the warnings were moot as sounds of alarm began rising from the valley below, horns and bells making their dire announcements. The assembly began stirring with uncertainty as Ferriman reached the Commander General.

"Sir. I think it best to adjourn from the hall. There may be danger. I've already ordered men to their posts."

Alarms began sounding outside in the reaches of Upper Bridash, confirming Ferriman's claim. The older man nodded and began escorting those gathered with him to the entrance. Ferriman looked back for Cerra and saw her tapping her way hesitantly towards the palisade overlooking the ancient upper bridge. She stumbled at the step down to the palisade but caught herself quickly as she reached the balustrade overlooking the falls and the valley below. Like a shadow, her black cat skipped behind her to launch itself up on the rail, eyes intent to the south. On the horizon, the blemish in the sky had become a seething conflagration which smote the air in ragged sweeps, a pulsing sunset dripping fire from its sinuous shape. Air lay dirty behind it, smudging the sky with bloody smokes.

Cerra had known the step was there, yet failed to account for it accurately and stumbled slightly as she made her way to the palisade overlooking the grand farmlands of the Lower Stands. The falls had a flatness of sound that disappeared into a well below. In spite of the warnings of Yutan to hide herself, her eyes remained riveted to the horizon.

There was no paint in her imagination to account for the crinkles of yellowed flecks that cut through her blindness like an enormous snake in flight.

Chapter 13

Flame dripped like spent scales in the wake of the dragon, floating down into the copses and pastures of the Lower Stands, the sparking flashes igniting any dry tinder they touched. The storm-red phosphor of its being sizzled, flaring the benign turbulence of the air with each coiling twist of its flaming tail, driving the phantasm forward to the towers and cliffs of Bridash, its flight unwavering and resolute.

Cerra stood against the balustrade, her blind eyes cast out over the valley below. The drone of the falls eclipsed her imagination, the strangeness of the surroundings making it difficult for her to imagine the tableau before her. A streak of flaming yellows, sickly in its appearance, cut across the blackness of her sight, flaring then sinking like scraps of paper. She could paint vivid and fanciful scenes, though this phantasm wasn't a creature of her imagination. Anxiously, her mind sought the rumbling connection with the demon.

'What is that?!'

'Vizier's work.'

Yutan's short answer confirmed her fears. The same potent recipe that had given rise to the demon had conjured the vision she saw before her, growing closer with each sweep of its fiery tail.

'Hide yourself!'

Yutan went silent in her mind, a sudden rumble of effort replacing it.

Even the vibrations surrounding the falls could not hide the disturbance created as the demon began to draw himself up from the lake behind the upper bridge. Thunderous clouds gathered in a boiling violence, a sudden turbulence capped the waters in white fury as wind spiraled upwards. Grasping at the sky, the demon rose in powerful turns, holding as much saturated airs as he dared. A monstrous waterspout emerged, an angry twist that thrashed the shoreline and swamped boats as the wind tore at the water. The tempest rose from the lake, dripping with monsoon rains as it cast itself over the city. A simmering cascade trailed it, laying down heavily on the shingled rooftops of Bridash.

Kamir leapt down for the safety of the pavilion while Cerra remained riveted to the baluster, even as the drenching rains of the demon passed overhead. Violent gusts of wind tore at the curly thickness of her hair, ripping it from her braids, the storm sliding quickly beyond the city and towards the approaching enchantment. She clutched her staff fiercely, bracing herself against the wind. The familiar light of the demon came through as a broiling mass of argents and blues. There was something both beautiful and terrifying about Yutan when he became one with the elements, when he became the Demon.

Her Demon.

Air churned in fiery sweeps, the dragon's tail and talons shedding flame like water sluicing from dipping oars. The demon felt the pull of the heated air and he propelled himself toward the conflagration. Sodden and heavy, he strained to keep himself lofted above the pinnacles and spires of the city. The skirts of the great city could be seen as they clung to the cliffs in chunks, connecting Upper and Lower Bridash as the demon crested over the pavilion that spanned the Emerald River before it cascaded to the valley below. The flaming dragon bore down inexorably, its path direct for the pavilion. Yutan could sense the blind woman below, could feel her reaching out, feel her uncertainty. Her awe.

Her Love.

There was a gathering force and the waves of her emotions crested throughout the turmoil embodied in the storm he had created. The air wanted to drift him apart and the water was doomed to succumb to the pull of the earth, solid and immutable. He knew fire, a part of him that itched and sparked with passion, hot and irresponsible, ravenous in its short-lived existence.

He closed the distance on the creature, placing the storm of him between Cerra and the incandescent heat of the approaching dragon. The eyes that guided the flame bore through his stormy essence, intent on the pavilion beyond. They became like beacons to the demon's flight, growing larger as they closed on each other, until the pupils gathered their own nimbus, a fire circling the eternal deep. Yutan felt the collision imminent, reaching out with the vapors of his gathered storm to enfold the dragon within his gales and drenching monsoons.

Ferriman rushed out to the balcony. The promenade, as

well as Cerra, had been drenched by the ferocious spate of thunderous rain, which now boiled in the direction of the fiery sweeps that cut the air. The phantasm had approached close enough that witnesses could clearly see the flaming shape of a dragon bearing down on the city. Some said later that the dark, fuming mass of air that collided with flaming beast, bore the face of an underworld god, fearsome and deadly. Punctured with lightning, the storm roiled with demonic precision toward the flaming dragon as though flung with a catapult.

"You must come inside!" Ferriman sought to move her away from the parapet, but Cerra resisted with a shake of her shoulders, keeping her unfocused eyes fixed on the scene beyond.

"No! Wait." Cerra's mind was trying to reach Yutan's. The enigmatic phrase *Ddraig och* came to her and then she could detect nothing further from him save the intention to quell the fire that consumed his sight.

"Ddraig och" she repeated aloud, a voice lost as she stared in disbelief at the impending collision of majics that invaded her blindness, the boiling argent of Yutan and the flickering tears of gold lights that marked the dragon.

The demon sought to embrace the fires in his smothering blanket of cloud and rain but the dragon seemed to loom larger and fragment as it bore down on him, spaces of white air eclipsing the solidity of its form. There was no turning back. The force of his violent storm demanded collision. He struggled to match the size of the beast, to overpower the sorcery that created it. Created him. As though filling his lungs for a plunge into the deep, the demon leapt at the beast, the storm cloud of his form wrapping the flames in his embrace.

The fire should have been dashed, consumed by the water and torrential winds he embraced, consumed by the demon in him. Instead, the conflagration sizzled and torched with increased fury, blasting the vapors of water into capricious steams that exploded at their release. There was heat, a shocking incendiary blast that tore at his memories like the moment he had been reduced to the elements, a soul shriven and torn from his being. Shredding apart, he continued to bear down on the fiery incubus that seared and crackled with a hissing roar, weighting it in a sinking diversion that left it arcing downward toward the face of the cliff.

Yutan sought to encompass the fire as the rains left him, driven to vapors, though the flames confounded him, sizzling from pressures within thin strips of light. The very particles of the flame became apparent, a firing of unstable metals, as the inferno of the dragon began to envelop him, casting him out in particles that lacked bonds, a gas within the spaces that had no ties to the weight of the earth. The demon's thought passed through the center of the dragon, a core burning with rims of flame as curls of charring parchment.

A word remained, the script grew as he fell further in: *Ddraig och.* The letters were written in dark inks by the sorcerer that created him and loomed over him like a colossus, before rushing past into the space beyond his thought. There was nothing more, not even the edges of his being, soaring outward in weightless abandon. There was nothing left to hold on to. Nothing.

Cerra felt a wrenching turn in her mind as the sharper blues surrounding the demon began to turn to nebulous vapors within the thin, crinkled yellows that marked the presence of the dragon. The colors merged and bloomed, a fuming mixture that burst at the edges from the impact. The wave of colors expanded, fighting for dominance in their explosive mixture. Cerra caught her breath as an abrupt surge of Yutan's argent light seemed to quell the dry yellows for the span of an instant, long and uncertain, before falling apart in a burst the shape of a silver orb that trailed nothing behind it as it expanded and was lost. A thunderous clap erupted from the burst, echoing in long rolls across the wide valley below, slapping the surfaces around her with an ominous pitch that shook her blood. The wave ripped past her leaving no trace of the demon's vibrant hue.

"Yutan!"

The cry partially escaped her lips as the buffeting winds of the detonation tore at her. Behind the flare of light, tainted yellow talons emerged from the flare and resumed their relentless approach. Ferriman pulled her roughly, away from the railing towards the dubious safety of the great hall. He lifted her up the two wide steps as they approached the interior. Most of the gathering had already left in a controlled rush, guided by the urgings of the General and his aides. A few dignitaries and their associates remained, who, like Cerra, had been drawn to the balustrade by the flaming sky to the south.

The ominous cloud confronting the dragon had been reduced to vapors in a spectacular clash. Fuming mists hung for uncertain moments before the fiery spectre of the dragon finally emerged from the remains, its flight lower and yawing at an uncomfortable tilt. Steam blanketed some of the flame as it began to arc down towards the cliffs, causing those remaining to retreat in a rush into the great hall, intent on the main doors leading to the courtyard. Cerra was jammed and knocked from her feet in their panic, her staff flying as she lay her arms out in front to catch her fall. Ferriman went down too, buffeted heavily by the rush.

Holding the red-haired woman close, Ferriman shot a look back to the promenade as the last of the panicked onlookers ran past. The burning dragon continued to pitch downward, thrown from its trajectory and arcing in slow majesty as it lost inertia, dipping from his sight as it smashed into the cliff below in a thunderous gout of boiling fire. The percussion shook the chandelier from the ceiling, shattering on the floor in a thousand prisms of fired light.

The colored glass windows of the great hall blew outward, revealing splashing waves of dripping flame, sparkling fury that spurred Ferriman to lift Cerra to her feet. He froze in horror as he saw the open courtyard ahead. Those who had dashed outside were hit with the shedding flame and reduced to cinders within the molten wash, the gaseous cascade rushing through the open doors. He dropped in close behind one of the marbled columns, wrapping Cerra within his arms as the incendiary remains of the dragon bloomed through the air of the great hall. Outside, a palisade and its arching bridges began to collapse as their wooden timbers flared with an enchanted combustion, abrupt and intense.

Cerra felt the Captain wrap her close amid the cacophony and heat. She hid behind her senses, rolled into a tight ball, scared and depleted by the disintegration of the demon, whose final argent bloom had dissolved into the darkness of her sight.

It was not pain that the demon felt at the last, but a detachment from all as the waters of his being steamed into gas, an explosion that left nothing but vapors to float into the ether. A satisfying peace enveloped him as he drifted into the thin motes of gas, dissolution not to the Void but to the edges of everything. No vestige of earth or water remained, just the expanding freedom of space.

❖ iv ❖

Flickering light played on the inks, making them pulse with energy, their depths momentarily unknown. As the shadow of the mage's hand passed over the card of *Ddraig och*, the glimmering reds and golds were extinguished, snuffed into lifeless design, though the fired inks of its frame remained. The marks framing the *Tower* card flickered weakly while the opposing card of *Abaddon* showed no life, subjugated by the power of the *Ddraig och*. The box that encompassed it on the arena was equally devoid of life. The appearance of *Abaddon* had been a disturbing revelation, a dangerous card to have in play. There was a sigh of relief from the seer as the card was slid from the arena and split into the safety of the deck. The *Knight of Swords* remained, resolute, though apparently with nothing left to defend.

The seer moved as though to finish the session when the arena cast a new light, lines simmering around the remains of the *Ddraig och*. Another card was destined to be drawn and as if cued, the Book flipped to a new page with a dry rattle.

"Draw the top card to complete the divination."

There was a thoughtful pause before the seer's hand uncovered the card and a longer one before its face was revealed. *Nuith*. The *Queen of Quills*. The candle light made the inks appear fresh as though newly drawn and wet to the touch.

The royal card showed a blindfolded woman with waves of fiery hair, seated with her hand resting on large cat. Her other hand gripped a staff topped with a pine cone. A crown of quills hung behind her as though a crown or a key to the gateway marking the infinity that lay beyond her throne.

The card was laid down carefully, whilst the book shuffled to a new page. The left depicted the Queen, drawn in sepia inks while the right page was given to description of the virtues of the powerful card. On the parchment of the arena, the marks of the two Queens were poised in opposition to each other. The card was an equal to the *Queen of Roses* which lay as the avatar of the seer and in play as though guarding the deck. The seer's finger traced the ancient Jimalian describing the *Queen of Quills*, the floral embellishments of the script adding drama to the language.

> *Nuith, before she knew who she was, had hair of ebony and walked with a black panther by her side. As she learned her nature through discovery, her hair turned lackluster and her panther showed the spots of a leopard. When she fully realised who she was and expressed herself fully in the world, her hair became red and luxuriant. The panther returned to its true self though spots hidden in the dark coat of the great cat remain as a reminder of the dark times experienced in the past.*

The seer read on, the hand stopping abruptly at the end.

> *The Queen of Quills represents the process of self-discovery and awakening, even though this means one will have to experience possible dark periods in life. Unaided she is powerful though susceptible to her shortcomings.*

Surrounded by her suit, she may become the most potent
card in the Royal Houses.

The Seer contemplated the final stipulations of the card,
the last words of particular importance.

Weakness:

Nuith will want to control and dominate her environment.
The Queen of Quills must fight the tendency and find
the ability to adapt to get on in the world. She knows her
contradictions and perseveres in their spite.

Her paradox: True power comes in serving others, not
dominating, so she must strive not to control events.

The Seer picked up and studied the card, the brilliant inks
twitching with life under the flickering candle. The *Queen of
Quills* was dressed in flowing green, and despite the blindfold
covering her eyes, seemed to gaze directly as though reading
the intentions of the viewer. Her red hair flared out like the
radiance of a morning sun. The card seemed to pulse with life
and the seer set the card back in its position next to the *Knight
of Swords* as though reluctant to handle it further.

The flaring inks of the arena began to fade as the Book
fluttered shut, signaling an end to the divination. The Seer
rose to light another candle while still contemplating the lay
of the cards. Without the wavering light of the single candle,
the cards seemed lifeless, their inks worn and scuffed with age.
The cards were gathered and returned to the box. Relieved of
its burden, the parchment of the arena folded crisply along its
creases, ready to slip into the box lid. With the contents stowed,
the box was set aside on the desk, left among the scrolls and
papers like a money counter's coin box.

Chapter 14

Wood smoke permeated the air, cindered dry and hot. A crackling like dozens of campfires dotted the space around, her orientation slow and breathing difficult. Cerra wanted to stay curled and safe in her soft, dark cocoon. Movement within the cushion that wrapped about her forced her to consciousness, the churning of events flashing through her mind as her senses returned. The dripping tongues of fire and incendiary heat had encircled her, the demon driven from her sight. A rush to safety by … Ferriman, … his movement coming behind her finally added coherence to her whereabouts, accompanied by the choked intake of breath. His protective arms loosened, a relaxation of exhaustion rather than ease.

"Cerra." The Captain's tense voice was barely a whisper, not question or statement, hope or acceptance.

She flexed in response, not trusting herself nor the surroundings. The wet nose of Kamir against her cheek prompted her to speak.

"I … I'm fine." Her voice cracked. She felt as desiccated as a cured herb and the image of her cottage lake surfaced in her mind. Just the thought of water rejuvenated her some, moistening her lips enough to talk. There were no searing pains that she could identify. She wasn't sure if she had been speaking to the cat or Ferriman. As she lay there, gathering her courage to move, she desperately tried to understand the circumstance and even where she was within the great Hall. "What was that?"

Ferriman's response was a dull grunt, incomprehension mixed with relief. "Don't know."

Talking stirred the both of them as Ferriman disengaged himself from his defensive shield. The sleeves of his shirt were dried cinders that split and rent apart as he moved. The leather of his tunic felt warm on his back. Had it been cloth he had no doubt it would have flamed. He rolled himself to his knees and stood. Wisps of thin smoke still escaped Cerra's dress, ragged and singed from where it was exposed to the vaporous erup-tion. The proximity of the stone pillar and the lower position of floor upon which he had thrown them, had saved them from the ferocity of the blast. Shingled panels still torched like prick-ets along the walls and the beams holding back the high open ceiling of the pavilion had tenacious fires clinging to them. Painful groans began to escape the timbers.

"We can't stay here." Cerra grimaced. She reached out as though she could feel the angry and uncertain space, then braced herself to kneel, trying to hear a quiet spot or feel a cooler breath of air as she turned her head. Kamir could be heard making anxious mewls to her left and she began to rise, with Ferriman helping her stagger to her feet. Cerra caught the cooling scent of water and coughed as she started moving in the direction the cat was indicating. "That way."

The Captain was fortunately urging her in the same direc-tion. He gathered up her cane, which had clattered against the steps, then gave her cues and warnings as they negotiated the smoldering debris, which lay in shattered mounds on the stone tiles. Waves of heat and crackling commotion pocked the air around her, confusing her ears and balance as she stumbled forward in the arms of Ferriman. Through the din of wreckage came the smooth sound of water, a clarity that added to the coolness and smell. The river was near. Amid the rush of water, the sounds of anguish and loss emerged. Other survivors had found safe refuge in the shallows where the river was bordered in cut stone and sculptured lawns, one of the many esplanades that skirted the backwaters as the Emerald River passed through Bridash and over the falls.

"There are steps just over here, leading into the lake for the water carriers. I'm afraid your gown is still smoldering. My back might be too for all I know. Careful, there is some moss on the stone."

Ferriman led her down stone cut steps until Cerra felt her slippers get wet. Just the immediate smell of the water acted as a balm that enveloped her, calming her disorientation as the hem of her gown swayed in the water. The Captain held her carefully as he stepped her further into the edge of the lake.

"Sit here for a moment." Ferriman guided her back, sitting as he did so. She felt like a dowsed poker, fresh from the fire as relief flooded her skin, caked grimes she hadn't noticed washing clear. She spit water from her mouth, her singed hair laying heavy and cool on her back.

"*Eesa sa.*" Cerra found her breath. The phrase she used was more an expression of a feeling than a word, something used in the Trader language when deeply moved or exhausted. She felt fortunate to live and relief was evident in her voice. "I'm not used to the rigors of government."

"The meeting got out of hand, I'll grant you that," Ferriman felt the same grimace inherent in her remark. Once dowsed of the incendiary heat that seemed to permeate their core, the cold water of the lake made itself known with an icy touch. It would be best to move before a chill set in. He stood, lifting Cerra to her feet before she had a chance to protest. "Here ... one of the benches at the top. Just four steps."

She was grateful for the count and sat with relief. The water had rejuvenated her and her sense of place had returned. What confused her most was the telltale traces of color that she had come to understand were not born in her imagination. She turned to face the Captain, seeing him with the same tell-tale colors, a knight with a sword eternally gripped in his hand and leading her forward. She had to know what her imagination had missed. She feared the reality was far more heinous. "Tell me. Please. What did you see?"

Ferriman waited to respond as her black cat pushed around her. She began to stroke it as it burrowed into the sodden folds of her gown, weariness and concern evident in the tight furrows of her brow.

The dragon-like effigy had been coiling directly at the pavilion that bridged the top of the falls. At their conference, Ferriman thought grimly. Instead, the monstrosity had been deflected by the clash with the storm that had risen from the lake like a counterstroke. Even though the brief, but raging tempest had been steamed to oblivion, the impact of it had sent the fiery spectre careening off course, dropping below the edge of the upper bench. The long tail of the blazing wyrm had smashed into gleaming towers and manors of the wealthy where they clung to the tall cliffs, but much of the beast had plunged into the great falls of the Emerald River. Shards continued to blaze like livid metal from a forge as they dropped with the water, the scorched remains of the dragon still shredding away with the relentless cascade. Pockets of fire remained seething at the perimeters, though the clouds of steam and billows of black smoke indicated most of the worst fires were already being contained by the emergency brigades. The torrential rains left by the sudden storm cloud had, by good fortune, soaked much of the area in its passing, else there would have been a firestorm within the stone and timber architecture.

Ferriman had little idea where to begin with his description. The sight of her calling to the storm that had collided with the fiery dragon made him think that she had witnessed far more than he did. What power did she possess? Of the many dignitaries that had been gathered, she remained the most unassuming, retiring early to the side and engaging in very few conversations. A joy had pervaded her demeanor, as though she communed with another force that engaged her heart. Now, as she gazed blindly at the flow of water in front of her, humor and wonder had been cast aside, a loss far greater than exertion.

"I am a Captain of the Gate. I am trained in battle. I know men and swords. I don't know what I saw. A dragon, yet not. A sorcerous wyrm of flame, intent on destruction as surely as the stones from a trebuchet. It crashed into the Middtons below us. The fires of the collision washed over the pavilion. Much of it hit the falls, thank the gods for that. Had not a storm ..." Ferriman turned to face her, questions evident in his voice, he wanted to see her reaction. "… a storm? … a sudden conjuring? … but had that 'storm' not met the fire dragon first, the pavilion and all inside would have been consumed."

Cerra nodded blankly. The collision remained emblazoned in her mind, the argent glow of Yutan dissolving into nothing. She heard a note of resignation in the Captain's voice as he continued.

"That is what I saw. If you can add to that …" Ferriman felt beyond a doubt that her presence or interference had somehow saved them from the worst of the collision and fires, he had seen her shout out to the storm … a word he did not know, a summoning … a name, a word of tremendous power. Yet, at the moment, the red-haired woman seemed as vulnerable and defenseless as he would expect from someone small and scared and blind. However, there was an air of resolve about her as she stared unfocused, the way some do when lost in thought, a look he knew better than to discount. She was not as defenseless as she seemed.

Cerra tried to recollect the image that had invaded her sight, the yellow and red crinkles that overrode her usual fanciful assumptions. The movements had been stiff, countless scraps folding in continual shreds of livid inks, like sun-damaged silk or …

"Paper and ink." Cerra talked softly out to the lake, the image of the dragon at last frozen in her mind. The sensation of ripping parchment into thin strips confirmed the notion. The answer sounded ineffectual, a weak solution, yet the idea persisted.

"I saw paper and ink."

Chapter 15

Luxury offers little comfort, Cerra decided. She missed the warm closeness of her cabin with its captured scents of living, a pleasure which seemed lost within the open courts and marbled walls of wealth. She could hear the ends of her room at home, feel the closeness of the thatch and beam of the roof, the glowing comfort of her cookfire. Here there was no companionable air nor close wall to hear her thoughts. Perhaps those deemed fit to rule needed more room for their lofty notions and grand ideas. There had been little opportunity to expand upon the notions of affluence and power, for the attack of the fire dragon had turned the serene and stately halls into boisterous and quarreling taprooms.

"You're stewing over something. You are unusually quiet." Captain Ferriman's voice came through unexpectedly. She hadn't forgotten he was there, or had she? Her contemplations and reflections had taken over. Kamir shifted a little. No matter the size of the accommodations, he would find her lap the most suitable spot.

Cerra let out a little snort. "A good stew has many ingredients and takes time to develop flavor." The tumult of the fiery attack still occupied her inner visions; the dissolution of the demon had left her energies depleted. He had been lost before. Was he lost now? Or … she let out a deep sigh.

"Maybe my plans for you weren't the best. Yet after this latest attack, I have no better option." Ferriman again interrupted her thoughts.

"Plan?" Cerra turned her head as if hearing a new and confusing idea. "How is it that anyone can make a plan ... make any arrangement. The force ... the enemy ... whatever it might be ... is most baffling. You don't know the who of it, nor their motives."

"Which makes me want to continue with the only plan I have." Ferriman clearly had no alternatives. His voice was as direct as a sword.

"*Phff* ... Plan *'Me'*." Cerra said dismissively and tried to imagine the comfort of her chair and preparations table, but failed. The dissolution of the demon had drained her senses of a vibrancy that she had grown accustomed to. She had become a pawn within someone else's game and comfort was not on the board.

Ferriman hesitated, thinking of his own daughter of nearly the same age as Cerra. Would he put her in harm's way? He thought not, though his daughter had not the quiet resolve that the blind woman had shown. "Yes, you."

Also, it was the unseen that seemed to make her blindness all the more valuable. His country was at stake. It was not the first time he had required a soldier to risk everything. He trusted her, even though she had not divulged all she knew. Who did? He wanted to understand her unexplained talent better, which meant broaching a subject he had mostly worked to avoid.

"When ... how long has it been ... since you've been

blind."

Cerra chuckled dryly at his reluctance. "Not a hard question to ask, Captain, be reassured. Any anxiety I've had about it passed me by long ago." She paused, the memory wry on her features. "When I was seven. A fever I was told, though I don't remember much before then. The fever also claimed my mother." Cerra shivered slightly, for she had envied her mother's death at the time and had wished to follow.

"You didn't take to it kindly." Ferriman prompted quietly. He could hear her voice change as memories poured forth. He didn't want to interrupt whatever revelations might be disclosed.

"Oh. I'm quite sure I was a hellion. *Heh* ... I remember one time hiding in a closet early on, refusing to come out, convinced that it was the closet only and when I emerged, in my own time, I would see again. But only if they left me alone. I was traded to many charities and orphanages, different voices and different towns, yet always in the same dark place. I truly hated it." Cerra felt a warmth penetrate her smile. She paused a moment as she let the memories of Susinna flood through her. "One day, I was led away by a woman, another in a string of forgotten moments and blank memories. I may have been sold, I don't know. I caught the clink of coin before I was handed over, though they may as well have been paying to have me taken away." Cerra tittered a little mordantly in conclusion.

"I can tell the memory of her is much better."

"Oh yes." Cerra agreed with a flash of merriment. "She was so patient, yet demanding. Everything I know, I know because of her, especially the knowledge of plants. Oh, of the knowledge of myself too. *Essaaa* … she'd give me a bit of a lecture about not admitting that first. She taught me the Trader's speech, though I couldn't imagine at the time why it would ever be useful, as no one I knew of in the Stands speaks it, except the traveling potters. She taught me games of concentration, like bagamon and chess. She did the impossible for me … she made me patient … patient enough, anyway … to understand who and where I am with everything I have at my disposal. Everything, except my eyes."

"You 'see' more than you reveal … and I'll not forget that," he added in what he hoped would be a reassuring tone. "More importantly, others won't be aware of this talent of yours. As you aptly pointed out before, people tend to overlook those that don't possess all of their faculties."

"I'm guilty of a lack of faculties, I'll grant you that." Cerra chuckled. "It's been brought up before."

"As with me." Ferriman admitted, feeling genuine connection with the young woman. "Especially when I am sure of my direction, though others might not view it that way. My sanity has been called into question more than once. But I get results." Ferriman thought of the many hard decisions and calculated risks that he had taken, sure of reaching his desired ends. Human battles were easier to assimilate. He felt as though he were trying to convince a fellow officer of his mad plan. His slender hope of success depended upon the audacity of placing an ill-prepared woman into the pit of nations and intrigues. He felt he had to convince both of them. "Now my sanity has been challenged with the unseen, the thread of majic, whatever it is, that makes your *'eyes'* valuable. You might not appreciate it that way. You have paid for the talent in ways I doubt I could endure. But here we are."

She shifted a little to turn her attention more towards the sound of Ferriman's voice.

"I don't do this often ... there are many that I only care to see by the picture of them I've formed in my mind. I should tell you, as we've journeyed I've often painted you as a knight on a horse, *heh* your sword always out and pointing as though leading the way. I should dispel such a fanciful image." Cerra raise her right hand tentatively. "Would you let me touch your face? If anything, it helps me see properly. It's the touch of my hands that really sets the picture in my mind ... and I would see you completely, Captain."

"I ... of course." Ferriman was overcome by a sudden emotional context he found surprising, an attraction like facing a lover. He gulped quietly, feeling somehow coarse, as she set her cat aside and turned to face him. The apprehension was driven away as she leaned forward and her fingertips touched lightly on his cheeks. Her unseeing eyes fluttered shut as if gaining additional insight, her touch spreading slowly across the rest of his visage, a delicate brush that seemed to liven his skin.

Cerra let her hands wash over the Captain's face. The tension in his brow, the twitch of a smile as her fingertips crossed his cheeks, all filled in lines of detail in her perception of him. His features constituted a chiseled firmness, though she hardly expected to feel any fleshy excess of soft living. His jaw, like his voice, was accustomed to command, the creases at his eyes spoke of his humanity. Surges of power emanated from him and she was reluctant to maintain her contact for very long.

Cerra allowed her fingers to trail away from his skin as they descended his neck. A tension, an unspoken examination of energy passed between them as she returned her hands to her lap, sitting back with a comforting smile brightening her features.

"I suppose I'll always see a knight of swords but the painting is gone and there is a person in its place. *Hmmm* … I am thinking you are what they would consider a handsome man."

"Most of my acquaintances would argue that."

"*Heh,heh* … oh I'm sure it's not the first thing they're concerned with," Cerra agreed. "And the gray of your hair at the temples adds to your charisma."

"You could tell that by your touch?" Ferriman looked at her sharply.

"Oh, no." Cerra laughed, her introspection momentarily forgotten. "I remember that you have a daughter my age. If you didn't have the gray there, I'd be very much surprised. I'm having you on a bit … and thank you for your indulgence."

Ferriman let the brightness of her smile relax him. The rich auburn of her unruly hair and freckled cheeks gave her a youthful glow. Her unfocused but rich brown eyes always appeared lost in thought, though he could see the mixture of curiosity and concern come over them as she framed her next question.

"What am I to do? I am reasonably sure your plan doesn't go much further than the next step, so a lot of detail isn't necessary," she added with a just a slight bit of sass.

Ferriman was glad to hear it. Her cat regained her lap and settled back in. Her absent-minded strokes on the cat's black fur spoke of home and hearth. He hated to dispel the notion, for there was no hearth and home in the ...outlook.

"There is a small delegation being formed to attend to the courts in Abbysin. I am regarded as the military adjutant to the delegation. I propose to take you as an advisor."

"Advisor? Do you want good advice? I can give you that, because I'm certainly not using it." Cerra chuckled a bit sourly as she returned to stroking Kamir's sleek fur, gaining some reassurance from the familiar touch. "Can I ask who else is in this 'delegation'?"

"In official capacity: Westre and Moors, with their escorts, Commander Holder and three of his general staff ..." Ferriman's voice rose slightly, revealing a touch of resignation as he obviously saved the bad news for last. " ... and representing commerce, so he claims ... Denalo Pryan. He paid entry into the delegation."

Cerra felt her stomach churn slightly. His sanctimonious attitude had been immediately hard to bear. Flashes of painted facial features and harsh shapes clouded her thought and she shook her head to clear them. "One I'd prefer to be better strangers with. He was taken with my 'observer' role. I'm sure he'll be absolutely thrilled with my 'advisory' position. Probably term it 'shortsighted'." Her nose flared, as if catching an awkward scent. "Well ... I can tell it's not meant to be a pleasant outing then. I've heard his notions and he plots to suit himself, though he says it is to arm The Stands."

Ferriman didn't disagree with her. He had heard similar intelligence, though considered it good policy to have the worm within sight. "He assigned himself by way of an edict issued by the Prime Council"

"Alder Histon? That surprises me. He didn't seem a sup-
porter of Pryan's interests."

"Indeed. Pryan insists that, in the interest of trade, all
the issues will be resolved. Another advisor as it were. As for
Histon, he is feeding the beast, convinced that Pryan will
reveal himself in some way. It's his opinion that Pryan is part
of the larger issue, whatever it is, I can't say I disagree."

Cerra felt herself at a crossroads. She felt the immediate
draw of her cabin, the familiar warmth. Everything had its
place, including her. Beyond it … an ocean of uncertainties.
She had been drawn out once with the demon as her guide,
though now, Yutan had vanished. Had he overestimated his
power since his release from the wizard's spell? She sank a
little as she considered his loss, while also sensing the attraction of destiny, a more subtle and insidious pull.

If Yutan yet lived … anywhere … it would be involved in
the mysteries surrounding his loss. Her cabin held no solace
for that and she could see herself tied up with her regret. There
was no choice but to chase the thread before her. For Yutan?
For her own peace of mind? Or for the sake of the captain
and his duties to the Stands? All three perhaps, though at the
core of it, the mystery of Yutan remained central. If there were
hope for him, she must somehow remain involved. She took a
deep breath.

"It would do me well to steer clear of talk of commerce.
Hmmmm … the best way to divert Lord Pryan's attention is to
talk of something other than him. I can tell you, I have topics
that will dissuade his conversation soon enough." Her words

were spoken softly, as though predicting a distant future. She finished with a self-deprecating laugh. "It seems my path lies before me … should I choose to step in it."

A succession of marks appeared, stacking in a pyramid formation as the outer knots of the arena arranged into new alignments. Fresh inks glistened in wet sepias that sizzled, highlighting the uppermost frame. The Seer sat in the shadow of the lone candle, covered by a hooded cloak the same ambered browns as the marks in the arena.

The deck waited, the top card destined to fill the mark. The reverse face of the deck was dark-bronzed with age and laced in omnidirectional waves that seemed etched in their brightness. Feathers overlapped in their broken pattern, drawing the eyes in with a trance-like fascination. The flickering candle played with slight colorings, making them appear to move like scales on a writhing serpent, adding to the allurement. Somewhere in the turns of light, a pattern threatened to shimmer into something distinct, a clue to the face beneath it.

At last the top card was drawn. *Nepethe, Queen of the Roses* was revealed. Under the influence of the lone candle, the white of the roses took on an amber cast, as did the brilliant ermine of her cape. The golden frame of her shield gleamed as though freshly polished. Glimmering in the inks and almost unseen, a fractured image caught the Seer's eyes and the card was drawn in for closer inspection, to reveal a thin spider, its web captured at the base of the shield.

The Numinon shuffled its delicate pages to reveal the written endowments of the card as though anticipating the Seer's intent. The symbology was quickly scanned until the Queen's shield was cited and then the Seer hunched tighter as the Book was read carefully.

> *'Her shield bears a Rose upon its steel, speaking of the*
> *necessary union of fragility and strength, though the*
> *shield is captured by a spider's web, an indication of her*
> *systematic intrigue.'*

The remaining text was read with more care, the tracing fingers of the Seer stopping at the heading of *'Weakness'*, written with a heavier stroke, so as to attract attention.

> *'The Queen of the Roses has the ability to be overly*
> *critical, cold, judgmental and cynical, allowing emotion*
> *and old obsessions or internal identities*
> *to get in the way of clear judgement.*
> *Past hurts can distort her intuitive psychic qualities,*
> *leaving the Queen unable to find herself as she becomes too*
> *lost in another identity.'*

The card was scrutinized a few moments longer, held lightly as though pleased with the weight and flavor of its message. Finally, *Nepethe* was placed within the frame at the top of the pyramid with a show of vindication. There was no mistaking the position of dominance within the pattern.

Once the card was in place, the Numinon shuffled towards the front, within the indices of instructions.

'In Opposition … select cards at random to fill,' scrolled in simple script, as three frames fired their inks on the bottom row of the pattern. The centermost frame gleamed brightest, as though

eager to be filled.

The deck was lifted and, with a sweep of the hand, the cards were fanned in an arc next to the arena. A long pause preceded the extraction of the next card; there was no telltale sign forthcoming from the impartial mesmer of the backs. The seer hesitated, then moved with more conviction, slipping a card from the arc, one tucked back as to remain unnoticed. The *Knight of Swords* was revealed and laid down in the center of the three marks with a grunt of disapproval. By the position, the Knight showed himself to be in direct opposition. Though *Briah* was a dangerous card, as yet he had proved impotent. The seer paused and reflected for a moment as the next frame abutting the Knight flared for attention. To the side, it reflected an attendant or subordinate role and a card not to be feared.

The next card was drawn from the center of the spread with more determination and set down on the mark before due notice was taken. When the card finally gained attention, there was a twitch of nervousness from the Seer within the long-backed chair. *Nuith.* The *Queen of Quills.* The Seer made a motion to remove the card then stopped. Though the powerful card had shown itself once again, it had not been effectual and now it assumed a lesser role next to the Knight.

One card remained. The candle flickered like a tapping finger, marking the time before the Seer turned the final card. The *3 of Quills* faced up and was laid down to the left of the Knight, with satisfaction. Another weak and ineffective card had reappeared. The two frames that occupied the middle of the arena, separating Nepethe from the threats below, began to flare, waiting for the cards to fill them. Ruffling its pages with a snap, the Numinon flipped to a new leaf, the inks severe and demanding.

'In defense, draw two cards.'

The seer traced a hand along the deck, seeking hidden clues in the touch. One card was slipped away from the spread, then another a few cards away, before both were turned and placed in the glowing frames.

The *7 and 5 of Cups* were laid in their defense, powerful in themselves and for their unity in the suit. The Seven, in particular, showed its deadliness, the liquids dripping from the rims of the chalices were painted with livid inks meant to repel. Rendered in liquid color by the flickering candle, the ichor spilled from the chalice to the Cups below with no drop wasted. Less overflowed until the final draught was cut in twain by a single sword. A thin trickle of droplets was left to find the Lotus which lay beneath the drip, both fulsome and diseased by the feast. Cued by the placement of the Cards in the arena, the Book turned its delicate pages to first reveal the properties of the Seven.

> *"The 7 of Cups, called 'Mastery', shows reliability to settle disputes or conflicts. Mastery of emotion is depicted by the overfilling cups, marking the memory of past lives, past atrocities and useless recollections, sadness from loss and induced bitterness. What exudes in the passing are refined extracts, poison in their purity."*

Having revealed the first Card, the Book shuffled two pages over to expose the Five: *'Distraction'*. Though not as powerful as others, there was deceptive brilliance in its exposure. The *5 of Cups* displayed the face of a juggler, looking in both directions while keeping five cups flung between his hands. Like the onus of the card, a number of conflicting accounts appeared within the description of the Five. The Seer's hand stopped at the most hopeful passage.

"The 5 of Cups represents the conflict of the actual and the desired. Within the cups are found Courage, Audacity, Bravery, Will and Creativity. They are juggled by a jongleur who faces backward, while the visage incorporated in his hat controls the spin of the juggle.

The 5 of Cups invokes the powerful use of words that inspire calm.

It will avoid conflict wherever possible.

Allied by their suit, deception and distraction became paired with the mastery of emotion, which for now, became the powers defending the reign of *Nepethe*.

Chapter 16

Passing through the ruins of the Black Gate, Ferriman was reminded once again of how the gates had been destroyed during the last demonic cataclysm. And how they had been restored, rising from dust and turmoil to stand once again, guarding the fertile Stands. To his eyes, there was no majic or omen greater than the colossus that had replaced the ancient king. Benign vigilance was the hallmark of the new carving, gazing outward with sightless eyes towards the lands of the Abbysin. With no dignitary to lay claim to the monument, it came to be known as '*Nuith*', named after the mythic Goddess of Change. Some saw the massive statue as the beginning of a new age. Ferriman wasn't so sure. Though the gate lay destroyed again, the colossus remained unscathed, change and constancy both displayed starkly before his eyes.

Ferriman, at last knew the identity of the guardian, though he had never disclosed what he had witnessed, for the explanations defied him, as did the woman who rode in front of him, her black cat placidly at rest in the fore of the saddle. Her song had brought on the storm of the Gate's restoration. The blind woman likely knew of the arcane forces behind the destruction of the Gate, he was sure of it. Yet, he had broached the subject enough to know that explanations seemed to be beyond her as well. She had no motivations for gain, her secrets seemed to lie on different ground. Ferriman had patience brought on by years of command. He would know more before the mission was over, a deeper secret to be sure.

Cerra had felt the closeness of the cliffs, the steep walls pushing the river into the narrow confines of the gorge. The Emerald River had its own sound, deep and solid, a fluid hush that lay heavy on her ears. She had trusted Sugar to keep pace with the rest of the entourage, pausing only occasionally to gather in a sense of the air about her. Lady Moors and Commander Holder were in formation ahead, accompanied by their aides and guards of State. Captain Ferriman rode respectfully beside her, though he seemed unusually quiet for most of the journey. In all, the procession seemed to have a funereal air.

Pryan gravitated towards Westre as she had hoped, for the aristocratic Lord was the only sympathetic ear to the overbearing noble within the small company that comprised the Standish Embassy. It was evident that more than camaraderie fueled their fellowship, as much of their talk was guarded conversations, hidden by the shuffle of travel. Cerra was grateful that the boastful Pryan regarded her and her defects, blindness and lineage both, beneath his self-absorbed attention. In spite of their exclusion, she had captured enough snatches of their exchanges to know that the two Lords had come to some sort of arrangement and were convincing each other of their acumen, which she considered 'selling the skin before the bear has been shot,' as the potters were fond of saying.

Pryan kept his personal servant close, a quiet, hawkish man who attended him and two laden pack-horses that the boastful lord proudly claimed to require for his comforts. Westre and his second seemed equally as guarded. There was little attention paid to whatever luxuries the pack-horses might provide on the trip, though the parcels were closely watched and never disturbed nor unpacked, as far as Cerra could discern.

Much of his conversations with Westre were simply curious bits that smacked of opportunism, though there was little of any solid intelligence to impart to the Captain. Cerra kept the mental nuggets stored away in their tidy compartments, drying like the herbs in her closet at home and, for the moment, forgotten. She felt her mission, or whatever it was to be called, would begin in earnest with the conferences they were traveling to attend. She ached for her home, though she had reconciled herself to this venture as there was hope that détente, rather than war, could result from their efforts. The mystery of the sorcerous assaults lay at the mission's core. Given the disappearance of Yutan, Cerra felt personally involved in ways that no one else in the company would be able to comprehend. The Captain may have her in his charge, yet it very much seemed to her that she was being compelled by her own mission. Cerra quietly hoped the success of one would satisfy the other.

It was not until they were past the wreckage of the Gates and on the threshold of the veldt plains, wedged between the mountains and the desert, that Captain Ferriman was obliged to halt the entourage in order to await an escort from the besieging Abbysin army; the host to accompany them to the conference being held at the Vale d' Houri.

Cerra withdrew the hood of her traveling cloak, the versatile robe of the Cherros. Listening carefully, Cerra heard little of the expected hum of activity that should attend such a large force of arms. All she could sense was a recent telltale of cinder and carnage that left bleak images of charred paper in her mind, devoid of color and life, the same desolation that had pursued her thoughts since the fiery attack on Bridash. It was a stark tableau made even emptier by the impatience and disregard she heard coming from Lord Pryan. The Captain drew up close to her right side.

"The Abbysin army seems neither sizable nor determined." Cerra noted quietly to Ferriman. "They've been … damaged … and there's too much char in the air for campfires."

"Indeed. Some form of heavy fire erupted here." Ferriman responded in the same low voice. "I'd guess the same time as the attack on Bridash … and victims of the same beast. Their army is lesser for it as you noted, yet the fact that they still camp at our Gate shows enough of their determination." Ferriman touched her lightly to indicate a direction. "Our escort approaches. By the look of them, those that remain bear the expression of those that have seen dire things. Their determination could be either to wish us dead or themselves home. I would tread softly until I know their intentions better."

"Not all of our company are diplomats." Cerra observed drily, then added with a sidelong grin. "I shall manage my cat as best as I can."

Ferriman chuckled. There was little to be done about the boorish Pryan. In his experience, given time, the graceless Lord would dig his own grave, using his words as the shovel.

Katarin Moors sat mounted to Cerra's left. The Standish aristocrat had been an attentive companion for much of the trip as they had followed the Emerald River across the lower Stands to the Gate. Moors was always solicitous, if not painstakingly proper, as Cerra imagined a Lady of the ruling classes must be. In spite of her singular attention to detail, Cerra found her warm-hearted and generous. It was easy to paint her with aristocratic, aquiline features. Even Moor's voice spoke of elegance. Cerra rather liked her clear and measured diction.

"I shouldn't let this out, but Sir Holder informed me that the Jimalian contingent is en route. He must have good sources. I think it's unfortunate, in a way, that the summit is not in Abbysin. More than twice the journey, mind you. I've been there before and the oldest parts of the city are quite lovely. A shame that it isn't closer…" Katarin spoke with a hint of gaiety, yet Cerra could hear the uncertainty in her voice.

"I should love to visit the spice markets," she offered without commitment. Cerra well remembered her own experience in the imperial city. She pushed the thought of Yutan from her mind. "I can tell you, from my point of view, there is little more than the city could offer. The aroma of a hundred spice carts would be a vision in itself."

"I should visit the markets more often. Too often I have a servant attend to my needs instead. I would make it a point to accompany you. *Ah* … it's just as well we go to the Vale. Our mission has nothing to distract it. Diplomacy is our only attention."

"I have diplomacy well in hand, dear women. I am a deal maker. You can trust me. It is what I know." Pryan had sharp ears when he had a mind to. "You can spend all of your time in the spas if you wish. The men shall work things out, you can depend on it."

"We shan't be there to record your splendid efforts, then … sadly." Cerra kept her voice light, though she had found the man's continual company abrasive. Cerra caught a soft chuff from Katarin that heartened her: the Primayor of the Lower Stands would not be so easily put aside in negotiations.

A heavy jangle of harness and clomping of hooves marked the approach of horsemen. The measured gait indicated a closed formation that spread laterally in front of her as they drew to a stop. A handful of men on either side, perhaps two dozen by reckoning.

"They have us in numbers," Cerra observed quietly, leaning to Ferriman. The delegation seemed less secure and another layer of insulation was formed between her and home. She pushed away any thoughts of the excesses of barbarian hordes, as portrayed in any number of old tales. The Abbysins were a proud empire, known for their traditions. Hospitality was said to be one of them. Ferriman confirmed her thoughts.

"Security is the price of diplomacy." Ferriman observed, dryly. "However, they won't violate their own vow to protect."

Cerra found some consolation in that as Ferriman and Commander Holder rode forward a few paces, claiming charge of their small delegation.

"Collenel Lazaros of the Imperial Paladon Crussars." There was a snap of leather and a jangle of harness as salutes were exchanged. "You will not need your own escort. You have the protection of the Empire. Please dismiss them."

The Collenel's speech was thick with Abbysin intonations, the *'p's'* getting lost like *'b's* and a rolling of the *r's* that caused Cerra to listen with care. She held her head slightly down, the better to catch the negotiations directed at the two soldiers and not the rest of the party. Kamir was equally as attentive for she could feel him rocking his view side to side past Sugar's neck. Holder replied in a much clearer Abbysin, a belligerent edge to his tone, one accustomed to having his word enforced.

"It is our custom to travel with an escort. We have the women to consider and their comfort. One of them is blind, mind you … she requires extra attention. We are under your aegis as you say. As the Abbysin own their honour, we will own our men-at-arms. This is not for negotiation."

Cerra hated being singled out and she could feel the scrutiny of the Abbysin troop as their horses shuffled a few steps with impatient snorts. There was an aside she didn't catch, an Abbysin slur she figured she was better off not knowing, as a slight round of snickering was heard to pass along the right side of the Abbysin line.

"Their behaviour is your responsibility." There was no sourness in the Abbysin commander's voice, apparent to Cerra that he had expected that very reply and was ready to assume charge of the complete detachment.

"What's he saying?" Pryan called out impatiently to Holder from the left side of the assembly before turning aside to Westre, still speaking loud enough for Cerra to catch his words. "Why can't that tinman speak decently … or slower at least? Can't trust a one of them."

"Who is that? He looks like a freshly slapped arse." The

Abbysin commander's accent wasn't so halting with the question. Derision was an oil for eloquence and Cerra smiled inwardly, the Abbysin officer had a better facility with language than he let on. Pryan continued his observations to Westre, who was wisely silent.

"A minor Lord ... and the least of our embassy, I must add. A man of business." Holder paused in response, as though that were explanation enough, his discomfiture evident. "He is my responsibility."

"*pssht*. Not an enemy, hey? ... but none of his friends like him either. The one to watch is also the one to ignore." The commander spoke aside in quick Abbysin to his aide, before replying to Holder. "See that he does not embarrass your company."

Cerra concentrated on the sounds of the Abbysin escort as their leader gave a gruff command. No one spoke, yet the horsemen moved in unison to the right and the motion passed throughout the Standish horses like a current of water, as they all sought to follow with the turn of their heads. Ferriman voiced his own short command and the embassy moved forward. The singular screech of a hawk or eagle, high overhead, seemed like a cry from the heavens to proceed. To Cerra, it sounded like an invitation more than omen and she let herself imagine the scene from a lofty height.

The gyrfalcon was settled on a gnarled branch that clung tenaciously to the cliff face, across the river from the monolithic Guardian of the Gate. The speckled brown and cinnamon tints that laced through the falcon's white feathers made the bird difficult to spot against the rough stone of the cliffs. The large raptor had established a nesting cove days before, drawn by the lingering residue of bewitchment within the narrow defile. Patiently, the raptor waited, settled down within the spent atmospheres of the sorcery that had bedeviled the Gates in recent days.

The bird watched the activities below with intense, unblinking interest. Grounded ones had passed through the narrow defile, exposed like voles in a pasture. The falcon's sharp eyes focused on one that rode in the center of the group, brilliant red feathering exposed when the figure's hood was dropped. The alert gyrfalcon shifted its glance across to the monolithic guardian of the Gate, the figure's serene gaze a beacon of welcome. The bird's attention darted back to the mounted figure as the collection of riders began to move away from the defile, out towards the open airs of the desert. With an energetic flap of its wings, the large raptor launched itself into a soaring glide away from the cliffs and cried out the triumph of its discovery.

Chapter 17

Early starts were the order of the march, especially now that they were in the company of an escort. Cerra preferred the brisk order of morning for it set the tone of the day for her. She worried a little about Kamir among all of the unfamiliar horses and arms, though he invariably found his meal before she was done with hers and quick to let her know he was close. He seemed to gather most of his sleep rocking in the saddle, half-nestled in her lap. She wished she could doze as effectively. Holder and Ferriman had ridden forward, presumably to confer with the Abbysin commander and Cerra prepared to wrap herself in the cocoon of her thoughts when Katarin shifted alongside her.

"We'll be on the plains for the rest of the morning," offered Katarin helpfully. "Once we cross the Moon bridge, it'll be mostly desert from then on ... until Vale d' Houri. Two days I should think. Three is likely, though our escort keeps a good pace. I tell you, I would have preferred to go to Oskara, had we gone on to Abbysin. One merely has to take a boat across the Sultan Sea."

"Men have been going to sea for ages." Cerra commented ruefully, reluctant to share her past experience on the ocean, then brightened with an entertaining thought. "*Heh, heh ... I'm sure things improved when they started using boats.*"

"It must have occurred to them at some point. Likely, their wives pointed it out." Katarin enjoyed the blind woman's off-beat humor. "Still, they've become good at it."

Cerra decided she preferred most any mode of travel to a sea voyage. "I think flying would a be much better option."

As though summoned by the thought, the thin cry of a hawk shrieked from high above her. She let herself imagine its height. From such a viewpoint, it was easy for her to conjure up a vision of the plains of rough grass that wedged themselves between the river and the Granite mountains behind them.

Katarin laughed at the notion of flying and diverted the conversation back to the wonders of Abbysin. Cerra was glad for the noblewoman's attentive company. Ferriman had his position to maintain among the Abbysin command and the unpleasant Pryan, thankfully kept close company with Lord Westre, who seemed eager to latch on to the many mercenary opportunities that the voluble Lord Pryan identified as a result of the unrest.

Once across the long arch of the Moon Bridge, they left the Emerald River behind. The desert had none of the deso-lation she remembered from the crossing of the Hellesmere, a flat, hardened plain of salt that invited the death of all who attempted to cross it in the light of day. Instead, there was the smell and rustle of dried shrubbery, competing with the parched soil and stone that crunched under the horse's hooves. Despite the descriptions that Katarin added, highlighting the sparse trees wielding thorny branches and mesas that stood like lone sentries in the distance, Cerra continued to visualize the drained surfaces as so much broken pottery, baked and painted like wares in a market.

Early on the third day, just an hour or so after they had formed the ranks, Cerra caught a faint whiff of moisture in the air, a breath of evaporation that seemed fresh. A flash of verdant pools floated in her imagination, happily interrupting the sameness of the desiccated airs. She leaned slightly to Ferriman, who was riding at her side.

"The oasis must be near, or I am smelling a mirage?" Cerra chuckled. "Tell me true so I know if my nose needs repair."

Ferriman raised an eyebrow at her remark. They were still a half day's ride from the oasis of the Vale d' Houri. The scarred mesa, which marked the beginning of the rift cradling the deep lake, was visible in the distance, though the oasis itself would not be seen for some time. "Near enough to be reached before the worst heat of the afternoon. I think your senses are adequately attuned."

"I'm glad I haven't caught their cookfires yet. My stomach would growl and scare the horses," Cerra snickered. "I'm famished."

"The delegation will take apartments at one of the hostelries. Your appetite will be satisfied, at least better than camp fare."

She had no quarrels with the food. The constant riding exercised her more than she remembered and she seemed to be hungry often, quite imagining she had lost a half a stone since they had left the comforts of her cabin.

"Kafi ... within reach of my bed. What luxury. Though Katarin claims the baths will be invigorating too."

Ferriman allowed himself a dry chuckle. "Heh. A day of

luxury. The term is different for everyone. For some it would be the attentions of servants. For others it might be the solitude of one's thoughts."

They could hear a loud guffaw behind them as Pryan regaled Westre with another tale of his accomplishments, laced with mean-spirited jabs at his hapless opponents.

"I think the quiet of solitude is the best choice, one of the few luxuries that costs nothing." Cerra grinned, looking ahead as though already sighting the oasis.

Water and shade were chief among the luxuries provided by the hostels and inns surrounding the Vale d' Houri. The graceful walls of the imarets girding the blue waters of the oasis were molded as if emerging from the rusty sandstone, sculpted smooth and rounded by the winds. The bleached colors and heats of the desert were held back by a lattice of arbored walkways covered by jacaranda and orchids, dappled with fountains and decorative pools. Patios, balconies and courtyards were adorned lavishly with awnings and colorful umbrellas. The tall palms that guarded the oasis rustled like green banners proclaiming a midsummer's faire. Caravaners mixed with smugglers and roisterers, for the Vale was a law unto itself, wedged in the vacant lands between the Stands and Abbysin. Although it lay within the Abbysin realm, the rulers claimed it a Free City State, protected by strict rules of autonomy and greed, written long ago. The Vale was an oasis of both water and pleasure for those congregations that suffered from their drought.

Sinjin had often waited in the shady bowers of the oasis, a crossroads of information and intrigue. In his occupation, observation was paramount, even when not in the pay of a benefactor as he was at the moment. The gold coin fresh in his purse was more than enough for a few more days at the Speckled Drake, a lesser but still lavish inn, which lay too near the stabling lines and servant housing to be attractive to the richest of the royals and revelers. He sipped on a cup of melon juice infused with hashin. The drink rendered subtle powers of timeless and tireless observation, the basis for the brand of his Guild, the Hashini. The Assassins.

Trained since childhood in the arts, Sinjin was raised devoid of pity and compassion, traits that had no function in the roles he must play while in the service of those who had not the ability, nor stomach, to wield the knife themselves. Even within the cold and secret brotherhood of the Hashini, he was feared above others. He had no great height, nor imposing stare, yet he commanded with his cold objectivity. His unassuming looks allowed him to blend in, with little attempts at disguise necessary to create the character he wanted, although this would only work if he didn't remain long in the company of strangers. Then, the coldness of his character would creep through, a subtlety that kept any budding friendships and comrades at bay. However, time rarely was an issue, for he always managed to get close enough to earn his stipend. He demanded a high price, though by all rumors, his fortune had been made long ago.

For now, he was tied to the purse of the Chancellor of

Abbysin, of that he was sure. There was no direct payment of course, however, the intermediary was a known subject of Chenli's cousin, Patan, a magistrate of the Armorer's Guild. The target of his mission was among the diplomatic contingent from the Stands, which was expected within the day, or the next, or another if they lacked ambition. The traveling habits of the wealthy and elite often bordered on sluggery.

As he waited for their arrival, he quietly gathered in the news and information spread by the caravaners and agents who frequented the commons of the Speckled Drake. The talk of armies and strange majics had circulated the breadth of the empire, from the eastern ends of the Jimals to the southern borders of the Trader States. Caravaners had found less to trade as merchants had begun warehousing many of their goods in fear of unstable times and possible losses. He didn't wonder that the embassy he awaited would be of importance to the Chancellor. It was the targeting of one of its members that had him thinking. Not of the validity of the assignment, merely of the repercussions. To stay in the game, one must anticipate the moves ahead.

Ferriman joined the ranks of the Abbysin Collenel as they descended into the deep rift that captured the oasis. The rustle of palms and the sultry envelope of humid air was a welcoming change to the arid grit of the desert. Cerra could already feel herself swimming in the cooling waters.

The procession along the main thoroughfare leading into

the Vale seemed a lively affair after the stark passage of the desert. The Abbysin escort had been as stern as the arid lands they passed through, without excess or vibrancy. There was an air of expectation within the oasis, as though a revel or feast might begin at any moment.

The aromas of the northern caravan lots and paddocks were quickly replaced with the cooler scents of rushes in shallow pools, as the embassy neared the inns and imarets that framed the aquamarine waters. The company was halted in a courtyard, where liveried servants rushed to attend to their mounts as penned horses and camels created a brief din of greetings and snorts. Cerra waited until Ferriman drew to her side before dismounting.

"Don't get lost," she advised Kamir. "I've been assured that dinner is soon."

She turned in a circle, closing her eyelids as she absorbed the surroundings. After the sterile scents of the desert, the air felt rich, rife with the smells of water, flowered hedges, hay and manure. One rank tendril wormed its way into her senses, past the bouquet of the oasis, the feeling of being watched. She dismissed the notion quickly, as she had been the object of speculation since she had begun the journey. All she wanted at the moment was a refreshing swim or bath and some food.

In a palm near the reeded shore, a majestic brown and white raptor settled and watched with intensity at the activities below. The gyrfalcon was distracted for a moment by the flash of a large fish just beneath the surface of the water, but its hazel eyes darted back to the gathered forms, intent on the red-haired creature that shone like a prized jewel among so many stones. Spreading its wings, the bird spiraled in a soft drop to the ground behind the sculpted towers. With the attention being given the official entourages, no notice was given to the lithe young woman with feathered brown hair and shawl, slipping onto the patios of the imaret with a lively step.

Chapter 18

S hadows lengthened with the afternoon and a mixed caravan of Jimalian and Eastern traders had just settled into
the stalls of the northern quarter, when the watch called out the
approach of a party with a large armed escort. The banners
were announced shortly after, the crossed palms of Paladon
Crussars, along with the Standish mark of Inana. Sinjin took
a last draught of his melon elixir, satisfied they would soon be
at the northern approach. The Crussars were Abbysin troops,
not mercenaries engaged as a result of the recent escalation
and considered elite among the corps, trained severely in the
martial arts. It was an escort wasted on the Standish royals,
though their rigors had apparently aided the party in making
a timely crossing of the desert.

The entrance of the Standish embassy into the Vale d'
Houri would have certainly drawn attention, even within the
busy and often raucous stabling arenas at the north of the Vale.
Though battle-stained and torn, the tawny leather armor of
the Crussars flashed with polished golden vambraces and blue
lacquered sheaths. Banded in gold and inlaid with the crossed
palms of their order, their compact shields and peaked helmets
glittered in the brilliant sun. The Standish troop, though not
clad in battle attire, looked no less capable with their crisp discipline, tailored moss-green and dark maroon uniforms and

flowing capes of dusky jades.

A dusty avenue opened up among the carts and shifting pedestrian traffic as the detachment trotted forward through the gate.

Sinjin had found a comfortable place in the shade of an awning of one of the many vendors gathered close to the gates, offering food and last moment trades. He paid for a kabab to justify his loitering, for he wanted to observe the bearing of the detachment, especially the mien of the Standish Lords, fresh from the harsh sands of the desert. The Crussars looked hawk-like and alert, leading the contingent past the stall where he sat. The Standish commander, marked by the brocades on his uniform, wore a frown etched across his face, a look of internal discomfort. The lieutenants at his flanks exhibited more curiosity about their surroundings than exhaustion, as though the trek across the heated sands was nothing out of the ordinary. It was the wave of red hair that caused his blood to chill, even before he focused on the body beneath it, the kabab he had been picking at nearly slipping from his fingers.

The witch!

His eyes narrowed to a flinty sharpness. There was no mistaking her as his memory sought to validate his conclusion. Red hair was uncommon enough in these lands and a rarity even in the Stands. The wayward tangle of her tresses made her identity a certainty, though as he watched with more scrutiny than he wished, her face bloomed into his consciousness as well.

'You will remember some of this.' Her low voice had been soothing, even as the pain lanced through him, sending him into

oblivion.

Sinjin rubbed his right thigh, still scarred from the event. She had saved his life, he gave her some measure of honor for that. In the few years since he had deposited her at the wizard's estates in the imperial city of Abbysin, he had scarcely thought of her, having more immediate concerns to occupy him. Seeing her again sparked his basest fear, facing an opponent armed with weapons that he did not possess and could not master. That made her most dangerous.

For the first time in his professional capacity, the target of his surveillance was forgotten, his attention diverted like a crow on a shiny object. He watched her pass, engaged in conversation with one of the Standish officers. Other than a bit tousled, she looked unaffected by the harsh passage, a hint of bemusement and inquiry intent on her face, as though straining to hear the officer's words.

Rumors and tales of dark majics and fell creatures had circulated in every corner of the empire, from Maabi to the western shores of the Sultan Sea. In the imperial city, the talk of war was on everyone's lips, the unrest giving rise to a sudden rattling of arms and cries of nationalism. In every corner of the Empire, grave doubts had been placed upon the various priests and seers, regardless of their association or house. The Greycloaks were especially viewed with suspicion; their reclusive monastery in the hills above Bridash, most of all. That it lay hidden deep within the Stands was but one of the mysteries that surrounded it. Now, in the midst of these troubling circumstances, surrounded by omens, the Standish witch makes an appearance. There are no coincidences.

Sinjin let the remains of the kebab drop to the ground. A scruffy dog, tawny as the parched sand, was quick to snatch it up behind him as he began following the legation to the main plaza, fronting the most exclusive of imarets that edged the water of the oasis. With practiced command and discipline, a large portion of the embassy broke ranks in formation, to settle at nearby hostels and tend their mounts and stores. Those that remained appeared to be Standish Lords, who dismounted within the receiving gates of the Night Candle. The imaret featured a sculpted series of three elegant towers buttressed by tiered patios, the most exclusive villas that hedged the water's edge. Snowy white egrets stalked in the reeded shallows, while elegant flamingos sifted the silts alongside the arbored walks, scented and colored with flowering vines.

Sinjin spent no time perusing the grounds as the legation dismounted, stablehands and servants emerging in well-ordered procession to accommodate the arrival. He waited only until he was certain the red-haired woman was a guest, escorted inside with great deference by the Standish officer.

He would revisit the imaret in a few hours.

Cerra again felt the chill of observation as she walked with the polite assistance of Ferriman's arm, up the broad steps heralding the entrance to the imaret. She paid the notion little mind for she had been watched constantly since she had arrived in Bridash, either by curiosity or concern. Kamir uttered small mewls as he trotted up in front of her.

"I know you're hungry. I'm warning you, the mice might be too fat and rich for your blood." Cerra redirected her conversation as she patted Ferriman's arm. "It's said a hungry cat hunts best. *Heh* … I'm famished as well. I'll fairly pounce on a tray."

An attendant met them on the portico and directed them along an arching path near the water's edge. The floral notes of honeysuckle and trumpet vine were a wonderful elixir after the dry scents of the desert. Gentle breezes shunted down the pathway, holding a mix of sand and water within their puffs. The turn from the path wasn't far from the entrance, some forty paces. The coolness of earth and stone washed over her as she entered the chambers of her apartment. Keen patches of scent indicated arrangements of freesia and lilac in sculpted vases. The balm of a pool or large bath, was another enticement.

"*oooh* … if I can stay here a bit, I'll be ready for anything … ring for me in a fortnight." Cerra enthused with a satisfied smile.

Ferriman guided her to a cushioned divan, a further luxury after the stiffness of the saddle for so many days. "I have to dispatch the company. I'll check back later if you wish."

A young woman in a simple shift and loose weave shawl stood near the bed pallet. "'I'm here to look after you." she offered.

Ferriman gave her a quick glance. The attendant spoke in practiced Trader, obviously not her native tongue, thick with the accent of the Luminars, which lay far to the east. She was barely of age, though with her slender, exotic look, it was hard to tell. Her mocha skin with a passing of freckles was unusual, as was the feathered cut of her light brown and cinnamon hair, though Ferriman got immediate reassurance from the intelligent hazel eyes, so looked to excuse himself. Cerra had no other desire except to lay about and gather her sense of place as she had been moving for days.

"Oh, Captain, yes … attend to the men. You've done me enough of a service. I intend to bask in this rare extravagance while I may."

There was a short click to his heels, indicating a customary bow that made her smile as Cerra heard his departing footsteps. The attendant took immediate charge, sweeping back the drapes and directing the servant in placing Cerra's small travel cache. The servant left with a murmured bow, though the presence of the attendant lingered. Kamir hopped up onto her lap to settle himself.

"Don't get too comfortable, little one. I've a mind to wash the dust off of me." She shifted to speak to the young woman who had placed herself near the door. Cerra spoke in Trader, for it seemed the attendant was fluent enough, using very correct phrasing, as though learned from a book. "There's a bath in here … or pool. I'd truly enjoy a soak … if that is allowed. What's your name?"

"Haviana, milady … Havi, if you wish. *Uh* … please indulge yourself as you wish." She pulled aside a thin white drape to reveal a terracotta deck beyond the room. "There's a pool just here, adjacent to the waters of the oasis and it extends to the patio beyond your bed. I'll attend you if you prefer. I have robes and toweling." Haviana sounded unsure of how to continue. "I'm … relatively new here. As I understand it, there are other services you may enjoy, a masseuse or inamorato?"

Cerra blushed slightly. The thought of a small romp and pleasant recovery would be a further luxury, though it only made her think of Yutan and enjoyment faded with the thought.

"No ... just a soak. If you orient me to the bath I'd be grateful. I'm fairly good once I know my whereabouts."

"Of course."

"Kir? Or any white wine would be nice."

"I'm sure there must be Kir. Would you like some finger foods brought with it?"

Cerra thought that a good idea as there would be plenty of choices for Kamir and no fawning cook to lament the final resting place for his efforts. "Oh wonderful! Please do." The cat hopped from her lap as she gathered herself to rise. "Place me next to the bed and I shall be right as I can be."

Cerra had the bounds of the room nearly placed in her mind. She had carefully noted the movements of the Captain and the attendant, putting measures to their footsteps and voices. Havi guided her across the room, leading her to a corner before reaching the pallet. "There is a water closet, lavabo and dressing station just here. Your bed has a drape around it, the gnats and mosquitos must swarm sometimes in the evening hours. Your bags and things are in the dressing station."

Cerra felt the corners of one of the posts that held the drapery, a fine and sheer fabric judging by her touch. The attendant took her hand and guided it to a bell cord next to the forepost of the bed.

"Pull this for anything you might need, I'm told no matter the hour. Likely rings the master of the imaret. I'll be back soon with your Kir and noshes."

"How long have you been here?" Cerra asked, curious about the girl's history. She sounded young, though earnest and assured.

"I'm here specifically for this gathering." Haviana answered amiably. "I was requested by … my superior … to watch over you personally. I imagine it is because of my sharp eyes and I am fluent in many languages. I have no other assignment."

"I'm grateful for the attention … I guess … though I hope not much will be needed. I'm certainly not used to this."

"*Err* … neither am I, though it is my privilege to serve."

The response left Cerra wanting to know more about the young woman, for she didn't sound like one used to a servant's role. There would be time later. "Thank you … Havi. I'm most content."

Cerra wanted to sink back in relief as soon as Havi left the room and the temptation to nap nearly claimed her. Rousing herself, she considered losing the grit of the road the greater relief and began removing her Cherros cape and riding skirt. Normally she would fold or hang them carefully in their place; instead, she flung the clothes on the bed as she shed them and paced carefully to the pool. The air immediately around the pool was noticeably thicker and rich with moisture. She felt the edge with her toe and eased herself down, sitting on the edge, as her heels slid into the water.

"Ahhhh, feet!" She let out a pent-up sigh she didn't know she'd contained.

Another satisfied groan escaped her as she let herself slip completely into the water. It was shallow enough for her feet to touch the smooth tiles before the water reached her breasts. She pushed off into the pool, turned gently and floated on her back, eyes closed in sublime contentment. Her hair flowed in a thick weight, a halo of fire around the pale moon of her face. With ears muffled to the world, the liquid world carried her, floating in blissful release. As wayward images blanked in her mind, so did her thoughts. She let her inner vision wash clear, floating in dusky spaces, until the darkness seemed complete, a connection with the eternal.

The water caressed, a susurration that spoke of passages between the gases gathered in the air and enrichments reaped in the soils. A light sparkled in her mind as she absorbed the welcoming moistures and watery embrace. Yutan knew. He had told her that the water had life, was life, a creation like no other.

"Yutan. Where are you?" Cerra let slip the quiet murmur as she floated, allowing the thoughts of the demon to buoy her.

White light filled the space, intervals of nothing captured within opaque illumination. An emptiness of weight and color, save the minute points of light that infused the air, spread thinly across the heavens.

A speck, brighter than the rest, garnered attention, a germ of brilliance that attracted. The emptiness of the immaculate space suffered a mote, a diamond speck of moisture that gathered a coating, traces of mist not yet resolved to the gases of time. It continued to sparkle, an insignificant beacon flickering in the vast emptiness, until an awareness awoke around it, linking in curiosity to the earthbound bead of water lost in the ethers.

The bead spoke of cycles and torrents and nurturing mists, gathering grains and crumbs of its likeness as it passed through the heavens. The weight of its being garnered a thought to relive the course, to sink back within the watery depths of the greater whole.

An echo of another age passed through the glimmering idea, a sound formed from the emanations of another light.

'Yutan.'

A struggle ensued to hold the sound, to persist within the weight of the growing fleck of ice. Another alliance was formed, another coating of rime adding substance to the thought. The accreted weight pushed the gases further away, the element of earth tentatively engaging the imagination, for now the pull of its core was inescapable. The notion would carry itself, an accumulation of being, scattered throughout the firmament, settling as the thought took form.

Pressing the acorn activated the inner clasp, a trail of vagrant light tracing along the knotted edge. The top opened without a sound, the joinery precise and clean. From the lid, the parchment extracted itself, its folds extending like a moth finding its wings, to settle on the escritoire, open and simmering along the traces of its inked arena. The lone candle hung from a hook in a metal cage, a storm lantern without its glass. The vagrant light of its dancing flame pulsed life into the inks of the knotted borders, which shimmered as though ready to flow away.

The Cards and the small grimoire marked Numinon, were lifted carefully from their velvet lined nests and placed on their marks, livening the next band within the arena. When the sparse lightnings settled into the inks, the Book opened, it's thin leaves of onionskin, fluttering to a page marked by the image of the Queen of Roses. Immediately, the arena scoured out a mark glowing near the Eastern badge, demanding the card be set.

The deck lay under the fingertips of the seer, the top card slid away and turned onto the parchment, revealing the Queen in the upright position, one of strength. Patterns in the border edged out, forming into Jimalian scripts and signs that evaporated as the inks drooled with fiery resolve into three frames, an effective wall that divided the Queen from the center of the Arena. Without further instruction, the cards were drawn and laid within their marks. The familiar *10 of Roses* held the top frame, with the *7 and 5 of Cups* taking up the column beneath.

As the frames that guarded the Queen cooled their inks, a fresh mark was being drawn, in the West. Without provocation, the Numinon shuffled the few pages away from the *Queen of Roses* to her sister, *Nuith, Queen of Quills.*

The card was slipped from the top of the deck with a precise move and laid on its mark. The cowled figure sat back, contemplating the reappearance of the powerful card. Her position on the cardinal point was an equal. The allies of the blindfolded Queen were beginning to reveal themselves as the glimmering around the *Queen of Quills* continued, embers that refused to die until a new line was sparked. It extended in front of Nuith, making a barrier of one, the card to be played in her defense. The motions of the Seer indicated uncertainty. At length, the *Knight of Swords* was revealed again, gaining the forward position, a staunch ally of the powerful Queen.

The second mark came to lie against the NW corner, the Point governed by the Suit of Quills. Sitting away from the powerful Queen, the mark showed little strength and the final card was drawn quickly, the space filled by the weak *3 of Quills,* the *Messenger.* The Seer shifted as if to stand, when a bloom coming from the Arena's frame indicated another card was to be revealed.

No immediate move was made as the Seer sat back and contemplated the patterns. Given the power that was showing in the East, there was little to fear from the reading. The frame settled itself in the South, away from either clutch of exposed cards. The Numinon waited patiently to reveal its knowledge the moment the card was released from the deck. At last it was drawn, turned with reluctant curiosity to be viewed.

The *Ace of Swords* pulsed under the vagrant glow of the single flame, which stretched as if reaching more potent fuel. A bright sword, nicked with age, dominated the card, piercing the fragile petals of a flower held between two dark bladed crissknives, which arced to either side of the pierced bloom with wing turned handles of purest nacre. The purples and indigos of the background swirled in a turbulence of water and sky, energized by the wavering candle.

The card was placed in the spot determined by the Arena as the Numinon shifted its pages deep into the Minor Arcana, at last settling on the singular Ace.

> *The gleaming sword resembles the purity of the weapon*
> *also represented by the Ace of Roses,*
> *although here it is scarred by use.*
> *It pierces the fragile petals of a flower which is held*
> *between two crissknives in front of a dark and chaotic*
> *background, neither deep ocean nor sky, yet both.*
> *The knives hold the flower by their points in a delicate*
> *balance as the sword pierces it, holding it in place upon the*
> *blade, whose hilt is inscribed with the word of the law.*

More described the lone sword, the words reviewed hastily until a line caused the perusing fingertips to halt.

> *Alone, the Ace of Swords has little power. Adjacent to the*
> *Major Arcana, it increases the power of the ruling card*
> *and its own ten-fold, such is the weight of its sword.*

No other marks presented themselves upon the Arena. The *Ace of Swords*, neutrally poised in the Southern mark, had the point of its sword dividing the board between the two formations like a judge at a tilt. The name of the card was *Sorrow*.

Chapter 19

Ruling classes were all the same from the assassin's perspective. Their sole objective in governance was to maintain their control, whatever the cost. Sinjin considered himself one of the necessary expenditures they must bear, a pair of hands willing to endure the soil of treachery. His benefactors could claim no moral high road by their disassociation and Sinjin had no opinion one way or another. The integrity of the deed lay with the one holding the tool. His job was merely to be sharp.

Those benefactors also liked their mysteries, as if the cloaks of concealment could somehow absolve them of their corruption. The noisy taverns fronting the caravan pens kept secrets trapped within the din and distraction of their commons and the shuttered doors of hastily rented rooms. The assassin wondered briefly if the lesser accommodations made the men that approached him uncomfortable, for those that ruled were seldom at home among their subjects. Master Armorer Patan, his current benefactor, was still known to work his own forges and had the grained features of a working man. Regardless, he held court within the Smith's guild as though he were the emperor himself. The Guildmaster looked as comfortable in the tavern commons as a caravan potter.

Sinjin hadn't expected to see the other man accompanying

him. Though dressed unobtrusively and without the badges of his office, the Chancellor would likely appear the same in a hall of kings, as he carried himself with manifest authority and a churlish disregard for all else. Sinjin took a sip of lemon water from his mug while the two men took up seats on the bench. He was not given to drink alcohol, both as a matter of personal and professional choice. It could well be another tool loosening the lips of someone else, while his judgement remained unclouded and his speech guarded. However, the growling Chancellor was unlikely to let loose any choice revelations, regardless of his sobriety.

"There had better be a good reason for this. I hate the smell of caravaners." Chenli growled, looking around with disdain. Patan sat comfortably like a judge, waiting for the closing arguments to be done before offering his mind.

"The Standish contingent arrived less than an hour ago. There are concerns you should be aware of. I thought it best if you knew directly. I can hardly knock on your doors in the daylight."

"What is it, then?" The Chancellor had no patience for a long introduction to the story. Sinjin voiced his main concern and most valuable piece of intelligence first, regardless of how dubious it may sound. "They have with them a powerful witch."

The Chancellor regarded him with a piercing look as if ready to strike. "A witch?! And you know this … how?"

"A patron of mine … a necromancer, though he never said as much … was at odds with her in the past … two years ago, three maybe … his name was Rovinkar."

Chenli started visibly as he recalled the upstart conjurer, who had been full of promises and even more laden with disaster. His remains still were graven within the abandoned tower in Abbysin. Not even the crows would set foot in the place. Sinjin noted the Chancellor's reaction. It was plain he had known of the wizard. Considering the wizard's directives, it wouldn't surprise him in the least that the Chancellor was well versed in all of them.

"Rovinkar. The name is vaguely familiar." Chenli admitted nothing, his snarl unchanging, though curiosity sharpened the flint of his eyes. "What of this ... witch."

"It is my opinion that it was the witch that defeated him." Sinjin took a sip of his drink, relaxed and sure of his assessment.

Chenli's nostrils flared as if he didn't believe a word. "*Pfah!* There were a lot of tales floating around regarding that wizard's demise...... and not one included a witch!"

"She was there, that I know for a certainty ... and she disappeared from his dungeons in the process. Vanished." Sinjin flicked his fingers apart like a dandelion expending its fluff. "Believe what you like, I've dealt with the woman. She has uncommon powers." Sinjin offered nothing more about his experience. That was another operation, another client and he'd revealed too much already.

Chenli assessed this new piece of intelligence. The events on the borders these past few months, spoke of the interference of mages and their arcane weapons. It had the same taint as the powers Rovinkar had employed. He had seen the wizard's reward.

"Then, something will be done. Who else rides with the Standish?"

"By the banner ... and her semblance is correct ... the Damen of Ceniago, Katarin Moors. The other Bridash flags ... they represent the Standish Guard, a general, an escort of twenty ... and three minor lords. Their names aren't known to me but they look the part, important and well fed."

"One of them will be a man named Pryan." The Guild-master spoke quietly, a stark contrast to the gravel of the Chancellor's harsh manner.

The two men gave each other a sidelong glance. Obviously, the information had not been shared or there was something about the lord that involved them both. Sinjin took another sip of his lemon water, waiting for their assessment.

"If there is an opportunity, the one named Pryan could be observed as well, though his purpose is known." Patan made the remark, offhand, as though the request were a small matter. Sinjin knew there was nothing too trivial in the land of princes. The man Pryan would be a chief concern and the Chancellor reaffirmed the notion.

"Yes. Mark the man. I want to know who he talks to while he's here in the Vale. Especially if he is closeting with the Jima-lians. As far as this ... *witch* is concerned, I think her presence is not needed at the negotiations, nor the Lady Moors, for that matter. Women cause trouble." The Chancellor growled, looking about the crowded common room as though someone would offer further agreement. "There is to be an informal dinner tomorrow evening, preceding the summits. Inconvenience them, nothing more. Are we clear?"

Sinjin allowed himself a non-committal nod under the demanding gaze of the Chancellor. The Abbysins were notoriously skittish of women in their ruling midst, unlike the Standish, so the request came of no surprise. Soporifics were easily administered. "Of course."

"Keep that witch under your eye, for as any common dolt can tell you …" Chenli looked around again with distaste, lowering his voice to express the confidentiality of his words, loath to admit his lack of information and hissing with the effort. "… there are sorceries involved in the events that brought us to these summits. What I *don't* know is the flavor or who is mixing the brew. I have no use for seers and sorceries. None. Maybe this witch is at the root of it … who can tell? What I *will* tell you … use a great deal of caution sticking your nose into that honey tree. You will most certainly stir up something that will sting you if you aren't careful." Chenli well remembered his last arrangements with a conjurer. He felt fortunate that he had managed to distance himself enough from that affair, but the webs of intrigues run deep, especially where the ways of mages were concerned. He snarled, his hard eyes boring into the assassin to make his point. "I don't want a failure flying after me."

Haviana draped the colorful sattika over Cerra's body with practiced ease, covering the bone-colored silk bodice and underskirt. The smooth texture felt delicious on her skin, fresh from bathing and the expert masseuse by one of the many exponents employed at the imaret. She felt refreshed by the short nap and this attention further energized her. Havi spoke of the bright color and intricate pattern dyed into the cloth. Cerra's mind brightened with response as she painted the colors enriched by the soft, fluid touch of the silk. How the colors appeared in her mind were more like layers of land-scape than drapery.

"The central color is green, like fresh celery, the accents are ecru and a rich deep purple, such as royals are fond of wearing. There is a band of cloth that looks like silvered gold trimming on one edge and at the last yard, the color is all purple with dashes of the green, thin enough to see through, for this last drape, pulled over the head, acts as a hood and when drawn across the cheeks, becomes a suitable veil."

"Oh, I shouldn't need a veil." Cerra laughed, laying her hands along her freshly dressed mop of red hair. "Unless it's to keep my hair away from my food while I eat. Oh … my hair feels well done, I might add. Not even half of it out of place."

"Your metal pins are marvelous. You'll find it bound to good effect." Haviana gave the red curls another soft pat to finish.

Katarin Moors sat by comfortably and observed as Havi finished adjusting the dress and headwear. Cerra fussed at the drape and texture with her hands, clearly unsure of the cos-tume. "This is a traditional dress … or sattika. The veil for your hair is proper for women in a formal setting, particularly among the Abbysin."

"I have my Cherros cloak … the hood would have been more than adequate." Cerra complained, though only halfheartedly. "You didn't have to provide this ... though I confess, right now I have no arguments that my skin would agree with."

"*Pshw.* That cloak is for travel and has no color at all. I'll not have an ambassador of the Stands looking like a vagabond."

"I'm a mere aide to Captain Ferriman. I shouldn't want to be noticed at all."

"Anyone in the party is an ambassador by default. You will attract attention in any event, not the least of which is your stunning red hair. It is as rare as a winter swallow on the Twelfth of Never." Katarin added in a confidential tone. "However, I must tell you, once they admire your dress and the heft of your bosom, the men will become more interested in themselves and their pissing contest than they will be in you ... or me ... and I am central to the delegation. You might note that I'll be largely ignored in the proceedings, an irritation I have to accept when dealing with men, especially with the Abbysin."

"I prefer the councils of Aleston, I think. I can't imagine Merilinn ... that's the innkeeper's wife ... keeping quiet when there are issues to be discussed. Why, I've even spoken myself ... I believe to good effect. The point is that there was none to gainsay us." Cerra flashed a smile in the direction of Katarin. "There are a lot of us women about and we are to be reckoned with." She heard a most un-servantlike chuff come from Havi.

"I do my best to even the odds but it rarely works in direct negotiations." Katarin commented, as she stood, motioning the young servant girl away whilst she added a little dust and brush adjustment to Cerra's dress. "I have my ways of having my way. Come. You look fit for royalty. Let's not make a late entrance. There are plenty ready to assume that dubious honor. We're to gather first with Commander Holder."

Cerra heard Kamir make a plaintive mewl from the middle of the bed.

"No, cat ... I've got things to do before I lie down. You'll just have to wait. I promise to sneak you some morsels from the kitchen."

Haviana returned to offer a tentative touch on Cerra's elbow. She held the blind woman's slender stick, which was turned from a dark hardwood and topped with a small carving of a pinecone set with a bronze ferrule. It had the look of a slender scepter.

"You *do* look like a queen. It's fitting." Haviana remarked softly, a touch of awe in her voice. "Your walking cane, milady."

"Havi, you anticipate me well, one luxury I could get used to. A Queen! Oh my ... after the attentions of the spas today ... and this dress ... I must confess, I feel a little bit like one." Cerra turned to embrace her, then grasped the cane, a broad smile beaming across her face. "Both of you ... *heh* ... I feel well-tended, if that is what Queens are accustomed to. Others will have to judge the dress, *ahh* ... ... to me it feels divine," she thrilled as she fanned the fabric in a half turn.

The girl's remark gave her pause even so, spoken as sincerely as if she were addressing royalty. Cerra had a rare vision of herself, dressed in these queenly robes and seated with a black panther at her side. As if privy to her thoughts, Kamir meowed to voice his approval, prancing around the sweep of her skirt. "Yes, little one … you're definitely part of a queen's retinue … the way I see it, anyway."

A fanciful portrait of the soft-spoken girl had arisen in her imagination as well, that of an attentive falcon that missed nothing. The image persisted, an oddly satisfying one as she thought of the eagles that guarded the air.

Chapter 20

Cerra remembered the pace and direction to the central plaza of the imaret, easily defined by the wash of water-scent from the oasis to her left. As they walked, Katarin listed the Abbysin dignitaries they would likely meet, if not by name, then rank, for the Abbysin were meticulous about form and convention.

The shaded area of the central courtyard was apparent, as well as the awakening scents of the night blooming jasmine, coming to life in the long glow of the setting sun. The heat of it lay soft and low on her cheek, giving Cerra a sense of soft colors mixing with the brightness of her sattika.

The murmur of close conversations and rustling of numerous bodies, replaced the muffling splashes of the courtyard fountain as they entered the central plaza. Cerra heard murmured excuses from Captain Ferriman to an aide, then his sure movement towards her.

"Captain. I hope we didn't keep you waiting?" Cerra held out her hand.

Ferriman could still be startled by her perceptions, even after weeks in her company. She had cued on him immediately, again making him wonder what uncanny vision formed behind those sightless eyes.

"Not at all. Mostly it is the guards and armorers looking at each other from the corners of the courtyard where they stand watch. Those of us from the Stands are in attendance. The Abbysins won't appear until everyone important has arrived."

"That's why I am rightfully early." Cerra chuckled. "But I hear more voices finding partners to greet and they dance around in pleasantries. Is it a gathering yet?"

"Not quite … and it will be a little larger than planned."

"Excuse me, Cerra. I see Westre at the wine. A good place to start is to slow down his cup without him knowing it." Katarin gave Cerra a reassuring clasp of hands, then left her in the care of Artis Ferriman.

"The surprise guest, of course, is the delegation from the Jimals." Ferriman confided quietly, as though giving instructions for a coming operation. Cerra could hear his voice going outward, indicating he was surveying the room as he spoke. "They were not expected by the Abbysin. It's my guess they found out while on the way here, as we did."

"A surprise? A good one I should hope. If the back-fence talk I heard in Bridash is true, they are as affected as we."

"True." Ferriman admitted. "It has only raised an issue with Ser Pryan. He must have an issue with Jimalians."

"That doesn't surprise me. Has he met one? Or just on principal?"

"Principals only, such as he has them. As for meeting them … I did some checking on his supposed business. I gathered rumors that he owes a great deal of stock and trade to a Lord from Tenigra, one of the major Jimal trade centers … Andigar Cianon. Rumors are sieves, but there are morsels to be caught in them."

"It's how we collect news in faraway Aleston." Cerra chuckled. "I'm unsure of the ways of lenders, though I've heard them called sharks, presumably by those who owe. Come to think of it, if you're looking for 'principal', there it is."

Cerra wondered what other pieces of information floated about the halls of power. She was sure that secrecy must run deep. She was attending a performance and knew none of the troupe. There was a muting of conversations with a wave of attention directed towards the entryway. Ferriman gave her the clues she needed.

"The Abbysins are here. There will be a round of introductions and formalities. Only a few are known to me … the Chancellor, Chenli, to be sure. His generals and staff are a standard lot … some I've served under. They will follow the line of Chenli. There are a few, dressed richly, who undoubtedly represent the trading guilds."

"I don't know the secret of politics between kingdoms, yet I wager that in the end, the trader's voices will speak loudest, if not in volume, at least in effect." Cerra observed. "Gold talks … it can also sing. Probably dance if one let it."

"No matter how deaf, one can always hear the sound of gold." Ferriman agreed. "The Chancellor and his guards are circling the courtyard making their introductions … they'll be here within moments. He is exchanging words with Westre and the Lady Moors. Behind him is a man who looks to be a lord of the Armorer's Guild … he has the marks and the build for it."

Cerra picked up the solid reassurance of Katarin's voice from the entanglement of conversations. She was dismissed with a gruff acknowledgement. Her immediate picture of the Chancellor was one of a bear, irascible after rousing from a long sleep. His presence closed on her, the rustling moves of the detachment surrounding him seemed to extend the aura of his power. The image of the bear only strengthened when he spoke, the harsh tone more apparent when standing near.

"Captain Ferriman." Chenli spoke as though Ferriman had long been in the Chancellor's service, though they had never met. It was the Chancellor's way of letting the other know he was informed and likely knew of the Captain's entire career. Cerra could feel when the cast of his gaze fell upon her. She looked down and sketched a reasonable curtsy.

"And this must be the blind girl," Chenli spoke in Abbysin. Her knowledge of the language was rough, though serviceable. She didn't need translation to hear his tone, mixed with derision and curiosity, as if unsure there was any advantage to himself in knowing her.

"My aide." Ferriman said formally. "Cerra of the …"

"Cerra." Chenli broke in. The title had no meaning to him. He switched to Standish, speaking with none of the usual Abbysin lilt. "I've heard of you. A curious addition to your embassy. Exactly what do you do… aide?"

"She is …" Ferriman stopped his introduction abruptly. Clearly the Chancellor had frozen him into silence with a look.

"A planner, your lordship." Cerra spoke brightly and without hesitation, as though pleased with the introduction. She was uncertain of the best address, but 'lordship' never failed as an honorific. "A mere advisor."

She could feel his scrutiny and held her sightless gaze to where she thought his heart might be. She heard a muffled snort as if her status had been further rated and found wanting, the status of Ferriman as well.

Chenli moved away, intent on reviewing the rank and position of each person in attendance within the confines of the central plaza. A shadow of movement followed him, his personal guards, Cerra supposed. She waited until they had moved well away.

"I don't think I've improved your standing with the Chancellor of the Abbysins."

"I would not have much rating short of a Commander's bar in any event. When the discussions are boiled down to where treaties are made, my words will count as only so much salt, added to taste." Cerra could hear the wry humor in Ferriman's voice. He again spoke outward as he surveyed the courtyard, yet softly as only for her ears. "The Abbysins are still filtering in … hold a moment … the next person you are destined to meet looks to be a little spicier … the Ducesin Linarest Mirbek, of the Jimals … 'Queen', if you will. She is coming this way. Maybe I shouldn't tell you this, but right now she is looking at me in a most unwifely manner. Her husband, the Ducet Risherade, is the titular ruler of the Middle Jimals. He's circling behind her, yet likely has the loudest voice you'll hear within the courtyard."

The sound of a smooth wash of silk preceded the arrival of the Ducesin, along with the vaguely floral scents of rose and piney wood.

"Milady Ducesin," Ferriman spoke in Jimalian and

sketched a bow befitting a uniformed officer.

"You are Captain … Ferriman. Your Commander has been kind enough to name his staff. He tells me you were once stationed in the Jimals."

"True enough, milady. Without that I shouldn't be so proficient in the language and the art of the people there. I am quite sure that is why I have the honor to be included in this embassy."

It was a tactful lie, for the Jimalians were not expected when they departed. Ferriman saw no reason not to imply that Standish military intelligence was accurate and extensive. A rustle was all Cerra needed to hear to know that attention had again been placed upon her. There was another, quieter form that moved close to the Ducesin's side, felt by the wooden scent in the air, one far removed from the sands of the Vale.

"Your … 'aide'?" The Ducesin was soft spoken and dry of throat. The image she cast came through as a papery thing, her diction controlled and smooth, though Cerra felt if she were to talk louder, her voice might sound more crow-like — harsh and demanding.

"Cerra Meadows." Ferriman replied. "She … is an advisor to the court and my staff."

"I see."

Cerra refrained from answering. Her command of Jimalian was sparse, so she was still forming the thoughts for response when Ferriman touched her and offered the introduction.

"Cerra … the Lady Ducesin."

"Dear girl. Quite lovely. Remarkable, very lovely, really … even with the odd cast to her eyes."

The last comment slipped out as her voice slid back towards Captain Ferriman. Cerra felt herself tear up a little but she kept a smile warming her cheeks as she spoke in Standish, holding her hand out to accept the Ducesin's hand in greeting. "It's an honor, your ladyship."

"Of course, it is." The Ducesin spoke in fluent Standish, taking Cerra's hand. "Where are you from? Surely from the Eorin Isles. They may be the only ones with such red hair as you have. If it wasn't so rare, the color might even be popular."

"Thank you, milady. I've heard of the Isles, to be sure, yet I only know my home ... in the Stands."

There was a long pause, a detail being analyzed. "That is an interesting cane. Almost like a scepter." By her tone, it was apparent the Ducesin found the idea both humorous and curious.

"It helps me see ... to find my way." Cerra offered. *'I can see whacking your ankle with it'* crossed her mind and she was fair certain she could hit it on the first go. The thought made her smile genuine as she nodded politely, accepting the apparent compliment. It was obvious when the Ducesin turned back to the Captain. "I hope she gives good advice." Her words practically had a wink and a nudge applied to them.

The Ducesin's husband, who crowded in like a stockman looking for a pint, had Cerra taking a step back from his pressing bluster. "Here, what's this? Woman, for the moment our interests lie across the courtyard."

"I see no reason not to mingle while waiting for the Abbysins to lay out their banquet," the Ducesin replied indulgently, obviously used to her husband's brash assertiveness.

"Formal talks are tomorrow … you can make your decisions then. And you shan't need me for that either. You know the Abbysins … the idea of 'Queen' is a foreign one to them."

"A Queen … the tapestry that hangs behind the throne, rich and lovely to look at, don't you agree?" Risherade pushed close to his wife, claiming proud ownership. Linarest's response was non-committal, but cold, a bantering that had lost its zest long ago. Ferriman responded with a light click of his heels, his voice tight and formal.

"Excellency."

Cerra felt as though she had walked into an ongoing family squabble, made more uncomfortable by not being able to readily make an exit. Risherade, thankfully escorted his wife away before an introduction was necessary, proclaiming forced pleasantries to the bodies near him. Cerra pictured a large ham swinging in a butcher's cellar, as she listened to him cross the courtyard.

"Pleasant couple … they go well together. As Annie the Weaver would say: 'at least they won't spoil two homes.'" Cerra snickered softly. She leaned a little closer, her curiosity piqued by the exchange. "Tell me, there was another with them … who said nothing."

"Ah … that one. According to my intelligence, it is her chief servant … one both deaf and mute. Perhaps the best qualification for the job," Ferriman added dryly.

"Oh? Well, she felt like a shadow. It must be a difficult position to … "

"He … the servant is a man. A slender man, who I daresay could pass for a woman with little disguise." Ferriman clarified. "And yes, he shadows her carefully. Not someone you'd want to talk to at any rate. He has a forbidding look about him, as though food and people are merely necessities to be tolerated."

"I'm happy to have missed it … as much as I'm happy not having the trappings of power. *Heh* … I've nothing to guard. Such constant attention would make me feel suffocated."

Ferriman let out a small snort. "I think attention is what power craves. That and feasting … the Abbysins have released the servants bearing the oil that will lubricate the proceedings … plates of food and by the looks of it, jugs of wine. The fate of worlds is decided over appetizers."

Cerra caught succulent drafts amid the perfumes and scents of the gathered dignitaries. "Do not the deliberations begin tomorrow?"

"Officially, yes. But the promises and bribes will all be made in the circles that form while the wine is flowing and stomachs are filled. Tonight, is when alliances are formed."

"Which circle will you be observing?" Cerra noted that Ferriman's voice was seldom directed at her. He was certainly on constant watch, making his own observations regarding the notables in attendance.

"I have just one concern. The Stands. Holder is voice of the Standish forces. I hold my own."

"Then I'll surely hold my own opinions too." Cerra chuckled softly. "Else I should create new conflicts. The ones on the table are dire enough for now. I've no good feelings about war and I should like to bend the ear of the Chancellor."

"You'll not get debate from me. The agonies of battle are

enough of an argument." Ferriman lightly touched her arm. "Speaking of Commander Holder. He is engaged with the Abbysin Collenel and by the marks, a master of the Armorer's Guild. Pryan is with them too. War may be a bad situation, but there is coin to be made in prolonging it."

Cerra plucked the voice of Pryan out of the murmuring threads of activity awash in the courtyard. He was well into a boast she had heard too many times during their journey to the Vale.

"A better conversation to be had than here, gossiping with a lone girl. Steer me to a seat ... I must confess I'm tired of standing ... and use your rank to advantage. Besides, I can hear much better that way. I'm not in your service to 'keep an eye out'."

Ferriman responded, a smile evident. "You see more than you let on. It's why you have value ... the rusty tool you're so proud of."

"Rusty," Cerra snorted. "In this gathering, I'll need the eyes of a true cynic in order to improve my vision."

"You see well enough to sidestep intentional traps. I noticed you didn't respond except in Standish to either the Chancellor, nor the Jimalian Ducets. Your command of their languages is better than that."

"I'm trying to match your level of tact." Cerra offered. "A new challenge for me."

He made a brief chuckling sound. "I've made the observation before, that I'd do well to not play at cards with you.... ahh, there's a bench near the arbor walk that isn't occupied ... yet."

Ferriman guided her to the edge of the courtyard, a shift and freshness of the air letting her know the waters of the oasis were once again visible.

"I'll send a servant with a plate …"

"And wine …" Cerra added helpfully as she sat facing the courtyard, the dappled breezes sparkling the scene in her mind.

Her walking cane momentarily stood erect like a ruling scepter in her grip, causing Ferriman to smile at the semblance of royalty that she managed to attain in the instant before she slipped it down alongside the bench.

"And wine."

The Captain's footsteps mingled into the stir of the plaza, a square some sixty paces across. She reached out to feel the column next to the bench, one of many bordering the small courtyard. It was textured with many small tiles that Katarin had described as a mosaic, patterned and colorful. Cerra felt the precision of the inlay remarkable, every tessera felt smooth, as though polished like a gem before being set. A servant brought her a small tray of fingerfoods and she marked the spot where the glass clinked down on the bench beside her.

Cerra sat, idly sampling the foods and sipping on the wine. It was very good Abbysin fare, roasted morsels of lamb and pork with succulent glazes, along with spiced vegetables. Cerra wandered through a light smear of goat cheese on bread, a nibble of grapes, a delicious baked small tart and a sip of wine finished the round of tastes. *'I would eat here again,'* she chuckled to herself and settled back to sample more from the plate and assess the room.

Chapter 21

Power glittered throughout the assembly, as polished and colorful in their regalia as the tiles that covered the archways of the plaza. The lowering sun and guttering torches cast a blanket of warmth over a conference layered deep with tension. The informal conclave was officially underway, though most contingents huddled together like feuding relatives at a family gathering. Sinjin could already spot those whose eyes shifted to other camps, waiting for their opportunities to close ranks. Those glances were the secret ones, the ones not meant to be noticed. In the subtle exchanges that followed, deals would be made while the celebrants cut the cake.

None of the looks were directed at him, dressed elegantly as one of the majeure-domos to direct the staff. His hair was curled and oiled, as befitting of the office. He didn't worry about challenges from the other servants and staff, as they all had their own tasks to fulfill. The Lords of the Vale noticed nothing unless it inconvenienced them.

He lay about his task early, making his presence known among the staff before the arrival of the dignitaries. Importantly, he was there when the witch made her entrance along with a few of the Standish officers, earlier than the rest of the diplomatic parties. He allowed himself to watch her as he moved about the room. Her red hair drew him like a moth to flame, even though it was largely contained by the veiled headdress of her attire. That she was blind saved him the uncomfortable possibility of eye contact, yet he still wanted to avoid notice by the officer that accompanied her. Her blindness had not been revealed to him until after the downfall of the wizard. A stunning revelation in itself, making her all the more powerful in his mind. He pulled aside a liveried servant.

"The Standish Lords … serve them well. If they have any special needs … any at all … let me know immediately." He waved away the servant as he considered his opportunities. Sinjin gave the same instruction to another servant and perused the serving tables as the fingerfoods and delicacies were brought from the kitchen and arrayed. Fish from the oasis, along with crab and oysters from the Sultan Sea lay at the center, as well as slivers of meat in savory marinades. The wines and ports were decanted in the kitchens, well stocked as the focus of the evening was to loosen tongues. As food and drink were in abundance, meant to ease the negotiations, food and drink would become his tools. Negotiations could take a strange turn.

He ran his thumb along the ring that held the soporific. He'd see if the witch had the same constitution as the other Standish Lady. The venins laced into his mixture would leave them cramped and to their beds for a day or so, nothing more. When the meetings were over, everyone will have dismissed the discomforts as 'woman's time' and be forgotten.

The gathering gained momentum quickly, the occupants drawn into the whirlpool by the events. The threat of hostilities hung in the air and some would try to mitigate the issues.

Other would try to profit by them. Sinjin cast a look for the Chancellor and the Abbysin Guildmaster. They were not yet in attendance, though he doubted either would notice him. Servants gained a certain amount of invisibility among the wealthy and powerful, not recognized until something was needed.

Soft echoes, the agitation of air from the people gathered in groups and knots, bordered the space in front of her. The expanse of the pavilion allowed a picture to form in Cerra's mind, a fluid space awash with the water of sound and scent much like the lake near her cabin. She sought first to isolate Captain Ferriman, if she could. It only took a moment to place his even, confident pattern.

The other members in her party were easy to locate, for they were still grouped together, speaking of harvests and the various struggles facing their many holdings, to a group that must be Abbysin by their accents. There were smatterings of Abbysin spoken here and there, though much of the discussions she captured were relayed in some varied degree of the Trader dialect, favored by the caravaners and sailors that lay claim to no country except the vessels of their trade. It was common among some of them to speak a patois of both. Like a misplaced note in a song, Pryan's voice wormed into her consciousness.

"I don't worry about kingdoms. I worry about my purse and so should you."

It was the one voice in the gathering she could well do without. Yet once it was there, she let her hearing chase it down. Jessan, her mentor, had long ago encouraged her to follow sounds; a departing horse or far away bird, for as long as the vibration held in her ears and even a bit beyond as her imagination took hold. In her sightless world, acute hearing and a sensitive nose took the lead in painting the spaces around her. Touch, was a more private brush.

The person Pryan addressed was unknown to her, though that held for most of the three score in attendance. There was maybe a score more, given the guards immobile and quiet at their stations. Cerra formulated the size and disposition of the group by quartering the gathering and making rough assessments, based on the volumes of sound and motion. She smiled to herself as she thought of the many gatherings in Aleston, where families and clans came to mingle, yet spent the time largely with their own familiars and relatives. She sought the voice of Katarin, easy to identify in the buzzing undertones of the courtyard blooming with male conversation, then again, her attention was caught by Pryan, his voice given sudden volume by exasperation.

"The debt is exaggerated."

"It is not for me to say, I merely pass on recommendations." The reply was quieter, in fluent Standish though the accent was unfamiliar. "Further delays can affect your health, as I understand it. Perhaps you would like to speak with him directly."

Pryan's reply was more restrained but Cerra was now sharply attuned with curiosity. "The original sample is still intact. I have made arrangements, to the benefit of all. Very likely the best you will see. Ever. Mark my words. Has Andigar heard of patience? It is the nature of business and I am distressed by these accusations. Since you press … *mmmmph* … I have an alternative that will satisfy us both. Tell him this …" Pryan's voice dropped to an indecipherable babble, impossible to follow, but insinuations of conspiracy coated his words as he retreated to close parley. There was also the vibrato of fear. She pictured him breaking into a sweat and turned to face the origin of the voice. The puzzling, yet apt image of a two-faced juggler once again crossed her mind. She took a sip of wine, closing her eyelids with the smile of her satisfaction. The mixture of good wine and information made a curious palate.

Cerra kept a mark on the area and ventured her awareness out to where she had last heard Katarin. She caught flecks of conversation, even a remark directed at her, spoken in Jimalian, noting that at least one person was enjoying the moment. A growling voice snarled close by, the unmistakable grate of the Abbysin Chancellor.

"Give him what he wants. Just make sure the accounting is accurate and you see the stamp of his gold." The reply was muted, yet it had the tone of agreement. "And send Patan to me."

The Chancellor's voice turned away from her, talking to someone behind him in hushed tones that she could barely catch. Another voice trickled in, the Jimalian who had accosted Pryan if she had her guess, causing her to spark her interest in that direction. " … given the revenues … perhaps more mining will …"

A rolling mewl at her ankles broke her concentration and she was just able to ready herself for the inevitable leap into her lap. "What are *you* doing here?" Cerra admonished Kamir quietly, as he turned two circles in her lap and quickly settled into a comfortable repose. She set her wine down to feel for a gobbet of honeyed pork from her tray of foodstuffs and tore a small shred, letting Kamir worry and lick it from her fingers.

"Now make yourself at home … and don't purr," she cooed softly. "I can't hear anything above that racket and I'm trying to be alert. I've lost two tidbits of food now … that and a shred of gossip." She kept her voice low so only the cat could hear, while she sought to relocate the sound of the Chancellor's voice.

It took only a moment for his gravelly snarl to mark him, walking away and moving towards the rear of the courtyard, his words indecipherable. On impulse, she sought the voice of the Ducesin and was quick to locate it by first identifying the more robust conversations of her royal husband. His remarks were self-promoting and her responses were perfunctory and dutiful. The likenesses that evolved in her mind were of opposites. She appeared cold and immaculate, festooned with roses and closely attached to her corpulent husband by the lacing of a spider's web.

Cerra looked away, puzzled at such a vivid image. The ham likeness she had formed of the Ducet persisted, one that favored the plumpness of a distillery pig. A slight twisted grin was evidence of the guilty pleasure of her imagination as she took another sip of wine. The image cleared as she heard the Ducesin compliment a nearby courtier. There was an inclusive warmth that indicated a long association. She never said so outright, but a magnitude of discovery was evident, a prize that could only be hinted at. Clearly infectious enough to lace their private conversation but not enough to share from a foot away. There followed an agreeable response, the word 'gem' uttered as a seeming compliment for the Queen.

Cerra couldn't catch the length of the reply, for Risharade interrupted loudly and began steering the group beyond her range, adamantly insisting that negotiations were pointless in any event. He was *'ready to leave and there was none to stop him'*. Cerra was certain he was speaking for the benefit of his group, though he clearly included any Abbysin that might care to hear as well as the stablers well beyond the courtyard. An even stouter ham emerged in her mind as she shifted her attention to where Pryan could easily be heard, now much closer to the water side of the courtyard where she sat.

Cerra caught the self-satisfied tones of Sevekin Westre, in conversation with Pryan. She turned her right ear slightly towards the two, easing the other sounds of the courtyard to the side as she sought to catch their words. Another was with them, the same voice as before that had questioned Pryan's debt.

"You have assurances?"

Pryan's voice rose slightly, puffed and important. "You've heard them."

Again, the voice of Sevekin Westre could be heard, mumbling his replies as though reluctant to agree. Pryan interrupted him with a flare of impatience.

"There's no issue, as you can see. We support a strengthened army ... a necessary accommodation ... and to profit, where is the harm in that? It's done. Your share is already five-fold ... good bargaining."

Westre's response was unintelligible, yet the tone was one of agreement.

"You see. The arrangements serve all of us well."

The third person offered to relay the terms. Cerra wished she could follow the man as his footsteps drifted away into the muddle of courtyard sounds. She thought to locate Captain Ferriman if she could, yet Pryan's voice drew her attention back again. "Westre, you'll be happy your nerve embraced your purse. Most happy. No pact is complete without a bit of risk and no reward so satisfying. Take it from me."

"The Abbysins are notorious for ... " Westre's voice shifted low and wavered. He was looking around to notice those close, guarding his words. " ... they're notorious for saying one thing and doing another."

"Don't worry about the Abbysin. At the moment it's been arranged ... eh ... I've arranged ... for certain Jimalian, um ... 'liaisons' to be included until all the demands are met ... part of the conditions and solely on my properties, mind you." Pryan's reply was tense and hurried. He clearly did not like the terms, nor Westre's reply.

"My estates still include yours. I don't like it ... and I thought it was ten times ..." Westre changed his tone dramatically as a thought occurred to him. "What do the Jimalians need in the Stands? Observers?"

"Don't you think maybe that's what we need ... observers?" Pryan deflected the question with one of his own. "Ours is blind. *Hah!* … and as healthy as a miller's horse too. If she had her eyes right, I might give her a tumble myself… but … there she is … look at her, sitting by herself like a spinster at a dance with a bedamn cat on her lap. That's our collective military mind at work. Maybe some Jimalian observation is what we need, have you thought of that? Besides, it isn't permanent. Just business."

Cerra kept idly stroking Kamir's soft fur and took another bite from her tray. With her ear well-trained on their conversation, she knew her attention appeared to be directed elsewhere. She considered a lot of clever retorts, smiling as she panned the thoughts aside in order to concentrate on Westre's response.

"I'm committed to a strong army, you know that. And damme, you still owe rents for that estate. With those arrears in mind my 'investment' is feeling a little less attractive. …"

"You think too much, Westre. It's done. I traded today and the proceeds …"

"Oh Cerra, you have been ignored horribly." A rush of fabric and Katarin's enthusiasm blocked the reply Cerra was straining to hear.

Chapter 22

Sinjin moved smoothly about the gathering, watching those he deemed most important, even catching what he could of conversations. He never gravitated far from the witch as if he were held within her circle of influence. The opportunity to approach both her and the Standish Royal, named Moors, would come soon enough, once the wine and foodstuffs were circulating in earnest.

At the moment, she was sitting to the side of the pavilion, the water of the oasis reflecting the early moonlight behind her. Sipping her wine and nibbling on her small tray of finger-foods, she appeared lost in thought, showing subtle reactions like a momentary smirk or tightened brow, as though listening to a conversation. Her cat sat nestled on her lap, poised and comfortably alert, judging the assembled nobles with disdain.

Sinjin studied her again in a new light, then looked about to the immediate audience near where she sat. Snatches of phrases and repressed laughter came through the general din of conversation. The Jimalians and the Standish Lord were in close huddle. If he strained to hear, he might …

His attention was drawn back to the red-haired witch. The Lady Moors had approached her again. They sat for a moment and Sinjin toyed with the vial briefly, sensing the moment to act was near. As though paying attention to the quality of service, he kept himself close.

~ ❖ ~

Kamir stretched and settled back on her lap as Katarin sat next to her on the bench, clearly satisfied with the proceedings thus far. "There are more emissaries here than planned, as you know. I've not talked to half of them yet and I can't remember half the names of the half I have. But a good thing. Everyone is talking and not shouting as you can plainly tell … though no one really knows what is going on. I didn't mean to ignore you."

"Oh, I'm fine, I assure you," Cerra replied sincerely. "I really hate standing for long. Sitting allows me to enjoy the surroundings more… and I'm only bumping into rumors," she added with a little laugh.

Katarin was relieved to see the ready smile on Cerra's face. Her deep brown eyes, though sightless, always appeared to have a merry demeanor. Her gaze was never guided in quite the usual directions, though it seemed to Katarin, it was a focus given to seeing beautiful things.

"Your cat has found you, so you are not lacking for company at any rate." Katarin gently laid her hands upon Cerra's wrists. "Let me take the glass for a moment … here's your stick. Willem … Commander Holder … is in debate with the Abbysin Collenel. He's asked me to have you join the conversation."

"I can't imagine what he should need my opinion for. I have no head for military things at all," Cerra puzzled as she grasped her light cane and made motions to rise, nudging

Kamir into motion. "Here, cat. Sneak a prize from the plate while you can and before someone shoos you off." Kamir dutifully skipped to the tiles at her feet as she stood. "Shall we make opinions together?"

Katarin laughed, impressed to note that Cerra faced exactly the direction it would take to reach Holder across the courtyard. They locked elbows, Katarin leading Cerra to the tight knot of men where the Commander was engaged.

"You'll do well to make headway," Katarin remarked with a little sigh. Clearly, she had already been slighted in the conversations. "Generals and Collenels and Khans are men who have armies as their voice. They don't raise their voice, they have a spear cast instead."

"May the gods help us if they take to swearing. So far, so good" Cerra said, offering encouragement.

"Personally, I think someone has. And in the worst language possible." Katarin observed with a sudden change of tone. "The attacks on Ceniago and the Gate … Bridash … feel like the work of oaths spoken in the dark."

Cerra felt her mood drop as well. Catastrophe and ruin had been left in the wake of those extraordinary events, even the dissolution of the demon, a loss Cerra had been shunting aside with the same methodic certitude that helped her cope with her dark world. Powerful majics, more compelling and forceful than even her dear Yutan, were at play.

"I don't think dark majics are the work of generals and their attendants." Cerra countered softly. "Leastways not of the sort I know. I believe they're content with their slings and arrows and shaking their spears." She picked up the voices of Ferriman and Holder, still yet a few paces in front of her, mixed with a group of five or six. They were standing near the entrance of the courtyard from the west side that faced the desert. No stir of conversations could be sensed past their knot. "However, … those that employ the spears …" She gave Katarin's hand a reassuring squeeze as Ferriman turned to greet them.

"Cerra. So good of you to join us. The Lady Cerra of the Meadows …" The Captain's voice trailed slightly as he turned away to introduce those standing within the circle, officers of Abbysin origin by their names, their ranks of similar grade as the Captain.

"My pleasure, Gentlemen."

Turning slightly, the Lady Moors signaled one of the staff and was rewarded with an eager nod in response.

From his station close by, Sinjin motioned to the servant who had answered the summons, drawing him aside before he could begin his task. "The Standish noblewoman. What did she want?"

"Sherry, Majeure," replied the servant. "She wants the Luminarian. Of course, we have it handy … though I told her it was a scarcity and I was daring my luck."

"Well done. It will show better on the charges later." Sinjin glanced quickly at the witch and Lady Moors, engaged in conversation with an Abbysin Collonel. Judging by the curiosity in the witch shown by the officer, they would be caught up for the moment. "Show me the bottle. I'll deliver it to them personally."

"Of course, Majeure." He turned immediately, intent on

the timely execution of his errand. Sinjin had to hurry to keep pace to where the steward kept his wines and spirits racked in one of the ante-rooms. Another servant, slender, with intent eyes and tonsured like a mendicant, passed them bearing a tray with two poured glasses, an ornate ceramic carafe balanced between them.

"Ah … I see the Luminarian is popular tonight." remarked the servant with a grin, then changed his expression to doubtful concern. "Then again, maybe that was all of it. We will have to see."

He doubled his pace, though something made Sinjin stop before they reached the steward's door. He turned back to satisfy his curiosity.

Cerra spoke in Standish, holding out her hand as they accepted it one by one, the last officer even placing a chivalrous kiss upon a knuckle before releasing it.

"I am enchanted. You are a picture of beauty, a grace to your companions." The man spoke in Abbysin, a courtier's voice, oiled and used to compliments, the very same Collenel that guided them to the Vale. He struck a much different tone in the company of royals, separated from the faces and rigors of his command. "Your captain … an able man … he tells us that you are a player of chess."

Cerra smiled at him, uncomprehending. As he spoke of chess, she immediately felt as though she had been placed on the board and the voice claimed the shape of the paladin in her mind. Her command of Abbysin was sketchy and not given to nuance, so she held her reply, unwilling to reveal a slim advantage. Captain Ferriman quickly translated and Cerra was careful to show her delight at the words.

"Yes, I do! And I have so few opportunities to play. It's a game not much given to those in the crofts where I live. Not like One-a-Twenty Pegs or Bidderkins. You were in command of our group … I've forgotten your name … but a Collenel I remember." Cerra had excellent recall, yet gave the officer a chance to introduce himself again. He would no doubt begin speaking of himself, to cement his legacy and qualifications. If indeed she were in a game, she would learn the players and pieces as best she could. Ferriman had positioned her as a pawn, stepping forward to confront the powers of the line.

"Yes … Collenel Iakobi Lazaros, at your service." This time, he spoke in Standish, the smooth certainty remaining.

"Collenel. I have to thank you for your spirited crossing of the desert. It made our trip so much more enjoyable with early starts and a good pace. As I understand it, the rank of Collenel comes from an Abbysin word … for 'column'. Was I told true?"

"Indeed, Lady Meadows." Lazaros warmed to the curious woman in front of him. He had given her little thought during the chaperone, which he considered an odious affair, his elite troops playing nursemaid to foreign royals. Once engaged though, pride was involved and he had made sure his command was as polished and resplendent as possible after their encounter with the Fire beast at the Gate. His column had shown well upon their entrance to the Vale. "It is so. I am proud to lead the Paladon Crussars, all fighters from the western hills of Abbysin. We are known for our ... ferocity."

"I am grateful to have met you ... in the calm." Cerra nodded slightly in his direction. "As for chess, I play, true enough, yet I can hardly claim any expertise."

"I had not thought women capable of the game." Lazaros responded, a trace of arrogance lifted his voice. Cerra quelled her first response. *'Better my teeth are sharper than my tongue'*, she thought as she smiled back at him.

"I play as well." Katarin broke in smoothly, giving Cerra a reassuring touch on her shoulder. "I shall have to challenge you."

"Oh good ..." Cerra giggled, grateful for the momentary diversion. " ... an opportunity to sit for an hour and not move a muscle." She faced the Collenel with a brighter smile. "I'm not sure I truly know the game, ser Lazaros. I merely understand it."

"What then, is the object?" The Collenel pressed.

"Why, victory, of course." Cerra countered, hoping that would be answer enough, as men center on the destination more than the path taken.

"What else? Victory is the purpose of everything. What could you possibly find interesting in such a strategic game?" Lazaros still maintained his superior air.

Cerra couldn't resist a strong counter. "You mention strategy ...it's a good test of imagination and there is much to work with in chess. Everyone has their particular strength. I find it curious that the King is the weakest piece on the board ... even the pawns have a stronger purpose. Conversely, the Queen is the most powerful ..." she gave Katarina's hand an unobtrusive squeeze. " ... and can go anywhere she wants."

"*Eh* ... but all are at the King's service, are they not? How is it that you play? Not only a woman, but ... *ah* ..." Cerra could feel Lazaro's self-satisfied smile turn his voice. " ... you play at a disadvantage."

"I can only rely on my perception." Cerra tapped at her head. "If I have a strategy, it is to see the distant pieces as if they were close and to take a long view of those things near at hand. I have to remember where everything is ... I suppose that helps too."

There was a moment of silence. Cerra could feel the Collenel scrutinizing her. She wondered what the object of his focus was ... her dress? Her blind eyes or red hair? Or her apparent effrontery? Cerra decided she would attract less attention with a modest conclusion. "I've not played an expert such as yourself, Ser Lazaros ... a military man. I have no doubt I would learn much from the experience."

"No doubt." A smug acceptance oiled his voice. She could tell he remained curious about either her mien or her game, when someone close brushed past her. Katarin immediately voiced her enthusiasm.

"Oh well enough! ... I had sherry brought to us, Cerra ... Luminarian Dry. The staff here claimed they had to raid their cellars ... I *knew* they had it. Captain ... Cerra. Ser Lazaros ... a pour for you too." A glass was handed to Cerra as Katarin turned aside to speak with Lazaros. "It's frightfully hard to find in the Stands."

Cerra's raised her glass and her heart jumped as she parsed

faint odors, a fruity elixir mingled with the very slight tang of bittered tomatoes, a sharpness she knew too well from her practice with herbs.

"*Stop!*" She reached out in alarm, knocking Katarin's arm before she could raise the glass to her lips. Both goblets fumbled and dropped with a tinkling crash, the obvious sound of expensive crystal making her cringe. A slight hush floated through the courtyard as she felt all eyes turn momentarily to the group. She hadn't meant to speak so loudly.

The shout of alarm and crashing glass riveted Sinjin's attention on the witch and her entourage. Despite the confusion, his sharp eyes knew better than to focus on the alarm. Clues would abound in the faces and movements around her. A furtive movement to his left drew his attention, the subtle insinuation of hand signals which brought his eyes in contact with a face that registered. The mendicant. Sinjin registered the man's features, ingraining them into his memory.

"Damme! Have the servants bring Lady Katarin another." Cerra could feel the General's disapproval directed at her. "What is the meaning of this?"

"Captain. Don't drink your sherry." Cerra didn't give anyone a chance to come to her defense. "Poison … sir." She spoke low, afraid to let her words carry.

"Oh, my word …" Katarin grasped Cerra tightly as Ferriman looked at the amber liquid in his glass, then knelt to inspect the small puddle on the tile. A small man, clad in the desert tan livery of the Vale's caliphate, rushed over, brushwhisk and cloth in hand.

"Many pardons … please, allow me …"

"Take care not to touch." Ferriman warned.

The servant looked to the bits of glass scattered in the amber liquid, which now glistened with an oily sheen, giving the Captain a last skeptical glance before setting about undaunted to remove the spill.

"Here ... give him some room." Ferriman guided Cerra to the side as the group shifted away from the servant. An aide stood near and Ferriman directed him to search out the man who had brought the wine. Cerra could think of nothing to say. What else could she have done? Katarin filled the gap.

"It appears we have more than chess to talk about."

"If it's any consolation, I think the poison would likely only make us all a little ill. At least they could have put it in a cake, chocolate if I had my way. If I'm to be done in, I'd rather go from too much dessert." Cerra tried to put Lady Katarin at ease with a smile, for the draught would certainly be deadly if too strong. She had her doubts about the dosage.

"This is an insult!" Lazaros sounded genuinely angry to Cerra's ears. "A coward's weapon laid against diplomats ... and ladies of note."

"The obvious question is 'who'?" Cerra muttered to herself. Lazaros had regained Holder's attention with his promises of vengeance as the honor of Abbysin had been breached, leaving her for the moment centered on her thoughts. The presence of the one that had delivered the tainted sherry had a familiarity that she could not yet place. She had met too many individuals throughout the course of the evening. Another question sifted into form as she wondered who the sherry had been meant for. She felt for the Captain's arm and leaned close. "It seems we've attracted someone's attention."

Sinjin's attention was riveted back on the witch, stepping towards the group that had gathered around her, when a hand gripped his arm. He nearly grappled back in self-defense, catching himself at the servant's triumphant exclamation.

"Majeure. We have yet another bottle. That was not the last as I feared."

"I'll take that." Sinjin collected the ornate carafe, capped with the appropriate seals and guild labels and dismissed the servant, taking a quick look back to those surrounding the witch. The mendicant was nowhere to be seen and the witch seemed forgotten and lost in thought.

For the moment, the din of the gathering muted in Cerra's ears. One thought persisted, driving the gathered conversations back into an unintelligible buzz, that she was getting closer to the source, though she could hardly even assess her place in the game.

Chapter 23

Jasmine and Kahil ginger scented the air, a level of color in her imagination that was sparkled by the chirping of crickets. Cerra layered the sounds beyond her, like moonlight glistening on the waters of the oasis. She lay comfortable within the bed, crisp linens welcome on her bare skin. The pallet faced the open terrace, framed and hung with fabric netting from above, creating a gauzy screen to deter any flittering insects seeking refuge in the coolness of the room.

Sleep escaped her, snatches of conversation overheard during the informal summit invading the placidness of slumber. The notion that she was getting closer to the power brought Yutan to mind, that in some way, displaced remnants of him yet existed and that somehow her efforts might draw him back. Her thought was held out like a light for him to see, for she seemed as lacking in direction or solutions as a lost mariner.

'*Yutan.*'

With beads and wisps of vapor, water coalesced around his intellect, drawing the memory of the earth closer. Remnants of his being found their common energies and bound together to his will. Like a vibration carried among the droplets and mist, a word came through, a vagrancy of thought, a calling as inevitable as life and death.

His name.

As her mental cry faded, she wished she had invited Havi to stay for some company, a diversion from the chaos of her thoughts. Kamir lay nestled in a furred round against her waist, no misgivings troubling his nap, even as she absently trailed her fingernails along the fur at his neck. Cerra gravitated back to the sound of the crickets, chirrups floating in the air like so many stars. The trilling calls again pulled her thoughts to Yutan, lost to the world, divided like so many sounds. Far outside the safe confines of her cabin, like the demon, she was lost to elements beyond her knowledge. A stew of intrigues and unanswered questions fought for equal resolution. She lay still, concentrating as she might on the nocturnal sounds of the oasis at rest; the music of chirping crickets and tinkling fountains creating a hypnotic mantra which she hoped would allow sleep to embrace her.

The slice of air, indicating a body in motion, may have been missed among the enchantment of sound, had she been closer to slumber. Cerra's blood froze for the instant that it took her hearing to locate the movement, cautious and cloaked in stealth. She fought the urge to speak, *'who's there?'* stifled to an anxious thought. The dress she had worn lay on the bed beside her, thrown there as she had stripped, exhausted from the summit. She eased her left hand across to feel the length of silk, for her belt knife lay beneath it. Her heartbeat quickened as her fingertips felt the leather of the sheath. She strained to sense the movement, a step that landed soft as down, closer … inside now … coming from the terrace. She walked the belt along with her fingernails until the hilt slid beneath her hands.

Silence washed ahead of the figure, no sound apparent until the soft pad of leather soles was sensed near the foot of the bed. Cerra held her breath shallow as a thin scrape of metal revealed a touch on her long metal hairpins, which lay on the bedstead beyond the netting. Another light *'click'* told her that it had been laid carefully back in position. A flavor of his scent came to her, a wooden note that she thought she should recognize, supplanted by the man's musk. Her hand tightened on the hilt of her knife, a scream ready at her throat. Kamir tensed at her side, a low growl whining at his throat. She felt the tension next to her change as the cat started to move.

"Stand down!"

Cerra couldn't help but blurt out her pent fear as she heard Ferriman's commanding voice come from the balcony. "Artis! *Ware!*"

The body next to her bed rustled with quick movement at her shout, the slick scrape of metal escaping from a sheath, unmistakable.

Ferriman caught the swift reaction of the shadowy figure, years of battle and combat ingrained in him and jerked his head aside as the whistle of sharp metal flew past his ear. Another dart was flying and he flared his cloak in front of him to divert it as he whisked his sword free. He advanced without word on the dark figure, masked in black like one of the dread Guild of assassins. The intruder had loosed his own sword with a slow and methodical scrape. He too withheld comment, bringing his curved sword to ready, a silver slash that reflected the moonlight. The assassin stepped forward carefully, poised in *'chedan'*, the steel door, marking him as an adept. Ferriman mimicked the position as they closed with guarded balance, watchful eyes assessing each other's form and intent.

When it came, the attack was blinding, even with Ferriman's experience in battle. He barely was able to parry, two strokes slashing from opposite sides followed by a sweeping downward swipe at his head. Ferriman, driven down on one knee, pressed beneath the blow, rising into the attacker before he could turn the curved blade back in. The arced blade was favored by calvary troops, particularly the horsemen of the Cherros, deadly at slashing, but less effective in pinion. Ferriman slid a quick jab in towards the ribs. A spiral counter at the last instant diverted the thrust, a thin weal of blood tracing the rent. Ferriman swept aside the riposte, opening up the attacker as he drove in again, delivering an open palm like a striking cobra into the attackers' chest. The dark shape flew back against the wall next to Cerra's bed with a harsh expulsion of breath, Ferriman sweeping into him with a downward slice to the neck. The assassin reacted swiftly, catching the blow with the pommel of his sword. The impact caused the assassin to lose his weapon, clattering to the terra cotta floor.

Ferriman coiled to strike again at the exposed chest when the assassin dropped his left hand and twitched like a scorpion. A needle of pain bolted through him, a flash of energy that exceeded the bounds of his skin, a sublime pleasure that could only be felt once. The sounds that entered his ears came from another time. The intensity of the light increased, taking the pain with it.

Ferriman crumpled onto the bed, pulling the netting from overhead, the hairpin driven like a stake into the soft spot at the base of his sternum. Cerra screamed as he collapsed on top of her. The razoring clamor of their swords striking blows had only lasted mere moments, the Captain driving the unknown assailant to the wall. There had been an instant that she had felt saved from the danger, a moment lost with the laden sigh of a last breath.

She heard the scrape of a sword leaving the tiles, anxious that it may again turn towards her, but brisk silent steps rushed towards the balcony and were gone among the sounds of alarm. Cerra struggled to release herself from the bedding and netting, pinned by the weight of Ferriman's body.

"Oh … oh no … Captain. *Artis!*"

Her voice wailed as she pulled herself clear, ripping and tearing away at the thin scrim of net. She felt the metal of one of her hair pins, embedded in the unmistakable heat of fresh blood which flowed from his chest.

"Oh no, no no!"

Agony washed over her and Cerra collapsed sobbing on top of the lifeless Captain as guards stormed into the room. Hands pulled her away from the bed as she struggled to remain beside him, to somehow revive the Captain if she could.

"She's killed him." Pryan's voice barked through the angered confusion of sound. Soldiers responded to the accusation and she was wrenched further from where the Captain lay. "Put her under watch."

"No!" Cerra felt herself torn apart as she struggled in the guard's grip, like being hemmed in as a child, within the dark confines of a closet that refused to let her see.

Chapter 24

Darkness pervaded her thoughts. The rooms they had moved her to were plain and featureless with little to spark her imagination and crack through her bleak mood. She was grateful they hadn't placed her in some rank cell, as they considered her blindness cage enough. Her sole experience with incarceration had been one she had no desire to repeat. Yet, in spite of her protests and denials, the possibility remained. She sat on the bed pallet with her knees drawn up, Kamir curled faithfully at her hip. A small anteroom held the main entry to the apartment, a wide portal that allowed passage into the room where she sat. Other than the slight balcony that faced the coolness of the oasis, there was only one other window, facing in the direction of the caravaner's pens and stables. This offered a steady chorus of bleats and whinnies, alongside the gruff gutturals of camels that sounded as though they were near ready to sick up.

The image found purchase with Cerra in her desolation. Her agreements long ago seemed ingenuous and woefully ignorant of the hidden gears that run the world. She had accomplished nothing and her allies had fallen in the passing. She had felt Captain Ferriman's life seep out of him, each fade an agony. Yutan's fate was less sure. He was a creature of the elements, of majics far more powerful than the workings of man.

Cerra heard the door to her apartment hinge open. As yet she'd been denied visitors or council, though she despaired of any company at all. The sweep of cloth and stalwart pace reassured her it was Katarin Moors, even before she caught the citrus scent she favored. The Standish Lady could well be her only remaining ally.

"Lady Moors, I ... " she could not keep the anguish from her voice.

"Katarin. You're not in ill-favor with me and you know that." She sat without asking leave on the pallet next to Cerra and pulled a hand within her grasp. Cerra gave it a thankful grip. "I have been most adamant in your defense. I don't believe for a second ... not a second mind you ... the tale of some lover's quarrel that Ser Pryan favors. *Bah!* It makes no sense. There was no indication whatever of any ... "

Cerra let out a moan of regret in spite of herself. She felt responsible for his death even with the other voices inside of her begging her to not listen. Katarin heard the agony in the blind woman's voice and changed her focus, giving Cerra a reassuring embrace.

"Cerra ... dear ... I know. I know." Katarin waited for some long moments until she felt the tension in the blind woman's shoulders sink a little. She hoped she sounded confident enough to offer a little encouragement. "Pryan is an opportunist and I have no intentions of listening to his accusations. The legal issues, thankfully, rest with the Caliphe of the Vale. Neither Standish nor Abbysin holds sway here. You should know the Caliphe finds you a 'woman of mystery' as he puts it. The word he was using really meant 'oracle'. In any regard, he is reluctant to cast judgment or risk repercussions from any bad treatment of you … he looked to the heavens when he recommended your confinement … it's anyone's guess what he believes. And so, you remain here and not in the pens. Gods, what would that be like?"

"While others think to accuse me, my concern is for the fate of the Captain. He was there to save me. What of the assassin? Who would stand accused if it were me lying dead?" Cerra leaned her chin on her knees, trying to take the anguish out of her voice. It hurt even more to hold back the tears that threatened to break free when she spoke. "Why should I even be marked to die? I've done nothing and said even less. Whoever it was had no reason to be elaborate. *Pfft.* Any tale of my death would be sufficient if it was prefaced by … 'she tripped over her cat.' "

"When the courts are involved, there is no ready answer. You botched an attempt on my good health, did you not? Another issue entirely? Or the same … intrigue finds its own life and solutions. But yes, someone has marked you as dangerous and you are right to question it." Katarin patted Cerra's hand for reassurance. "Questions. This whole embassy has created more issues than it has solved…, and to put a feathered cap on it, the Jimalians have quit the discussions. They left the Vale this morning at first light and in quite the hurry. They must have been all night preparing. They claim the Vale is too dangerous to remain and blame you … you'll hear that soon enough."

"Me?!" Cerra turned her head towards Katarin, brow

furrowed in disbelief. "That's absurd. I'm as harmless as a skink."

"Dear Cerra, I know that. I think they just wanted an excuse and … well, Captain Ferriman's death provided them the exit they desired."

Cerra snorted and thumped back against the wooden headboard, her blind eyes searching the unknowns of middle distance. She spoke not to Katarin, but to the room, reviewing her own internal dilemmas.

"Dear Ferriman wasn't the target. It was me … or the both of us … there was the sherry as well. It was a little stiffer potion than I let on, if my nose is still accurate. Also, the perfumes of the rich are far too strong" Cerra growled, … "as long as I'm in the mood to complain. Someone thought I was important enough to be a danger to their plot … or an instrument. But who? Who has most to gain from the conflict? Given the preparations necessary, I believe the Jimalians would have left regardless. Their king was ready to leave before the lamb was cold in the buffet at the embassy party, as well as a few of their courtiers. They seemed reluctant to give any considerations at all, as though they had already won their position."

Cerra mulled over what she had overheard in the informal gathering. Last night? Another? The lapsed time had been disjointed and exhausting, driven by loss and confusion. The unofficial conclave was to precede the official negotiations, now in question with the departure of the Jimalian embassy. The only talk of profits had come from Pryan. Most of the other conversations she had overheard were suggestions of solution, or merely the exchange of mutual interests.

"In any event, I would not trust Ser Pryan in discussions. He has no interest in the welfare of the Stands, merely his own pockets. If I were to guess, his pockets are as empty as his promises and those lie in the East."

"I can well believe that." Katarin agreed. "Only a fool would believe otherwise."

"There is no shortage of fools." Cerra considered the avid interest of Sevekin Westre. "Fool or not, he found the receptive ears of Ser Westre. They have struck a bargain."

"I hear nothing of their conversations. They are careful not to include me. I assumed they were gathering support for arms, though Westre let on that most of their talk of conquest regarded women. I get much the same treatment from the Abbysins." Katarin sniffed her displeasure. "I'd have done better to remain in Ceniago where at least my authority and opinions are recognized. Mind you, Pryan has only the authority to make suggestions, though Westre can drive policy if he wishes. I can well imagine he might be swayed by castles in the air."

"I think he's been persuaded to live in one," snorted Cerra. "And has already paid handsomely."

Cerra knew her opinion of Pryan was clouded by his overbearing opinions and belittling statements. She had no use for the man at all. Both Westre and Pryan would likely deny anything she might say. Plots had no teeth until the meal was ready to serve.

"Forgive me for saying, I'm in a sour mood … at best Ser Pryan is a dog under the table looking for scraps. A better question is who prepares the feast."

"All fingers point to the Abbysins." Concern muted Katarin's voice, layers of evidence sifting in her thoughts.

"They have more to lose than to profit, at least as I understand it. In the simplest terms, I can only think of who stands to gain. What I 'don't see' is that fortunes and treasure count more than the land and those that dwell in it ... outplaying the other is more important than the price of victory. It's like cheating at cards with a sleight of hand, when the opponent had occasion to sneeze. Someone wants to win very badly and my guess is there is a great deal of wealth at stake. *Heh* ... the fact that Ser Pryan is rooting around is adequate proof. If gold talks, it whispers lewdly to him and is beckoning a bare arse for all to see from the Jimals." Cerra snickered dryly. "With me, it doesn't talk at all. Hells, I can't even see it wave at me from someone else's pocket and that's just fine. That's my mind. I don't have the experience of nations that you do, milady ..."

"That is an uncomplicated view, maybe a bit cynical ... and as you mention the Jimalians, it makes for an interesting subject. They have a long history of denouncing the Empire's taxes and levies, though I understand their roads have never been better." The noblewoman gave Cerra's hand a reassuring squeeze. "... and it's Katarin."

"I'll try to remember." Cerra curled a reluctant smile as she returned the gesture. "But you make my point. I am not in my world. I am not given to ruling over others. Am I just simple folk then? One of the lesser cards good only for topping the smaller ones beneath us? One of those that doesn't matter as their game is played? Us small folk have little concerns except nurturing our little plots of ground and making them productive. We need to rely on each other and feed our efforts, or there is no harvest … or for me, no value in my ointments and herbs. There is no luxury to misuse our trust. Forgive me for saying … Katarin … that as I consider everything … those that rule seem to have little interest in those they lord over, so long as their coffers are full."

"Not all of us." Katarin insisted. "Like a field, Ceniago thrives because I divert most of my rents into its maintenance and well-being. I well meet my needs in any event. For me, the richness comes from the vibrancy of the life contained within my borders. Would it be the same place if half the citizens were beggared? *Hmmmph* … nor would it be safe. Instead of being honored, I'd be envied and forced to guard myself more. I'd rather spend the rents of my land on my land."

"You may stand alone, then." Cerra returned the reassurance with the touch of her hand. "I have gained a dubious advantage by not seeing. There is no glitter to distract me. I didn't hear every word at the gathering, of a certainty, though what I did hear had very little to do with good of all, only veiled jousting's looking for advantage and admitting nothing. If there was any plain speaking at all, it was only among those like-minded in their intrigues."

Katarin raised an eye regarding Cerra. The blind woman's eyes had lost their merriment and were now lidded with grim thoughtfulness. She often mis-judged her disability and the red-haired woman had proved to be remarkably astute. She had done little more than sit alone and contented during the enclave. When her cat had appeared, Katarin had felt a little relief that the blind woman had her familiar companion. Yet she seemed to have gained a great deal of knowledge. She had never really questioned Captain Ferriman's choice for his advisor, even if it seemed a little odd. Through the weeks of their acquaintance, the decision had gained more weight. There was much more to Cerra of the Meadows than met the eye. The apt turn of phrase in Katarin's thoughts made her smile and she leaned in close to the blind woman.

"And which intrigues might those be? If I cannot get good intelligence from my counsel, maybe I can learn something from gossip."

Chapter 25

Fragments of dust collected a circling aura of moisture, adding weight and substance to the thin gasses. Awareness settled with the density, as though each mote held a rare significance of thought, collecting themselves in a thin and gratifying reunion. Substance added consciousness, as resolutions found balance and the weight of life took hold. There was no extent of being yet, a dissipation that extended throughout the skies. It was the light and spread of lands below that stirred consciousness. Beyond it, a starry sea extended far beyond his nebulous reach, arced within the weight of the earth below. The nebulous expanse was vast, though no comparison to the sightless and timeless ink of the Void.

He could feel his survival, the element of air in full command, abstract and fluid, given to deep imagining far beyond the embraces of earth and sea. He felt as though he had been in a coma of an endless idea, a vast realization just beyond reach of anything held to earth, touching the consciousness of the universe in the vastness of space.

Yet all is held within the mantle of earth, even the thin gases that protect it. More dust drew him down, dry and sterile, attracting the elements of water, held captive by the heats of the day. He pulled them to him, embracing the fluid circle of its life. He knew that, as he settled into the thicker ethers, he would find the frictions of fire, kindled by the tempest of the elements as they collided below him.

The cosmos of light and dark continued to cycle, perhaps blinks in his awareness or the passage of time that extended as he gained substance.

Fire was the last element to gain purchase, a bolt of blue flame that shot through him with enlightenment. The shuddering infusion thundered the sky as he could sense himself gathering shape and form with the clustering of his demonic elements. Shades of memory collected, animated by the immediacy of fire, sparking his thought and energies.

'Yutan.'

In the time of his being, the name had been uttered, spoken in one of the many realms that exist in the ether. A thought could carry in some of them, like an arrow to its mark. Familiarity lay in the summons, an attraction that the naming demanded.

The spread of vision below him was a tableau of unnamed lands, patterned and broken by the rough tools of nature and man. Within the order and chaos that churned below, one light burned clear in his thought, somewhere from the core of his essence, a coriolis of ambers and soft golds surrounded by fiery brilliance streaming outwards in its embrace. An essence attached itself to the calling.

Cerra.

The name of the blind woman had become an anchor to his consciousness. He gathered his memories, spread across the vast skies, and collected them around the thought of her. Within the atmospheres, the waves of her presence would be found, trailing from the breath of her movement. The flavor of her would remain, a taste in the air.

He let himself continue to gather, circling lower in the ethers as a gathering storm.

Chapter 26

It was important to arrive at any meeting before the benefactor, especially in the rough environment of the taverns bordering the caravan camps. Waiting implied a superior position and afforded the opportunity to survey one's surroundings. Advantage meant everything in Sinjin's profession and he created one at every opportunity. He pulled aside a serving girl, telling her how to prepare his drink … lemon and water on shaved ice. She gave him an odd look, hearing something other than the usual pour of cheap Oskaran wine favored by most the clientele. The Chancellor was not long. Though he apparently arrived alone, Sinjin knew that the Chancellor's personal guard lurked nearby. Two had been salted in among the patrons even before his arrival, easy to spot by their martial carriage.

The Chancellor looked angry, more dispossessed than his features normally revealed, sitting across the heavy weathered table with an impatient shove of the seat. The Chancellor's eyes pierced along with his snarl, the hooded warning of a dangerous animal. Sinjin kept his face impartial. The Chancellor would be the first to speak. He had but to wait for the conclusion and it was quick in coming.

"Tell me about the Standish woman."

"You've surely heard the accusations." Sinjin replied

smoothly. "The witch. Likely in a moment of passion. Who can tell with that sort?"

"I've heard. Now I want to hear from you."

Sinjin took a sip, looking at his iced drink as if contemplating.

"The accusations serve well enough."

"The Damen of Ceniago seems well enough too, and supporting that 'witch', with everything she has at her disposal." Chenli grated. "What of her? I ask one thing, I get something completely different. Now I'm sure I don't want that woman interfering in the proceedings."

"That is where it becomes interesting. Someone else made the attempt. Curious, is it not? Have you a confederate? … or is there someone else in the same game. Naturally, I had no chance after that. As it was, the witch interfered, either by accident or design." Sinjin gave the Chancellor a look that said he should have known. "I think design. I warned you about her."

The Chancellor growled, ramming his fist into his palm, his eyes darting as though the answer lay in a fight with anyone that might give him an odd look. Sinjin waited. He knew what the solution would be.

"Get her out of here. The Caliphe of the Vale has done nothing to secure her … a token guard. The Caliphe believes her story, the Moors woman is convincing … and eventually, so will others. So, the accusations don't serve well enough. If there is another … agent … accomplishing the same end, I shouldn't be too worried. If it is one of your brotherhood, the answer lies on your neck. Either way … it would serve us both well to find out who it is."

"I can guess."

"Who?" Chenli's eyes glittered, avid for information like a money-changer for gold.

"Who left the Vale of a sudden before dawn? Therein lies your ally. For the moment."

"The Jimalians?" Chenli didn't know whether to give credence to the idea or not and his momentary perplexed look came out as disgust. "*fah* ... do you derive your schemes from fortune tellers? They are particularly hostile at the moment."

"The Standish Lord, the arrogant one. He left with them." Sinjin watched to see if the intelligence registered. It did. Sinjin could see the Chancellor adding the thought to a tally like an accountant at his beads. "Whether willingly or not is a matter of guess."

Chenli cursed roundly. "Make no further move on the Damen. This summit is falling apart like a beggar's cart and it won't do to have more disruptions."

"The witch?"

"Right now, she is your sacrificial goat if you want her. Where you tie her is up to you." Chenli's cheeks tightened as another thought occurred to him. "Just keep her away from my armies."

The Chancellor's cold, even stare displayed a ruthlessness Sinjin found rare in those who normally required his services. The implication was not lost.

A dark slice of azure cut across the arid sands like a polished agate, water teeming with fish lazing at the surface. The tan and white gyrfalcon circled the fertile cut, noting the overhanging cliffs at one end and reeded shallows at the other. Perfect conditions for hunting, even though not in the verdant rainforests of home.

The hunt could wait, the ornate line of wagon and mounts that had been advancing along in the baked sands far to the north held more interest and once again drew the bird of prey away from the surety of the hunt and into the uncertainty of the barrens. Even with their quick pace, the column had yet to advance further than the gyrfalcon could soar in the cool of the day.

Closing on the human company, details again became clear. Banners waggled like injured parrots, a further distraction along with the richness that glinted from the trappings of the company. The arrangement was different.

The gyrfalcon circled, noting the division of the humans. A small group had separated, traveling at a faster pace than before and with less accoutrements. The bird stalled its flight and circled to note the encampment of those that remained. Familiarity lay about the tents and awnings like a molt. One banner held the raptor's attention, a white rose which beckoned like a mouse on a burgundy field.

Hot thermals continued to rise from the desert floor, holding the gyrfalcon aloft as though resting. In lazy circles, progress of the one group was noted while never drifting far away from the camp, though the uplifting airs would begin to weaken and dissipate before long. Sooner or later, like the rays of the sun, its presence would be felt. The notion of observation came like a sense of warning from the stationary camp. A Sister was awake and aware. Casting a long look back to the distant slash that marked the oasis, the raptor's eyes widened at the signs of a gathering storm. One last perusal was given to the encampment below, before bending wing for the distant water.

MARID

WATER SPIRIT

© Bluebird 2020

Tented walls held the candlelight close, as the arena flared the position within the center ring. The hooded figure, ensconced in the shadows, had met the demands of the Numinon, allowing the first card to be drawn and placed as directed inside the arena. A map of the empire lay within the fluctuating borders, and Castle *Destiny* was put to rest in its Western mark, trails of phosphor ink scorching a path across the arena and connecting to the *Queen of Roses*, which lay exposed near the Eastern mark adjacent to the deck. The card depicted a castle rising from turbulent waters, approached by eight causeways radiating from its center. The spire of the castle raised toward the sky in sculpted splendor, water cascading from its peak.

A new frame came alive alongside the *Caer Ri*, sepia inks emerging in scorched lines demanding placement. Within the Book, the pages shuffled briefly until the hierarchy of the *Enûma Eleiš* were referenced, though only one remained unused and livened with vital inks: *Marid the Water Shifter*.

The illumination depicted a figure of icy beauty emerging from a fog at her feet. Her features were smooth and perfect in their execution, her form protected by the icy veils of her robe. Her eyes stare into the distance, not observing the water she is pouring from a cauldron, cascading to the mists below. The water swirls away before the mists are reached. Behind her, a globe rests in the sky, colored in blues and indigos depicting fertile seas beyond her reach. Without waiting for approval, the Book shuffled to the description. The notes were studied briefly, fingers coming to rest at a telling phrase.

The cold beauty of Marid is her strength, defeating
those as they fail to take another risk or make effort in
the future, hiding away where they can't be disappointed
again. Goals of the material benefit from the energy.
When played well it can indicate favorable investment.

Beneath the notation, a final caveat lay ignored.

In the Inverse, the cold of her visage leaves the land
empty and nothing will grow.

Markings in the Numinon asked for acceptance with a glowering circlet below. The hooded figure touched the icon lightly, dutifully drawing the card from the deck and placing it across Castle *Destiny* on the parchment of the arena as the mark allowed.

The Book riffled back, the thin pages stopping short of closing. Unembellished script, with only the terse instruction to draw a card. In the arena, a box began to fire with fresh inks above the two marks. A defender had been identified.

The top card was slid from the top of the deck and turned over reluctantly. The seer tensed as the guardian was exposed.

Abbadon!

No move was made to place the card in the correct position. The hooded figure tensed, turning the card back over quickly to dismiss the offensiveness of the ominous portend.

It was returned into the middle of the Deck with a careful nudge. The candle flickered the passage of moments while the figure studied the silent deck.

With more determination, the seer drew another card. It was slowly reversed, as though being read by a gambler anticipating the richness of a desired fill.

Abbadon!

The card was flipped over with a speed driven by shock and pushed back into the deck. Another card was drawn immediately, the face exposed with a nervous turn, again revealing the ominous *Abbadon*.

Anger was evident as the card was returned to the deck with a shove. The hooded figure flipped the deck to reverse its array, the painted images flipping down as the fan completed. All bore the image of *Abbadon*. The hands swept the deck shut, leaving it in a stack next to the Rose Queen as the candlelight measured the moments.

At length, a breath escaped from beneath the hooded cloak, a sign of finality that signaled the moment to proceed again. The top card was drawn, the lacquered blue figure of *Abbadon* glimmering hotly in the candlelight, and placed with reluctance on its mark.

Chapter 27

Much of the desert between the western hills of Abbysin and the plains abutting the Black Gate of the Stands, is given to tired ground, with just enough life bound to the parched grit to hold a stubborn scrub in its grasp. Thin grasses and thorny trees cling in patches to the rocky soils, at odds with the wandering herds of thin gazelles and onagers that rip and chew on their leaves.

East of Vale d' Houri lies a more severe drought, where mountains of sand and stone shift with the wind, driven with slow and relentless destiny. Deserts of sand expel water from their grip, absorbing its liquids into the arid depths or wringing out the heated vapors in wavering mirages. There, no moisture holds the earth in place, nor binds the remains of lifeless things that invite new growth. Only the deep, expansive waters of the Sultan Sea inhibit the eastward march of the monstrous dunes, stymied by its shores and blown away in trails of dust.

The waters of the Vale provide the only flush of green in this hot and desolate arena. The slashing bite of earth that exposed the underground river fed by the distant Camelback mountains, also cut deep beneath the azure waters of the oasis, leaving cold, unseen depths at the far end of the ragged tear. Within its deep canyons lay the dark cavities and fissures where the river worms its way back beneath the dry surface of the desert.

The deeps had long been a source of speculation and fear. No fish were known to stray into those cobalt waters, where the cliff walls came together precipitously at the end of the long defile, overhanging the water in tentative, windblown shelves. The few souls that fished the oasis kept closer to the reeded shores, rich with fish and comfortably away from the looming and desolate eastern banks.

Kimber rarely dropped lines in this part of the oasis but he had been offered a good payment for a Scaleback; the armored, ancient-looking fish that lurked in the middle deeps, prized for their firm flesh and succulent roe. He could understand the price, as the meat was as rich and firm as the large claws and shelled tails of rock lobbers. However, lobbers were easier to catch and he had no concerns for the jewel-like sac of eggs within the Scalebacks that the rich patrons of the oasis so favored, far too salty for his taste. If the princes that visit the imarets enjoy it, then the price of their coin must enhance the flavor, for Kimber would be paid a lot for his effort.

His punt had a short mast with a high-slung sprit. Nudged by the light morning winds coming off the western desert, he worked his way along the ragged northern shore. The early afternoon breezes would likely shift to the East and aid his drift back towards the fisherman's cove. The bottom was beyond definition, though he watched the blue water carefully, looking for the deeper note of color that defined the canyon. He had the best hope of catching the Scalebacks by working the edges of the deeps. Mantled by heavy banks of sand and silt, they captured rich nutrients that filtered up from below. Other spiny fish collected there, much smaller though with a good filet. One just had to mind their sharp dorsals, which would paralyze the limb and afflict the eyes for many days. Even if he did not catch a Scaleback, which would weigh nearly as much as himself, the longer sail to these exotic beds to fish would pay for an easy day tomorrow. He would have to be lucky in his drifts, for his spool barely held enough line to dap along the bottom.

Kimber let the punt sail until the last breath of wind rose from the rippled water to disappear over the merging cliffs. The loose-footed sail hung limply as the boat coasted slowly along the water. The sun had not yet cleared the eastern canyon walls enough to warm them, which made the smear of indigo that marked the deepest waters of the oasis easier to see. As the boat drifted to lassitude, he worked a hook into a thumb-sized snail and added a light weight an arm-length above it. He spooled a length of line and tossed the rig away from the punt, letting the length run to the end. There was a basket of insect larva and worms stored under some rags where it would keep cool. Kimber considered using a pole rig for another line, then set it aside to look back towards the far end of the oasis, where the rich imarets gathered like stone reeds along the south and western shores. He judged his position and, satisfied he had chosen his spot correctly, settled back to grab a quick nap. The second line could wait.

A vagrant puff filled the sail enough to ease the punt into the deep while the fisherman dozed, the line trailing with a tickling wake. As the boat floated over the deepest water, the line began to sag as though captured by a heavier weight. A white haze began forming around the line, tendrils feeling their way up the slender cord. The ripples trailing the line crackled, leaving traces of a stoney hardness. Growing shards grasped at the water like a claw, crystals spreading like a bloom as the punt drifted to a standstill.

The tug brought Kimber to his nodding senses, scrambling awake and ready to spool in his line. The notion that he had a bite was quickly dispelled as he stared in curious horror at a thing he had never witnessed in a life spent within the waters of the Vale, the crystalline nature of ice.

It wove up his line like a braid of snakes, sliding with a crackling hiss. He barely had a moment to look about the boat to assess the clicking waves of frost that diffused like hard smoke across the surface of the water. He dropped the spool as the ice touched his hand, a numb cold that seemed to cut with a razored bite. His small punt was caught within the hard fractures, which started to creep across the surface and scramble up the side of his boat like crabs over sand. Eyes wide, he grabbed an oar and began to flail at the crackling ice, attempting to knock it away as it continued to pile over the gunnels in sparkling shards.

As he flailed at one side, ice mounded behind him. Frantically, he pounded at the surging crystals, for the hull of the small boat was beginning to splinter, crushed within the frozen vice. Traces of water in the bilge had frozen and his bare feet were becoming numb, the pain radiating up his body with a frigid ache. He was tiring swiftly as the chill blanketed him, more ice stabbing skyward from the water in swordlike thrusts.

A desperate blow shattered the oar and he tried to sit back. The ice propped him up, enclosing him quickly with icy flakes. His last vision as the water in his eyes began to freeze was patterns of lace extending out towards the shores. It was the most beautiful thing he had ever seen.

Chapter 28

Camels and pack animals shuffled nervously within the paddocks that edged the Vale. Horses nickered and pranced, anxious to be released from their pens. Cerra heard the restless unease moments before she felt tremors, no more than a thin quaver of air without the strength to rattle a teacup. She pressed her palms to the padded cover of the bench, making sure of her seat as an odd surge of energy trailed the vibrations like the livid air from a thunderstorm.

She bolted up straight as she heard distant crackling, turning her ear toward the source, still far in the distance. Kamir jumped to her lap, a movement that caught her off guard with a nervous jolt as she was searching her senses to explain the distant sound.

"*Ooofff!* Oh buggers, you gave me a start!" Cerra corralled the cat, who refused to sit, turning anxiously on her lap. "Aye, I know. Nerves. I think if I had a lap to go to, I'd be there too. You've got somewhere to sit for the moment … *heh* … though I can't tell you for how long."

The air was becoming cooler, as frigid as an icy wind driven from the mountains during the Spring. The ominous crackling seemed to grow louder, initiating another wave of discord from the animal pens and driving Kamir from her lap.

"Now I know how you feel near a rocking chair," she

groaned, uneasily. "I don't know what it is, but it's coming our way."

Cerra thought of the mysteries of Yutan, when she had first encountered the demon. Astonishing majics lay hidden in the world, wondrous terrors that struck dread and reverence in the minds of men. Cerra thought little of majic, for she didn't have the vision to absorb its fears. She had seen its soul in Yutan, pure and at a loss in a venal world that had tried to bend him to its will.

'Yutan!'

Her cry was silent and not the first time the vacancy she felt reached out to be heard. Her fertile imagination was usually enough to satisfy her and paint the world. Held with suspicion and feeling somehow responsible for Ferriman's death, she missed the piercing, argent vision of Yutan that invaded her blind eyes and filled the hollow in her heart.

Cerra stood as a host of voices were raised outside, curiosity and concerns chattering back and forth like the crackling sound that gained intensity as it grew closer. The balcony lay fifteen steps from her chair and she could feel the open space that allowed the usually warm morning breezes to slip in. Now, the draughts were cold, filled with biting needles of air that made her shiver.

At fourteen steps she put her hand out to steady herself against the gritty surface of carved sandstone that framed the doorway. Stepping forward carefully, grasping her cloak around her, she moved onto the balcony. The railing met her short frame low in her ribcage, so she felt in no danger of falling from the tower as she leaned to explore the activity outside, unconfused by the walls of her confinement.

She gazed out in the direction of the breaking sounds that snapped cold and sharp, surging inexorably closer. More voices were raised from the oasis, echoing loudly along the smooth walls of the imarets, this time with great alarm. The shouts told their own frantic story, giving her a frenzied description of a rapidly spreading sheen of ice on the oasis, which was now racing towards the shores and gaining momentum with each cracking advance of its frost.

As she gazed in the direction of the water, out of the enduring black of her sight emerged an image that grew with the dry, snapping sounds of the ice, as though it was a fire disgorging, rather than consuming its fuel. In the distance, the parchment dry image of a woman cloaked in snow rose in her vision. It was an extraordinary fabrication that colored within her mind like bits of paper, cast by the same hand that had created the dragon of fire.

The vision alone would have held her attention though it was the emergence of powdery blue into her blind sight that caught her breath, a coalescence of familiar energy that caused tears to suddenly well in her eyes. She cried out with a crushing joy,

"Yutan!"

Her shout was lost to most, for the violent advance of ice had now raised alarm all around the Vale. She knew that he heard, for the name gathered focus in the demon as though summoned, dissolute within the blowing sands of the desert.

There was one other that heard Cerra, for she remained under a watchful eye. From his vantage, Sinjin felt a violent urge to aim a bolt into her witch's heart, furious that he had no weapon handy to strike with at such a range. Her cry was triumphant, shouted like an invocation, a name, or curse. He followed her rapt attention toward the northern sandstone cliffs that guarded the oasis, where a swirling cone of wind-driven dust and sand raggedly danced along the edges. Motes and shadows within the roiling funnel captured a sense of being, as though there was a face to the tempest. It was no gusty fluke, but a djinn. The woman had proven before to be a witch of enormous power. He looked back to the eastern end of the rift where a glistening pillar was being fashioned like a live thing from the crackling waters, watching in disbelief as patterned ice advanced in broken fingers, toward the reeded shores of the Vale's imarets.

The storm was growing in ferocity as though the witch had summoned it, whipping the palms of the oasis as it circled the churning mound of ice, small lightnings dancing to the surface. The frozen pile growled with torturous aches as it continued to form, head and torso finding shape as crystalline arms jutted and spread as if to embrace the gathering tempest.

"Yutan!"

The cry rang within the demon's being, though there was little he could see beyond the ravenous sorcery that sought to devour. Awareness collected around him, adding substance to his being as much as the motes of dust and moisture added weight. Energies mingled in the ethers, the refuse of exertions and enmities, the vaporous filaments of joys and desires, all woven together in their exhaustion to form new bonds. Within those strands, Yutan felt a thread familiar for its fanciful images. It was flavored with the scents of skin and hair, flecks and fragments of word and movement. The specks traced an image and the awareness bloomed as emotion added gravity to his being.

'*Cerra*'.

He followed the tendril, a vine emerging from the tangle of animation and enterprise that fueled the life around him. A slash of sparkling water cut into the parched earth below. Nested along its shores, the rock stood in graceful columns, the manufactured habitats of man. The impression came strongest there, the familiar coolness and humor of the woman mixed with unusual anxiety.

Another emotion found purchase, dragging him closer to the binding earth: worry. The blind woman had insinuated herself into his very being, so that her distress became his own, without any tableau to give it reference. It called him to guard her as he would guard his own soul, with the last kernel of his being. Woven above all of those threads was one he knew too well, the spark of majic, its light powered by intention. Gravitating below him, the energy of the spell congealed and moved towards Cerra's essence, which lay contained within its neighboring towers. It had the same flavor of discontent that drove the fiery dragon into the towering walls of Bridash, another memory finding a niche.

The demon let himself gather weight, anger gaining

momentum, a turmoil that stormed the air around him. The magic of the dragon had dissipated his essence to the extent of his being. He could not exist as himself without the inclusion of all of the elements; becoming such a spread of gaseous air had nearly dissolved him of all thought. The dragon had been fashioned from more than the base ingredients of life and fueled by an animus of intention, spawned by the same mage that had created him. The thread of its sorcery was apparent, pushing forward the forces of its desecrated nature.

There was a deeper element to consider than the majics of their animation. Ice was a cold center that he rarely felt, water stripped of its fluid warmth. Water was the one element that coursed through his demonic form which had a voice easily heard. The embrace of it had been his ultimate acceptance of this world, for it permeated all, even to the vapors of fire that burned within him. Water was a spirit beyond the sorceries of man. This was an abomination. Like him.

He circled the icing form with caution as it continued to reveal its glistening being. As he passed over the edge of the advancing ice he let accumulated heats discharge in its path. The ice blossomed into a gout of steam, which crystalized in an instant before falling back to the surface. Fresh ice formed and began a rapid freeze, outward from where they touched.

He abandoned the heat of his efforts as he continued to circle, gaining speed and fury as he fought to contain the wild fluctuations of his elements and keep the sorcery of the ice within his bounds. The icy monolith in the middle was fashioning itself into a cold beauty, armored by knives of frozen water that cloaked her form, razored icicles hung like hair around the dispassionate gaze of the colossus. The waters of the oasis were glistening with frost, white dust beginning to coax its way up the sand and stone of the shoreline.

The demon was immersed in the lasting knowledge of water. To be a drop in her oceans was to be all of her, an unrelenting lover. This avatar, borne of sorcery, was stripped of life. The dragon of fire, still fresh in his thoughts, had taught him caution. It was already apparent that to use more heat would make the icy incarnation more powerful, for she would spread a hundredfold with the vaporized snow left in his wake. The elements that raged through him depended on their inherent natures, as well as the majics that kept him embodied. His hope depended on the nature of water that he knew. Ice, under pressure must occupy a smaller space, to become water only and not face the fate of its extremes. Once liquid and in the embrace of 'her', the incubus would lose potency and purpose. The demon could feel the threads strung beyond the colossus; the weavings of a mage, strings forged by his creator.

He let himself gravitate downward, shedding heat as he settled in constricting turns, holding back the suspended sands and silicas caught up in his tempest. His turbulence created a dense fog as he collapsed. Frigid cold lashed through him as he brought the metals suspended within him together, covering the frozen colossus like a lover and wrapping it in his embrace. The intrusion carried the frigid heat of its magic, a fresh agony that caused the demon to hold tighter in a desperate heave to shed the consuming pain.

Struggle was hard to identify, for he bore down on the frigid avatar with a suffocating certainty, wrapping tighter as the sands found bonds and welded within his compression. It was the coldness of her features as he wrapped her icy body, clenching tighter, that illuminated the center of the struggle within her, without life, without caring. If she tried to push against him, he didn't feel it. He didn't allow for the possibility as he contracted further.

The face of the avatar came into view as he closed his embrace, the sharp edges of her features smoothing with moisture. Crystal surfaces lost their sharp edges, surfaces rounded and wetted as rocks in a stream, the gleam of water adding a trace of emotion and sensuous embrace. The demon continued to squeeze, his binding storm covering the ice-bound colossus. The presence of 'her' was felt and the demon let it flow through him like a lover, allowing it to overwhelm him as he pressed.

Cold analyses and vaporous angers assailed the demon's perceptions, trying to break his concentration, pushing at his resolve. As the fumes of his tempest shed itself in tepid rain, he continued to press with the violent encroachment of an invader, the fierce grasp of a lover, urging the solids held captive in his storm to hold their lock about her. The mold of her body became lusher, more vibrant as the flush of water overtook the ice of the spell.

A voice came from somewhere deep within the press, a voice that belonged to all,

"*I am ...*"

A droplet trickled away from the corner of her eye at the moment the colossus gave way, as though dropped to the knees in collapse. In the release, an exhaustion that felt like a purge, he heard a cry, nearly lost in the rumble of his screaming currents. Crackling shards fused with a resounding knell as the ice sluiced away in a liquid torrent that took the demon with it, crashing into the embrace of water. The churning tempest howled, a screaming wind that pierced in its agony.

"Yutan!"

Stars swept the air in front of her blind sight, the demon swirling pinpoints of light, becoming more substantial as he formed. The nimbus of the demon wrapped with bat-like wings over the sorcery, the papery light flickering through his argent blue in stubborn flashes. Cerra was rapt, bounding between awe and fear as the tempest froze in time, an agonizing balance between the majics. As she willed Yutan to triumph, the maze of colored form collapsed in a low, heavy flush of sound. The demon fell apart in her sight like gases at the end of a flame. Tumultuous gusts pulled at her hair, the sounds of the battle coming as the shrieks and wails of tortured wind.

The blue aurora of the demon's light had riveted her gaze. His presence had been sorely missed, an emptiness she had done her best to ignore. In the moment of dire need he had effected a return, only to be torn away from her again. She gripped the railing as she cried out his name.

A warning?

A cry for herself?

From within the din came an anxious shout and the assassin shot his glance back to the sandstone tower holding the witch. She stood facing the conflict, wild red hair whipping about her head and reaching out in seeming desolation. Sinjin had long guessed at the woman's power and now he was witnessing it first-hand. She cried out again. The assassin could not determine whether in agony or a profusion of power, if she was saving the oasis, or preserving it for her own brand of destruction. She was too dangerous in any event.

Scores of observers looked on with fearful curiosity, lining the imarets and shores as the sorcerous battle raged, the violent funnel cloud cloaking the frozen enchantment. Sinjin held his vantage, eyeing both the witch and the spell she had cast over the oasis, where nothing was to be seen except the swirling chaos of the storm. Hot and cold currents of wind swept the oasis in erratic gusts, tearing at the palms as the center of the cyclone tightened itself into a dark and dreadful mass.

A crystalline peal rolled through the air when the storm dissipated in an instant, sluicing like a tipped vat in a mad rush of foaming water deep into the oasis. The shattering break elicited another cry from the witch. From jubilance, or terror? A quick glance back to the waters of the oasis revealed the turbulence of the storm had collapsed, the icy monolith sinking into the waters of the oasis, gleaming like a goddess being born. It lowered with magnificent splendor, but it was the huge foaming wave, caught up with the remains of the storm and surging the length of the cliff-bound oasis that spurred him away from his vantage near the reeds.

The guards at the base of the imaret that held the witch

joined the rush away from the patios and shores as the churning wave raced towards the imarets of the Vale. Sinjin sprinted toward the entrance to the apartment holding the witch, hoping to gain entry before he was swept from his feet.

Chapter 29

Yutan!" The word seemed to hang in the air, caught in her ears, a tone that over rang the howling of the storm. The cacophony left no room for the soft sounds behind her. There was no warning when strong arms pinned her, a warmed pad soaked with evil smelling fumes bunched over her nose.

'Bryony ...mandragora and hemlock ... opium ....' Cerra had only the fleeting recognition before she collapsed.

The hooded man caught her under the arms and dragged her back into the tower, towards a heavy armoire that lay open against the sandstone walls. He kicked briefly at the cat that hissed and clawed at his ankles, then stepped into the closet, dragging the limp body after him.

A panel slid open at his touch. A narrow slit of stairs descended in a curve against the outer wall, barely wide enough for his shoulders. Within the Vale, a honeycomb of passages had been maintained for those who wished to keep their trysts and exchanges secret. Without a word or wasted gesture, the armoire was closed from within and the hooded man squeezed himself back down the steep curve of the staircase, easing his burden along carefully. At the bottom of the narrow steps, a cramped rabbit-like warren was carved into the sandstone, each narrow tunnel leading to some secret tryst.

He grabbed the torch he had left and began dragging

the inanimate body after him as he backed down the tunnel cut into the rock, pressing through a narrow cut as a sheen of water-darkened patches of the stone walls and began collecting in rivulets along the passage. A shift to an adjoining corridor allowed for better movement, the hooded abductor lifting the body over his shoulder as he moved along, marks etched into the stone indicating the direction of the stable-house. The abductor's only concern was discovery by another finding secrecy in the hidden chambers, for a killing under these circumstances would be an inconvenience. He continued to shuffle the limp body through the stone channelings, until at length a carved post revealed the stables.

The horses of dignitaries were kept apart from those of the common caravaners, posh quarters meant more for the prideful satisfaction of the owners than the horses, who required nothing more than a few flakes of hay and a bit of grain. A short rise of rough-hewn stairs revealed a trap with a hay sile.

A snort of recognition came from one of the horses, though it was ignored as the man dragged the limp body into the stall next to it. A canvas lay out on the ground and the body was rolled onto it, then tied and slung over the back of a waiting mule.

Astride his horse, the figure emerged from the stable wearing the dun robes of a desert trader, a laden mule trailing on a lead with docile acceptance.

The door marking the third level was unguarded and no

lock sat in the hasp. Sinjin crept to the ornately carved door
and pressed, listening carefully for any activity within, expecting the witchery of chants and invocations. There was nothing,
just the empty hollow of a lifeless room. The latch softly clicked
free and he held the door as a brace as he eased it open, ready
to use its fulcrum as a weapon if need be.

As the door began to peek open, a slot no wider than his
fist, a black cat shot past his ankles, dashing down the steps
as though pursued by larger prey. A surge of fear and elation
jolted through him as though he had just cheated death, the
motion a dark arrow that had narrowly missed its target. He
keyed to the danger, his skin properly alive and senses alert.
No further sound transpired from the room and he caught
a reflection from the dressing mirror inside that revealed
an empty chamber. Nothing was sensed save the windswept
sounds from beyond the open balcony.

He thrust the door open, the room empty as he had feared.
The witch was gone. He scanned the room quickly, observing nothing save a rumpled pallet, a gilt-edged mirror and a
few belongings, which lay neatly against the armoire. His eyes
darted back down the tiled steps, wary of attack, yet there
was neither witch nor cat to be seen. The powers of the blind
woman confounded him and the escaping cat brought to mind
the shapeshifting Sybellines, who generally kept to their convents nearly a half world away. It would explain much. The
woman was far more dangerous than he'd realized.

Jolted to consciousness by the expulsion of breath, Cerra's mind spun, churning from disorientation as she was turned, rolled and uncovered, rough jute pulled free of its cocooning wrap. She lay still, her head throbbing with a gripping ache. Slight groans escaped her lips as she sought to find her breathing and quell the pain that gripped at the bones around her eyes.

She began to focus as her breath steadied, hearing tuned for movement and clues to her whereabouts; outside in the dry heat of day, the scent of horse nearby, the rustlings of a few spare trees in the light wind and the unmistakable creak of harness. There was no sense at all of the oasis. She was no longer in the Vale. The crunch of five steps on the pebbly ground circled her, someone who had been standing next to the horse. There were two mounts, a horse and mule by their snorts, no sound of other souls. Just her and ... the question formed quickly ... 'who?'

The noxious fumes that had left her senseless, still lay like a vice about her head and she pulled herself up to cradle it with her hands, trying to massage in some relief.

"Oh gods." Cerra groaned. In a moment she might be more concerned with her condition. For now, the residue left her head pulsing and her temper short. "If you meant to kill me, you've done that. Now leave me alone."

There was no reply, just the sound of the person ... man ... kneeling next to her. Her right hand was pulled from cradling her head and forced to grip a wineskin.

"Oh, no more for me." Cerra pushed it back. "You can have it all."

The response was rough and immediate as the skin was pulled away and her face roughly gripped about the chin, forcing her mouth open. A stream of plain water coursed into her mouth before she was released with an impatient shove. The skin was again forced into her hands.

"FINE ... fine." Cerra tried to shove the man away but it was an ineffectual swipe as he stood back away from her. She took a sip from the skin, letting the cool of the water slow her temper as well. "Just no more of your wine. Save it for removing stains."

Even though a touch stale from the skin, the water felt wonderful, seeming to course into her as she drank. She poured some of it on her brow, hoping to ease the throbbing at her temples as she collected her thoughts. It was late in the day, judging by the heat of the ground and the lower angle of sun felt on her skin. She had been abducted. How long ago? An aftertaste of the acrid fumes sorted through her mind. No more than a half day she would guess. She had inhaled sharply at the surprise of her capture. Her cheeks and forehead still felt hot and her head weighted as if she'd had too much to drink. So far, her captor, whomever he was, had yet to mutter so much as a word. His accent might give her a clue. She took another cooling sip before she spoke. He was next to the mounts; the sound of a rope being run over a pack. Arranging the load.

"Where are we going. Or rather, where are you taking me?" The throbbing in her head left her disoriented, ill-tempered and not ready to believe anything. "Tell me we're going back."

The footsteps crunched back to her and she flinched as his

hands grasped her and lifted her to her feet.

"Hey!"

Cerra was heaved astride the mule, where she fought to gain her seat within the few packs burrowed out like a saddle. She growled to herself as she settled in. The leathery creak ahead of her indicated the man had mounted and, without warning, her mule was yanked into a trot, held in tow by the man's horse. She had a firm grasp on one of the jute lashings or she might have pitched backward.

"A name. Give me something to call you. If you don't, I'm warning you, I'll make up a name. I'm quite good at it." She knew she sounded shrill, but didn't care. There was no response from the man in front of her, just the clop of hooves as the two mounts moved forward. Cerra groaned, her head still throbbing. "I'm not in a mind to be complimentary."

There was no response and she wasn't sure she expected one. She thought of a few vile curses she had heard from the potters, but couldn't bring herself to say any of them. The silence elicited by the man was uncommon, not even a grunt of air when lifting her to the mule. *'Well it isn't like I weigh a lot, anyway,'* she considered. It seemed as though he was entirely incapable of speech.

"Don't play hard to get. You're already hard to want," she badgered him, though her remark didn't even register a snort. "Which is unusual in a man of few words."

Her first inclination was a wry admission that he likely couldn't hear either and she began to suspect very soon that might be the case. There was one soul that she had come in contact with in recent days who fit this description. Her mind refused to picture a man and didn't care to put a face to him. No sounds nor language existed to define him. Instead, the flat imagery of spilling cups persisted, draining waters devoid of expression.

For now, she urged herself some patience to be led on, for there was little else she could do. She didn't fear much for herself. If she had been marked for a death other than by the grinding headache, she'd have suffered that fate already.

"Hey! We have to go back and get my cat." She gave her voice a purposeful whine, knowing she'd be ignored. Cerra managed a hurt smile. Kamir had a way of turning up.

As she had surmised that he was indeed both deaf and mute, by all estimations he was without emotion as well. She tried a few times to engage him in some kind of contact but it proved fruitless, he could neither hear her words nor was she able to see any gesture he might make. His sole communications were to lift her to the makeshift saddle on her mule when ready to ride and to place a tin of food in her lap when it was time to eat. She determined he must be an awful cook, for all that was proffered was dried meat and hard, savory biscuits.

Cerra retreated into the monotony of the ride, letting the painted visions of the prairie occupy her inner sight and the occasional shriek of the hawk fill in the other side of her conversations. It was a familiar call, high above her, and she was happy to feel the connection with another live thing, one not being led to an uncertain doom. Given the deaf and mute abductor, it didn't take much of a leap to conclude that the Jimalian Queen was responsible for her abduction. It was a cold realization that Artis Ferriman had likely been killed preventing the first attempt at abduction, at the hands of the same silent wraith that held her now. It added a stony weight to her silence, an angry burden she found hard to bear.

She sought to dispel the burn and pain of the loss, by engaging the Captain's spirit in the mission she had been left alone to discharge. The brief introduction to the Ducesin at the Vale must have made a curious impression indeed. Cerra remembered the meeting well, mulling it over with little else to distract her, though she failed to recall having said anything remotely worth intrigue. There was no sense of anger or hurry evident in the cold presence of the mute, only the precise gears of a mechanism at work. She was being drawn in like water from a well. She lived. If there was danger, it would be in the offing.

A puff of air threatened to extinguish the candle, causing the inks to waver and wash upon the parchment arena like a fanned blaze. The glowing marks steadied, laying back into their crisp lines. Alone at the top of the pattern stood *Nepethe, Queen of Roses*. The worrisome *Nuith*, the rival *Queen of Quills*, was covered by the deadly *7 of Cups*, laid sidelong across the top of her like a crux. Below, the *5 of Cups* stood marked as a sacrificial ally, given the inverse lay of the card.

Below the captured Queen, another frame beckoned as the candle flickered again, a victim of the capricious air. There was a certain slow reluctance to the turning of the card, then evident relief from the seer when the *3 of Quills* was revealed. The Book fluttered to the appropriate page, though the Seer didn't look at the notations as the *Messenger* was placed in the frame. The weak trey was not of interest and *Nuith's* most powerful allies had not returned to the board.

The round cage of marks that girded the arena sizzled as the edging knots sought new alignment. Once the position was determined, a last frame presented itself, arrayed near the *5 of Cups*. The position allowed itself to go either way, its allegiance unknown. The reverse face of the top card fluttered, its markings hypnotic under the wavering candle. The *Ace of Swords* was drawn and though a minor card, was studied for a long moment by the Seer before being placed. Dutifully, the Book shuffled its pages, crisp and thin, leafing open to describe the lowly Ace. Its singular nature paired badly with others in its suit, a curious revelation that the Seer studied closely, taking advantage of the candle's last moments. The card's nature was known, so the Seer read quickly then turned the page seeking conclusion, though stopping with a tap of a finger on the last few lines, the ending note as two-edged as the blade.

'When positioned in the positive, the Ace of Swords finds moral purity and innocence in the flaws of its nature.'

The Ace lay within its frame, removed from alliances, the tip of the sword pointed directly at the *Rose Queen* and *5 of Cups*. With ominous timing, the candle glimmered out, exhausted of its wick. The Numinon flipped shut and the inks of the arena dried like a stain laid long before, marking the end of the divination.

Chapter 30

Dust settled in waves beyond the northern rim of the rift valley that formed the Vale d' Houri, the leftover trailing's of the wind's vigorous sweep. Low and narrow ridges of sand had been strewn across the road leading to the Vale, along with broken remains of scrub left in the track of the blustering storm. As the skies began losing the brown cast of choking dust, the murky disc of the sun reluctantly started to show through.

With widely measured beats, the grits merged and sloughed, legs and arms compacting into shape, eddies leaving voids for vision and sound. A figure emerged from the settling fog, a confluence of dust and sand as Yutan molded himself into the familiar form first sculpted by the blind woman, long ago. He stood on the brink of the valley, looking down on the domes and thin, graceful towers that clung along the cobalt blue shores of the oasis.

His dissolution within the healing embrace of water had felt brief, a mere smattering of time, though Yutan knew too well the odd passages of days that occurred outside the constructs of man. He searched the Vale for the tell-tale air of the blind woman, the one person who had never wanted anything of his power, the one person who had shown him love, even before he knew what he was; an abomination of forbidden majics. She

had restored him in every way he could count. He gave voice
to the vision in his mind.

'*Cerra.*'

The very word was a guidepost and he let his senses chase
the name out over the valley. Scents and sounds came back
to him like trailing vines. She was there and not there, left
over traits that could have been absence or sleep. He would
find her. Yutan knelt, flipping a few small stones aside until he
found a handful agreeable for his purpose. He pressed them
one by one in his fist, releasing the gem within, facets formed
by the strength of his grip. His time in the human world had
taught him the value of ready coin, riches a trait prized above
all others. A rag hung from a short tree, a head wrap snagged
from the tempest by a thorny branch. He lifted it away and
wrapped it around his waist.

It did not take long to reach the lesser hostels that gathered near the stock pens. Behind their doors he traded quickly
and emerged wearing the practical trappings of a seasoned
caravanneer. In this human form, Yutan aroused no attention
passing among the denizens of the Vale. Confusion still mud-
died the lanes leading to the richer estates and imarets girding
the lake, as well as the sand and muck that yet pooled among a
bywash of debris from the towering wave. Merchants and servants alike conspired to restore order, while those that deemed
themselves guests of the estates gathered in safe cliques, critical of the efforts and mindful of the inconvenience.

The impressions of Cerra were written in the air as though
she had etched her name in the stone. Listening, he sifted
through the fragments of speech that came to his ears of the

dire events that had transpired that very morning. Yutan felt a grim satisfaction that his elements had not transcended the notion of time in the final moments of the ice demon's collapse. The core of the demonic spell had discovered its true self in that instant and became one with her that lived in every drop. His separation from the spell had been swift, expelled like spume as the remains of the feral majic sloughed back into the water like a calving glacier.

The events were fresh, for the clash of sorceries was on everyone's lips, conjecture and news still spreading with a mixture of fear and excitement. The rapid growth and advance of the frozen monstrosity proved especially dire for those who had never seen the ice and snows of the northlands. Old gods received a new wave of believers and new ones found favor once the demonic storm had cleared. In its wake, the ice-bound colossus had been forever sculptured into a pristine, crystalline form, a goddess reaching for the heavens which had come to rest, half submerged in the middle of the oasis. It came to be regarded as a fitting monument to the Vale and the spirits that protected it, though no one could agree on which of the gods was responsible.

It was in the clothier's shop that he heard about the murder of a Standish Captain and the disappearance of the witch, who was said to have slain him. Unused to the press of humanity, Yutan kept his comments short, offering no more than gruff asides and observations as he gathered the threads of recent events. The idea of Cerra's involvement and fault in murder had no credence, for doing harm at all was beyond her capability. By the time he reached the imaret where her presence was felt strongest, he had painted enough of the picture of events, that he was certain the blind woman was no longer in the Vale. Nonetheless, he followed the trail of her scents as he advanced up the tower to the room she had last occupied. Her presence remained as surely as the stone.

The door was open and unguarded. Her belongings lay positioned neatly on a table and stand near the bed, laid out as she would have done, meticulous in her habits. Yutan went out on the balcony. Had he seen her standing here? Was it his name she called out? He looked out toward the blue slash of the lake to regard the avatar that now glistened with the purity of crystal, blessing the blue waters, it's magic spent. He thought of the final moment of their joining, the return to life with the release into water. The joy. Into her. The sands and micas he had gathered into his storm remained, forced from the water and fused under the pressure of his embrace. The cord of the sorcery that created it had been cut, a thread that found its origins in the east.

Returning to the room, he gathered up Cerra's few belongings, each containing a sense of her that he could feel as if she were yet in the room. A few small jars of unguents and tied packages of herbs, small clothes, her Cherros robe and a length of new silk, a smoking pipe and menses sponge. There was little more than would be held in a pair of saddlebags.

The last item was one of the metal engraved pins she used to hold back her hair. He considered it as he reflected on the rumors of the Standish captain's death, that he had been stabbed by a metal skewer. He slipped the barre into her pack. Her walking stick, topped with the carved pinecone, lay propped near the door. He felt a dark anger pass through him. There was no doubt she had not left of her own accord.

Once back at the broad pavilion fronting the lake, he turned in a circle until he faced the northeast. Air transcended the spaces in between and he let himself filter its notes. The sense of the blind woman came from that direction, divined as surely as a mariner's needle could find the ends of the earth. The threads of majic had been woven from those points as well, a spider's silk drawing her in. Yutan considered the small collection of belongings gripped in his hands, then looked off to where the stables and pens were located. There were still remnants of Cerra evident. *'The cat.'*

Few things gave Yutan cause to smile. Cerra was one. Her self-assured black cat was the other, fierce even in the face of his most terrifying transformations. Kamir vigilantly guarded the blind woman and, in that regard, they recognized in each other a common bond. Nearing the barns reserved for dignitaries, Yutan spied the cat, perched alert on a shelf, as if impatient for his arrival. He mimicked the whistling call Cerra reserved for her horse and heard an answering nicker from within the stalls. Kamir arched and stretched as he approached, pushing into him as he gave a scratch about the ears.

"That accounts for everyone. You have done well."

He was about to slide the bay doors open, when a stable boy edged between the fence slates and came to stand beside him. The boy's hesitation was evident, his eyes wide in a mixture of awe and fear.

"Kin I help? Which one's yer horse, sir?"

Yutan looked down at him, stern face unreadable and

repeated the whistle. An impatient neigh and snort returned immediately.

"That one." He handed a silver coin to the stable boy, whose eyes widened at the sight. A ha'copper was the fare if he was lucky and the wealthier the client, the thinner the coin.

"Th-th-thank you …y-yes, yer excellency … at once."

The boy disappeared into the barn in an eager rush, leading Sugar from the stalls only moments later, freshly saddled. He turned over the reins with a relieved look. Yutan allowed a slight smile to crease his face.

"Open your hand." He did with reluctant curiosity and Yutan dropped ten more coppers into his palm. "Save the silver for need."

The boy nodded vigorously, pocketing the coins as Yutan gained the saddle. Kamir leapt up, using Yutan's leg for purchase, and nestled quickly behind the horn.

"Boy." The stableboy glanced up as he swung open the paddock gate, alert and curious eyes wondering what might come next. " … forget that I was here."

A bright grin crossed the lad's face as he grasped another silver coin thrown his way. "Not likely, ser ... heh heh … but as I think on it, I know I h'aint never seen that horse a'for … which is too bad, as'n' she's a beauty."

Chapter 31

He was more than ready to put the Vale d' Houri behind him, a place with little more than water and intrigue to sustain it, for Sinjin gave little thought to the dalliances of the rich. Decadence was the hallmark of their existence and their regrets were often the source of his income. The pursuit of riches kept the Brotherhood of the Hashini steadily employed and by far the most reliable incentive for their services was acquiring power and keeping it. The courts were occupied by well-groomed faces with agreeable smiles masking treachery and betrayal, intentions hidden as well as a carder at his tricks.

The man across from him had none of those motivations. The Master Armorer was coldly comfortable in his position, with no worries concerning rivals or the size of his purse. There was but one thing that exacted the need of a killing stroke for the Guildmaster: fraud.

Sinjin could see the cold reasoning in the Armorer's eyes, a man not above slaying his own enemies, as few of the Hashini's clients were. Sinjin accorded him that respect.

"He left with the Jimalian court. I've said before … whether he went willingly, I can't say."

"I think willingly." Patan calculated. "He avoided the primary payments. I fault no one but myself there, a lapse in judgement. The promise of a better price paid to allow for the abeyance, drew me in. It arrived … a chest of freshly coined gold majores with Imperators layered on top. The Imperators I can spend. The Majores are worth ballast for the man's boots." Patan snorted, looking about as though considering other past sins. "If I ever do that again, I'll give up the Guild."

Sinjin raised an eyebrow, not used to Lords admitting their faults. He relaxed with a rare show of kinship, two men discussing a failed sporting wager. "The Standish lord has a face that is always uncomfortable … a good shitte would do him well. I think the hard dropping will be into his own bluff."

Patan turned his attention back to the assassin. "He's a *wenk*," using the vulgar term that means either a big or small mouth, usually both at once. The reference was clear. "The man has cheated me and with open intent. Frankly, you could forgo any payment and simply deal with the pocked arse as a boon to all."

"Expenses only then." Not a man much given to humor, Sinjin kept his chuckle brief. 'Expenses' amounted to a loose accounting that was never questioned.

"The caravan bearing the Standish arms left yesterday. Ahead of schedule." Patan continued as though planning a simple task. "I can get my wares back easily enough, even if a little war breaks out to accomplish that. There is a troop already dispatched."

The master armorer paused, gaze leveled at Sinjin to make his point. "That Standish prick is a fraud who thought he could cheat me and hide behind his fecking Gate. A trophy isn't necessary and would be worth nothing. I've been fouled enough by the man. If he's going to get his due … "

The Guildmaster paused and Sinjin groaned inwardly, for it was obvious that another, more entertaining thought had occurred to Patan as he settled back with a satisfied look.

"There are fates more appropriate than death, don't you think? When you find him … take him to Oskara."

It would take no more than a few days to locate the Standish lord and leave him for the carrion birds. Easy and done with. Anything else involved more work and risk … and cost.

"Expenses only." Sinjin put his fist to the table, accepting the commission. The witch had disappeared and the Standish lord in the hands of the Jimalians. Given his experience with the intrigues of the powerful, he would bet his expenses that the two yet traveled in the same circles, the trail of one leading to the other. "I'll see you in Oskara."

Round eyes, unblinking and intent, glared down on the two riders as they neared the copse of sparse oaks, tucked within a fold of the grassy steppe. A circlet of tawny feathers framed the white head of the raptor, powerful brown flecked wings tucked in close as it perched in the broken top of one of the trees. The fierce bird, a gyrfalcon common to the southern jungles, darted its head aside, bringing its focus on the string of horses that stood tied near the stone well. Colorful tents flying long banners from their peaks nestled within the spotted shade. The copse was one of the few arbors along the caravan route that crossed the plains above the northern reaches of the

Sultan Sea. The bird's eye's darted back with stark intensity, drawn by the motion of the two-legged ones.

Linarest Mirbek emerged from the center pavilion wearing black riding leathers, her buckled boots rising high on her calves. A maroon top skirt covered her upper legs, the bodice laced over a crisp linen blouse. Guards dressed in the maroon and white livery of Marsena flanked her tent and remained stiffly at their posts as she stepped from the treeshade into a patch of sun, to await the riders near the horse line.

The ostler gave her a deferential bow, avoiding her glance and stepped from the lines as the riders stopped. He didn't trust the lead rider's stallion and wanted to place him at the end of the tether. The mule would be fine anywhere in the herd and he gave a glance to its burden. Curls of riotous red hair framed a lovely face, the fair complexion freckled and ruddy from the sun. She looked as though waiting for something as the other rider dismounted.

"Can I give you a hand … milady?" The ostler tentatively raised his arm to help her dismount.

"She's blind. Treat her with care." Linarest spoke as though she were having a piece of fragile art moved about. "Her tent is the one next to Ser Pryan … the red awning. We will be leaving in the morning after we break fast."

She gestured to the lead rider, fingers moving in quick patterns, then turned and retreated to her pavilion, her mute servant in tow. The ostler inwardly cringed, then looked back up at the woman still perched on the mule. He couldn't tell if she was smiling or resigned to exhaustion.

"Well, then. What would you like?"

"Can you help me down?" Cerra spoke in the Trade tongue, though she knew enough of the Jimalian dialect to get her by. As she wore further into this journey she was becoming far more reluctant to share any of her secrets, Captain Ferriman the last of her confidantes. She felt for the horse-tender's hand, calloused and firm. He grabbed her under the ribcage and easily swept her from her perch atop the mule. He set her down beside him and straightened her skirt with a brush of his hands, as though swatting the dust from a saddle.

"Thank you." Cerra smiled up at him gratefully.

The ostler felt his heart cave at her crooked grin, ready despite her obvious exhaustion. *I've been with a dour group too long*', he mused, preferring the company of his horses. The older man felt as inexperienced as he did caring for his first colt, though likely not as ready to run at his approach.

"So, you're ... *eh* ... blind then. How ... what should I do?"

Cerra patted his arm in reassurance. "Lead me to the tent. Give me your arm and take your steps reasonably and I'll do well enough." She leaned in a little closer to him, sharing her joke like a confidence. "I only get in trouble when important people tell me where to go. Look where it's gotten me."

The ostler snorted a laugh. "*heh* ... me too."

"I'm Cerra, otherwise known as 'the blind woman'." She introduced herself as the horse-tender took up a slow pace, cautious in choosing his direction.

"Samenlia. They call me 'Sam' if they call me at all. Usually 'hey' ... which is to be expected, as I tend the horses."

"Or neigh" Cerra giggled, encouraging the horse-tender's

jest. The two days of silence in the company of the queen's mute executioner, had been almost unbearable. It had been hard to form any sort of picture of him in her head, a silent wraith that beggared description. The more she had tried to focus on him the more he became a papery cutout of cups running dry but refusing to empty.

"Sam. A goodly name. Well, Sam, lead me to my quarters and you can return to the joys of your charges … and chargers. How many horse have you?"

"Lady Cerra … just the twenty-five now, and glad of it. We were traveling well enough, though not because they're mindful of the stock, *heh* … but too slow for the King. He left some days ago with half the party, all the lords except one … the Ser Pryan. He claimed the additional speed of the horses would aggravate his gout." From the ostler's tone, it was evident he thought little of the excuse. "So, what's left is manageable for one at any rate. We've been waiting … and I guess you're the reason. Here … watch your step."

Sam passed her through the flap and made sure she was seated comfortably. He sounded apologetic as he paused before leaving. "Her queenship is traveling light, not with her usual trappings or I'm sure you'd have been assigned a better tent."

"It's well enough. Thank you."

The flap whisked shut, trapping in the musty air of the tent. Cerra plumped back into the meager cushions, ready to sleep the remainder of the day away, though she doubted she'd have the chance. Hearing the name of Lord Pryan, only added a further exhaustion. Even if she didn't have to bear his company, the fact that he was nearby was enough.

His presence here was more than a curiosity. Playing the role of agent, for which Ferriman had paid with his life, gave her reason to draw further conclusions, if she could. She may be as misplaced as a fish out of water and likely ages away from the powers assaulting the realms. Yet, here she was and as yet to discover a reason for it. Cerra let her thoughts coax her into a little doze, a frown settling as she relaxed. She missed her cat.

The gyrfalcon remained watchful from its perch, its keen stare following the red-haired woman until she was guided inside the tent. Casting about with darting turns of its head, the raptor watched for attention from the camp. The horses at their lines quit their shuffling as activity about the encampment tempered into an early evening lassitude, they would not decamp tonight.

The gyrfalcon launched itself in a silent glide to the ground, landing near the outer edge of the copse, away from the spring. There was a brief instant when the bird's quills flared, like quaking leaves on a birch, a shimmering into a plumed cloak.

Then, the same intense, hazel eyes peered out from the feathered hood, skin lightly bronzed beneath a short, feathered crop of cinnamon hair.

Chapter 32

Finding the witch's apartments cleared of her belongings was a mild surprise. To learn that none of the staff nor her confederates had been responsible, gave him more pause. Unseen forces circled the woman like ripping currents beneath the surface. A quick inspection of the stables revealed her horse as missing. The stableboy, who appeared bemused and simple-minded, had seen nothing nor was it evident that he had even seen the horse. He found the woman an unnecessary distraction, one that nagged him like a small sliver difficult to pluck.

The Jimalians, with Lord Pryan in tow, had taken the northern caravan route, the best alternative to circle the Sultan Sea. Even though his target had been shifted to the Standish lord, he feared the witch would somehow end up in his sight as well. There were ominous powers at play and the game had not concluded. Her powers were reason enough for concern, even haunting the emptiness of his dreams. He subconsciously rubbed the scar on his leg. It was as well the Guildsman had no use for the witch, only the head of the Standish lord.

Before the bells of Vesparana marked the dinner hour, Sinjin had made his reports and settled his debt at the hostel. It was a twelve-day journey to Safrasco. He did not doubt he would catch his prey long before that.

Yutan sniffed the air, his nostrils flaring to catch traces of her scent. Two days had passed since he left the oasis. He had ridden hard, covering the leagues in a stoic silence, matched only by that of the black cat nesting on the saddle in front of him. Beyond the arching Moon Bridge over the Emerald River, the route divided. To the northwest lay the Black Gate that guarded the Stands. Even leagues away from the narrow entrance, he could smell the verdant fields that were home to Cerra.

Instead, the sense of her came from the track headed east, the caravan route that skirted the upper reaches of the Sultan Sea. Her presence lay clearer, sharper, so he had made progress. To have followed her using the winds would have been fast and sure, though there was more to the woman than just the core of her. There were the trappings of her life, a satisfying conclusion to his thoughts as he gave the horse a firm stroke down its neck, wet with exertion. The horse held its own devotions. He had conjured the image of Cerra as a reminder of the bond, knowing the dependable mare would seek the one it regarded as the lead of the herd. The black cat was as single-minded as he was, rarely stepping away from their camps or infrequent stops. Even now, the cat looked at him as though questioning the need to stop.

"She's closer. Have patience, my little friend."

Kamir settled himself, satisfied with the remark. A nudge from Yutan's heels prodded Sugar into an eager trot.

Chapter 33

Stale and musty canvas was all Cerra could smell, a cluttered vision of cobwebs and dust leaving her mood equally untended. With the mute, demands had been no greater than to eat or ride as directed, for that she was grateful. Now, between the measured marches of the daytime, the closeness of the tent made her wish for the open breeze of the plains. It offered much more for her imagination as it whispered with grasses, leaving trails of scent, both plant and animal, while announcing the approach of bigger gusts and larger turns of weather. Not much was heard over the rattle and shuffle of harness as the Queen's procession advanced, though each day she had heard the skree of a falcon or bird of prey high above her, reminding her of the cliffs and spires of her home. It was a different call, from a hawk or harrier she wasn't familiar with, one that demanded attention and had done so, she mused, since passing through the broken Gate. When she heard it again, recovering from the mute's vile potion, she felt as though it was speaking to her. The regular cries became a welcome distraction, for her escort had not spoken at all.

The Queen had an atmosphere of entitled superiority and her silent escort had exhibited the same soulless character. There were but twenty-five horse in the company, as the horse-tender had revealed. King Risharade, not content with the

Queen's slow pace, had separated from the company after the Moon bridge, along with the rest of the nobles. Dire business was all that would demand such haste and Cerra was certain that the Queen's pace would quicken now that the retinue was complete, and that proved to be the case.

At least the food was marginally better than the mute's offerings. A servant bringing a meager dinner signaled a change of the guard at sunset, where she was left in her tent without even a watch. They rightfully considered that her blindness was enough of a defense against flight. Cerra found herself bored, not by the inattention but her lack of busy work. Her herbs and potions gave purpose for her sensitive hands. She felt a pang, missing the familiar sheen of Kamir's fur with his nuzzling affection. There was nothing in the musty confines of the tent that created interest in her mind. Too early to sleep, she lay back, letting her imagination piece together the fragments of events that had led her here. Yutan had been strongly curious at the beginning. If not for his encouragement, she'd be still in her comfortable cabin.

"With my pipe and cat, you right bastard," she mumbled aloud, thinking with a wry smile of his detached and resolute demeanor. "*ahhh* ... by the gods, I hope you don't take too long catching up. I'm fine for the moment, though sure not going to my debutante in any event. I know you're about. I can feel it."

The most curious thread that was wefting through her thoughts was the insufferable Pryan. To discover he was among the party felt like undue punishment and she snorted to herself at the idea she should complain to the staff. As distasteful as the thought was, she found herself analyzing what she knew of the aggrandizing lord. Was he even a lord? Boorish behavior was no measure of royalty.

"If it were, he'd have an empire," she chuckled, " … and a thousand foolaminies to sit at his feet, waving …"

A rustle that sounded like flapping wings interrupted her musings and she sat up sharply as she cued to the static of it. Quiet movement brushed against the canvas and the flap whispered open and shut.

"Who's …" A jolt of fear shot through her as the presence seemed to hop to her in an instant, a graceful arm wrapped in a feathery sleeve clamping a cool hand across her mouth.

"*Shhh.*" The voice was feminine and soft. Young. Familiar. "I'm here to help."

The hand released from her mouth, a finger tracing lightly on Cerra's lips to encourage her quiet compliance. Cerra quickly grasped the hand and held it to her cheek.

"Havi!" she whispered, giving the hand a pat before letting it go. The young woman stayed close to her shoulders. "What are you doing here? You nearly straightened my wig! You can't be from the Queen. You have none of her flavor. How did …?"

"*shhhh shhh shh* …. Haviana soothed, her voice low and anxious. "*heh* … you have that right, I'm not with these folk … all the more reason I mustn't be seen," .

"You're in the right place. I haven't seen you at all." Cerra joked quietly, laying a hand on the other woman. The touch revealed a thigh, light and long-boned, the young woman's presence spry and agile. There was a moment of silence before Havi replied, her voice tentative as if searching for answers.

"*chff* ... I've been little help, though I think all I'm supposed to do is watch." The young girl sounded irritated with herself and uncertain as to what to do next. "I feel that's going to change."

"Everyone seems to be watching me." Cerra couldn't help but put a little annoyance into her voice. "Now ... please ... tell me who you really are. I'd very much like to know who finds me so interesting. These days, it seems to make up a clan and I feel like we're heading for a reunion."

The girl let out a reluctant giggle. "We don't get to choose our families, do we? My name ... full name ... is Haviana Gaines. As my Sisters know me."

Cerra repeated the unfamiliar name. "Hah vee ah' nuh. How unusual."

"After my father, Xavier. He's from ... well, I'm not sure. Just call me 'Havi' ... as he does. I usually hear 'Haviana' from my mother when she's mad."

"I'm happy to side with your father, then." The image of a bird persisted, a caricature that formed erratically making the girl hard for Cerra to visualize. She turned to face her, hands raising gracefully toward the young girl's face. "Havi ... if you don't mind, this helps me to see you better. I think ... I think I need to make sure of you."

She heard Havi catch her breath. "Oh ... there isn't much time ... " the girl whispered fiercely.

"Please." Cerra's fingers were poised near Havi's cheek, relaxed as if biding welcome.

"Y...yes, of course." Havi whispered, mirroring Cerra's hand for a moment as it settled on her cheek.

Cerra's finger's brushed over the young woman's face, so lightly that Havi could feel the tiny hairs being grazed. It felt like a blessing as the blind woman traced her skin, almost as though she could feel the nut brown of her complexion or the hint of freckle that marked her.

Cerra beamed as she let her fingers riffle through the girl's hair, which was cut in short straight auburn and cinnamon tresses, layered like so many feathers. Their feel helped dispel the papery construct about the girl, which had plagued her imagination, though the image didn't entirely fade.

"Smooth … feathered as a crested bird." Cerra grinned. "I wish I could get my hair to do that." She pulled at the mop of red hair that seemed to double in size if there was too much moisture in the air. "I tie it back or corral it and move on."

"I am … "

Some rustling and conversation came from without the tent. Havi froze mid-sentence, her sudden alert tenseness further convincing Cerra that the girl spoke the truth; she was not only in her tent, but in the camp, without the knowledge of the guards. The pacing of the feet outside continued past the tent and in the direction of the cookfire, by her estimate.

"I am … what?" Cerra encouraged quietly. "Besides here to watch."

"I don't know where to begin, for the cards have already been played and you are marked."

"Well, now all is clear … as mud." Cerra whispered dryly. "Who would have you watch me? You say 'cards'. A game master with a bet on the table?"

"There's no money on the table, though the stakes are

high. And no gambler sent me." Havi paused, uncertain how to continue. She let out a quick sigh, deciding. "I'm a Sybelline. The cards I speak of belong to us."

Cerra knew very little of the Sisterhood. They seemed more tales of faraway lands, for if they dwelled in the Stands, their numbers were few. It would be hard to know in any event, for they were shrouded in rumor and secrecy. The influence of the Sybellines was heard of more in the distant lands of the Golden Coast and the Trader States of the Luminaria, where they kept their convents and priories. It was said the Sybelline Oracles could exhibit great powers; and, if the rumors were true, shapeshifters. She felt a rush of questions. She let her curiosity about the girl trail her more immediate concern.

"How is it that I'm 'marked'?" Cerra considered the various images that had come unbidden into her imagination since her trail began at Bridash, as though paintings done by another artist than herself.

"It's a tale long in the telling." Havi whispered, shifting slightly as she looked around, tense for any wayward sound. " … and it will have to be briefer than it was told to me in preparation. I hardly know everything, either … I'm young for the sisterhood."

"Yet here you are. *Heh* … Were you entrusted with a task unsuitable for someone older? My guess is you were chosen for your skill." Cerra added, certain of the girl's aptitude.

"Maybe you're right with both." Havi admitted, her tone signaling the inevitability of her situation. "My … skills … include very good eyesight. Now I wonder if the choice is ironic or necessary."

"Not necessary, yet welcome." Cerra gave the girl a reassuring grip. "Now, before we're both caught and beaten, tell me ... these cards?"

Havi rose and briefly peeked beyond the tent flap, before resuming her spot close to Cerra on the cushions of her palette.

"The deck ... The Deck of the Numinon ... has been put into play. It's a divining deck, only it was created by sorcery... in the wrong hands it can be used to design events, rather than foretell them. It was commissioned by the Sybellines long ago, a magic left over from another age, guarded by the highest circles of ... our sisterhood. I don't know the age of the Deck, that wasn't in my preparations, only that the sorcerer was powerful." Havi quieted even more, aware the majics of the Deck could touch more than its own power. "It's even claimed that he died at the hands of a demon he created. It was stolen some years ago."

Cerra's mind raced as she slipped these pieces into the puzzle she had been creating of the events. The reference to a demon ... there was little doubt who that could mean ... it offered proof as to Yutan's singular interest in the fantastic series of events that began with the destruction of the Stands by the stone giant. If she had felt under someone's observation before, she felt more exposed than ever. It is one thing to be near the stage as audience and quite another to be on the same stage with all eyes on your every move.

"You say I'm 'marked'. Tell me what you mean."

"You are embodied now in one of the cards and it's in play."

"Someone's controlling me?"

"Oh no. It's not like that ... I think. It is more an avenue set down for your actions. Sorry I know so little ... just what I've been told ... but once in play, the cards come to represent the strengths of the person's character, not the sorcerer that created them. Cards can be played but they take on their own life, not one controlled by the user of the cards. It's a very dangerous deck to play with, for the outcomes are uncertain. The deck can turn against the player, depending on the strength of the spirits it attaches to in play ... and what they choose to do. Even the Sisters say they would not use it once they understood its perils. So, you see, you can be swept aside or change the course of events." Havi spoke even softer, as though revealing a secret within a secret. "That also applies to the one using the deck. I think the sorcerer that made it played his own clever joke on them."

"I wonder how it is that I haven't been swept aside already ... maybe I'm in mid-sweep. I certainly feel ruffled." Cerra mused dryly. "Do I also have a broom?"

"*Heh heh.* I'm pretty certain that the card that has you marked is Nuith, Queen of the Quills. It's a ruling card and can't be cast aside so easily. It's interesting that the card shows the Queen as blindfolded. I thought it a metaphor. I confess, upon meeting you I was surprised to find it to be true."

Cerra snorted. "*pfft!* If I were your Sisters, I'd have the cards reclaimed. I only have 'Queen' residing in my bottom ... where she rules supreme, mind you. Right now, she's not comfortable ... nor amused."

"Please. Nuith is ... very much like you in spirit." Havi's

voice sounded hurt, anxious. "She's not just a name in a deck of cards. All creation comes from her … a vision that only she can see. I wish I could tell you all of her qualities but there's no time … now. Every card has a quality and purpose in the divinations. The key to them lies in a book that measures the portends the cards reveal, the Numinon."

"I'm sorry. I don't mean to belittle your efforts. I never feel 'Queenly'. Just 'me'. I'm content in my little corner of the world. It's a small realm. I should be a poor choice for a queen."

"But you are not there now." Haviana observed. "You have moved onto a different stage."

"Are you on this 'stage' too? A card in play?"

"Oh yes, there was no avoiding that." Havi's voice displayed her confidence, an enthusiasm engendered by youth. "A low card, as I was told … which is suitable. I'm not very old, you know." She let a note of caution return to temper her tone. "Of course, I can bollix things up too. I may have already…."

"We all have our strong features." Cerra gave a light grip to Havi's arm. "The … creatures. What of them? I've been spared their sight as I've encountered two of them. I could conjure nothing in my head … and I can be pretty inventive … nothing except dry things, like paper. I …" Cerra stopped, thinking of the images that she had painted, the fire of the dragon, the cold ice of the womanly creature at the oasis … all papery cutouts inspired by their dry, lifeless impulses. The oily Lord Pryan conjured up a similar fabrication in her mind, the Queen as well … Cerra made an intuitive leap that seemed logical to her. "Linarest. She is in play too."

"Yes. She's certainly a power in play... I can only guess at her card, a Princess or Queen ... a royal at any rate."

"Who? Who is 'playing' ... is that the word for it? ... this deck?"

"I don't know. It's why I am here. *Heh* ... it was first thought it might be you."

"Me?!" Cerra was incredulous. "Oh bother ... Why?"

Haviana shifted on her seat. "There's another card linked to you, that of Abbadon. That worries ... my superior, for it is one of the four most powerful cards in the deck, the demon of the Underworld. They believe it represents one of the sorcerer's most arcane creations." She gripped Cerra's hand. "She feared you were being influenced by it."

Cerra could feel the girl's scrutiny and thought of Yutan and the torturous existence he had endured.

"Well, that isn't the case. We're all in play and ... who is using who? Or whom." She turned to face Havi, both puzzled and chasing the quandary to some conclusion. "It isn't death nor demons that worries me ... as you say ... I'm here and still in the game. The outcome. That's another story. Abbadon, if that's the name, may save us all. I hardly feel like a major player. *Pssht* ... I don't know anything ... and right now, all I have is a musty tent and a pot to piss in. Why should the Ducesin bother to abduct me at all? ... why not just kill me outright? ... Though I do admire her restraint in that regard, mind you."

"She fears you. You may hold the higher rank.... a Queen. You cannot be cast aside so easily."

Cerra considered Pryan and the vacant, one-dimensional

image that persisted in her sight. "Others are in play and one of them is holding this 'deck'. The … "

Havi's hand clapped over Cerra's mouth as footsteps approached. She froze, hearing one of the Jimalian officers giving instructions to one of his aides as they approached.

"*shhhh.*" Havi murmured, releasing her hand as she slipped off of the cushions. "I'll return."

A shifting wave of fluttering accompanied the whisk of the tent flap being pulled aside. Cerra's heart was in her throat as she feared for the young girl's safety.

"Gad, it's dark in here. No candles." The soldier began to slide his sword from its sheath as though wary of attack. "You. Wake up."

"I'm here … and quite awake." Cerra made herself sound cross at the rude entry and rose quickly, the guard shifting nervously in front of her. "You don't need your sword."

"The Queen would be wanting to see you …" The sword slipped back into its sheath with a razored hiss and a rough hand grabbed her arm, jerking her towards the tent flap. "… now."

Chapter 34

Crisp and clean air filled the demon's nostrils. In the early morning, the plains that skirted the northern slopes of the Sultan Sea lay frigid and brisk until the sun was well up on the horizon. The grayness of the false dawn filtered through him, cooling his heat, the earth eternal in its grounding. In his humanity, the elements had attained a balance that he could appreciate in their complexity.

Yutan drank a cup of kafi as he waited for the black cat to return from its morning prowl. Cookfires and food were conventions he had rediscovered, bringing him closer to her and to his humanity. The demon needed none of those things for the elements provided their own fuels. He looked at the cup with amusement, another pleasure discovered at the hands of the blind woman. She had provided the slow return to his humanity, though the curse of his demon-hood remained, which could neither be un-learned nor forgotten. In the aftermath, Cerra had left him the creation that was himself and not the tool of the unscrupulous and powerful.

The nicker of the horse caught his attention for the moment, a flick of its grazing head as the blind woman's black cat scampered from the dried grass with a vole tightly clamped in his jaws. Her mare shone like burnished chestnut in the early light, the flecks of white across her chest and haunches that gave the horse her name, glowed as though she were lit by inner coals. She looked at him, shuffling with impatience.

"Sugar. Keep your nose on that herd ahead of us … we'll be riding soon, so take your ease while you can." Yutan gave the cat a brush as it hunkered down next to the small fire to finish his prize. "Kamir. You've done well."

He enjoyed Cerra's quick wit to spare for the little animal. She would likely have asked him to go out and get something bigger for the both of them. He scratched the cat again, who looked at him with predator eyes. The blind woman had slowly eroded his taciturn nature with her bright quips. He could hear her now, so gave the cat the response it expected.

"None for me. I've eaten. Don't take long, we're riding when you're done."

Talking with animals was much easier than with his human counterparts, whom he carefully avoided beyond the devoted Cerra. Animals were direct with their desires and affections; their communications lay deep in realms where humans failed to listen. He stood and scratched some dirt on the kindling, then squeezed some water from the air to douse the fire. The stone that he had crushed into flame within his fist would lie in the wet ash until it expired.

His kit was quickly stowed in the saddlebag and Yutan mounted the horse as the sun was still a flattened orb, glimmering fat and red on the horizon. He tossed the knotted rope and chirped in the manner of the blind woman, a sure prompt to spur the cat to its place on the saddle. He scratched and settled the cat as he sniffed the air, letting it invade his pores. She was closer. Two days of prolonged riding had freshened the scent. There was a new cast to the atmosphere. Cerra's essence was no longer tied to her captor's alone, there were many. Yutan let a hard smile crease his features, for a large party would move much slower.

Behind him to the west, another presence lurked at the fringe, an essence he would have ignored save for the nagging familiarity left from another age. Like stone, he remembered; the ages collapsed within moments and stored like gems. He cast another glance to the simmering orange ball, threatening to release itself from the grip of the horizon, wavering lines already twisting the airs.

Yutan leaned close to the horse's ear. "Troubles ahead, troubles behind. Follow the herd and I'll see to the blind."

He nudged the horse into an eager canter.

The familiar presence trailed in the west by one days' ride, where Sinjin scanned the horizon ahead of him. The plains made distances deceptive, for the distant Granite mountains to the north never seemed to change their stance nor did the carpet of grass that spread out over the flat prairie. It would be many days before the horizon betrayed the purpled spires of the Jimals.

The Standish Lord was traveling with the Jimalian contingent. The Guildmaster had been clear about the fate of the man. He could well believe Patan would exact the proper fare for his transportation to the next life. Sinjin favored killing. It was simpler and required no further effort.

The witch nagged at him, for he remained certain that somehow, she would reappear. Such things were fated and unavoidable. He scratched the scar on his leg, a constant reminder of her other skills. Reluctantly, he knew he owed the witch his life. It would be fitting not to have a reason to kill her.

Chapter 35

Stepping into the Queen's tent, Cerra quickly sensed a broad, fresh space, so unlike the stale accommodations she had been assigned to. Carpet cushioned her feet and sound was slightly muted by the richness of the tent walls, draped with the soft textures of rich fabrics. The scents of rose, sandalwood and wax, mixed in the air. The warmth of candles came from the opposite corners of the tent, the arid and featureless voice of the Queen coming between them, as dry and vacant as the space.

"Show her to the cushions next to the bump table and leave."

The guard hesitated for a moment. Cerra could feel his shoulder turn a bit as he looked to the side before he gripped her upper arm.

"This way." A trace of nervous discomfort gave a rough turn to his voice as he led her, a bit harshly, she groused to herself, seven paces before being set down.

"You're too kind." Cerra felt like slapping him away but brushed at her skirts instead as she settled, calming her irritation with another cursory examination of the Queen's tent. The flap fluttered shut behind the departing guard, though someone else remained inside with them. The guard's hesitation had made that evident and no guesswork was needed.

She could feel the mute's silent presence as surely as she could sense his breath and smell his musk. Turning briefly to scan the area, the chill, dry image of poisonous cups resurfaced in her mind as she marked his location.

"Thank you for joining me." The queens voice was perfunctory as Cerra sank into the cushions, rich brocades distinctive for their luxurious feel.

Linarest gave the blind woman a critical examination as she settled herself. Her riotous red hair and freckled complexion gave an exotic look, one that would add conversation and interest in court. Her lack of sight made her more amusing and compelling, for she seemed quite capable otherwise. The odd cast to her eyes never gazed directly. Linarest felt as if her heart was exposed by the kindly orbs that didn't register what they saw. The Abbysin dress and shawl made her appear like an oracle, a notion that gave her pause, for the soldiers had already taken to regarding the blind woman as a diviner, an omen that they could not decide for good or ill. While the woman had a ready smile that was difficult to associate with dire consequences, her warm, brown eyes seemed to catch sight of visions unseen by others and therefore, a mystery.

"Thank you for insisting." The blind woman spoke with a warm contralto, a trace of impertinence in her voice.

"I hear that you play chess. I thought I would indulge in a game."

Cerra thought quickly. Her chess game had only been mentioned in conversation with the Abbysin Collenel, a piece no doubt overheard. She wondered what other tidbits of information had been relayed to Linarest. Not for the first time, she wished that she had no one paying attention to her at all. Information was the game and she had been recruited by Ferriman to fulfill the role. To that end and to respect his sacrifice, she must at least try to gather more than she gave away.

"I hear you didn't kidnap me in order to gain a gaming partner." Cerra felt like purposely testing the Queen's motives and patience. "I'm sure I play poorly to anyone that knows it."

"Enough. You are here because you were seen by many as being an interference to the proceedings." Linarest spoke as though Cerra was merely an inconvenience in scheduling. "So, I removed you. We don't 'kidnap'. Now I am merely trying to decide what to do with you."

"If one of your options is to send me home, I would choose that. This has become a most disagreeable journey."

Linarest gave a short, dry laugh. The woman was clearly not intimidated by her royal presence. She gathered up the board and placed it on the table between them. "I intend to keep your company a while longer, so I thought I'd test your skills as a diversion. Which side do you prefer?"

"The right one. As for the game, you've already made the first move, so you must be white." Cerra offered flatly, not wanting to play under the circumstances. "That leaves the other for me."

"They are black, carved from the finest onyx." Linarest turned the board. The mute remained standing at his place near the door, leaving Cerra with the feeling of a silent spear pointed at her back. Black suited her mood as she resigned herself to play at the Queen's game.

"That helps." Cerra retorted drily, turning her attention to the board in front of her. "Black is easier for me to keep track of."

She carefully reached for a piece, a knight by feel, the carving elegant and weighted nicely at the base, then let her hands graze the edges of the pieces and board to gauge their shapes.

"How shall I know your moves?"

"I shall give them to you, of course." Linarest seemed irritated by the question. The pleasure of a game was obviously not the Queen's focus. Cerra could already feel a line of questions being queued up behind the demanding tone. "Are you ready? As I have the opening move … Queen's pawn to the fore, two squares. E4."

A grid was a very easy thing for Cerra to imagine and she used it often as a device to sort her jars. The Ducesin's opening move was a common one, delivering multiple options. Cerra again felt the backs of the pieces closest to her to gauge their orientation. She pulled back the drape of her sleeve and countered by sliding her Queen's pawn up two squares to face it. She felt the edge of the opposing pawn with a light brush of her fingers, confirming its placement in her head.

Linarest followed the move immediately, using an aggressive opening, wanting to finish the game quickly. "Knight to F3."

Cerra paused as she focused on the numbering of the grid. She carefully mirrored the Ducesin's action, placing her own knight in front of the acolyte's pawn. She would move the acolyte out with her next move. For the moment she wanted to concentrate on the center of the board as she had been taught long ago. Linarest announced her next move and Cerra countered, dutifully moving her acolyte along four squares to land near the center.

The Ducesin moved a pawn forward and Cerra matched it as it helped again to orient the pieces in the grid. Her inner sight immediately caught a diagonal that lay open to the king and easy to exploit. She moved the other pawn to a vacant square, a thoughtless move that she knew would be sacrificial, but might draw attention away from that side.

Linarest was mechanical in her making her announcements, as though disinterested in the game. Cerra was well aware that she was much more the object that occupied the Queen's mind. Cerra cleared her back row then made the 'king's leap', in which the castle and king were exchanged to one side of the board. The white queen hovered to the right side of the board, along with the knight, the brunt of her attack. The Ducesin had left her King exposed with the weak diagonal as Cerra had hoped. She set her other castle to force the white queen off, a move that irritated Linarest.

"Queen to E1." Linarest retreated the piece, placed back to the original spot as Cerra had spoiled her planned move. Her annoyance was evident as she returned to a line of questioning instead. "I wish to know why you are here."

"I'm here at your direction of course." Cerra countered, grateful that Linarest has come to the point of the whole charade. "As I said, my home …"

"Yes, yes.… your home. It's far behind you. I am not the one who placed you in the Standish embassy." The Queens impatience was clear.

"Howsoever it occurred, those fortunes are indeed mine," Cerra admitted. She moved her knight to take an unprotected pawn, another diversion away from the weakness on the left of the board. She lightly touched the immediate pieces to confirm the positions in her imagination. She was beginning to warm to the challenge. "I feel like that pawn. Your move."

As expected, the Queen countered with an acolyte, forcing Cerra to retreat or lose her remaining knight. There was no sentiment, except that the piece had taken on the valiant nature of Ferriman and she wanted him to last the game. A dangerous position lay in the center, protected by the castle. She located the knight in the square, bargaining against the exchange. The Queen ignored the move and drew her own queen out again, her same ploy as before.

"Queen to B4. Did you follow that?" The Queen's mind was clearly not on the game, her tone abrupt, as if the interview had taken longer than expected. Cerra nodded, considering her next move as she lightly touched the rook at her king's side. It did not surprise her when the queen returned to the topic that was evidently most on her mind. "I am curious … about your purpose in the embassy. You are neither a trade baron, royal, nor ruler of any domain …"

"My cat reminds me of that almost daily, another reason to return me to my humble home."

Linarest ignored the quip. " … yet you have the ear of the Standish rule."

"I was merely enlisted as an advisor. Advice is one of my strengths. I fair give it away, as I seldom use it." Cerra laughed with a genuine warmth, though Linarest was well aware of the evasiveness of the blind woman's response as Cerra eased a pawn forward, blocking the move Linarest had anticipated for the queen. It occurred to Linarest that, as the chess game was proving, Cerra of the Meadows would not give up her secrets easily.

"And what advice did you have?"

"Watch your acolyte. Check." Cerra measured the distance carefully and snagged the piece deftly with her fingertips, replacing it with her knight.

"Pawn to B4," grumbled Linarest. "That is not what I meant."

Cerra set the considerations of the horrific spectral events and the subsequent rattling of sabers aside. Her opinions were incomplete, too much was unknown and she felt very much like a fly in a web. There was one subject that brooked little argument which, given the presence of the pompous trader, was a fitting diversion for this conversation.

"Advice? I'll share a piece that all should heed ... put little stock in the words of Lord Pryan." Cerra moved the pawn again, positioned so that the Queen's acolyte and knight were both under attack. She would have to lose one of them. Cerra was gambling on the second acolyte's demise.

"You were hardly included among the Standish embassy in order to be his watchdog." Linarest snorted. "Knight to C5"

"You asked for advice. I gave it to you. Advice that I'm actually using myself." Cerra responded dryly. "He's got more twists than a bag of snakes." She slid her acolyte up one diagonal. It appeared to guard her knight, though when he moved, the White King would be exposed again.

"I'll bear that in mind." The Ducesin sounded non-committal as she considered the next move.

Cerra could tell that the Queen faced the mute rather than her as they talked, the servant no doubt discerning their conversation by the movements of their lips. Cerra's imagination had become emboldened by the game. If the Queen was expecting a quick victory, she was being disappointed and her clipped speech indicated a growing concern over the match. She was managing better than she thought she would. *'I'm still on the board'* she mused wryly, *'and not swept aside … so there's no reason why I can't make inquiries of my own. Who said royalty held all the cards?'* The imagery that came to mind made her think of Havi's warning.

"I would ask why you sought to kidnap someone as unimportant as I to the proceedings? My sort of advice is easily gained by the most simple of souls, even your staff."

"Castle to A6." Linarest ignored the gibe as another of Cerra's pawns fell. "Someone thought you important enough to include you in the Embassy … a nobody. I'll tell you this, there is no such thing as a 'nobody' in any embassy. You either have power or information. Whose ears were you to report to?"

Cerra thought of the dead Captain, a sudden pang of loss quelling the small level of enthusiasm she had garnered. He had led her with confidence into this affair and what she had learned would remain in his trust. The Queen had earned nothing.

"Ears no longer among the listening to care," she murmured, tempered by the memory. "All the more reason to release me. Are we near Oskara? I have a friend there. You would do us all a service."

"Your move," the Queen prompted.

Cerra carefully placed her queen near the edge of the board, backed by her acolyte, the two pieces an arrow pointed at the White King. When her knight uncovered, the game was in reach. She lightly grazed the remaining pieces closest to her, reaffirming the pattern that she had kept pace with in her mind. The Queen was attacking on her right side, though it would take her at least three more moves to make the ploy work.

Linarest had observed during the game that the blind woman was not directing her attention as one normally would. At first, she attributed it to disorientation. The Queen even closed her eyes briefly to imagine what the Standish woman was experiencing, though soon deemed it too cumbersome to do for more than a few moments. As she had the chance to observe her over the game, the blind woman's movements were subtler than confusion would allow, turning slightly to various sounds, like the ears of a cat.

At the moment her head was slightly tilted in the direction of Steban, who stood resolute and motionless next to her palette. Linarest glanced over to the mute, who signaled briefly with quick, silent movements of his hands, then turned her attention back to the blind woman. A better opponent than she had anticipated, though she was leaving herself in a weak position on the board. She crossed her knight into the fray.

"Knight to C6. What advice would you give the Captain … if he were here?"

Cerra turned her head towards the Queen, the word giving her a little start as she had not mentioned any rank at all. The slight friction of the mute's gestures had made their communication evident. A curious language of sight that gave her a moment of fascination. "The same as I give you now and I've offered before. Give Lord Pryan a wide berth. Unless he owes you coin … in which case, my advice comes too late."

The Queen had positioned her knight as expected, slapping it down with a little harder knock than before. Cerra had the feeling she had struck a nerve. The move left Cerra's acolyte exposed and likely to be removed from the board with the Queen's next move. Cerra understood what it felt like to be left as bait. Her own knight would provide the correct counter, while opening the door for the black queen. She carefully ticked the jumping move, forcing Linarest to decide between her remaining knight and the exposed castle. Cerra was sure the Queen would guard the castle, needing it for the trap being laid.

"I will bear that in mind." Linarest paused for a moment, warily eyeing the blind woman, suddenly aware of her exposed King. She sniffed as she quietly slipped a pawn back one square while making a definitive move on the board. "Castle to A6. I was looking for something reflecting a grander stage, perhaps, an opinion regarding events of the past season, which by all accounts are terrifying. The Lord Pryan may be worth a caution, yet he is hardly the source of such sorcery."

"True that." Cerra agreed. "A minor player in a game that surely demands more subtlety than he is capable of. A sledge has more touch. However, there is always someone who benefits from these … *eh*, inflicted turmoils. The only benefits seem to be money and power. One has to look no further than that. Where would you look in such a case? I believe this is checkmate."

Cerra picked up her queen and slid the diagonal necessary to mate the White King, trapped behind the pawns in the back row. She nearly fumbled the piece within the light grasp of her fingertips as she tapped the wayward pawn set in its path.

"Oh … I'm sorry! … my mistake." Cerra was genuinely abashed, an unaccounted jolt of fear passing through her as she quickly replaced her queen. She could not have forgotten such a placement and it astounded her that the Queen might cheat. She let out a chuff of disappointment, as though her own mistake, then returned the queen to remove the wayward pawn from the board. The Queen could either take her queen or advance on her king. Either way, the game had turned. Her black queen fell with the next move.

"You've misread the board in more ways than one," the Queen observed.

"Yes, I have." Cerra admitted. She moved her knight, a failed attempt to guard the king as the Queen had placed her castle well and defeat lay in the next move.

"Castle to C8. Checkmate." Linarest claimed with quiet finality. "You play a decent game, for one blind."

"I once said that the goal of the game is to win. It's apparent that I don't understand the game well enough. A Queen learns differently, I suppose." It was unthinkable to Cerra that cheating to win would create any satisfaction at all for the victor, that winning was more important than the merits of her game. It was the trait of someone that would … Cerra felt a piece of the puzzle fall into place as surely as a missed pawn. She couldn't resist laying an innuendo. "I imagine you play at cards with the same determination."

Linarest felt suddenly exposed, as though her ruse was witnessed by the entire court, instead of this sightless peasant. She didn't even steal a glance to Steban to gauge his reaction. "You are impertinent."

"I don't mean to be, milady," Cerra replied with a slight smile, though she very much did so. "I merely suggest that you are much better versed in perils of court than I. I think games are like that."

"An interesting choice of words … suggesting cards."

Cerra could feel the wariness in her voice, a curious blend of curiosity and uncertainty. It was the tone of someone who knew they have been seen and hoping yet to distract attention.

"Cards are games for gamblers, hoping for a bigger payoff than they would have by spending their efforts on the price of bread and kafi. It's a game that I'm ill-suited for.

Cerra caught the rustle of the Ducesin's sleeve. A stillness settled as she heard the stone pieces being laid into their box. Cerra imagined Linarest's mask of politeness being cast aside with the distraction of the game, for her next question was much more direct.

"What of these recent events? What do you know of them? You evade my questions."

"Do I?" Cerra paused, thinking she had answered well enough, though her words for the Captain would have been much different. She could hardly tell the Ducesin to look to herself. At best, she wanted some impression that she had cracked the woman's icy demeanor, yet no change could be felt, much like her silent confederate, who poised like a statue within the tent. Save that Linarest spoke aloud, the cold indifference was the same. If she had to lay odds, the player of the deck was in this room.

"I can think of nothing more to say. As anyone can see, powers beyond the world have been called into play, powers beyond the scope of you or I. If a game is afoot, look for who has the biggest stake in it. I assure you it isn't me … nor the Stands. That's my advice. Other opinions may be forthcoming, from those less vocal than I. His advice may be entirely different."

Linarest and Steban exchanged a hard look. The queen shook her head slightly, negating the thought that ran between them, before turning back to the blind woman. "Do you have a stake in this … game?"

"Yes, of course!" Cerra felt suddenly animated, as though it might be the slight opening she needed to crack the woman's veneer. "My small claim is the same as everyone's … a peaceful place in which to enjoy myself. I can think of no better ambition."

"Thank the gods then, that you do not have to make the decisions of rule." Linarest scorned her naiveté. "The world is a bigger board, yet nothing more than a game of chess. Or cards."

"I'll remember that." Cerra let out a short, dry laugh. "*Heh.* If I had another move, I'd as like forget my place again."

"It would be wise to consider yourself nothing more than a pawn, while I consider what to do with you." Linarest nodded to the mute, signaling that the interview was over, a cold finality that Cerra could sense as well.

The tent flap was whisked aside and she was led out with rough indifference by the guard. The smells of the open camp were a welcome relief after the cloying purity of the Queen's tent. Cerra didn't mind the gruff company of the guard back to the tent, at the very least it exhibited more emotion than the Queen or her mute had shown. She was reassured as much by the presence of Havi, as the willingness of the Queen to consider alternatives for her, other than being swept from the board. They were still some distance from the Chained Lakes and Safrasco. Regardless of what game was played, Card or Pawn, someone was sure to make a move before then.

Chapter 36

Scent left trails in the air as surely as footprints cast on the ground. The steppes were laid out as a crumpled dun blanket of swaying grasses, whispering and dry, the breezes drifting with the scuffling of grazing herds and scattered speech of its human denizens. Sugar nickered, flicking her head with a snort that rippled her russet mane.

"You sense her too. Patience." Yutan patted the horse's neck, damp with sweat. Kamir sat nestled in the saddle, looking up at him with feline intensity as if demanding he continue on. "Patience for you as well."

He gave the cat an absent scratch behind the ears. The Jimalians were close by, a half day's ride without effort, their spoor and bouquet fresh amid the warm breezes that pressed up from the south, filled with fragrant salts from the sea and traces of industry and waste from human ports. It wasn't those markers that concerned him but the essence behind him, drawing nearer as the day had passed. The dark figure had been visible in the distance since morning, the aura hard and familiar. The open steppes offered little opportunity for ambush or surprise. Yutan had been exercising a slow control of his own, damping the fires of his impatience with the calming ground that the blind woman had molded into him. He nudged the horse forward along the caravan trail, following the wagon ruts filled with fine dust the same color as the dry grass, to where a lone oak, thick and ancient, shaded a fold in the terrain. Water lay just beneath the surface, the prairie grasses sprouting lush and green in the shade.

"We wait here. For now." Yutan gave the black cat a nudge, who stretched in an upward arch before alighting to ground.

He dismounted, letting the mare wander to the tender shoots within the shade of the oak. Pacing slowly, he found a natural shallow along the ground where he knelt and pressed into the earth. He shaped the ground, allowing the dust and grits to remember the age of stone as he hollowed out a bowl. Crystal, azurite and granite layered the surface as his hands sculpted.

At last, he urged the water from beneath the surface, promising the earthbound water the rejuvenation of air for his intrusion. It bubbled into the waiting basin with a cheerful gurgle, cooling the hot rock with a sizzle, causing the demon to smile with almost fatherly affection. Water was a spirit, an intelligence, sustaining and unforgiving. As the oasis was proof, it had the power to reclaim the most virulent majic. It had the power to reclaim him, if he allowed it. He stared at the pool a moment, knowing that he could lose himself in her embrace.

Sugar left her grazing momentarily to sample the spring, then paced away, tearing at the grass as she went. Kamir was hunkered motionless near a small hole burrowed in next to one of the oaken roots. Yutan mirrored their calm by settling back against the broad trunk to wait.

Half a league distant, Sinjin regarded the lone oak with skepticism, a grazing horse silhouetted beneath its broad mantle. He marked the rider as the one he was closing distance on, seen since the morning. Lone riders were rare this far along the caravan track. Oskara and the Sultan Sea lay two days ride to the south and the Cherros were ever in small bands that ranged constantly as they policed the grassy expanse of the steppes. This rider was no Cherro.

Sinjin slowed to a canter as he approached, eyeing the pool of water that nestled wet and inviting within a clean stone basin and cooled by the shade. The refuge was relatively unused and ungrazed, save for the horse that contentedly munched on the verdant grass. Sinjin's hackles shivered with current as he felt himself come to guard. Watering spots were rare enough when crossing the wide plains of the Cherros, that the ground should be trodden with hoofmarks, or the forgotten leavings of the caravans. He debated passing on. He had water gained earlier at a sump creek that bore enough of a trickle to be palatable. The Jimalians were close enough ahead that he would overtake them before the last light of day and he wanted to observe their camp with light to spare. The ensuing darkness would take care of itself, a condition he favored in executing his commissions.

Within the umbra of shade, a black shape darted, rounding up with a scamper onto the grazing horse. Sinjin's blood froze in an instant when he saw the intent eyes of a black cat, staring at him from atop the saddle. He pulled his horse up short in the same sharp breath. The witch!

He scanned the patch of shade and another jolt passed through him as his eyes froze on a man standing as solid and unmoving as though he were part of the tree itself. He reached to draw his sword.

"Stop."

The voice resonated as Sinjin tightened his grip on the hilt, neither shout nor whisper, a sound that compelled him to cease his motion.

"Draw not the sword."

The voice sounded from another time, formal in address. The assassin stayed poised in the saddle as the man stepped forward, appearing to grow as he moved through the filtered light under the heavy oak. Long dark hair in thick locks framed a chiseled, clean-shaven face. Unarmed, he was dressed in the solid leathers and cloths of a successful caravanneer, one who hid his wealth carefully. The sword seemed locked as he tightened his grip, unwilling to extract itself from its protective sheath. The man's eyes showed no fear, holding him in a steady gaze without anger or demand. Instead they welled with unspoken secrets of a thousand lives. They were familiar eyes, deep brown and haunting, the tender eyes of love conjoining the luring invitation of death. Sinjin cast a glance to the black cat, who remained poised atop the chocolate mare, before shifting back to the traveler, who had taken another step closer, looming larger and more substantial than before. His hands twitched slightly before he released his grip on the sword, a reflex against his nature.

"I noticed the water. I want nothing more." Sinjin allowed carefully, then slid from his saddle, a slight nod from the man granting the favor.

He led the horse over to the basin, water pooling clear over glistening stone. Sinjin knelt to take a sip that he cupped in his hands. It tasted fresh and pure. His horse nosed in gladly and began drinking its fill. He emptied the slack water from his skin off to the side, then let it fill from the pool. He kept the man in the corner of his vision while performing the task, ever wary of attack but knowing with a certainty that a truce had been wrought, so long as his sword remained undrawn. No sword was in evidence, the man had nothing more than a stave tucked under the saddle flap to protect him. Even so, there was an unyielding presence he had only witnessed once before, from the Hashini master of deception; Han Kesslmen, named 'the Ghost', for his age and lineage was unknown. Kesslmen was an examiner all Hashini must encounter in order to earn their dagger and cup, a man who possessed the same implacable eyes: knowing, forgiving, yet merciless. Sinjin soaked a cloth to wipe his face and neck, then stood to face the lone traveler.

"I will trouble you no further." He turned back to his horse, who had moved companionably nearer to the chocolate mare as they munched on the shaded grass. He had not taken but a step when the man's voice stopped him.

"What is your intent?"

"My own business." Sinjin bristled as he turned, his hand slipping inside his jerkin for a flechette, yet he stayed his motion as he met the man's eyes, his every purpose laid bare. "Show some gratitude that it is none of yours and you do not have the weight of it."

The witch's black cat stared, waiting in judgement as the bronzed man regarded him, judging his answer.

"I would have you remove the weight of it all together if

it is the blind woman you seek." The man's voice was deep and resonant. There was no demand in it, only the surety of conviction.

"It is not her that I …" Sinjin stopped. The codes of the Hashini are strict, scorning and ostracizing any that divulge knowledge of their clients or objectives, yet he had already made an enormous admission by claiming to know of her at all. "I am on the road to Safrasco. Sorry to trouble you. I'll take my leave."

"You'll go nowhere."

Sinjin felt an instant of outrage at the command. He skillfully palmed the flechette, flinging it into the air with a snap of his wrist, a whistling blade that crossed the space between them in an instant. The man moved only to brush at his throat, a brief swipe over the spot where the blade should have impaled him. The assassin felt his blood run cold, for there was no gash of impact, no grimace, no clatter of the blade on the ground. There was nothing, as though he had thrown a wisp of air.

His eyes riveted on the bronzed traveler's face, bearing the same deep presence as though he carried within him the souls of the dead. Holding his gaze, the bronzed man slid the dagger into view as he had removed it from the palm of his hand, polished and gleaming like fire in the mottled shade of the oak. It flickered like a star, disappearing in the flash as a slap of pressure edged his boot. Sinjin knew even before he glanced down that the knife had impaled the leather. It lay imbedded to the hilt, having sliced cleanly between his ankle and the side of his boot as though sheathed. The handle shown like a jeweler's clasp.

"You dropped that." The traveler's voice bore no trace of rebuke. Sinjin bent carefully to slide the knife away. He had no doubt the man could have placed the blade in the center of his eye if he had chosen to and he had not seen so much as a quiver of the man's muscles.

Yutan regarded the assassin with remote detachment. That he was of the Hashini was apparent. The slight triangle, mistaken for a scar on the wrist, was the secret cipher of the Guild even in the ages of his youth. The taste the man left in the air told him he was the very one to follow Cerra on her trek through the mountains in times past. That the assassin lived to this day was a testament to the blind woman's unwavering kindness. She had stayed his hand before, promoting caution and gaining insight. His mouth twitched slightly in a smile at the thought. She had molded him more surely than she knew. He repeated his command.

"You'll go nowhere until I know your business. Otherwise …" Yutan paused to make his point. The blind woman's influence only went so far and the man felt like a danger to her being. The color of the assassin's field seared with obsession. " … you'll go nowhere at all."

"Not her." The assassin's reply was short and business-like, a price uttered at the end of unsatisfying negotiations. "A Standish Lord in the company of the Jimalian Troop. One of those who would be better off culled from the herd."

"Only the welfare of the woman concerns me." Yutan gave the assassin a hard look, watching for the sly shine of duplicity. There was none, only the cold determination of one set on his goals. "They have stopped less than an hour's ride from here.

The outriders circle within a bell of their camp. We can travel together."

Sinjin gave a thought to how the traveler knew the location of the troop with such surety. Riddles surrounded the traveler. He may even be a fabrication of the witch and for the moment he felt outflanked by the mystery. There was little he could do at the moment except go along with chain of events. The traveller watched him as impassively as the ferryman of death. He would need no sword to exact his fare.

"Agreed."

Chapter 37

Cerra set her bowl aside, putting it down harder than she intended with a brush of impatience. The lack of palatable food was not what tried her patience, rather the rigorous isolation she had faced during the past three days on the road. None would talk with her, regarding her a mystery better ignored, no more than a parcel to be moved. The horse-tender offered the only kindness, small considerations as he took charge of the mule at the end of the days ride. She had little energy and no audience for the quips and jests she imagined, which was just as well, for they were becoming more biting as the days progressed.

She ached for the familiarity of her home, the welcome weight of Kamir lapped in front of her on the saddle. Losing the companionship of her black cat felt a little like losing her sight, a sense easy to take for granted until it was no longer there. She had been stripped of her possessions and worried over the fate of Sugar.

"I swear I'm never leaving home again," she muttered, flipping the wooden spoon into the bowl.

She could tell by the clatter that it had hit the edge and bounced clear. She didn't bother to collect it. Her frustrations had been mounting and only the curiosity regarding the Ducasin's intentions kept her senses alert. The Ice Queen, a character in many folk tales, wormed into her imagination whenever Linarest crossed her mind and it was hard to imagine her as anything else but the cold ruler in the stories. The cold papery forms in her mind reinforced the opinion and Linarest and the Ice Queen formed into one.

It seemed as though nothing would change until they arrived at Safrasco. She had none of her usual pastimes and distractions to take her mind away from her impairments. Without apparent purpose, she found herself more and more bound by the cage of her short-comings.

'*Little wonder they don't even see fit to put a guard on my tent to prevent escape,*' she groused silently. Her brooding was brushing on despair and she was thankful for the presence of Havi. The young girl had never disclosed her secret, though Cerra had come to realize with a certainty, that the young Sybelline and the Gyrfalcon were one and the same. She now found the occasional '*kee-aw*' that pierced the high airs during their trek along the caravan route, even more reassuring.

Campfires were in evidence long before they reached the Jimalian camp. The red glow of them, pressed low by the cooling dark, hung in the air just a league ahead. Sinjin fell in behind the quiet traveller, who wove his way along a shallow course in the grass that kept them off of the caravan track and beyond the sight of their outposts. The traveler had assured him there was but one, and pointed the shade out, though Sinjin could not see him in the dark.

There was no temptation to waylay the traveler. He had little doubt, the man, if that's what he was, would turn the attack on him and succeed. The stronger check was that Sinjin's curiosity had caught him up as soon as the truce had been reached between them. It seemed the traveler's interference would make his commission easier and one did not discard tools freely offered. Rid of his obligations to waylay the witch, he was equally curious about her fate. For the moment, the traveler had a willing ally.

The shallow draw wasn't evident to Sinjin's eyes, though the traveler had no trouble remaining in its vague cloak as they approached the camp. The silhouetted horse lines framed the near edge of the camp, across the wind of their approach. As yet their own horses had not been recognized by the herd.

The tents of the Jimalian company, piped with the maroon and white of the Queen's livery, took on a hazardous red glow from the three low campfires roughly framed in pits. There was enough firelight reflecting on the fringes of the camp that Sinjin had no problem spotting the two perimeter guards when the traveler pointed them out. The assassin nodded, placed in the long-unfamiliar role of second. There was a moment when they were nearly on the verge of the firelight that Sinjin thought they might rehearse a plan, though the moment passed quickly when the witch's black cat suddenly bolted from its perch in the saddle and dashed into the dark shadows.

The cat disappeared like a wraith, the traveler dismounting as soon as Kamir lit to the ground. Sinjin pulled up and slid from his saddle in one quiet motion. The traveler handed the reins of his horse over with a quiet nod.

"I'll call for the horse."

Heavy footsteps interrupted her thoughts, the familiar plodding of Lord Pryan. She thought he might pass her tent, already thanking the gods that he never ventured into conversations with her, when the crunch of his boots stopped. He didn't move for an empty moment, causing Cerra to catch her breath when the tent flap slid aside.

"Who's there?" She demanded, knowing full well whose voice she would hear.

"Lord Pryan." His voice was low and invitational. The flap whisked shut as she heard the heavyset Lord step inside, the creak and smell of a lantern swinging in with him. "I'd prefer you called me Oylay"

"Lord Pryan, I'd prefer to be left alone." Cerra had her guard up, tension heightening her perceptions. "I'm feeling … indisposed. I fear the food and the smell lingers. If you would, clear these dishes for me on your way back to your tent."

"After we talk, I'll send a servant. I thought to bring my own light, you see. Thinking ahead. It's what I do." Vanity oozed from him, as if his words were gold. There was a brush of metal on the table as Pryan set down the watch lantern and without leave, sat close on the cushion beside her. "You know, you're quite a beautiful woman."

"I wouldn't know." Cerra clenched a small pillow to her chest, looking away from his voice. "Please, sir, I …"

"I suppose you wouldn't." Pryan tried to sound companionable, as though he often found himself in the same position. "You must miss a lot. I remember being laid up more than a fortnight, my feet you know... very painful ... I hated that people made concessions for me like I was crippled, like they do you. That must bother you too." He paused, his voice a hand span closer and lower as though exchanging a confidence. "I think if you were able to see me, you'd be impressed. I've been told I'm a handsome man."

Cerra felt his hand settle on her thigh. Her stomach did a turn. "I'm sure you've been told that many times. I've often wished we were better strangers because of it." Her nerves caused her to move askant, to worm out from under his hand and he thankfully withdrew it. "Do you have some request ... some business with me? I do not want your company, so if ..."

"I can be quite generous." Pryan eased a little closer and replaced his hand on her thigh. "You'll find me a very generous man."

"I have no need for generosity." Cerra cringed. "I have all I need, except being left in peace."

"You misjudge me. I'm here to help you. I have influence with the Ducesin. You don't seem to be in her favor."

"If you please ... Lord Pryan ... I'm not at all interested in currying favors ... from anyone." She tried to lift his hand away. The man was pushing himself on her, a condition she found repugnant. His hand reclaimed a grip on her thigh. "There is enough to give displeasure in the world already, without you working so hard to give me more. It would best if you leave."

"I'm not through here ... and when I am, you'll be thanking me."

"I'm thanking you now, if it's praise you want." Cerra turned to face him, her anger growing. She didn't bother to keep her voice down. "Now leave! ... Before I also have occasion to praise the guards for their attention."

Pryan lifted his hand from her thigh but didn't move away. His voice lowered, sounding more dangerous and intimidating. "Linarest ... the Ducesin ... claims you advised her that I'm not to be trusted. I have no idea where you would get such an idea. I'm wealthy ... treat everyone like a king ... like they were my sons ... my daughters. I merely wish to change your mind."

"It is an opinion I was asked to share. Good that she shared it with you as well, for I can imagine silence is golden in your, 'family'." Cerra felt herself growling, furious at his intrusion and shameless advances. "My mind is changed by solid evidence ... and you don't need to make a point to come back with your evidence later, if you can find any."

"I'll leave when I'm ready." Pryan said gruffly. "I can see you're ... upset. I must say, you look quite beautiful when you're angry."

"Then, I'm going to be truly magnificent in just a moment." Cerra felt herself ready to yell out, but too angry to. "Leave."

"You're not talking to some bumpkin ... I know that's what you peasant girls are likely used to."

Pryan leaned in, trying to snatch a kiss on her lips.

"I said ... Leave!" Cerra's voice was near a shout as she turned and pushed at him.

His hand clapped over her mouth, forcing her down onto the cushions. "I said … when I'm ready!" His low voice snarled with determination.

She bit down hard on one of his fingers and shoved him back with a yell. Pryan muttered an angry oath and wrenched her arm behind her, forcing himself down onto her, his hand locked again over her jaw. He pressed himself close and grunted into her ear. "You'll like this better if you relax. Like I said, I'm a generous man."

Cerra, flamed with alarm, let out a muffled scream as she tried to knee him but he lay like a dead weight upon her, gross and unyielding as his free hand pulled up on her skirts. She tried to wedge her arm between them, churning and bucking her torso to evade his clenching arms. His hand felt wet and cold against her thigh and she tried to scream through his muzzling grip. Far from deterring him, her struggles seemed to energize him further, his weight pressing down as he clambered over her.

Chapter 38

Sinjin gathered in the mare's reins and directed his attention to the Jimalian horse lines, nearly in front of them and masking their approach to the camp. The traveler marched forward without hesitation or concern for the numbers. The assassin estimated there were an even two dozen in the company, odds that he found too rich for his liking. He didn't carry that many knives. The traveler was different though, and Sinjin doubted that any number would matter to him. The assassin could no sooner turn away from what was about to happen than ignore the moment of his death. A cringe went through him like a knife blade, knowing that the traveler was likely some conjuring of the witch and not of this world. He felt as though he was in the middle of some sorcerer's spell and the last words were being spoken.

The traveler's horse snorted with agitation, causing the Jimalian horses to shuffle and shift at their lines. He could see the obscured shape of the traveler approach one of the tents set at the edge of the camp. It seemed to storm with intensity as he disappeared inside.

"Hey what … what's going on here?"

A voice broke through the horse lines, a shadow of a man ducking underneath a tether to approach him. It proved to be an older man, unarmed and dressed in simple riding clothes, neither guard nor lord, no doubt the stabler. He looked ready to call for the guards. Sinjin slid his hand away from the hilt of his sword and held it up in a common gesture to 'hold the thought'. At that moment, a large falcon swept into the hellish glow of the cookfires, screeching alarm as shouts arose from the camp. For some reason, he grinned at the man.

"It will be worth your time to gather up Lord Pryan's horse … and make it quick. He'll be leaving very shortly."

Cerra growled and fought, trying to free her mouth to bite when she heard a familiar yowl, followed by an angry curse from Pryan.

Kamir! Cerra's heart raced.

Pryan swiped at the cat and Cerra used the momentary freedom to yell out and punch as hard as she could, connecting just below his nose. She didn't hit him with much impact, yet she felt the weight of him fall back as though being lifted away, a bloom of argent eclipsing the black of her sight, erasing the blank terror of Pryan as his mass was wrenched from her. Rage fell away along with his turgid weight, surprise churning the emotion into a rapturous joy.

Yutan! Did she cry his name aloud?

"Unhand me, you …" Pryan's angry protest was blunted into a gurgling swallow as he was lifted by the throat as though a trifle. The face that gazed at him was more than a man, a fire burning in dark marble, a vision of death. Pryan felt himself go slack in fear as the merciless eyes bore into him.

The demon's grip began to constrict about his neck as he was dragged roughly from the tent. Cerra clambered to her feet, the commotion outside raising as the camp stirred alert.

The low light of campfires whiskered his features in a hellish cast as Yutan turned to face the gathering camp. Temper began to torch his surface as the Queen's guards moved forward uncertainly. He lifted the Standish lord from his feet and growled, a rumbling noise that caused the Jimalian troops to freeze. Cerra emerged from the tent as the demon turned slowly, holding out the hapless Pryan like a warning, daring the Jimalian guard to come closer. Yutan mimicked Cerra's whistle, a sure call for her horse, though never took his eyes off of the Jimalian company, who hesitated getting closer, unsure of the apparition before them. He could feel the fires of the earth threatening to consume him as he struggled to hold back his anger. It was all he could do to not torch the offal in his grip. He tightened it as a shout bore through the red haze of his thought, either fear or lack of breath causing the heavyset lord to at last cease his weak struggling.

"No!" Cerra cried out, recoiling from the demon's seething emotion that flared in her thought. "Stop!"

'He will not die. Yet. Take to your horse.' Yutan's reassurance came into her mind as she heard the clop of Sugar's hooves approaching.

The screech of a raptor again cut through the din, soaring within the halo of firelight and circling the demonic scene, cutting down in a wide arc towards the figures emerging from the most ornate tent. The Ducesin ducked back as the raptor shot past her with a piercing cry, then elbowed past her guards, followed resolutely by her mute companion. She froze as the blind woman raised her hands in a shout. A chestnut horse, speckled white on chest and rump, trotted in from the darkness, the night air eclipsed by the glowing figure whose demonic eyes compelled fear.

Linarest watched in disbelief as the blind woman mounted, a dark shadow leaping to the saddle in her wake. The red-haired woman turned the mount and galloped into the darkness, past the horse lines and beyond the glow of the campfires, the large raptor screeching and soaring in her wake. She focused for an instant on the hawk, it's essence and angry cry, a warning from another age.

The igneous creature appeared to gain size as it held Pryan out like a severed head, scanning the camp with a pitiless scorn. The sculpted stone surfaces of the demonic form seemed fused with live magmas, a heat pulsing deep within its core. Its eyes at last fell upon the Jimalian Queen. Shadows and densities meshed to reveal the heated bone and muscle of the beast. Linarest was held aghast until the demon turned away, breaking its torturous hold on her gaze. Gasping, she gripped the shoulder of her mute companion while croaking for someone to shoot at the departing apparition. A round of arrows flew at her command, though the shafts burst into flames well before they found their mark, the demon following the blind woman's path.

The witch had passed at a gallop, no doubt headed for the spring, but Sinjin couldn't take his eyes off the traveler as he approached, the heavy Standish lord a pittance in his grasp. The traveler seemed to have grown in size, traces of the camp's firelight fracturing around him like a storm. The assassin turned to the ostler, who was caught up with the same astonishment as he led Pryan's horse, a cantankerous mare, away from the lines.

Sinjin gathered the reins from the ostler, the traveler's eyes blazing with a cold anger that seared his features. Sinjin was glad the menace was not directed at himself as the limp Pryan was dropped to the ground at his feet, discarded like a waste-bag. The traveler, or his avatar, continued on without even slowing his step. Sinjin quickly heaved the drooping lord across his horse, tying his wrists in a hobble about the horse's neck. The ostler had an unsure look about him, his eyes darting back to the encampment on the other side of the lines, where the company was making a lot of noise, but as yet, no attempt to pursue the apparition.

Sinjin swung up into his saddle and yanked his mount's head around to follow the traveler. If it was the witch's magic, she provided a memorable show. He still had the same unchar-acteristic grin on his face as he turned to the ostler and flipped him a gold piece, caught deftly by the old man.

"I said it'd be worth your time. I think you'd better see to your horses."

The old man nodded with a crinkled smile and turned to the horses, joggling and shuffling anxiously at their lines. He directed his attention back to the Ducesin as he came into the fireglow of camp. She was signaling her mute shadow with a twist of her fingers as their eyes followed the wake of the departing fiend with grim intent. She barked orders to her Pursar before she addressed the Captain of the Guard, a sure sign that they were striking camp immediately, then glared in his direction. There was no need for a command. He would have the horses ready.

Chapter 39

Her horse slowed to a trot soon after they were clear of the Jimalian camp. Cerra didn't know which way she was going, only that she was on the caravaner's road. She let the horse have her head, for Sugar's gait was even and direct, as though she were heading for the barn. The familiar weight of Kamir nestled in front of her was even more reassuring, for he seemed calm and unconcerned. Her extraction from the camp had left her disoriented, her directions confused, though freedom from the sterile Queen was an enormous relief. Lord Pryan's attack on her was another memory she'd rather leave behind her.

The argent glow of Yutan striding up to her gave her encouragement as well, proving Sugar had fled in the proper direction. A whisper of wind in tree leaves and the scent of fresh water lay in front of her. Just as the horse slowed, she caught the sound of other horses coming up from behind and a knowing call from the raptor above.

'We are at our camp.' Yutan's voice came through to Cerra with the lovely touch of his mind. *'There is another present. You will know him.'*

As though cued, Sinjin rode into the bower leading another horse. He came alongside her as she brought her mare to a stop, bearing the rare flush of excitement. "I would have planted myself for days and paid dearly to see that."

Cerra knew the voice instantly. "Oh my. You trail us again. I admire your persistence."

Sinjin caught the radiant glow of her smile, wondering if it was her witchery or sincere. The woman had identified him immediately at the sound of his voice, though it had been years since she had heard it. He was unsure how to respond, her unfocused blindness gave him nothing to control or intimidate.

The large hawk that had been circling settled down silently within the stout branches of the oak, instantly camouflaged by its welcoming embrace.

The traveler circled Pryan's horse and cut the thongs holding the Lord to his saddle. He lifted the Standish lord and slammed his wrists one by one into one of the oak's spreading branches. As Pryan sagged on the branch, a light step came from behind the tree, a cinnamon-haired girl appearing as though shredded from the bark. Her presence baffled Sinjin, for he had no inkling of her approach at all. His training and arts prepared him for the mortals he encountered. Mystery and power surrounded the blind woman like the lances of the gods.

Her demon black cat bounded from the horse to inspect the shadows as she dismounted with ease. The horse paced slowly forward to the stone basin, Cerra holding to the saddle as it walked. When it paused, she released her grip to kneel carefully and took a sip of the spring water, cupped in her hand. Sinjin was captivated watching her. She finally played a wet kerchief to her face, easing the concerns etched there, then stood to face him, visibly more relaxed.

"We've met … twice … though never properly introduced." Cerra looked in the direction of Yutan, then back and smiled warmly. "Since you're alive, I can only assume you mean me no harm."

Sinjin cast a glance over to the creature he only knew as the 'traveler'. The man had lost the spectral glow, which seemed to reduce him to a more appropriate size. He returned his gaze to the witch.

"My intention always is to stay alive." Sinjin gritted. "Your guardians are persuasive."

"Then I'm glad you've come to a like mind," the witch replied with sincere warmth.

The blind woman's confident cheer would captivate many, drawing them into her circle, further evidence of her witchery. At the moment, her life was held beyond his reach, a relief, as he had plenty reason to spare her. Sinjin scratched at the old scar, then nodded at the figure hanging limp from the tree.

"It is my good fortune that the Standish Lord is my assignment … and that's enough. I'll be gone before the sun is done rising and trouble you no more."

"You're welcome to him." Cerra was relieved. She had been in the overbearing Lord's company far too much. "A hard man to ignore but, I daresay, worth the effort. I imagine he has much to answer for. If you're the hand of justice, you might take him to the Stands first, to make an accounting."

"That is not for me to decide," Sinjin replied. "The Stands will likely not have an opportunity to find judgement."

The blind woman gave him a puzzling look. "I can't say I'm surprised."

"He owes my patron a great deal of gold. The coin he left was not worth a tinker's scrap. I expect he has it with him."

"Oh, I doubt he traveled with any large amounts of gold." Cerra replied.

"I would like to determine that myself."

"You'll have to go back, then ... though, if I were to venture a guess, they're already breaking camp. But I can save you a trip, for I assure you, there was no large amount of gold within the Queen's party."

"You seem convinced, yet I find your certainty suspect. You may have missed something," Sinjin growled, making an oblique reference to the witch's lack of sight.

"You're quite right." Cerra chuckled. "I do miss a great deal. I haven't lost the capacity to ask questions, however. The horse-tender of the Queen's company was most informative." She thought of the journey with the Standish embassy to the Vale, the laden horses with Lord Pryan's 'supplies'. "The amount of gold you suggest would have required an extra team and created an additional strain on the company, don't you think?"

"I am the better judge," Sinjin insisted. "I rely on what I can see to make my beliefs."

"You must have remarkable eyes," Cerra countered, a pensive look crossing her features. "I have to rely on my heart for something so deep as that."

"Then what does your 'heart' tell you?" Sinjin made an attempt to keep the skepticism from his voice. He wasn't used to treating with someone who knew of his reputation and yet conversed so openly. Curiosity tempered his patience.

"If it's the gold you seek, I would look first for a trader in the Vale who deals with jewels and stones. There cannot be many that could support a large transaction." Cerra wrinkled a complicit smile. "I'd wager there's only one."

Sinjin did not need to review a long list in his head. There truly was but one merchant in the Vale d' Houri that would accommodate a large amount of gold, the Paso Reblais, not one, but three brothers, well-ensconced within the private cartel that governed the Vale. He had seen the Standish lord visit their shop. If the gold was in their hands, it would stay there forever.

"There is just the one as you say." Sinjin's answer was dismissive. "There is no future down that road. The Standish Lord, without that pile of coin to prop him up, is not worth the effort to cross a lane, much less taking days in tracking him."

"You're welcome to check the Jimalian troop if you like, but you might consider it's no longer gold. Look instead for jewels, something much easier to transport."

Cerra gave her unruly hair a twirl behind her shoulder. Sinjin looked down the caravan path in the direction of the Jimalian border, then back. The witch was confident and tight with her knowledge, doling it out piecemeal should he ask the right question.

"I may be good at my craft but I am not one to waylay a score of royal guards. There would surely be three left ere I die."

"Only three left to acknowledge your skill. It'll be a short rite in your honor then." Cerra smirked. "But I can save you both the ceremony and effort, if you wish."

"How so?"

"The Lord Pryan is a very guarded and suspicious sort. He trusts no one, for he believes that, as he's a liar and cheat, so too must all men be. He would not trust another to carry such a burden. Take one of your many knives to the puffed sleeves of his surcoat." Cerra paused, shivering as she thought of the oddly hard edges of his soft, heavy weight pressing against her. Her intuition led her on. "Mind you check his waist belt, as well."

Sinjin walked over to the Standish Lord, hanging by his wrists from the branch, his feet kicking weakly for purchase a handspan above the ground. He pulled a blade from his hip sheath and held it to Pryan's stomach, regarding him as though deciding which way to filet the hanging gibbet.

"I … I can make you rich." Pryan wheezed. His head lolled, though the venal eyes remained, looking for kinship.

"I am already rich." Sinjin's knife shot up in a slicing motion, like a fishwife gutting the catch. The padded middle of Pryan's garments separated and clumped to the ground, as a thin red line traced the silk of his shirt. "My knife … it slipped. My apologies."

The assassin bent to the wrap and slit the seams, exposing pockets of jewels carefully wrapped in velvet pouches. He looked to the blind woman, who stood patiently as though waiting for a conclusion. He regained his feet, circling the hanging Pryan. The Standish lord tried to follow him through half-lidded eyes, exhausted.

"C-cut me down. You … you don't know … who you're dealing with."

Sinjin took a step closer to face the Standish lord, the knife held at his throat.

"You are wrong. I know exactly who I am dealing with. Which mouth are you speaking from, *wenk*, big or small?"

With another slash, swiping across the front of Pryan's neck, Sinjin cut at the vest, severing one side then the other at the shoulders. The surcoat fell to the ground, two more thin slits of blood appearing below the cuts on Pryan's shirt. Squatting, the assassin picked at the seams with the point of his blade, exposing two small pouches on each side. He opened the pursed end and slid small, finely cut gems into his hands that glittered like green fire.

"You found them all." Cerra had heard the tickling sound as the gems spilled into his hands. "I'll wager there is more than the value of the gold."

Haviana and Sinjin both looked at Cerra with surprise. Yutan remained in stoic vigilance, much like the black cat that glared intently at Cerra's feet.

"I'm no judge of fine gems but I would not take the bet."

"Then you have all you need."

Sinjin scooped up the bags of jewels and stood facing the suspended Lord. "It's as well I don't defile this place by slaying him here. He might even make it to Oskara."

"B-big … mistake." Pryan's face, wedged between his uphung arms, was blanched white with strain and fear as he choked out another plea. "I … c'n … help you … make you rich."

"You repeat yourself. I have no need of these baubles." Sinjin tossed two of the bags towards Cerra, as though not worth his effort to retrieve. "I don't need any of this. How is it you can help me?" Pryan gurgled at the flagrant display, the bags that were flipped so haphazardly bore the Tenigran crest.

"He sounds horribly distressed." Cerra turned to Haviana. "Does he need some water?"

"He needs to be a touch closer to the ground. He's hanging from the tree." the young girl replied, loud enough for Pryan to hear. "Deservedly so. *Shest* … not distressed enough as I see it."

'He will not die.' Yutan bespoke her mind, the simple terseness of his thought always without artifice.

"Well, we can't leave him hanging, can we?" Cerra stepped forward. Sinjin backed away, respectfully giving her room to face the suspended Lord. There was no longer imagery emanating from him, the bold colors depleted. "You once referred to business as a game, Sir Pryan. I'd say you've lost the game. I think you lose most assuredly when you don't respect the other opponents in the game, the other players. There isn't anyone left to cover your cards if need be." She heard a slight rumble, the unmistakable sound of hooves. She turned towards Havi. "We'll likely have visitors."

"There was a herd not two leagues away. They must smell the spring." Havi offered.

"If they gather here, the Cherros won't be far behind," Sinjin grumbled, curious how the young girl knew the location but the witch's acquittal of the Standish Lord brought his attention back, addressing Pryan as though there were an attentive audience behind him.

"He was very intent to establish a lucrative and I imagine, very exclusive, trade. He inflated the value of both his wares and his worth with both parties and used gold ... cadged from worried Standish dukes and due to your benefactor, I imagine, else you would not be here ... to pay a debt he could not avoid." Cerra turned towards where the assassin stood. "Some of these proceeds rightfully belong to them ... the Jimalians. I wager they haven't been reimbursed by some artifice or another. He was freely in their company of course, so the bulk of his riches belong to them and he likely made even grander promises regarding repayment."

"*Mmph.* I have not the scales nor the eye to value his stones." Sinjin replied, a trace of sarcasm in his voice. "You might be the better judge, you measured the value of this fake far better than most."

"A piece of glass ... easily seen through." Cerra smirked in spite of herself. She was worried about his fate, though Pryan had likely never considered the repercussions of his actions on others. "What is to be done with him?"

"Do you want to know?" Sinjin answered harshly. "If it were up to me, I would leave him staked to the prairie as food for whatever carrion beast could stomach it. It isn't for me to decide ... nor worry about."

Cerra turned to catch the blue shimmer of Yutan in her sight. He looked back in stoic silence, a tacit agreement that larger fates were at play.

"You're right. I have no need to know anything beyond my own fate," admitted Cerra reluctantly, facing the suspended Pryan once again. She didn't want to carry that weight, nor the burden of revenge. There was none in her heart and she didn't want to feel the thread of his passing. She could hear Pryan's breath, shallow and labored. The tremors in her feet were more telling, the pulsing earth of an approaching herd. "At the least he shouldn't suffer more at our hands. Please … cut him down before the horses arrive. His escort is here and capable and the Lord's only weapons are empty promises. I daresay we've heard them all."

She stepped back as Yutan came forward to grasp the thick branch, releasing the grasping shoots that pinioned the Standish Lord. The heavy man dropped limply to the ground, reluctant or unable to stir in his exhaustion. Sinjin wasted no time, for the man was drained of any fight. He propped the heavy man up on his horse as before, bracing him swiftly to the saddle with an expert hobble.

The cantankerous mare bucked at her reins as the growing thunder of hooves pulled up near the oak, rounding and restless without the benefit of their riders. Cerra eased back towards the bole of the tree as they approached with caution and began circling the spring.

"We can safely say the smell of the spring caught their attention." Havi grinned.

Sinjin scanned the horizon, dim in the morning light. "The Cherros won't be far behind their herds. I have no need to delay and await their presence. Vermin such as this attracts unwanted attention."

"Then you should take the opportunity to leave while you can." Cerra turned to the assassin. "Fare you well. Your path at the least returns you home."

"I have no home," Sinjin replied, trying to keep a rough edge to his voice. Staying in the vicinity of the witch seemed to weaken his resolve. "Just places familiar."

There was a slight tremor in the ground, a subtle vibration that was seconded by Yutan's thought. *'They come. Riders from the north.'*

"I think you should find a more familiar place while you may." Cerra cautioned, then added thoughtfully. "I would wish you well, yet I think your success is another's sad end. Find a home if you can."

There was no immediate answer, just a long pause where sorrow hung in the air, a sublime silence that was brief and clipped. She could feel his eyes on her when he mounted and raised her hand in farewell, imagining that he did the same. She heard no movement other than the turning of horses to gain the caravan track.

"My name is Sinjin." An admission, a secret reluctantly given. The assassin allowed himself a rare smile as he turned away. The two bags of jewels remained untouched at the witch's feet. A king's ransom in esmeraldes. He rubbed the scar on his leg. It was a suitable offering for the favor of the gods.

Haviana approached Cerra as the assassin cantered off to the west, the Lord Pryan tied and straddled across the reluctant trail horse's back. "I fear there might be more to deal with," she said quietly. Cerra could sense immediately that the young girl was unsure how much she should reveal, spoken in the same breath as young secrets.

"What? We've no secrets here. *Pssht* ... you've witnessed one of mine I daresay." Cerra felt an odd relief that at last, someone other shared her most private treasure, that of Yutan.

Haviana was in awe of the man's presence, the simmering power that manifested such tenderness toward the blind woman. The Sybelline mother would have to know of this. Or would she? The events were still unfolding. "One of the Queen's company is … one of us … a Sybelline. I wouldn't have been certain but then, I felt a change, a sense of when a shaping occurs."

"A shaping … like becoming a falcon?" Cerra observed quietly as she leaned against the young girl. She felt a flush of comradely pleasure from Havi. "You make a most marvelous bird."

"I …"

"We'll both keep our secrets here, won't we?" Cerra interrupted, giving her hand a reassuring pat. "But tell me, before the Cherros arrive. The Cards … they once belonged to the Sybellines. It stands to reason the thief is one of them."

"Yes. But it is the shaping that confuses me." Havi admitted. "We can tell when a Sister is 'in form'. It was only when the Standish Lord was in his stocks that I felt it. Now I'm certain. I know of many shapes … we know far more than we can accomplish … but nothing I've experienced. An older Sister might understand." She considered for a moment the dynamic influence of her father and the rare command that he had of the animal and person within. "I should mention that men can be Sybellines, though it's rare. Whatever I felt, it was watching us, and not far away."

Cerra felt the short hairs on her back rise, for even Yutan had not gained notice of the observation. His awareness quickened with her sudden alertness as Havi added with surety. "It's gone now."

In the fragmented light of dawn, the figures under the tree had appeared dark and anonymous as they chattered with the incessant energy of crackling intent, directed to one gibbeted to the limbs like a succulent feast. Watching, the carapace twitched as there was temptation to draw nearer with a few more angular steps. It began to move then paused mid step, the sudden knowledge that it had somehow been recognized halting the motion. Instead, it turned to the east, slipping away in quick, vanishing flicks, scuttling across the soft, windblown grass like a cloud-cast shadow.

Chapter 40

Little time was available before the Cherros arrived. A faint rumble that might be mistaken for some distant storm, came from the upwind and a nicker from Sugar confirmed Cerra's notion that the riders were near enough. The exposure of Ser Pryan and the subterfuges of the Queen and her company, had given her much to think about. Without the guidance and ear of Captain Ferriman, she felt like a valuable book destined to be left unread.

"Havi. I wonder …" Cerra trailed off, unsure how to continue as she attempted to sort through what she knew. The young girl was an intriguing glimpse into a world she didn't know, much like the introduction of Yutan into her staid and protected life had been, just a few years past.

"Wonder what?" Haviana was quick to engage with Cerra's thought as though each one would be a new revelation, an education the equal to her school.

"Could you deliver a message? I don't know how to ask, for I don't know the extent of your … range or abilities … if I may be so bold."

"Be bold. It suits you." Haviana smiled. She doubted many would have the blind woman's steady nature given the trials she had faced. "A message sounds easy enough, but hurry and ask, for the riders are on the way and I don't want to … be here, so to speak … when they arrive."

Cerra lowered her voice as though there were someone to overhear their vital secrets. Yutan kept his attention directed towards the north from where the Cherros approached. She could sense his urgency. "Can you find the Lady Katarin? *Er* … from the skies?"

"Easily done … I know the sight of her well." Haviana responded eagerly. Her senses came alert, focused on a new prize.

"I don't know where she is now, though I can guess by now she's returned to her estates in the Stands … and not shopping the markets of Abbysin or Oskara as she had wished. *Heh heh* … I would sooner join her rather than here … an unknown road yet in front of me. The threat of war would keep her away from such a trip in any event, for she values her people and property a great deal."

"What shall I say?" Havi asked, anxious to depart, for the sounds of the Cherros approach was beginning to thrum the ground.

"Tell her I'm well." Cerra gave the girl's hand a squeeze. "And then there's the matter of Ser Pryan and the Jimalians. Listen carefully."

The Cherros cut swiftly across the sea of grass, spread out in three ragged '*Vs*', their robes fluttering, appearing in the early dawn like a squadron of geese in flight. Lean and bronzed by the weather, their faces bore the bold stripes of their Horse clan, augmented by the colors of their house, those bestowed by the wives and mothers of the riders. Their hooded robes were a celeryed green that melded with the grasses of the steppes, turbaned or tented to their heads, though often worn loose, allowing their long black hair to whip free. Their saddling was thin, leather and weave chased with the colors of the rider, the bits for the horses no more than a light halter to guide.

The nomadic horsemen roamed at will across the steppes, which they regarded as their sovereign territory, paying tribute to neither Abbysin nor Jimal. They measured their wealth in the herds of horse and grazing beasts that ranged the wide Alatian steppes, stretching across the northern shores of the Sultan Sea.

The caravan route was a necessary scar across the Cherros lands and the caravaners paid their appropriate tithes. It was also a convenience that the route claimed nearly all travelers across their domain, leaving the wide grass seas largely free of intruders. The lone oak was a landmark along the route, three days southwest to Oskara and three days east to Maabi, the bustling seaport that lay at the mouth of the Darii River. The tree was an easy marker for the caravanneer route and a reminder to the Cherros that they neared the fringes of their territories.

Long rays of morning light, softened by the early haze, were cast low beneath the lone oak as the Cherros approached. A hawk gave out a forlorn cry and lifted from the tree as Seredan raised his hand to slow the other riders to a trot. It was not the sight of their missing horses grazing contentedly that gave him pause, it was the lone figure sitting next to a sculpted spring that pooled beneath the tree. He made a fist to halt the troop, which cantered quickly to his side.

"Thane. Those are your charges. Have them rounded to herd back."

"They've not wandered here before, have they Seredan? Count me among the moon children if you like, but there hasn't been a spring here before either … has there?" Thane had a wary look about him. "That's what led them."

Seredan's eyes had not left the figure sitting beneath the tree, a woman with an unruly crop of flaming red hair, wearing the simple hood and cloak of a Cherros.

"You're right." Seredan spoke without looking at Thane, recollection claiming his vision. "The spring is new."

A red-haired woman had been captured years before within the plains. He had been there. She was blind and capable of enormous powers and had left their camp in a Cherros robe. He swallowed sharply. It was her, looking in his direction with unseeing eyes and a benign smile.

"The woman. Touch her not." Seredan said, his voice clenched, signaling the rest to remain on their horses. He trotted carefully forward and dismounted near the pool. The red-haired woman spoke to him as he approached her.

"Mana." Her voice was low and inviting, using the traditional greeting of the Cherros, which meant the same at either the beginning or end of a journey.

"Mana," replied Seredan cautiously. "You've anticipated us."

"Who else on these lovely plains save the Cherros?" She smiled at him warmly. "Your presence is a boon to all that cross your lands."

"You have crossed our lands before." Seredan made it a statement, sure of her response.

"Yes, I have. I confess it was a wonderful experience, all in all." The blind woman paused for a second, the memory brightening her features. "A horseman … Jadon, if I remember correctly … was most accommodating."

Seredan had little doubt of the woman's identity and the mention of one of the Council of Riders confirmed it. He himself had witnessed her sorcery, an uncanny confusion of nature, though she had left the camp in peace as was her promise. Two velvet bags lay near her feet and he stooped to pick one of them up, which weighed heavily like a child's bag of rounds. He poked apart the cord and peered in, the glitter of polished green glowing back like adder's eyes.

"Esmeraldo's" he whispered, entranced by the verdant glow that needed no light. He peered at the blind woman, questions racing through his thoughts as he looked around. A witch of legend appears at a spring where there was none … and with a fortune of gems laying at her feet.

"I sense a good tale." he offered, hoping for a simple explanation, but knowing far more was in store. There may already be spells attached to the stones for all he knew. He slipped the knot on the bag and dropped it with the other. "There are two bags at your feet. Gems. If they had the value of horses I would be King of the steppes, and maybe Oskara too, though I hate that place. Where did they come from?"

"Oh my … they must have been forgotten. The man was in a hurry to leave. His companion owed the Jimalians money, so I suppose it might rightfully belong to them."

"Who is this man?" Seredan tried to sound angry, yet the mysteries of the woman invited curiosity.

"I didn't see who it was," Cerra returned smoothly. "I expect I can find a way to give it back to the Jimalians, as that's where I travel ... the Queen perhaps, though I doubt she needs it."

"Ask about the spring." There came a voice from behind. The riders were getting restless, casting joking asides as they surveyed the scene. Seredan faced them, his sharp features grimacing as though they were breaking wind.

"Quiet! Remember your manners." He turned back to the red-haired witch. "The spring. It's nice ... but first I would know what you are doing here. If I had not seen you before, I would insist on taking you to the Camp," he could nearly feel the air crinkle with energy at the mention and hastily added, "... and that I will not do."

"That's well and good, for I have no intention of going," Cerra agreed amiably. "As for what I'm doing here, I've lately parted company with the Jimalian embassy. Just this very morning."

"Their camp is three leagues away."

"I suppose it must have been something like that. I'm also guessing it's vacant by now."

Seredan watched her with growing curiosity. Her brief appearance among the Riders had sparked both folktales and legend. A well had appeared at the edge of the desert near the salted mirror in years past, bearing the mark of this woman and again a new spring rises from the ground where she has appeared, bearing jewels like one of the Effreti, the spirits that live in the world deep beneath the roof of the Assai's sweeping prairies.

"And where are you bound?"

"It's my heart's desire to return home. As I think of it, I would most surely enjoy a visit to the Cherros' Camp. Your women are the treasures of your tribe. *Heh* ... the food alone would make the visit worthwhile. You're fortunate to call it home." Cerra's head dropped a little as she considered her destination. "Despite my early exit from their company, I fear I have another appointment with the Jimalian Queen. As I said ... that's where I'm to go."

The blind woman exhibited a compelling innocence, her presence a tale yet to be told. Seredan felt as though he was on the brink of leaving a foal unguarded, spelling certain death at the teeth of the direwolves that emerge from the northern forests in the Spring. "Safrasco? I like it less than Oskara. Forgive me for claiming the obvious, you are alone ... and blind. I cannot leave you here, unescorted."

"I'm quite content with the escorts I have." Cerra replied. "My horse and cat have never failed me." *'And my love,'* she added silently.

'There is nothing to fear here,' returned Yutan. *'I would feel it.'*

Seredan stooped again to retrieve one of the pouches, his men murmuring with expectation as he stood and extracted two of the esmeraldes from the bag. He drew it shut and held up the small green stones as a reassurance, a worthy trade made for the benefit of all.

"Two stones. A token of the bond between us." Seredan

glanced around to the other riders. "Gradan. Take your hand and the horses and keep them near. Send a rider to the Council with the message that we've taken a contract of passage, then wait for our return."

He turned back to the red-haired witch, a mixture of innocence and mystery milling about her. He was never one to stifle his curiosity. "I will escort you to Safrasco …with the Hand that follows me. You may trust your cat … and your fine horse … but I don't trust the road to Maabi. Bandits prey on small companies in the hills before the road makes its descent to the harbor. They are not to be seen until too late."

"I tell you true, I have no fear of them. You do me a great kindness to offer, though."

Seredan well remembered the encounter with her, a tale still told. The blind woman had easily held a score of Cherros at bay. He did not doubt her powers. He let out a small laugh "*mmph* … I understand. I think instead it will be a service to others, to not die unnecessarily because of a bad choice of quarry. They will not attack Cherros under any circumstance. To scratch one of us is to cut us all. And now … you have a trust." He swept his robe aside as he knelt on one knee with the two pouches of stones, laying them carefully in her hands.

'It is unnecessary.' Yutan's voice was clear in her head.

'As long as I have you, I fear nothing in this world or the next. Yet, if I have learned one thing, it is to accept the help that is given freely. Or reasonably cheap.' Cerra mused with a dash of humor, trying to put Yutan at ease as she considered the majics that had transpired. The metaphor that occurred to her seemed more than appropriate. *'We are in an unknown game and we must view carefully*

the cards that are dealt us.'

Yutan gave a thoughtful concurrence and lay quiet, patterned into the ground surrounding the oak. Cerra felt a wave of appreciation course through her, one that returned in a diffusion from beneath her feet.

'I love you.' The earth heard and acknowledged, a wave of pleasure that had no words.

Seredan watched as the woman's face seemed to glow with a sublime beauty, a smile that was at peace. The other riders were watching equally transfixed, even the skeptical Thane. Fate and destiny were entwined with the witch like the curled chaos of her strange red hair. Great things would follow her footsteps and Seredan found himself wanting to bear witness to those tales. When she spoke, her soft, low voice added to the spell of enchantment that seemed to pass over them all; one that called them to guard her with their lives.

"You are too generous. Truly. You turn from stranger to friend. I am grateful."

As the diviner waited, the knotted border surrounding the
arena sought new alignments with the braid, runes and
sigils finding more secure bonds and alliances. When the edges
locked together with a fresh arrangement, threads of gaseous
light wormed out to illuminate the cold remnants of the last
reading. The boxes came alive and shifted, moving the peak
card to the center, while those that had lain in pyramid fashion beneath it, drifted with fired inks to assume new positions
surrounding it. The center block pulsed like a live thing, demanding placement of a card.

Dutifully, the top card was drawn and *Nepethe, Queen of
Roses*, was laid within the mark.

The Numinon shuffled its thin, crisp pages, stopping to
reveal, '*Threats*' heading the page in elegant script. Within the
narrative, long passages revealed the nature of each threat and
their guiding principles. The Book turned a page without bidding, to reveal a pattern of cards interwoven as though each
spoke to the other with hidden lines, shadowed glimpses of a
spiders' web.

The arcane references and chartings continued as another
page turned, more complex than before. When the book finally
revealed a new page, presenting another choice to be made, a
square was illuminated on the parchment of the arena. The

next card was drawn from the deck and, for a moment, held face down within the box. Upon the reveal, the graceful hand of the seer clenched as *Nuith, Queen of Quills*, was displayed in the arena, once again in direct opposition. A second box illuminated next to her, demanding placement.

Once again *Abbadon* was revealed with the draw, the indigo inks limning the horrific ruler of the mythic underworld, glowing with molten freshness under the light of the lone candle. A slight murmur of alarm escaped the Seer's lips.

Two more placements opened up on the arena, one directly aligned with the *Queen of Quills* and her frightening ally, exerting further pressure upon the central mark.

The card was drawn with little enthusiasm and placed within the glowing box next to the Queen. The *9 of Quills*, a new power revealed, though of the minor Arcana, yet especially powerful as it resided in the same House as *Nuith*. The Numinon flipped briefly to denote the quality of the card which showed eight crossed quills, straight and pointed like arrows in the background with a large dominant quill in the foreground, where the moon showed at the nib and the sun represented as the golden spray of its feathered end. The seer's hand traced the writing below the illustration while its words were absorbed.

> *'The Quill is ever damaged, a warrior wounded and the*
> *eight behind stand ready to replace him.*
> *The energy of the Nine represents not a short burst*
> *of quick ideas, instead the long and slow release of*
> *Endurance.*
> *The 9 reveals a situation that tests*

its influence to the limit.
Its companion and support shall have a very different task
in front of them, requiring all resources to see through.'

The final card, the *3 of Quills*, was placed off to the North-west corner where the sign of the Quill rested in the border of the arena. The trey, denoted the *'Messenger'*, again was positioned as though out of play. The presence of the persistent *Nuith* and the demonic *Abbadon*, was far more worrisome.

With the cards in their spots, the Book flipped pages once again with a fluttering shuffle, finishing at one marked *'Protection'*. Below the titling script, a selection of cards with the powers necessary to thwart the challengers was revealed, their small depictions appearing like imprimaturs and seals. A number of the images were dull, as if the impressions were old, eroded by time from the thin paper. The remaining icons shone bold and vibrant, as though the ink was still fresh from the pen that laid them down.

The seer considered the resources the page revealed, the lone candle guttering down in drips the only measure of time. The wick of the candle continued to burn lower, passing below its dripping remains that lay piled along the molten rim, like ruined castles of wax. The light was nearly spent before the seer finally made the choice. *Babalon*.

At once, the Numinon shuffled its pages to reveal the nature of the selection, while two marks appeared on the arena, wavering to either block *Nuith* or *Abbadon*, depending on the placement.

Babalon resided within the *Major Arcana Cardinale*, an equal in power to the dangerous *Abbadon*. Her arms lay open and

bespoke of appetite and lust, her bare-breasted figure entic-
ingly arrayed in purple and scarlet drapes that fogged her
curves. Dark hair swirled outward in seven beckoning waves.
Her wrists snaked with gold and and an amulet of green light
glared like a beacon between her breasts. In her right hand,
an orb shined, the Eye of One glowing from within a vulvar
flower. Behind her, the wheels of prayer turned, marked in
ancient signs by their ruling passions. The card ruled '*Desire*'.

The qualities of the art were detailed, descriptions of the
symbolism surrounding the enticing figure explained. A passage caught the Seer's eye as the trailing fingertips paused.

All have a carnal side. Babalon knows if Desire is
repressed, it becomes as much a burden
as relenting to it would be.
It is the working of Babalon to believe what we want to
believe when we are under her influence.
When those are lost to Babalon in this way there is a
transformation of energy
and her victims die to the moment.

At last the card was drawn and *Desire* was placed in the
arena, laid to block the *Queen of Quills*, thus deemed the most
dangerous card in play. The inks of the arena flared around
it.

Chapter 41

Flying high over the Gate at the first light of dawn, the gyrfalcon let itself be caught in the vortices of air that swirled outside the ragged opening of the chasm. Its sharp eyes were focused on the colossus of stone carved at the entrance of the Black Gate, whose eternal gaze emanated kindly to the flat reaches beyond. The familiar semblance entranced the great raptor as it circled, then at last sent it on, the great bird breaking free of the toroid winds with lazy flaps of its white-speckled wings. The gyrfalcon soared up the canyon to the fertile plains of the Stands, head scanning below in constant search. Waving from a short oaken tower, a banner with a sheaf of golden wheat laid upon a green field at last drew the attention of the raptor, a fierce memory that brought it circling down from the heights.

The manor of Katarin Moors was enclosed on a large estate, surrounded by the barns and cottages of tenants and servants. It was bustling with activity, all involved with the late Spring laying in of crop and freshening the grounds from the winter's mulch. The raptor circled without a sound, finding an appropriate roost within the beams of the bell tower. It tucked in its white-speckled wings, rocking to a rest as it surveyed the wide courtyard. Patience and keen eyes kept pace with the morning until a slender, elegant woman appeared in the courtyard below, recognition sparking a fluttering of feathers as the bird adjusted its perch. The gyrfalcon watched with singular intensity as the woman crossed the broad expanse, unremarkable in her dress from the others contained within the walls. She talked briefly to a pair of crofters, then disappeared within the stout wooden structure that bore the pennant of her house. With a flex of broad wings, the gyrfalcon lifted from the bell tower and glided within a whisper to an opening beneath the pennant.

Haviana shed the memories and will of her second self, a dissolution and acceptance both. The articulation and thought of her human spirit took hold, finding her fingertips instead of pinions, her attentions diverting from prey to observation. The darker shadows lost their luster as her eyes adjusted quickly to the room, one given over to the presence of the one who controlled the surrounding lands. Light, measured footsteps marked the approach of the woman. Haviana was certain her intuitions were correct. She never missed a target once she had established her aim. In anticipation of the Lady Moors, she stood waiting like a maid, bowing when the woman walked into the room. She spoke first, hoping not to startle.

"Lady Moors … I'm sorry to intrude but …"

"Oh … lands ..." Katarina caught her breath for a moment but recognition changed her sudden surprise. "Havi! By the gods … what are you doing here? You look tired. Is everything well?"

She rushed her questions as she hurried to embrace the young girl. "Here … have a seat." Katarina pulled a cord as Havi allowed herself to settle on the corner of a low-slung divan. "I just rang the kitchen … they'll bring up something … now tell me … you have news of Cerra, I can see it in your face."

Haviana considered that Lady Katarina could see no such thing, yet there was little other reason for her to be there, unannounced. She smiled, relieved that her welcome came without issues. "Yes. I have news of Cerra. More exact, I have a message from her."

"Oh … knowing that she's well is a lift to my heart … she is, isn't she?" Katarin worriedly searched Havi's face, who smiled and nodded. Relaxing, Katarin came to sit next to the young woman, plainly eager to know more. "Where is she?"

Haviana could see that Lady Moors fully expected to hear Cerra was close by, for disappointment and concern was obvious when she explained the circumstances, concluding with her best estimate. "I imagine by now she is nearing Safrasco, likely a few days away."

"Oh my." The import of Cerra's whereabouts was not lost on Katarin and she urged Havi to continue, not wanting to form conclusions before she knew what she could.

"She said that she remains in the service of the good Captain and there are two things you should know. One is that the Abbysin are not behind the sorceries that have afflicted everyone. While she wasn't certain of the identity, all signs point to someone within the Jimalian Court." Havi sought to deflect any questions the Lady Moors might have about the powers involved with the Book of the Numinon, so she made her second point quickly. "The other is that Lord Pryan was in their service. Was. He's been captured for his frauds against the Abbysin. He won't be returning to your lands."

Katarin closed her eyes, shaking her head. Many of the lords had been taken in by Pryan's schemes. The news that their arms and fortunes both, were commandeered in some fashion rankled deeply, raising even more war-like rhetoric among them, especially Lord Westre, who had led the effort and contributed the most. He had already reclaimed Pryan's holdings, as was his due.

"It's good to know." Katarin felt some relief. "I have only a few allies that aren't willing to engage in open hostilities against the Abbysin. Everyone needs to hear this."

"Not from me, Lady, I …" Haviana wanted no part in being the center of official attention. "Please don't ask me to …"

"No, no. I agree … that wouldn't do." Katarin patted Havi's arm briefly before standing to pace, forming her thoughts. "News of Pryan's arrest will quell a lot of talk for the time being. If I know the Lords, their first concern will be the possibilities involved with getting their funds restored."

"That isn't likely." Havi offered. "I believe the Jimalians were meant to be paid with the proceeds. It appears they were as ill-used by Lord Pryan's debts and promises."

"I expect as much. Still … it will quiet the Lords and hopefully squelch their talk of war. They will find few volunteers if they have neither arms nor a rallying cry." Katarin returned to sit next to the young girl. "What of Cerra now. Her news is good but there is more. Else she'd be here to tell me herself."

"Lady Moors … I wish I could tell you." Haviana admitted, concern softening her voice. "I think her fate is uncertain."

Clearly Lady Moors did not know how to take that news for she stood again, obviously worried. A light tap at the door came and a cook's maid entered, giving her a momentary distraction.

"Some food and drink." Moors announced unnecessarily as the cook's maid sat her tray down on a customary sideboard and left without a word. "Rest here for a while. Is your horse taken care of? I heard no news of your arrival."

Haviana appreciated the open concern and hospitality of Lady Moors and eyed the tray of kitchen bits, gathered from what must have been breakfast an hour or so earlier. It looked appetizing and wholesome. She knew that if she lingered for too long, the questions would exceed her capacity to answer. "If I could rest here a little ..." She felt a little guilty feigning exhaustion, though it gave the opening she had hoped for.

"I'll leave you to the breakfast, then. I want to pen a message to the Prime Council immediately." Katarin had the look of one who has already formulated her next moves, eyes focused on an idea and on nothing within the room. "After you rest we can talk further," She came over to Haviana, who stood to accept her open arms. There was an unspoken inclusion of the missing Cerra in the embrace. "Thank you."

Haviana felt both like a wise woman and the young girl that she was, puzzled by the mix of feeling. The acquisition of knowledge and the power of only a few words could obviously carry a great weight, heavy enough to change the fate of nations. She realized it was a weight that should never be taken for granted and she felt older for the knowledge. The directions given by Abbess Susinna were the first grains of that weight and she felt certain she would bear more in the future.

The Lady Moors gratefully left her to the parcel of food on the sideboard, vowing to return once her messages to various counsels were dispatched. Havi sampled the tray, eating as much as she dared, wishing to linger but knowing she couldn't. Although weary from flight she wouldn't lay down, fearing that if she did, for even a moment, sleep might claim her. She could rest later, in the thermals of the afternoon.

Unnoticed by the occupants of the busy estate, a large falcon flung itself from a window of the keep and swept in a wide circle away from its walls, where it gained altitude with determined flaps of its wings, heading in the direction of the Black Gate.

Chapter 42

Wind played upon the grasses of the prairies with sonic brushstrokes, tracing among their blades and whistling over their awned crests in constant movement, creating layers of sound that painted slopes and expanses in passing. The breezes swirled in wide caprices about her and Cerra was thankful that it was generally at their backs, offering a gentle nudge or insistent push to aid their progress. It never ceased to talk to her, whispering when it nudged or moaning when it pushed, calling to mind obligations or insinuating lures of home. Riding across the expanse was at times peaceful, though often exasperating in its tedious monotony, almost like sailing an ocean of grass.

The constancy of the wind delivered such an insistent voice that the animals kept their silence in the face of it. So, ever mindful, Seredan had described them as they appeared; the antelope and karkadann that grazed at the tender shoots, the snakes and rodents that burrowed within the low-tufted grass forest of the plains. His stories helped give the emptiness pockets of life. Yet increasingly, she missed the dynamic sounds of her home: waterfalls cascading down the cliff, the meadow between the lakes that attracted artfully noisy creatures who splashed in the waters and reveled among the flowers. For the moment, it was Sugar's steady presence and Kamir tucked next to her in the fore of the saddle that supplied a welcome attachment to the far away comforts of her home.

Yutan drifted behind her, a tall trail of dust that swirled and kept pace like a djinn, causing the riders to stay on edge and alert. If nothing else, she enjoyed the pace the Cherros set, much livelier than the dignified progress she had experienced with the Jimalian court.

The Queen's company had apparently abandoned dignity for speed, as the riders soon came upon two wagons that the Jimalians had left behind, containing their tents and regalia.

"I wonder why they left all of this. Surely a boon for someone."

Cerra gathered the sense of urgency inherent in jettisoning such a valuable load. She chuckled as she thought of the woman's arid nature. "I imagine the Queen's blessings go with whoever finds her generous gift."

"*Heh*. If we were returning to our Camp, we'd pick it as clean as ants on a bone. Another insect gets the pleasure. The spoor marks your Jimalian troop taking a route east. From here it is two days ride to Maabi along the caravanner's road to the south … but only if you were to ride like a Cherros. A slow caravan, maybe four days. A Queen you say? *pfft*" Seredan chuffed with broad humor, citing a rather mannish phrase while inspecting the fractured path to the east. "It depends on the softness of her saddle. *Hah!* Make it five, at the least. Once in Maabi, the towers of Safrasco … another two days beyond to the northeastward. If they cut across, they save much of the distance. We near the edge of Cherros' lands but all know of the narrow defile leading down to the lowest of the Chain

Lakes. Our horses teach us the secret ways. *Hsiuh* … I don't think this Queen is quite so generous with her belongings. It is faster, but a path most unfit for carts."

'The earth still bears the marks of their passing. The Cherros is correct.' Yutan confirmed the rider's conclusion.

"They must be in a hurry to return home. I can't fault them for that. At the very least we won't have to concern ourselves about overtaking them." Cerra observed cheerfully. "Frightful company, really, save the horse-tender."

"What would you have us do?"

"Why, we should take the faster course as well. We will be done with this whole affair that much sooner."

The Cherros must have anticipated her answer, for she heard two of the riders immediately gallop off, where they would range ahead, scouting the open steppes along the route. She turned, facing behind to watch the argent form of Yutan hover and twist as he rose from the dried grass and dust of the caravan road. His blued image shone radiant in her sightless eyes and it ever gave her a broad smile.

Seredan watched the blind woman as she pulled her wild red locks tight to her head, raising her chin as if bathing in the breeze of a passing djinn. The other Riders agreed she was a powerful witch, a storm in a flask. Even her chocolate mare bore the smattered white marks of the ghost. To a man they were equally impressed with the power that seemed to circle about her. The curiosity of the Cherros and her unfailing kindness, drove them on to discover what tale was unfolding in their midst. Seredan did his best to describe their surroundings as they progressed, though he often considered she had already created a vision that far exceeded the world he could see. In a way it helped him reassess what he thought he knew as he worked to create the scenes for her.

"The peaks of the Jimals are visible now. They rise from the haze afar like the towers of the gods."

Cerra thought of the grand cliffs near her meadows. "The gods indeed make such a marvelous place as the mountains."

"I don't envy those that live in those closed spaces." Seredan disagreed. "Too many spirits hide in the stones and lurk in the forests. Broad horizons reveal all."

Seredan clicked his signal to advance and the small party resumed their gait, leaving the well-worn caravanner's road for the open grasses. The steady rumble of hooves as they crossed the plain confused Cerra's sense of direction, content to hold to the pommel and let Sugar follow the lead of the other riders.

Without the trappings of wealth, the Cherros traveled quickly, even curbing their speed to accommodate their blind charge. The meal at night was simple, torn pieces of dried meat pounded with currants and chokecherries. Cerra despaired at the lack of kafi, vowing never to leave home again without it. All the tell-tale odors describing her surroundings when she woke seemed to be leather, sweat and horses and she was quite sure it must be her own scent.

It was not until Seredan halted the company in the early afternoon that she could sniff the cool dryness of rock and stone. Everyone was tense and quiet at the sound of two horses approaching with a lackluster gait. She eased Sugar next to Seredan's horse.

"There's something the matter." Cerra stated, feeling the alarm from the men.

"We have arrived at the defile. The outriders, Sethin and Darinor … their horses return. They do not." Seredan shifted in his saddle, his voice grim. "A Cherros does not lose horse except in death."

Yutan and Cerra shared the same thought to look ahead and the sudden torrent of grit and wind indicated his passing.

"Do you think it is the robbers? We are far from the road to Maabi." Cerra had a sudden jolting thought that the Jimalians had left someone in ambush.

"If robbers, they are far from their profits and they are fools to match. A Cherros does not leave another behind."

Seredan signaled the company forward. Cerra sensed a close formation around her in a protective stance. Ahead, the spacious play of wind across the grasses whispered insinuations as it began trailing into the rift that would take them down to the Chained Lakes of the Jimals. The company paced forward expectantly, the horses alert and snorting their agitation. Sugar felt ready to bolt, her haunches tight as she trotted. Cerra patted the mare's neck, as much reassurance for herself as the horse.

"There now, Sugar. We've been through worse, have we not? … And not with the pleasure of such a company to protect us." Cerra imagined the rocky defile in front of them from high aloft, as Yutan or Havi might. "We have our eyes above as well."

The scent of pine and pelt, along with the chattering of birds flitting among the first ledges of rock, felt like a return to home after the empty sounds of the steppes. The horse's hooves sent their own pattern echoing into the air, revealing a canyon of majesty as they ventured further in. The wind twisted and turned, coming in subtle puffs. The way was not straight, as it weaved and curled like a snake. She doubted the Cherros would be able to see very far distant and they were obviously reluctant to send another ahead to scout.

Chapter 43

As the last inkling of the prairies disappeared from view in the deepening canyon, a low voice insinuated itself inside Seredan's head; demanding his attention, imploring him to stop. He drew the company to a halt after a snaking turn.

'That's better.'

The intonations he heard were soothing and richly textured, a voice that had never known distress. Seredan looked back at the witch. She was one to keep her own secret gaze upon the world, though she had no attention for him at the moment. It wasn't the blind woman who bespoke him.

'You have traveled far. Too far. You must be tired.'

The voice was closer. Ahead. He spun back and saw a woman sitting on a shelf of rock, not ten paces away. Her hair fell in waves of brown and gold, her face the light color of sand. How had he missed her? Stark grey clothes were sculpted tight to her form and glimmered with seams and marks that blended with the color of the rock.

"Cherros don't tire of the ride." Seredan said with a trace of contempt, though the woman cast an attraction on him that cooled his scorn.

"I shouldn't think so," replied the blind woman beside him. "I'm not even tired. Yet."

"Did you not hear … ?" Seredan looked quickly at Cerra

and then back at the apparition, which smiled as though it understood a deep secret between them.

'I am yours alone.'

"No … I didn't hear …" The blind woman turned her head quizzically as Seredan urgently glanced to his men. Each of them looked unfocused into the distance, enamored with unseen curiosity.

"We have trouble." Seredan growled aside to Cerra, then caused his horse to plunge into a tight circle. "Cherros! *Alala!*"

His rallying cry broke the trance, as the men's horses shifted nervously in the narrow gap. They looked at each other with uncertainty then around at their surroundings, as though seeing them for the first time.

"Maybe this route wasn't the best after all." Cerra murmured, feeling danger in the air, which smelt of petrichor and the ozones of lightning. The tensions that stirred the Cherros had also stilled the chittering and noise of the small creatures that poked among the rock.

"*Sardit!* This is a Cherros path." Seredan cursed before raising his voice. "Thane! What do you see? Speak! Do you have a turd in your teeth?"

"I think we should stay here awhile. See if she comes back." Thane leered.

"Who?"

"The woman over there." Thane jabbed a finger off to his left, irritated. "Why else did we stop?"

"She was on the rocks, just there." Cerra heard another voice behind her and disagreements regarding the location quickly arose from the rest of the men.

"What did you see?" Cerra quizzed the Cherros leader urgently.

"A woman." Seredan seemed caught in wonder for a moment, recalling something he couldn't quite believe. "Even without tribal marks … beautiful."

"All have seen her." Cerra remarked quietly. "Yet none in the same place. One? Or many?"

"I don't know."

"Where are the two missing? Has there been a sign?"

"No. Not yet. They would have …"

Seredan stopped as he was scanning the steep walls of the defile. He saw them, each captured in a niche, calcified in the embrace of women who appeared much like the apparition he had seen moments before. The statues gazed back at him with a satisfied bearing that mocked him with their superiority.

"There!" Seredan carefully gripped his bow, then with the abrupt suddenness of a striking adder, whipped an arrow from its sheath and fired. The arrow flew true to its mark, yet passed beyond the woman, shattering on the stone behind her. She didn't move nor change her gaze. She desired him. She was pleased with his marksmanship. The anxious words of the blind woman at his side cracked the spell.

"Seredan. Tell me what you see."

"Trouble."

He fired another arrow with the same lightning motion, this time directed at Sethin, the rider cast in stone beside the strange woman. The arrow struck at the man's throat as he had aimed, yet bounced away, a twig cast at a statue. As the arrow clattered down the rock, rumbling could be heard ahead and behind them, walls of stone beginning to fracture and collapse in ponderous slumps. The slides rumbled and shook the earth, sending gouts of dust billowing up the draw, trapping them within the narrow straits of the defile. The horses jostled and pranced seeking escape. Seredan worked to control his horse, though already he could see the men were again attracted and emboldened by visions that he now failed to see.

"*Alala!*" Once again, he shouted, the ululating cry meant to break the spell.

Cerra shifted with the others, jostled in unsure directions as the waves of dust washed over them from the slides. '*Where?*' she reached out to Yutan in her thoughts. The rumbling of the slides roiled with the thunder of him circling above. 'Where are they?'

'*I cannot see … them.*' The demon's thought reflected '*all around*', a dizzying notion she was trying to dispel among the jostling horses and the shaking ground. '*There is but one.*'

'One?!'

'*The center.*'

Yutan could be maddeningly succinct at times, yet she knew he was telling her exactly what he saw. A thought flashed of a beetletrap flower's core, colorless petals surrounding it, a poisonous shrub intent on netting them. As she turned her head, images became apparent, seven of them, encircled by light and laid out in a pattern. Whether her imagination or the sorcery seeping through the darkness of her vision, she couldn't tell.

"We are trapped in the draw." Seredan gritted, his horse

jostling Sugar as he turned. His voice changed to curiosity. "*Uunnhh* … she is over there now."

'*Here. I am here for you.*'

The same smooth contralto voice echoed from the shrubbed image directly in front of her, reassuring and succoring, though Cerra felt only the comforting tones of empty promises.

"What do you want?" Cerra called out. The Cherros were beginning to dismount, leaving their horses with quiet disregard. Seredan was still mounted beside her, yet he had become still as though preoccupied.

'*You.*' The response sounded like temptation, a lure of promise, though it sent a shiver down Cerra's spine, knowing it was a voice that only she could hear. Kamir growled and shifted in her lap.

'*I can give you anything you desire … if you follow me. And you must.*' The voice was honeydew vine water, sugary and tempting.

Cerra's mind raced. This was a majic born of the cards and laid in her path. Everyone had ambitions and cravings. To say she had none would not satisfy the spectre in front of her. She must answer the challenge with one of her own, glad that she couldn't see the vision in front of her.

"If you cannot give me what I desire, what then?" She spoke as an equal, demanding, as if daring the vision to admit herself to this world.

'*Nothing is beyond me.*' The voice continued to insinuate itself, luring her forward.

"I can tell. You radiate power." Cerra wheedled. "But I still fear you can't help me. My life has become a burden, for my deepest desire is a quest … one that I have devoted my life to discover. Look where it has driven me, so far from home. If you can't satisfy that quest, there's no call to follow you, and … sadly … I must continue on."

Cerra felt the angst of her journey, giving honest emotion to her voice. There was no scorn in the spectre's reply, just compelling allure.

'If I cannot fill your desires, I am powerless to hinder you. I can satisfy all.'

As if to illustrate her point, the world swam open in front of Cerra's eyes, the canyon walls clear, the colors bright and vivid. The woman stood in front of her, pulsating with force, naked in her beauty.

The sudden intensity of the vision overwhelmed Cerra, nearly causing her to topple from her horse. She gripped the saddle pommel, shaking with wonder and dread, as she raised her sight to the thunderous skies. The stormy cumulus of the demon, of Yutan, wavered above her. She could see his beauty shining through the roiling currents that held him together. As if in supplication, she clenched her eyes shut to the illusion, afraid yet desirous that her vision had truly returned. Emotion gripped her as though another life had been lost, a wash of anxiety that had her eyes watering in its pain.

In the throes of her agony she could tell the men had disbanded, for the horses were milling without direction. Seredan was still close to her side, murmuring. A mixture of frustration and misery drove her as she grabbed her walking stick from the saddle sleeve, slid it out and thwacked him hard, catching him just under the ribs.

"Don't look at her, wherever she is. Avoid her eyes!" Cerra

hissed, the sudden, fierce burst of speech staunching her tears. She felt a surge of relief, hearing his grunt as he regained his senses. "Look to your men. Quick. Ignore what else I might say."

Cerra turned to face the chimera, eyelids carefully braced shut and raised her voice, though she was sure the apparition would hear even if she whispered.

"Your invitation is ... worthy. In another time I might have ..." She heaved a sigh, shaking her head as if to banish the thought. "Circumstances change, do they not? My ... my most secret desire has been burning within me since I came of age ... to hear a truth, urged on me from one wiser than I. Perhaps you are the one to answer ... that my quest can finally end."

'You wish not your sight? Open your eyes. A greater gift you could not ask for.'

The words pulled at her chest, a groan she could not allow to be heard. The enticement persisted, though Cerra sensed a note of confusion in the woman's voice. She fought the turmoil within, unwilling to open her eyes and allowing in proof that her vision had been restored.

"A gift for another age. It is who I am now." Cerra said quietly, an admission to herself she knew to be true. When she spoke again, it was a plea, truly felt if only to remove the temptation. The anxiety in her voice was unfeigned. "A greater gift?! ... the answer to this puzzle would be a far greater gift, relieving me of a madness I can no longer bear."

'Ask, then.' The apparition's reply was short and dismissive, as though Cerra's time was running out.

"The question was told me, thus ... a koan presented by a

wise man who claimed the answer would reveal a secret to my true happiness." Cerra paused, fascination and craving heavy in the air between them, then intoned the phrase carefully.

" 'What we caught, we threw away; what we didn't catch, we kept. What was it we did keep?' … You see? It makes no sense to me … it beggars my mind."

'That is nothing.' The apparition scoffed, losing the sultriness of her voice.

"It must be a mortal root of philosophy I fear … I truly need to know. It has become an obsession I can't ignore. If you can't help me as you promise, then you can't satisfy me. *Awww*" Cerra insisted, disappointment evident in her groan. She kept her eyes tightly closed. To see the world again would be more than she could bear and she feared it would be her undoing. Suddenly, angry at the blunt temptation and sensing the hesitation of the apparition, she pressed back, like she was bargaining at the market with a seller she didn't trust. "These men are in my company and my responsibility. They aren't yours to keep in any event."

'They are becoming one with me. All must succumb to their desires … there is no other way.'

"*Hah!*" Cerra retorted. "You've done little for mine. Nothing, in fact. Answer me now."

'There is no answer. Consider another.'

"If all is knowable, then all must be known. Without an answer you must allow us to continue. As you can plainly see, I wish nothing else …" Cerra choked slightly, " … not even my sight."

'It … it …'

The unspoken thought died as it was uttered by the wraith, a brilliant notion lost in a boisterous room. Silence blanketed the narrow confines of the defile, leaving a vacant space that stripped her of dimension. Like her cottage after a snowy day, the air was muted and heavy without even the sound of a bird. Had she lost her hearing as well? If she hadn't felt the vibrancy of the horse beneath her, she would have thought herself swept away by the phantasm, though the insinuating presence could still be felt.

'Where?!' Cerra felt like reaching out stupidly with her hands to feel a wall that wasn't there as she cried out to Yutan with her thought.

'There is one!' His voice rang through the deadness like a shout, a cry of warning. *'Around you!'*

Cerra was frozen, afraid her ruse had failed as the apparition surged forward into her clenched eyes, a chill wind passing through her as the vision exploded. She shivered violently, the cold like a death rattle that shook free then dissipated about her in a thin steam that could hold nothing of substance.

Cerra's ears cleared, popping like a violent storm had passed. The sounds of nature returned as though slowly invited, giving definition to her surroundings. Kamir turned and shifted in her lap, pressing his head against her stomach.

'You. You remain.'

'What's left of me.' She felt drained and wanted to sink from the saddle. She leaned forward, her breath shallow, not enough for a sob. Unclenching the lids of her eyes, she opened them carefully, feeling a couple of tears escape with both a sense of relief and regret, as the familiar emptiness of her sight

remained.

She held herself up straight in the saddle after a moment, a new breath to fill her lungs and steady her resolve. The chasm began to refocus as she located Seredan ahead of her, heard shouting encouragements to his men, their horses scuffling and shuffling with uncertainty. The vividness of the vision remained though, a dizzying reminder of what she lacked.

'It is who I am.' She reminded herself, much as she had told the apparition. She felt a surge of power come from the demon, a measure of his understanding and recognition of her torment. She stroked the sleek fur of Kamir, a wistful smile curling her cheeks as she shook her head.

Seredan returned to the horses in the company of five others. The two riders he had initially sent ahead to scout the defile would remain ever as guardians, as well as two others, now etched indelibly in stone along the chimneys of the steep ravine.

"We have lost nearly a Hand of Cherros in this place." Thane grimaced, gathering up the reins of his horse. "I don't know whether to curse it or claim it for our own."

"It is claimed by the Cherros that linger. They'll ignore your curses like I will. Gather their horses," Seredan replied evenly. "Tabbor, the passage ahead is choked. Check the ravine beyond the turn … there was another slide behind us. See if it's passable."

Tabbor nodded curtly, still with a curious furrow on his brow, puzzling the chain of events and finding no answer. He mounted and trotted off to inspect the passage. Seredan turned to face the red-haired woman. He wanted to blame the loss of his men on her, yet he couldn't, for he had led them here himself, knowing that the woman was a pike to attract lightning. If not for her, he may as well be guarding the narrow chasm to the Lake with the others, with no one to remember their passing.

The witch sat on her horse, facing the sky with a look on her face that was a mix of deep sorrow and sublime joy, conversing with voices unheard. The skies above her broiled with storm, a djinn that quaked the thunderous dark underbelly of the clouds. It was moments before the rider cantered back around the near bend. His grim look told the tale. "The way behind is blocked too. Worse, I think."

"We may be doomed here after all." Thane grumbled. "Did you see the ..."

"You've old teeth." Seredan shot back with a snarl, scanning the rim of the defile. "We can climb our way out. Merely find the right chimney."

"And leave the horses?" Thane complained, without enthusiasm. He saw no alternative either.

'We are blocked.' Cerra implored Yutan, who circled above her like a swirl of stars. Would normal sight reveal anything as majestic?

'Can you clear the path?'

Yutan rumbled, a churning she knew as agreement. *'As you wish.'*

She leaned toward Seredan. "I really doubt I could make such a climb. The spell ... the phantom ... is gone. With luck, it's destruction will lift as well. We have but to wait."

"Luck?! *Bah!* There is no luck in ..."

As he spoke, lightning coiled about the billowing cloud, the dark underside shedding its weight among the strikes. The ground shifted with tremors beneath their feet as lighting cut at the ground beyond them, slicing into the rubble clogging the narrow defile.

Plumes of expelled dust appeared to scoop great slabs of rock in their embrace, dividing the debris in the defile like tall grass before a bull. Gouts of earth and stone rose up the cliffs, coiling in towers that expended themselves in wide arcs which threatened to fall back to earth in a thunderous roar. Waves of cindered dust, driven by the impact of the lightning, showered the riders, forcing them to turn their backs to the cataclysm.

Seredan wheeled around, trying to watch the dissolution of the spell if he could. The witch remained untouched and serene as earth and rock shuddered into place, arcing across the narrow divide like a stone bridge cast by the gods, holding apart the walls of the canyon.

The shaking subsided, dust and wind swirling away in vortices that rose again to the threatening sky. The Cherros regarded the red-haired woman with a mixture of reverence and awe. She sat silent, as if waiting for a new event, though nothing further happened. The Riders looked at each other, bird song and yelping announcements from the canyon walls returning to the muted air. She turned to Seredan with a bemused smile on her lips.

"The air is fresher. The way must be open."

"What of the spectre?" Seredan eyed the blind woman carefully. Sorcery lingered in the air like a storm that threatened on a clear day, though there was no distress marking the woman. Instead, a calm satisfaction lingered, such as he had only seen in old men, who had found wisdom past the frailties of the young. Even her cat had relaxed to curl within the pocket behind the saddle horn.

Cerra let out a little chuckle. "The gods aren't like us. That one didn't know the occasion of lice."

Shadows played across the stone walls, driven back and forth by the pacing form that paused in transit to view the arena, before resuming its nervous passage. At length, the candle began to sputter as it neared the edge of the cup and another was lit to replace it.

The cards lay face down, the grimoire lying beside and awaiting the judgement of the deck. The fresh taper laid an even, weak light close over the arena, which wavered as the figure sat, ready to view the results of the invocation. The pattern that evolved from the outer circles was much the same as before, the first mark shaping on the right quarter, requesting a card. The figure hesitated for a moment before slipping the top card from the deck and turning it face up on its spot, guarding the Eastern badge near the Deck.

Nepethe, once again revealed, occupying the same position established in the last invocation. Immediately, the next mark emblazoned itself upon the arena, taking a weak position behind the Queen. Another card was drawn, revealing the steady *7 of Cups*, the sole ally to be revealed as the inks on the parchment around the *Queen of Roses* lost their fire and dried.

From the West side of the arena, tracings shot out from the Quill and Western badges, leaving a mark waiting to be filled. The Numinon did a brisk shuffle, opening to the page of

Babalon. The seer drew the card requested and turned it with majestic surety, only to falter as *Nuith, the Queen of Quills*, was revealed, bold as if painted with new dyes. The lacquered card was slammed down on the mark with disgust. Only then did the seer notice the inverted position of *Babalon* on the page of the grimoire.

Two more marks came to simmer in the arena, adjacent on either side of the dangerous *Queen of Quills*. Dutifully, the next card was revealed and laid to the mark above her. As *Nuith* remained, so too did the fatal harbinger of the unknown. *Abbadon's* deadly image glowered back, illuminated with dark life by the candlelight. The last card was drawn and laid on its mark below the Queen.

Again, the *9 of Quills* showed itself, the matching suit indicating a staunch ally of the powerful Nuith. The Grimoire flipped its pages, combing deeply towards the last of the book before it stopped, allowing the seer to assess the continued import of the Nine, '*Endurance*' scribed in the ancient Jimalian hand.

> *The 9 of Quills provides for latent or hidden powers to*
> *become awakened and applied towards the practical.*
> *The Nine further represents a continued directed will*
> *power, which has been exerted over a long period of time.*
> *Despite all flux and change. the challenged persevere,*
> *finding strength within exhaustion.*

The seer turned to study the lay of the cards. Attention diverted, the Grimoire flipped ahead, stopping at a blank page that began etching its message as the candlelight flared upon its surface. The script lay itself like a question.

"Counter"

Runes and patterns ran in ghostly sepia inks beneath the surface of the paper as it waited for a response.

Chapter 44

Far below in the greened fields, ranks of groundlings lay adjacent to the sparkling divide of river, lined like ants and bristling with activity in their ordered forms. The gyrfalcon rotated her head forward to the soaring peaks that rose above the short plains beyond the river. The wind pushing against their walls would lift her higher and for a long span, the gyrfalcon allowed it, quietly soaring over the river dividing the armies of the Abbysin and the walled nests of the groundlings. Like moths gathered into their cocoons, they lay clustered tightly together with their tents and bags, hidden within the walls as well as sprinkled in patches in the narrow valley beyond.

The gyrfalcon tipped a wing, spilling pressure and finding balance to the left, dropping in a wide circle that would allow for an effortless route around an abutment, a soaring tower of stone, an aerie unassailable and majestic against the mountain that rose at its shoulder.

The raptor tightened the arc of the turn, picking up speed as she dropped. The great tower held an attraction, a detail that the bird's sharp eyes could not yet spot, a notion of change and being seen. The gyrfalcon dared a cry as it banked sharply along the north side of the tower. Swept balconies, turrets and domed towers graced its walls, save one, where a thin rope of web held fast to a balcony that clung to the north side, ever caught in the shade. A slick movement caught the raptor's eye, its head pivoting with aiming precision. Blackened spokes whisked away in the shade of the opening, the feeling of change dissolving with it.

Banking away and curving out over the sparkle of the lake, the gyrfalcon again sought altitude with the broad sweep of her wings, as much for safe flight as to escape the feeling of venom from that shaded place. Its eyes darted to the northwest. Along the far shores of the broad lake, a different beacon wavered, a familiar storm that lived under its own spell. The white-speckled raptor shifted its flight, taking measured strokes with its wings as it crossed the still airs above the lake, eager to rest after its long flight.

Cerra did not know what to make of the avatar that had confronted them in the narrow passage leading to the Chained Lakes, only that it had been meant to stop her. Forever. The powers of the Sybelline deck were showing themselves, regardless of who was turning the cards. The apparition spoke of desire and Cerra wondered when or where her desires had changed. Vision was a gift, as was the life continually around her, a life she had adapted to. Her inner vision created a world with paints of her own invention. It was a world that created her. *'It is who I am.'* The brief window of sight was already receding into a dizzying memory that lay like another vision she had painted, a scene to be marked and stored like a rare and precious herb she rarely had occasion to use.

She rode in quiet reflection until the smell of the lake drifted into the chasm, long before they were able to leave the narrow winding passage. The odors reminded her of her own cabin with its tiny lake, the images of which had become shaky and irresolute in her mind. Feeling the presence of the water freshened the memories and added to her mood. She reveled in the fresh musk that filtered in the air: trees, wet rock, … and fish. Cerra scratched Kamir behind the ears to make sure she had his attention.

"Smells like home, doesn't it? Surely there is widemouth in the lake, maybe even a goldfin."

Cerra was enthusiastic about a change of diet and when they had passed through the last of the canyon and the lake was before them, repeated the suggestion for the benefit of Seredan.

"Cherros are warriors, hunters, and horsemen." Seredan snorted, adding a small chuckle to soften his remark. "*Hmmpff.* We do not fish."

"Well, I do … though I admit I'm much better at fishing than I am at catching!" Cerra exclaimed brightly. The expanse of the lake felt open and airy after the close confines of the defile. "Still, I'm game to try … I may even catch one. I'll certainly, 'almost catch' a big one. We are able to camp here, are we not?"

"We can make camp here." Seredan agreed. "It is yet another day's ride south to the end of the lake. And just paces away is a likely spot. It is apparent the Jimalians have taken to the northern edge of the lake. It is not a faster route to

Safrasco, though they avoid the Abbysin army, who are said to be parked at their doors."

Cerra thought of her choices. She felt like she was being moved about like a piece on a gaming board, or … a card in play. The visions of the players that invaded the imagination of her sight had those qualities. Havi had made it clear that it was the sorcery of the Cards plaguing events, though if she was in play and didn't know what she was to do, how would the seer know what to expect? The thought gave her hope.

"I was told that the worst choices make the best tales." Cerra scrunched her face as though she tasted something sour. "There will be a good story no matter the direction."

"It was the threat of a good story that drew me in." Seredan admitted. "If the tale isn't done, then I'm not either."

"In the meantimes, there's dinner … and I'm not one to wait!" Cerra chuckled. "Could you have a one of your men gather some branches, whippy, thin ones like willow or vine maple. A rotted stump will yield a nest of grubs. I have no hook and string … and I assure you, I'm horrible at the spear. *Heh!* But I wager I can cage a fish in the time it takes you to boil a yam."

"I'll get your sticks and set Thaden on building a hot fire … perhaps engage him in a wager." Seredan snorted, not doubting the woman's mysterious powers.

Cerra was as good as her word. The grubs, along with a few shreds of the horsemen's cured meat, made enticing bait. She shared a little of the cured meat with Kamir, who patiently observed her efforts as if knowing a bigger, more savory prize awaited. She set aside her Cherros robe and hitched up her skirts to take the wonderfully squishy steps to where the woven cage could be placed. She thought the shallows, close to where she'd heard the stilting pecks of a heron, to be a good start for placement. Almost magically, the basket snared a set of angry perch from the reeds, even before the Cherros had settled their horses. She re-laid her trap and had another caught before she could clean the first two. There were still a few herbs tucked away in her bag and she was easily able to sniff out a nearby cache of lavender. That led her to quickly to some pennycress and young curlydock. There had been cattails by the trap and she tapped her way back to the spot, counting her steps as she went.

Cerra was sure the horsemen were amused, yet they respectfully held their banter while she filleted the fish and poached her catch in a shallow pan over one of their fires. There was more than enough for the company to share.

Seredan had watched the surety with which the blind woman had gone about her tasks; movements based on memory rather than sight as she paused and cocked her head slightly, gauging her next motion. The unruly mop of red hair marked her as touched by the gods, though her easy manner reminded them of their own cherished women. Fish was not a staple of the Cherros. Neither was the regular company of a foreign woman, yet she had long ago made them forget their normal traditions of meals, as the women ate separately. Seredan already considered her tale one that would take many nights to tell and well-laden with surprises.

The different fare brought some grunts and laughs but then agreeable smacks as the pan was passed around, leaving it scoured. Kamir had his fill of the freshmeats and was dozing by the fire, if Cerra had to guess. She sat back against a well-placed rock, picking at her purse to find the pouch of sweetleaf.

'*There is no time like after a good meal to delay decisions,*' she chuckled to herself as she lit her pipe. Cerra felt some of the aches of the ride fade as she let her thoughts drift to Yutan. '*Whichever way I am to go, I am grateful that you are here to give me strength.*'

His presence, a churning eddy of dust and storm, had drifted with the small troop. She longed for his touch, an embrace. The fire of him always gave her strength.

'*You would not be here except for me. There is no choice but to finish.*' Despite the stolid nature of his reply, she knew he was right and could feel his devotion finishing the thought.

'*I'd be bored silly, if not for you.*' Cerra smiled inwardly, enjoying the opportunity to tease him a little. '*And very likely quite content.*'

The sky rumbled softly as the demon responded.

Cerra let the occasion of a proper tea rest in her mind as she considered her options. While the royals played at their games, the wonders of the world continued unabated. She felt small and inconsequential. Kamir pushed against her then jumped to curl into her lap.

"Not content to sleep by the fire, are ye? As if I need a reminder there is always one smaller." She took another puff on her pipe. '*And you … are you content?*' Cerra cast her thoughts to the demon. '*You are both maddeningly close and impossible to touch.*'

'*I am all around you.*'

She smiled with the airiness of his thought. A demon of the elements, he reflected the mood of the ingredients that infected him most. The air and water soothed him, while his strength and temperament shone most when earth and fire held him heavily in their sway.

'The winged one is in the air.'

Cerra thrilled, a wide smile passing over her when she heard. Havi had returned. Not long afterward, Yutan took to the lake, shedding himself from the airs over the water in a shattering storm, fracturing the night sky with lightning strokes, appearing to the Cherros as feared Hellions, the mythical firebrands that could burn the steppes with their fury. Cerra knew he would sleep deeply, enfolded in the womb of the lake, a spirit alive and a lover she could not compete with, nor did she wish to. After her experiences with Yutan, she had come to understand more of her own intuitions, as though learning how to hear new sounds. The water and trees had long spoken to her, though she had only sensed a few of their thoughts. Now, she heard them much more distinctly. The occasion of witnessing the Void had sharpened all of her senses to keen proportions.

Curled up away from the light of the fire, her head resting on a saddlebag, she was near sleep when Kamir hopped from her lap, jarring her awake. A slip of movement caused her to raise her head, the start of curiosity replaced with the buoyant tread of Havi as she settled down next to her, light as a bird finding a limb. Cerra didn't need the calming touch of the girl's hand on her shoulder to reassure her or hold her silent. She pressed Havi's hand with her own. The young girl leaned in close, a soft voice to Cerra's ear as Kamir wove at the girl's knees with a low purr.

"I cannot stay … nor be seen. So, you know … the Lady Katarin has your good will." Her voice lowered further as if divulging a secret that shouldn't be overheard. "Armies lie in the fields ahead … one like a fat fox waiting for its prey, the other burrowed in like scared rabbits behind their walls. That isn't the worry for me, rather a great tower. Our Sister is there … and not at all what she seems. Sister … *shtt*… I say 'sister', but still can't guess man or woman. Sorry." Havi sounded both too young for the experience and hardened by it, a grim new piece of knowledge. Cerra could feel the tension in the girl's bones, like Kamir feels when ready to spring. She had a host of questions though knew it best to let the girl avoid the scrutiny of the Cherros.

"You're a most efficient messenger." Cerra whispered. "Go. I'll sleep even better knowing you're near."

Havi gave one last touch to Cerra's cheek, then slipped away as silently as she came, a fluttering that defied steps and aroused no more than a cursory glance from the nearby Cherros. Cerra slipped back into sleep as easily as Kamir returning to his curl against her.

The next morning, matters seemed clearer, her route decided. Directly following the Jimalians felt like endangerment to the Cherros, who had placed their allegiance in her hands and had already paid the price of four men. There was no risk to any of them at the hands of the Abbysin. If she was indeed a card at play, she'd be wise to add some strength to her suit.

Taking the trail south along the lake reminded her again of home. She let the familiar images occupy her thoughts, for the possibilities ahead of her were too uncertain and they all ended with dire consequences, if she let her mind chase them.

Chapter 45

Decorations and festive banners commemorating the Queen's return had been strung along the major avenues leading to the royal compound, which crowned the westward bluff bordering Safrasco. The attempt at celebration was shallow and short-lived for the city was still steeped in the uncertain fears provoked by the attack upon their revered guard towers, plus the presence of the Abbysin army, stationed just beyond the river.

The dour mood extended throughout the Council, tension snapping everywhere as both the Abbysin and Jimalian armies had been standing at the ready for too long, eating up stores and champing at inactivity. Though the route to the east remained open, the caravaneers had all but ceased their long treks to the far lands of the Regency Kingdoms, richly clustered along the Grand Coast, waiting for stability from the Jimalian territory. Goods and stores had been confiscated by armies many times before and they wanted to avoid that unnecessary loss.

Andigar Cianon, Margrave of Tenigra, seemed relaxed and confident in the midst of the strain that permeated the room. He sipped at his goblet as though attending an evening soiree. Makiel Ma'Gilrie, the Mayor of Safrasco, had the look of an elder philosopher, fresh from his books, his balding white hair in perpetual disarray. In close discussion with Cianon, the mayor's demeanor was far more incensed than scholarly, much at odds to his nature.

"Trade is suffering because of this stand-off and we are no closer to resolving it." Ma'Gilrie could scarcely contain his anger. Only his years of diplomacy held his temper in check and his long seniority allowed for strong criticism. "In as much time you have said the Abbysins are responsible and then in another, the Stands, as if that were remotely possible. Which is it? Since you've returned from the summit, the Abbysin troops have been mustering as though preparing for assault. Furthermore, ..."

"Furthermore, our armies are ready to repel them." Andigar Cianon interrupted. "They're waiting to prove their worth. I'm inclined to see it."

"Armies are not toys to be squandered at a whim." Ma'Gilrie growled. "Nor are the needs of the people. How are they served by any of this?"

"My lord Mayor, you've been doddered by age and no longer have the vision of youth." Cianon scoffed, as if announcing the obvious to a dimwitted servant. "The Jimalian kingdoms have more to offer by claiming their own rights and not being eternally beholden to the whims of the Abbysin."

"Tell me when we have suffered. Safrasco enjoys a good trade, as does the rest of the Jimals. A war ... this separatist cause, hurts us all." Ma'Gilrie was not to be intimidated by the cavalier regard of the entitled Lord. His spoiled manner would be hard to assail with logic.

"So, you say." Andigar sniffed, dismissing the arguments. "Your vision of the future is suspect, as I say. You'll see when we control the terms of trade … and the sanctity of our borders."

"Look. Look out there." Ma'Gilrie stabbed a finger towards the balcony overlooking the vale that led to where Safrasco guarded entry to the Jimals. The Abbysin regiments could be seen encamped along the river fed by the Pendant Mere, the hanging jewel of the Chained Lakes. In spite of the inactivity, they still looked ready and capable. "Is that the future you wish? Nothing good will come of it."

The Ducesin, Queen Linarest, edged up to Andigar's side. She had obviously heard their exchange and seemed as confident in the outcome as the Jimalian Lord. Her shadow lingered nearby, observing the Queen's company with mute intensity. Ma'Gilrie saw more mania than confidence in her calm, as though her thoughts were considering other conversations entirely.

"My dear Mayor. Of course, I have no wish for armies outside my doors. Exactly why we are pressing for sovereignty. I see a very promising future."

Ma'Gilrie didn't miss the complicit look exchanged between the Linarest and the Lord of the Tenigran Jimals. Given the confidence they acknowledged, it was more than a mere agreement of philosophy, it was the realization of some lofty goal set long before.

"I beg your forgiveness for saying so, there are few that agree. We lose the resources inherent in Abbysin, the freedoms to trade and receive goods for instance. Safrasco thrives in the passing. What do we have to replace it?"

"We have plenty, I can assure you. You may not agree. Someday if you rule, you can decide which agreements are worthwhile. It is not an easy path to walk." She turned to the Margrave of Tenigra. "I have the full support of Lord Andigar and he speaks for a great deal of the Jimals, especially the forgotten north." One eyebrow arched as though mocking the mayor's naïve view. "Who do you speak for, Lord Mayor?"

"As ever, my Lady, I think only of the people of Safrasco. Their success is mine. When they are put in harm's way, I become concerned." Ma'Gilrie replied humbly, though Linarest noted by the man's demeanor that he staunchly held to his opinion.

The Mayor was well aware of the Ducesin's scorn. She had more than just the moral support of Andigar. He was undoubtedly feeding her coffers, a hidden wealth lying between them. Her silent aide, the cadaverous Steban Mallbre, looked at him from his station with the eyes of a zealot, sharp and fervent.

He avoided the mute servant's cold stare with another look about the Council chambers. There were few allies to be found. Risherade sat on his customary dais as if bored with the proceedings. Ma'Gilrie knew the Ducet's mind had been fixated on retaliation since the attack on the Safrasco towers by the Abbysins, rather than whichever force or entity was truly responsible. Ma'Gilrie had strong doubts it was the Abbysins. The Jimals had been at peace since the time of Xerenon the Mage. Since being enfolded by the Abbysin Empire at the end of the Mage's era, the Jimals had been mostly forgotten by the empire as though a minor summer home and left free to govern as they wish. The taxes exacted were stiff, though not excessive, and used mostly to maintain the roads and communications to a fastidious degree. If nothing else, the Abbysin knew their survival relied on good arteries across their lands. Safrasco had flourished under the arrangement, as had the rest of the Jimals.

The Abbysin army had done little but hold camp since their arrival, positioned as though expecting to be attacked themselves. It was the glitter and clash of armies that fascinated the rotund Ducet, who fancied himself a consummate General. He only found interest in the proceedings if the subject of the discussions turned to attacking the Abbysin lines. What worried Ma'Gilrie the most was that the Jimalian officers were more than willing to toady to the Ducet's brash pronouncements.

The talk was turning to that of an offensive, to 'sweep the Abbysin from our front porch,' as Lord Cianon would have it. He had been one of the most vocal supporters of a new Jimalian sovereignty, even before the sorcerous assault on the towers. That attack had done nothing to alter Cianon's zeal or ambition, almost as though the attacks were well considered in his plans. Ma'Gilrie's own proposition, to stand the army down until further recommendations could be considered, fell on deaf ears.

Since the Ducet's return from the Summit, there had been a sudden rush of activity. Though nothing had been said, it was apparent that he was not going to be privy to the results of that diplomacy and Ma'Gilrie surmised that none of it was good, as they were maintaining one face while speaking with another. When ulterior motives lurked behind the good will of words, the mayor knew the trail to follow. His own path to authority, as Mayor of Safrasco, came from the levels imposed by the guilds. He felt fortunate to have discovered wood carving as a lad and a good craftsman to teach him the art. Lacking the fundamental joys of simple craftsmanship, the rich indulge in baubles, so when power struggles, someone is fumbling to hold the purse. Again, he looked at the confident demeanor of Cianon and made a mental note to examine The Tenigran Lord's resources.

Ma'Gilrie was more than ready to excuse himself from the council for there was little left but arguments about strategy and the sure probability of victory in each of their scenarios. He had heard all of their brave talk before, all the braver for them not having to wield the swords.

Arcane marks in rusty brown wove around the card placed in the crux of the pattern. Centered in the arena, *Nepethe* flickered vividly under the wavering candlelight, the roses surrounding her a white and sorcerous flame. Smoky threads began to blossom in curious tendrils, dissected script worming away from her mark as though seeking cues from the nearby Numinon. The smokes laid fresh inks in their passing, painting a stack of three marks to the West of the exposed card. The center box flared especially bright, inviting the next card within its borders. The seer turned the top card from the deck without hesitation, as if knowing the fate it would reveal.

Nuith.

The hands idled as the next card waited to be exposed, the inks of the arena shifting and demanding placement with the potent *Nuith*. The marks revealed the strength of her position. Nervous curiosity drew the subsequent cards, laid down in quick succession alongside the *Queen of Quills*, showing her support.

The *9 and 3 of Quills* lay exposed, the feathered edges of their suit bristling under the wavering candlelight. In line, the match of Suit showed tremendous power, the Queen's allies mated in their quest. Their qualities had been noted before and no move was made to consult the Book. Without provocation, the Numinon flipped its leaves slowly, advancing only a few pages before stopping at a bare page, its script lean and devoid of ornament.

'Allies'

Marks smoked in behind her in the East quadrant, leaving *Nepethe* supported yet exposed to the power in the West. The Deck revealed nothing, only the hypnotic imbalance that was the back of the top card. The seer drew the card, knowing the deck had determined the need. The *7 of Cups* was placed within the mark and the second frame beckoned. The card was drawn to fulfill the mark and the *10 of Roses* appeared, remaining a powerful ally. It was laid as pulled from the deck, in the inverse and the Numinon riffled through its pages quickly, to reveal the import. The *10 of Roses*, the most potent of the minor Rose arcana, was shown inverted on the page, indications regarding the weakness of the card written with heavier inks. The message was clear.

'On the occasion that Wealth becomes too important it
loses its value and becomes a burden,
a stagnation of remains.
Rather than yielding a fertile mulch,
instead it festers much as a cesspool,
too thick with waste to engender growth.'

In the formation, there was little immediate support from the two Cards as they lay behind her in reserve. Long moments passed while the Seer waited for more allies to appear. At length, the borders of the arena meshed and countered with new alignments, shooting fresh tracings, livid with a moisture that fractured under the trembling candlelight, to the Southern mark. The Seer's reluctance was evident as the next card was drawn. *Abbadon!* Again, the harbinger of death and rebirth showed, though in a neutral position as though a scavenger, waiting to pluck at the remains. It was laid down quickly, the Seer loathe to hold it.

The arena rested, its parchment securing the inks like an ancient document. The pages of Numinon flipped to the front, where the barest pages made their requests.

'Do you wish to Counter?'

Two sigils lay opposed below, the runes to accept or decline circled by inks that pulsed expectantly. The hooded figure laid a fingertip on the blazon, greened like verdigris copper, a trace of fire lingering with the print. The Numinon rifled its delicate pages into its references, stopping at an overleaf, dire warnings displayed with red inks and stamps. The leaf turned once more with an elegant pause, revealing the peerless *Arcana Cardinale*. Beneath the bannered title, a directive was written in red inks and framed with a filigree of drawn knots.

'The Suit of Quills is aligned against you and the powers
of Abbadon cannot be commanded.
The remaining Cardinale are the choices available.
They alone rank with the strength and power
to overcome the plotting.'

Seven cards, the ultimate ascendancy of the deck, were marked in small icons upon the page, their Realms limned in gold. *Harisphont (Knowledge), Alamed (Justice), Hermite (Soul), Aeon (Time)* and … *Jachra (Fool)* were exposed in dark, fresh inks. The depictions of *Abbadon (Death), Babalon (Desire), Magus (Unknown)* and *Empress (Creation)* lay dull and faded on the page, options not available to the Seer.

The hand lingered over the *Hermite* icon as the archaic Jimalian calligraphy revealed itself to define the choice.

'There is only the self to return to for all answers'.

The hand remained a moment longer, allowing yet more script to unveil on the arena.

'Alone and independent, the Hermite answers to no one.'

The *Harisphont* lay benign until the player's hand shifted to the left and hovered over its image. The nature of the card began to reveal itself, as had the other, writing curling into shape beneath it. *'There is need to follow rules and traditions …'* appeared bolder than the rest as if written with a heavier quill. The hand didn't remain, instead attention shifted quickly over Alamed, to the last card: *Obrōskō.*

Aeon.

Selecting the image, the Numinon shifted pages to the subject, exposing the full illustration and allowing more words to play out in their form.

'Obrōskō slays himself yet brings himself to life,
in seed and birth.
He embodies the One, who proceeds from the discord of
opposites, wherein lies the secret of the prima materia.
This can mean the ending of old ways and hence the
beginning of a new era'.

As the player remained in contact with the image, more writing curled across the arena, ancient sigils and cuneiforms of the mage, highlighting the script.

'Obrōskō is responsible for purification as the old is swept
away to make way for the new.

His spawn becomes the Horis of the day and the darkness
of Nuite and hence the cycle of time.'

The flame of the lone candle guttered and danced, keeping its shallow nimbus gathered close to the reading within the dark room. The Book shifted back to the directory exposing the *Cardinale*, whose active cards continued to beckon, livened by the flickering light. As the candle dwindled, the cards bearing the Quills seemed to gain depth to their inks, the colors swimming with vitality. The near shadow of the Seer lay across the Eastern portion, dulling the space. The shorter the candle burned down, the more the flame leapt and jittered. Small towers of wax, created by the drips and drizzles of the candle's life, rose from the edge of its molten crater like abandoned castles, ready to slide down into another ruin. The Seer made no move to select a choice until a scrawl appeared along the bottom of the page.

'Do you need more time?'

As if goaded by the Book, the selection was finally made, the image of Aeon simmering in amber fire for an instant as the Book shifted to a clean page, which displayed only a clear warning, without distracting embellishments, inked with the rusted color of old blood:

'Are you sure?'

A simple choice lay beneath it, scribed in the ancient Jimalian counters of *'accept'* or *'decline'*. The 'Accept' mark, instead of the coppery green as before, glowered with a dangerous carmine shine. The sigil was pressed impatiently and, with the connection, a new box appeared in the arena at the Northern badge.

The top card was drawn and *Aeon* played on its mark.

The arena fired with renewed energies, taking its cue from the coiling, eternal force of the card. As if marching a new course, the knotted borders of the parchment broke at the North and South and turned from the edges of the arena, circling in a wide arc of torching inks as it towed the knotted edging in its wake. The circling weave surrounded *Nepethe*, catching up *Abbadon* as it broke the Southern mark and isolating her from the other cards on the board.

A puff of air seemed to stir from the felted desktop and threatened to extinguish the candle with its sudden burst. Linarest, the Ducesin and Queen of the Jimals, remained in place as though bound to the chair, the currents of the arena spreading out seeking breadth, with patterns of light and sound converging in scales that wrapped the walls in their passing.

Chapter 46

Spread below her, the assembly of arms and humanity reminded her of the ocean, a surf marred by the metallic abrasions of sword and harness. The image persisted in Cerra's mind as they stood on a grassy hill, overlooking the wide valley of the Darii river where it meandered its way to the Sultan Sea. After the event in the defile, the Cherros riders had deferred to Cerra as though she were a paladin to be guarded by their sacred trust, coming to see her as a figure from legend, none daring to call her by her given name. She wore her treasured Cherros riding cloak, light and sturdy, tawny as the grasses of the wide steppes. Seredan rode at her right side, his sabre ever at the ready.

"There are maybe two thousand men in the valley, Neyith."

Cerra waited, knowing that he would paint the picture for her. Seredan rose to the descriptive task, like a storyteller with an appreciative audience.

"Two legions that look idle. I know none of their banners, though I see siege towers waiting to be lifted, a half-dozen sling arms and the camps of many foot soldiers." Seredan chuckled dryly. "Their sergentes are keeping them drilled and not lazy like the ones at the slings. The fields have been torn up by the encampments. The next grass will be foul. *Hmmph.* It's about time we've been recognized. Riders are coming … two of them … from the horse-lines behind. *Heh.* A banner I recognize: the, Patterned Horse brigandeers … Cherros mercenaries. It appears they are coming to greet us."

'Beware!' The sky rumbled as the voice of Yutan sounded within her. The demon had resumed his watch over the company in the early morning, rising like a mist from the lake and spreading himself into a forbidding cloud as the sun began to heat the day.

'Dear Yutan. There are only two of them and I have you overlooking everything. There is nothing to fear at all.' Aloud, Cerra questioned Seredan further as thunder rolled through the air. "What of Safrasco? Can we see the city?"

"We can. Towers that rise in grandeur, trying to mimic the mountains behind them." Seredan scoffed. "Only those who have not felt the open space of the Cherros steppes would be impressed."

"Do they show an army too? Surely all the men below are not on stage with no performance due…....." Cerra thought of Havi's quick assessment as her ears keened to the sounds below, keeping in tune with Seredan's description of the vista. "Likely behind the walls of the city and beyond in the fields if they don't show."

"*Heya* … I think you claimed it right. By the glint … it can only be armor … formations must be lurking behind. I doubt the army below can see them. My eyes are good, though not those of the great hawk that circles above us … *heh*, I wish I did … I can well imagine there are many more hidden at the back. Safrasco, the northern city … to your left as you are facing …

guards one of the two passes and the city nestles between them. The chains of mountains end abruptly, like they were sliced off with a knife … they nearly beg to touch each other. A wide valley is scooped out between them. From this vantage I see no end. The city called Saamed lies to the south of the opening and mirrors the towers of Safrasco in might and form," Seredan felt useless pointing to the left, though he did so anyway. "It is the northern towers of Safrasco that has all of the attention of the armies. Those great towers also watch the route that follows the Chained Lakes to the northern pass. They are the match of their brothers on the other side. *Shht* … some of them are shattered. Even a portion of the wall lays wasted, as though it were eaten away by moths." Seredan made a warding sign and looked carefully at the red-haired witch. "The work of sorcery. No rubble at the base … scarcely sand in a pile."

'It still remembers the moment of its collapse.' Yutan's thought interrupted Seredan's account. *'… and bears the mark of Xerenon.'*

Cerra thought of the assaults on the Stands. She spoke aloud, thoughtful and gazing in the distance towards the towers of Safrasco, though more to herself than the horsemen that gathered close around. "Many have suffered from similar fates." She leaned slightly over to Seredan, her smile returning. "Your fellows approach. They hail as though they recognize you."

"They should. We shared the same fosterage to earn our marks. You are in our care so you will have no lack for allies, Neyith"

"Then I am in good hands." Cerra reached across to briefly lay a hand on Seredan's shoulder in thanks as the pair of Cherros mercenaries crested the ridge.

The two Painted Horse riders expertly circled the horse-men, who were formed protectively around her, until one reined in next to Seredan with a clapping of arms and com-radely grunts of laughter. Cerra felt the other stop close to her, remaining quiet. There was no doubt she was the object of his attention. Kamir rocked in the saddle in front of her, returning the inspection. She stroked behind his ears, sure to ease him back to a comfortable seat. The first of the riders would be in charge and she turned her attention to him as he spoke.

"Are you out for a lord's tour?" Starrel Thott grinned ami-ably. "Did the lower platte finally leave you bored to tears?"

"I'd lay much to be in those fields now." Seredan returned the grin, though it had a fiercer edge to it. "Fate and the threat of a good story draws me here. The Neyith is in our care."

Starrel shot a glance back to the woman in their midst. The Cherros that made up the small company, all of the south-ern range by their paints, gazed back proudly, defiance and determination hardening their eyes. Starrel knew the look, the same fierce look he wanted to see from his own company of mercenary calvary before battle. Neyith … a name that had potency among the tribes, rumored a powerful blind witch, though much championed by the womenfolk. The name had spread like a windfire on dry grass only a few years prior.

He looked at her now, a shorter woman than his mind had painted, though well formed. Her cat looked to generate more ferocity, for the blind woman was unassuming, without the courtly airs of a royal and gazing off past him with a pleasant smile. A twisted mane of red hair was captured beneath her hood, an omen to be sure. The Cherros cloak she wore had been earned or she would not have it otherwise. He addressed her carefully, aware of how the other Riders had guarded her.

"And you … Neyith … you have the trust of these Cherros." Starrel spoke with a quizzical tone, though he must have given her a quick assessment for he didn't pause long enough for her to frame an answer. "Then you have the faith of us all. Still, I would like to know your intentions. I am Starrell of the Painted Horse."

"You must be the captain of your men." Cerra responded with amiable warmth. "You speak as though accustomed to lead. I shouldn't divulge my intentions to anyone less. It's a simple task really … to keep an appointment with the Ducesin of the Jimals. She is certainly in Safrasco." Cerra turned her head in the direction of the tower, an uneven smile bunching her face. "If you want to know, I'm pretty sure she's not keen on seeing me again."

"A burr in the queen's saddle, are you? A better recommendation than from Seredan." Starrel snorted. "But you speak true … the banners of the royal house were flying again at yesterday's dawn. You can see them … hells … well, they occupy the grandest towers of Castle Safrasco, which clings to its lake island rock like a fat tick on an old dog. What mean you to do?"

Cerra had never been sure what her actual mission was. It seemed to change constantly as the days transpired and the players showed their hands. The mechanical noise of the army at rest below her in the wide valley, seemed to give her a cue.

"To send armies home without bloodshed." She looked curiously at Starrel. "Though I suppose you then become unemployed. Do I upset your balance?"

Starrel grunted, clearly amused. "*Shht* ... not ours. We are paid no matter the heat of our blood, so if you go to stir the pot it's the same. Either way, it is a welcome change from the boredom of waiting for something to happen. The royals can't decide who wants to piss first."

"Aptly put. They can ..." Cerra snickered, though Seredan shuffled uneasily next to her on his horse at the other's rude remark. He must surely be giving the mercenary captain a hard look. She decided not to press the analogy "... well, I have no desire to wait around and find out who can't hold their drink. I'd rather be in my familiar chair ... *heh* ... and testing the strength of my own ale."

"We have no standing orders." She could tell the remark was directed at Seredan. "By yourself, you're a poor company to approach the gates. A full battle count of cavalry will make a better impression."

"That's hardly necessary!" Cerra exclaimed. Already, she felt the burden of responsibility to the Cherros that had guided her this far and for the losses to their numbers. "Please. I've caused enough trouble. I can present myself for this ... meeting."

"Trouble?! *Fah!* Maybe you cause trouble whether we are here or not. This way it is trouble close at hand and within sight of our storytellers, Seredan here at one time the most expansive of them all. By that I mean given to exaggeration. But first, we eat. It looks to rain at any moment ... and not a sprinkle. *Heh* ... an equal to the bladders of the royals. Join our company while there is good light and you are still dry."

"Gladly. It won't rain just yet, I assure you ... but we are famished, or at least I am." Cerra gave him a side-long grin. "Maybe I speak too soon ... I've not tasted army fare of the Abbysin."

Starrel laughed with genuine amusement. "It depends on the cookfire. If you want fowl, the archers who camp near the river do it well. If you want truly foul, then the sappers are your best choice. We Cherros cook the same as we always do within our home ranges. At the very least, all of my men live and they are fit."

"As good a recommendation as I could ask for." Feeling Seredan's agreement she added, "Please, lead on."

Starrel took a position to Cerra's left and began leading the party down from the bluff. He gladly described the scene for her, proud of his part of the assembly. The Cherros had camped high in the shallow valley near the bluffs, kept to the rear of the army as a strategic choice. Highly mobile, the Cherros Patterned Horse could be brought to the fore within moments.

The ranks of foot soldiers and scattered siege engines occupied the front, which had settled on the river as the neutral barrier. The grassy slopes leading to the towers of Safrasco and Saamed and the broad passes to the Jimal valleys behind them were clear of forces, the Jimalian troops tucked safely back from the entrances.

A tent was provided for Cerra at Starrel's insistence and the food, though rough, was nearly as good as what she remembered from the women's clutch in the Cherros camp some years before. She felt tired from the day's ride and exhausted from the tireless movement she had been exposed to. Yutan remained poised above the encampment and spread thin like haze over the valley, as the night fires of the army took hold of the light. He had grown quiet, saying only that the power of Xerenon remains, placing the center of power within the core of the castle towers, the royal towers if Starrel had described them correctly.

Cerra started in her reverie as Yutan shared a vivid light within her imagination that seemed a beacon from afar, for it sparked at misplaced intervals and disappeared before it could hold her attention. The flash, when it appeared, had the same argent glow that defined the demon, whose magic penetrated her sightless vision.

'There it is.'

Yutan could feel the power that generated from the deck, the sorceries common in their creation marked him. The residue of it vibrated through him, the night rumbling uneasily with no moon arise to give the agitated clouds form.

The argent mist of the demon was lost to the roiling and confused darkness, like a drift into the patterns of sleep, leaving Cerra viewing an empty room as though from above, a fly on a ceiling that had no surface to cling to. A lone figure was shadowed by the weak flicker of light, a dark form that caused her to drift with recognition as a card was laid, the curling scales of a dragon emerging and coiling to reach its tail.

She was awoken by the tumult of the entire army shaking awake at the first light. The clamor of mounts and arms being readied stirred her to movement, just as the flap of her small tent was pushed aside and Seredan hurriedly stuck his head in.

"The royal towers ... they're gone!"

Chapter 47

Confusion and alarm rippled across the armed encampment as troops, stirred from their comfort and lethargy, sought to regain their arms and formations. The Abbysin warlords and mercenary captains had raced to the command tent where the Strategos would determine some offensive or defensive plan, had not yet returned to their units to organize the effort. The practical Ushtars and Sargentes bellowed their readiness orders in the confusion, actions that demanded the most basic of attentions, regardless of what orders might come.

The graceful royal towers appeared missing, along with a large portion of Safrasco. All that remained were worn stumps of old rock, hewn relics left over from another age. Circling the remains were slim currents of air, mirrored and scaled artifacts that defied the eyes. A light, as though from the top of an unseen tower, circled in wide arcs, eating into the fractures of its passing.

Amidst the turmoil of the Abbysin encampment, an odd calm began to settle, first from the rear echelons and then through the camp, as the troop of Cherros mercenaries moved towards the front in stately procession. There were no banners of Abbysin allegiance flying from the thin spears of the lead horsemen, save their own colors, a roan horse on a field of tan that marked the Painted Horse legion. A fresh guidon, bearing the sigil of Neyith, preceded them all, held proudly by the tribesman that rode closely beside a hooded woman in a Cherros riding cloak. A gyrfalcon circled within a sky that rumbled with menace. The roiling cloud that loomed overhead seemed to flex with muscular strength as the column trotted forward.

Many of the closest foot soldiers, stationed in lined camps along the ordered front, made signs of warding as the procession advanced through the legions. The unbound red hair of the woman bunched like molten flame from beneath the hood of her cloak and riding on the pommel of her saddle, a black cat looked around with piercing eyes as if daring anyone to inhibit their passage.

Gusts of chill wind gave the procession a funereal doom and more signs of warding were made as they passed the last lines of the Abbysin, across the caravansary bridge and into the grassy slopes that led to the shimmering remains of Royal Safrasco. Rumbling ahead of the Cherros cavalry and spreading out in toroid billows, the thundering cloud crackled with thin lightnings as it approached the vague aura that circled the ruins.

A whelkhorn, sounding from the valley beyond, hushed the Jimalian Council meeting in the relative safety of Saamed. Drapes were pulled aside as the assembly drifted with curiosity out onto the veranda overlooking the valley that flanked the river. A vanguard was coming forward from the center of the ranks. By the banners, it was the Patterned Horse, a mercenary light calvary troop of the Cherros, renowned for their ferocity and skill. They weren't in the formation of attack, rather procession. An ominous cloud boiled behind them as if rising from the dust of the horses. From the distance, it took a moment to discern the figure leading the company forward. Once focused, Ma'Gilrie's eyesight was as good as any. He had seen many martial displays of pomp and ceremony, so did not expect to spy a woman with flaming hair, riding at the fore. He felt his stomach tighten. He could not guess what omen lay with the red-haired woman, though he thought it was not likely to be good.

Risherade, who had been seething over the sorcerous destruction of Safrasco, turned to Cianon, a zealous and tight grin on his face as though a hunt had been announced. "I believe it's time to … how did you say it?... 'sweep the Abbysin from our doorstep'."

"We are ready of course." Lord Cianon returned stiffly. The absence of the Ducesin, even that of Safrasco, didn't change his stance regarding the Abbysin. His domains lay within the remote but protected northern Jimals. Given the discovery of a lucrative mine, there could even be advantage. He was as anxious to secure his wealth as Risherade was eager to see the clash of arms.

Watching the column emerge from the ranks of the Abbysin army and cross the bridge, rallied the Duce to action. The skies were heavy with thunder, the ominous rumble shuddering the air with nervous tension. Much of Safrasco had disappeared in ruins, a glamour that none of the acolytes and generals could understand. They offered nothing but confusion and arguments as only ghostly fangs of stone remained, the destruction a broken artifact from another age. A small squadron had been sent to investigate, who rode into the thin glaze of air surrounding the waste and faded from sight. Some of the assembled court and advisors were still stalling, as if news or explanation might arrive at any moment.

"Send out the Buryats." Risherade jabbed a finger at the Cherros column advancing towards the pass in the direction of the ruins, directing his order to the commander of the armored horse brigades . "Now! We are under attack."

"But sire, they proceed cautiously, emissaries I'd judge by the ..."

"I said now!" Risherade cut his general short, a zealous anger flushing his face. "Do you see what has become of Safrasco? Look! Rubble! Fecking rubble if my eyes don't deceive me ... and they don't! My wife is ... was ... in there! Festering goats! It's foul sorcery and the Abbysin are behind it, you can be sure of that! That parade out there is just more of their fecking treachery. The Buryats!"

"Yes sire." The aging commander, the ribbons of office decking the front of his surcoat, clicked his heels with a hasty bow and turned to signal an aide standing at the door. Within moments a horn sounded: two long blasts followed by one short. Risherade strode over to the balcony to watch, an avid light piercing his eyes as though ready to watch the games.

Chapter 48

Cerra could feel the trail of men behind her, a force that was as much pushing her along as she was drawing it forward. Circling, argent fields cut into the black of her vision as she looked ahead, tearing away the frames of her imagination. The waves had shape and form, a beast of legend engulfed as it sought to consume its very being in continual struggle. Reflections of scales twisted the argent fires, as the great dragon advanced on itself with another ravenous bite.

'What lies ahead?' Cerra voiced her anxious thought aloft as she wrestled with her nerves, unsure of the twisting vision that insinuated in front of her. Like the demon, the sorceries of the cards penetrated her blindness with startling clarity.

'Time. It is time.' Yutan's word's bore none of his usual terse fierceness. Instead, a trace of wonder infected his thought. She wasn't even sure she understood his meaning. *'The deck lies at the center. I can see it's light.'*

'As I see you.' Cerra felt a surge of compassion for Yutan as she sought to imagine the magnitude of the toll that the sorcerer had exacted on him. In that instant, she felt the touch of his tenderness too, a powerful stoicism that calmed her. *'How do we get past it?'*

'You will not like the answer.'

'I haven't liked much since I left my sewing.' Cerra chided him

good-naturedly, deflecting her nerves. *'I already know there won't be kafi and biscuits waiting.'*

The sky rumbled ominously, the heavy, dark cloud beginning to find its way around the fractured lightnings that surrounded the missing tower, circling it like a maelstrom. Seredan leaned close to Cerra, keeping his eyes carefully ahead as they neared the reflecting airs that confused his sight.

"Neyith." His voice was low, infected with worry and awe. "We are nearing what's left of Safrasco and the gates of Saamed are no more than a quick gallop from us." Seredan hesitated. Cerra could feel his reluctance. "As we get closer, the air is more … the word I don't know … fluid, like a glamour. I don't trust it. What would you have us do?"

"I think we'd better stop for the moment." Cerra suggested. The bulbous and threatening skies that had developed with the dawn began to filter into the confused airs, causing it to boil with sodden grays and smokey whites seeking to define the sorcerous turbulence. Seredan was about to relay the message to Starrel, when thundering hooves could be heard coming from the towers of Saamed. The company halted of its own accord as scores of Jimalian cavalry rounded the heavy walls and bore down on them. Starrel didn't hesitate. A moment lost under attack is already a blow to recover from. The Patterned Horse erupted into a charge with but a shout. Cerra had no time to stop them.

From the porticos overlooking the walls of Saamed, the

Jimalian lords gathered expectantly as the Buryats streaked across the expanse. Conical helmets and slender spears glittered brightly in the early sun as the Jimalian horsemen cleared the bulwarks, horses decked in leather armor, richly braided and tasseled as if ready for the games of the Faire. A stark white rose on a maroon field flew from the guidon. The Jimalian cavalry rode straight for the Cherros procession, their spears lowering as they approached the ghostly sheen of circulating air that suddenly arced out in front of them.

"Look there! *Hah!* The Abbysin column is taking the challenge." the Duce snorted. "Anyone want to place wagers? No armor at all on them. Those twigs they call spears wouldn't hold a pigeon on a spit."

There was no coherent reply from the assembled council, just stifled muttering and consternation as they watched from the safety of their Saamed observatory. The opposing cavalries raced towards each other across the open slope, the Cherros column the swifter, crossing the span with astonishing speed and precision, forming like an arrow to split the lesser-formed ranks of the Jimalian charge. The thundering clouds that circulated over the battlefield nearly drowned the rumble of hooves as the cavalries sluiced together within the sheer of wavering air that surrounded the royal towers of Safrasco in a wide arc. There should have been a clash of arms and mortal cries as the horsemen came close to collision. Instead, they passed into the glamour as though one charge enveloped the other in its maw.

As Seredan cried out an oath, the two charges meshed like fingers in a thoughtful pose before vanishing in a current that swept them aside like dust. Cerra saw the dissolution like silvered feathers being swept away, the thundering hooves vanishing into some distant field. She could feel the riders around her bunch and shuffle, angry with their curses and ready for retaliation.

"Stop them! Please!" Cerra waved out her hand, pleading urgently to Seredan. "Hold your men!"

Seredan stilled them with sharp rebukes as the Cherros tribesmen held their anxious mounts and settled their attention back to the ruins and Neyith. The menacing skies, which threatened to release its lightnings in close fury, began settling on the coiling sheen of air that shivered in its wide circle about Safrasco. Slowly, the storming sky was absorbed into its weave, the sodden grays and spectral lightnings giving the circulation definition as the maelstrom was drawn in like clinging vines of steam.

Argent glows curled over the currents, a smokey light that gave them form as it advanced, etching out the lines of a scaled wyrm churning to devour itself. Sparks of lightning were pressed out as the coiling apparition squeezed and bunched, wringing the heavy air of its life. The image of the fallen tower within the wavering circle began to be blurred by the steams expulsed as the storm was enveloped within the glamour, revealing the extent of the ensorcelled beast. Definition gave the apparition motion, a persistent lunge of the scaled body with each successive gulp of its dragon maw.

"Neyith ..." Seredan's voice was awe mixed with disbelief. "We must leave ..."

Cerra raised her hand slightly to stay his speech, intent on the chaotic struggle in front of her, the demon's terse voice cutting into her consciousness.

'You must enter soon. I am … Time.' She felt a groan come from Yutan that could have as easily been her own. *'There is not much … left.'*

'What do I do?' She could tell he was trying hard to speak, the argent peak of him beginning to reach the dragons insatiable maw.

'Walk. I will show you … the path.' Yutan's voice in her mind was clear but seemed more distant as if talking over a barrier between them. Cerra held her hand out to touch Seredan's arm.

"No. Not yet. I … must … I have to go on." Her eyes stayed forward, intent on the weave of light in front of her. "Take me as close to that as you dare. Have your men wait. But … don't follow me. Please."

Seredan nodded, hearing the blind woman's quiet plea as a sacred command. He paced them forward until the fevered airs felt near enough to touch, a hellish cyclone that was gathering density, obscuring the ruins within. Cerra took a deep breath, scruffing the back of Kamir's neck.

"You have better eyes than me, so you know better than to follow," she murmured softly. "Damme cat … but if you do, please stay close … and not under my feet, mind you."

Cerra kicked her foot over the saddle and slid to the ground, grasping Sugar about the neck and nuzzling her for a moment, despite the urgency. A familiar scent that brought her cottage … and the thirty paces to the stables … to mind, a brief jolt of courage as she patted Sugar's neck. The sorcerous light that pulsed and surged in front of her held her attention, her cane forgotten as she absorbed the extend of its bright field. With a determined sigh, she turned to Seredan with a tight smile.

"I'll be back for my horse."

The Cherros horseman dismounted to take her reins as she stepped forward. The fractured air, threaded with the weave of the storming clouds, wavered like a wall of steaming scales. The ruins behind it were becoming less distinct as the tempest clouds were torn apart and absorbed. The blind woman threw back her hood and pulled the pin from her hair, letting her wild red mane disentangle. It whipped and fluttered in fits and starts as she approached the apparition. Her black cat trotted along carefully behind her, head up and alert with every step.

'Where do I go?'

Cerra could nearly touch the sorcerous anomaly. A humming sound, which made her think of metaled insects, was more a part of the air than something her ears could truly perceive. The silvery evidence of Yutan's presence was dissipating rapidly as he was drawn into the churning circle of the monstrous wyrm. Its head was moving away from her in its continual ingestion, the remnant trails of Yutan being inhaled into its maw. Her heart jumped with fear for him as his voice rang within her.

'Three steps will take you to the center of the sorcery. One to enter. One to be ... within. One to leave. I make the path.' His words were strangled. Determined. *'I am ... in Time.'*

'What of you?' Cerra pleaded silently. His dissolution was becoming more widespread, weaving within the sheer scales of the writhing serpent.

'*I am … Time.*' The demon sounded remote as though regarding another matter. A long moment hung in front of her, the humming persistent in her ears before she heard him again. '*You must succeed.*'

'Succeed in *what?!*' Cerra felt desperate.

'*Turn time.*' There was no profusion of word or thought from the demon. He was becoming very still in her mind. '*I … you … create the path. Remember. Three steps. One in. One within. One out. There is but one … passage … through time. You must be ready.*'

'*Yes-s.*' In an instant Cerra knew the dark and timeless passage the demon referred to and braced herself, not knowing if she could continue.

"I won't go back and I can't stay here." She growled to herself, stretching her arm out as she took the first step.

With the hammered resonance of a gong, the deeply rooted image of the Void flared out from the demon, a smothering blackness that consumed all, pulsing her mind to erase all thought. There was nothing. Her body was sliced with a chill that ripped her bones, awareness shredded of color and imagery. Memories fractured like broken glass, whisked away in glittering shards as her hips moved forward. A step, momentum borne from the last pace, lacked a footfall with no space to tread on. A weight caught at her ankles as she reeled, unable to fall, for there was no direction, no substance to her. Did she step to catch herself in the stumble or was it collapse? Three. A step? A turn? There was nothing, not space or sight, only an eternal ink that clutched at her mind refusing thought, as endless as the sound racing ahead of her that she could not hear.

~ ❖ ~

It was said that in death a light pulls one forth from the decay and insignificance of mortals. Cerra saw nothing of such relief. Her mind refused the notion of death within the long reaches of the Void. There could be no death when life was beyond reach.

It was a rasping pull, a sensation which tugged at the corner of her lips that gave her thoughts focus, a retreat from the emptiness. Mouth. The idea formed and she became aware of her lips, moving her tongue against them to give them a trace of moisture. The emptiness of the Void clung to her mind even as weight and fabric began to give her body dimension. Her head rang, a thin drone that sounded as though a distant teakettle needed attention. She moved her fingers, a touch that revealed she was lying down on warm stone, dry and swept, not the emptiness of the Void nor the thin grasses of the field. Another rasp was felt next to her eye, an insistent pull along her temple.

A push of soft fur along her cheek helped imagine Kamir in her mind, a shine of black that shaped a cat from the disabling ink of the Void. She shuddered, feeling as though she had worked for hours, exhausted from unknown labors. Her mind resisted hints of color, but the jade eyes of Kamir painted themselves in, a relief that the Void had not shriven her of all imagination. At length she realized her eyelids were shut in a tight clench and she let them flutter open. She moved her hand, a weighted effort, to scratch Kamir as he pushed at her.

"I believe you tripped me." Cerra groaned softly. "I'll get you for that." Her fingertips delivered another weak caress to Kamir's cheek, knowing she could never have managed the crossing otherwise.

A circular wall swam with scaled light, silvered like moonlight on water, a wavering movement coiled with tracings of Yutan. She shut her eyes and took a breath before opening them again, seeking a connection, though no response was felt. A sharp pang of fear shivered through her as her blind sight took in the residue of the spell, a hunching continuous flow that pulsed like something alive, the curling wyrm that had engulfed itself over the city. Yutan's words came back to her, *'center of the spell'* a thought that peeked out with others as her consciousness returned. Cerra was loathe to move, except for the hand she allowed to trail along Kamir's weaving form. His insistent purrs seemed muted beyond the hum that rang inside her head.

"I'm in it now. A foot in the grave and the other on an oily patch," she whispered to the cat. She allowed herself another stabilizing breath, taking in the scents of stone and polished wood before raising herself to her knees.

She felt like she was waking from a night of too much ale. The familiar acrid tang coming from the smoke of a burning candle, along with the soft amber scent of beeswax, marked her inside a room. Her mind sorted the possibilities as she willed the last vestiges of the Void's ink to dissipate. She was within the spell, within the very towers of the Ducesin. It was a small relief, as she sought her bearings, that there were no alarms or commotion to be heard over the thin ringing in her ears. She was about to stand when she froze, her blood chilling as she detected the clean rose scent of the Queen.

Seredan heard the approach of horses from behind him, yet could not turn himself away from the red-haired witch as she approached the wavering airs. The storm clouds that had glowered above them were being drawn into the glittering air, giving it definition as colored dyes added to molten glass. The storm began to roil in a wide arc as it was swept around the broken remains of Safrasco, churning in rabid fury. Soon the storm began to eclipse the mirage as it closed with the ground, gripped within the mirroring coils of the illusion. The circle evolved, the steams of the tempest revealing the slithering coils of a great wyrm, its giant maw gorging on itself as it approached the spot where Neyith stood, hand raised as though waiting to touch.

For an instant Seredan thought he saw a rip in the storm, a profound absence of existence as the witch stepped forward into the rent with a stumble, her black cat tangled at her heels. He blinked away the desolate sight and in that instant, the witch's existence seemed to end, sliced from the world by the empty tear.

The broken remains of the royal towers of Safrasco could no longer be seen, hidden by the writhing fury of the sorcerous enchantment. The Cherros eased their horses back from the tempest as three riders from the Abbysin camp halted in their midst. A field commander, by his ribbons, with two aides who roughly gathered themselves in. Their mounts, energized by the gallop up the long grassy slope from the encampment by the river and further anxious by the turmoil of sorcerous air that boiled nearby, proved difficult to settle.

"What have you done?" The commander bobbed and turned in his saddle as he tried to speak. "Who's in charge here?"

Seredan pointed to the broiling air, a long stone's throw away. "At the moment … that is."

"What is this sorcery? What have you unleashed?"

"Nothing." The Cherros horseman looked at the Abbysin soldiers, eyes widened by the storm. "It lay here before and you didn't notice. Things change."

"We saw a charge. We all saw it. By what authority …"

"The Jimalians sent a sortie against our embassy …"

"*Your* embassy? I say again, by what authority …"

Seredan would not be cowed. "The cavalry of the Cherros remains within that turmoil, or so I hope. Jimalians too. Rather than badger me, put your own men on alert."

"I am not to be ordered about by a tribesman."

"Do as you wish. I know one thing. When hunting pacaymas, a small spear will do. For the wild bristle boars that ravage our camps sometimes, we bring a bigger spear. Here, I do not recommend bringing a spear." Seredan turned away from the angry commander and looked at the spot where he'd seen Neyith enter the conflagration, the instant of blackness that made him think of the finality of death. He wondered about her fate, for the churning airs seemed to take on a deeper rumble once her presence was absorbed. He spoke to the storm, not caring whether the officer heard or not. "When faced with wizardry, bring a witch."

The commander backed away from him warily, as though the Cherros might be the next to be ensorcelled, yet the horseman kept his steady gaze to the churning storm that blanketed the towers.

Chapter 49

Cerra crouched on the stone, frozen for the moment as she sensed the Queen's presence in the chamber. It was no surprise to find Linarest at the center of the spell. She was reluctant to move, as though in a spider's lair, the Queen's unseen webs ready to entangle her in any direction. Her vision wavered within the spell as the edges of the room appeared to swim in silvered light, like water held back by an unseen wall.

Kamir pushed against her, purring and trying to stir her into further motion. A steady tone persisted, singing like the thin whistle of a tea kettle. She wasn't sure if it was within her head or the room. The suffocating depths of the Void had left her feeling empty, as though she'd slept too long in a restless sleep.

Taking a breath to steel herself, Cerra eased her arm closer to the shimmering curtain and let her fingertips brush the argent glow, expecting it to move like water in a stream. Instead, she touched reassuring dry stone, warm as an inner wall. She had no doubt that she was in the tower and stifled the thought of the gateway that Yutan had created. He remained, she could feel him like a memory, woven into the glamour that coated the walls.

'*Turn time.*'

His words came back to her, squeezed from him as he

embraced the coils of the great wyrm. It devoured itself in its endless spell, the magic sparkling within her blindness as she had seen it from the fields beyond, before the step through the Void that brought her here, both a moment and a lifetime ago.

She gave Kamir a reassuring pat and carefully stood, silent as a mouse and keeping the glamour of the wall within touch. No sound of movement, not even breathing could be heard, a stony silence as though she were entombed in a crypt. If the arc of shimmering movement was any indication, the room was no more than two dozen paces across. Objects within the room could be obstructing the effect, for the illusion wavered with boxy shapes as she let her eyes drift to the center.

Cerra took a few careful steps, inching along the wall until she felt a candle sconce. Easing past it, she touched slightly raised, rounded stones. A cooler, polished surface of wood lay just beyond the lintel, which she determined was either a door to the outside or a closet. A deft reach revealed the latch, polished and smooth with use. The sconce made it likely a door to rooms beyond and she was tempted to open it.

'Only madmen could guess where I'd end up.' she shivered to herself as she withdrew her hand. *'I'm not that crazed. Not yet.'*

Cerra eased past the door. Matching carved lintels marked the other side and another sconce graced the wall. The lack of heat and odor let her know that it too was not lit and had been cold for some time. She stepped forward, keeping to the glow of the wall, moving as silently as she imagined Kamir would. He would be making his own stealthy assessment of the room.

'Mind yourself, cat,' she chided silently, hoping he received

the message. She was vibrantly aware that she was sharing the warning to herself. *'What am I thinking? He's far better at this than I am.'*

The floral rose scent of the Queen persisted as Cerra inched forward. That she sensed the Queen, yet perceived no motion nor recognition was puzzling, as though the teakettle sound that persisted in her ears obscured her own movement. By count, she had taken a dozen paces past the door. As yet, no windows or other openings had presented themselves nor any stirring other than herself. A tomb pulsing with life but not showing the evidence.

The ghostly air made her hesitate, she held her breath as her skirt brushed a table. There were no signs of recognition. Four paces took her past it as well as adjacent cabinets, both laid heavily with the metal and wood casings of scrolls and leather-bound volumes of books. She touched a tabletop to her left, marked with a few tidy scrolls along with sheets of parchment, folded and creased like letters of correspondence. *'A writing desk.'* The presence of inkwell and quill confirmed her suspicions, set so as to accommodate someone sitting on the other side.

The scent of the Queen became more intense as Cerra inched forward, yet she still discerned no movement, not even the suggestion of breath. The lack of response didn't ease her caution as she edged along the wall, keeping her motions as timid as a mouse under the eyes of a watchful cat. The glamour persisted in cutting through her blindness with its scaled and argent currents. The ringing tone in her head had her wondering if she could be heard at all.

While the unfamiliar whine left her unsure of her senses, the pervasive intimate scents convinced Cerra that she must be within Linarest's most personal realm. Surely not her private chambers, which would be opulent and spacious. This space was closed like a secret. Even without the weaving of the spell, sinister purposes wrapped the walls, a notion that made Cerra shiver.

Another sconce bearing an unlit torch leaned out from the wall with a heavy weaving draped along the stones beyond it, a tapestry of some design. A desk lay close to her left that she dared not touch. Just yet. The heat of a candle warned her of its presence, though it was the wavering of argent glows, licking back and forth in foreseeable patterns on the desk that begged her to keep her distance. Cerra kept her eyes averted, brushing past the arras and ducking under the wall torch that was sure to be on the far side.

She felt herself the worst sort of thief, charged with the dread of discovery. Yet a perverse curiosity remained as she charted the room, placing the contents in her mind like chess pieces on a board. The second half of the room was unadorned save for two sets of manacles, which dangled from pins hammered with iron studs. A thick cord, sticky as a spider's web, held them close to the wall. Cerra anxiously slapped at the waft of cobweb on her skirt, the manacles rousing distasteful memories of her time in Rovinkar's dungeons. The thought of any torture to man or beast knotted at her stomach and she was surprised when she reached the lintels of the door again. She cleared her mind of the anxiety the room suggested and parceled out her next move.

Forty-three paces. No windows. Close to the center lay the magic surrounding the Queen. Cerra put her back to the door and directed her dark vision to the center of the room, letting the shimmer of the walls cast some definition. An area consistently brighter than the rest indicated a path without obstruction and she hoped the wavering glimpse was accurate as she stepped forward. Less than ten paces would bring her to the mark.

A soft pallet, covered with rich linens tucked carefully in place, marked a bed. Kamir touched her leg, a swift brush that caught her breath and made her stop short. The scent of the Queen was overpowering, as close as her touch. She reached out carefully, the high back of a straight-hewn chair with richly padded velour meeting her fingertips. Cerra peeked forward until she could see the thin argent glow coming from the tabletop, appearing like a reflection of the serpentine radiance that embraced the walls.

She held herself still and listened intently, seeking past the constant whine in her ears. There was scarcely the sound of a breath, even her own. At last she eased her head around the chair. The incandescence was fired by small images, figurines framed and floating within her dark sight.

'*The Cards!*'

Her hand brushed the long linen sleeve of the occupant of the chair, as the thought caused her to cover her mouth in surprise. Breath held, Cerra froze like a statue as Kamir moved against her ankles again. He wasn't anxious, merely brushing for attention. The familiar motion eased her as she gently let out her breath. There was a soft thudding as he lit up on the bed to afford a better view.

'*Stay off the table.*' She grimaced silently, hoping Kamir got the message.

Feeling no reaction from the Queen, she lightly touched along the cloth of her surcoat, following the arm across to the shoulder until she dabbed gently at her throat, fingertips barely grazing the skin, warm and alive. She touched the familiar small depression just below the jaw, the signal of life most apparent at that tender spot. Although it was present, the pulse was long in coming, a slow, painstaking resonance of distant impact.

She moved her finger away as Linarest's hand began to move, a slow inexorable motion, as though lifted with infinite patience by a skilled puppeteer. From the soft brush of moving fabric, it seemed to take an age for the hand to reach the spot Cerra had touched, fingertips grazing slowly to dispel an itch.

'*She's tranced.*' Cerra thought, though the mysteries of time surrounded her, its light pushed against the walls of the room. '*Or caught in her own weave and she can't perceive me.*'

Emboldened, she felt around the edge of the table, the glowing cards illuminated on a surface marked with similar vibrant brands. Cerra's nimble touch revealed a creased parchment mat, the cards placed within its pattern. A light tingle vibrated across her fingertips, the mat charged with vibrant air. The waxed scent of a burning candle was close and she centered quickly on its heat, a torchiere which stood from the floor and seemed to be the only light in the room. In spite of the Queen's stupor, Cerra knew her time was precious.

'*I don't care what the spell is, a woman knows when another woman's in the room.'* Cerra held the thought as tightly as her breath.

The pulsing suggestions of cards that leaked into her vision demanded her attention and she eased close to discern their shapes. The scaled beast, shaped in a figure-eight, was easy to identify. She had seen its simulacrum weaving from outside the tower and the glamour of the spell continued to wash over them. The card lay at the top of the arrangement, as though laid on a sundial and marking the noon hour. At the compline hour of nine, three other cards lay, including a figure that looked regal in her pose. Cerra's breath caught when she recognized the runes that identified the card. She lightly touched it, tracing the shape of the marking in a familiar way to make sure. *Nuith.* Her fingertips seemed to ignite in response.

Havi's words came back to her … *'at first I thought it might be you.'* The demon's thought before she passed through the spell was especially urgent in her mind. *'You must turn time.'*

'Oh, by the god's, I bet I'll be leading the pipers when I do.' Cerra gritted to herself. *'And true to tradition, a half-beat off the pace.'*

She was ill-gifted to be a card player and didn't know any of the rules. The role of thief was unfamiliar as well. Her nerves were on edge as she traced the edges of the array marked by the parchment. A carved box, lined with fine velvet, lay open next to a small book. Its dimensions would allow both cards and book to nestle in securely. Her fingers fluttered over the box, detecting the hinges and closure. The book lay open, weak fluctuations moving across the inked patterns. The parchment, if folded nicely at its creases, seemed likely to slip into the top. Her thumb crossed a button, shaped like an acorn, which made a light *'click'* when pressed. She checked a catch along the front edge, cleverly hidden within the carving of the edge and repeated the motion, satisfied that she could shut it securely.

The unused portion of the deck lay under the lax fingertips of the Queen. The exposed backside wavered with subtle geometries that rippled with a shallow gleam, drawing reflections from active cards spread in the arena. She eased the cards away from the queen's fingertips and placed the stack near the box, feeling a chill as she detected a slight stir in the queen, hearing the soft drag of fabric as she slowly began to readjust her hand. Tranced or not, Cerra was quite sure she had been observed by the Queen, perhaps even appearing like a ghost.

'You're not going to like it at all when you come to your senses.' Cerra thought. *'And I know you will … sure as I'm stacking the deck with some cards of my own.'* Linarest had set the standard for play during the chess game … she would no doubt understand. Cerra felt like touching the Queen with a reassuring pat. *'Don't go away.'*

She couldn't help but consider how much her role had changed since Captain Ferriman had appeared at her cottage. What would he think of his agent now? She gave him a thought as she backed away from the queen's desk. *'It was a long road getting here, dear Captain, and I'm pretty sure getting out is going to be a lot more difficult than getting in. I'll try not to let you down.'*

Counting her steps, she retraced the ten paces back to the door. The map of the room lay clearly in her mind and she moved to separate the oil lamp by the door from its holder. She eased along the wall to the next table and removed the candles, along with the striker that lay next to the candletree.

The argent wave continued to wash along the walls, making her reluctant to test the door. *'There might not even be a floor.'* she fretted to herself but pressed the latch anyway.

The door swung in on oiled hinges. The other side was fit in a stone pattern that would be a match for the walls and no frame was evident. The spectral blue that had pushed at the walls in the room filled the air as though in a pool. She half-expected the slithering current to carry her off as she touched the floor beyond as though testing water in a pool. Solid stone, smooth and squared as tiles, laid in the same pattern as the room.

Cerra didn't dare step beyond the door. *'Still not that crazed.'* she gritted, for the weight of the spell was stronger, leaving a heavier tone ringing in her ears. She eased herself back inside and let the door click shut. The handle was a lever that released the catch when pressed down. Her fingertips circled the shank and detected a small pin. She knelt and reached into her pockets for her knife, working the pin away from the slot that fixed it to the door. She worked with delicate care, for her slender knife was too big for the operation. She felt the pin move and she thanked the servant that maintained the locks. The knife skipped with a scratching release and she heard the small pin hit the stone lintel with a soft and satisfying pling. Kamir scampered past her ankles as she moved from the door.

"Mind yourself now, little Prince." she whispered, offering the same reassurance to herself. "We've got to be quick as a hiccup. There's no telling what will happen when I box the Cards."

Cerra counted her steps as she rounded the room, removing the oil torches from their sconces. When she returned to the queen's palette, she carefully laid one of the torchieres to the ground and pulled the top layer from the bed over it, a soft blanket of padded silk. She eased back to the desk, the touch of the queen's chair where she expected it to be. The glow of the cards seemed to bloom, becoming more apparent as she circled past the high back of the chair.

'*One last thing.*' She blew out the lone candle over the desk, sure that the room would be left in complete darkness. She would need every advantage she could get.

The book rustled through its pages and snapped closed with the momentum, giving Cerra a start, her heart leaping to her throat. Stifling her nerves, she reestablished the placement of unused deck with a touch, the back wavering with a hypnotic pulse as she felt the corners, feeding her currents as light as her touch.

She tucked the book in first, nestled perfectly to one side. The unused portion of the deck slipped into the adjoining section with her next quick grab. Her nerves flicked again as she heard a creak in the chair. The queen rustled with a sluggish lassitude as though she might be leaning forward.

Cerra tried to dissolve the tension inside her as she concentrated on the wavering glow from the table. The remaining cards had to be collected. There was little doubt that the vacillating depiction of the great wyrm must be the last. Not pausing to think further, she laid the cards marked with *7 Cups* and *10 Roses* on top of the adjacent *Queen of Roses* and placed them face down on top of the others in the box. She could only guess at their players, but *Nepethe*, the Rose Queen, was marked in her sight with the same dry papers she'd glimpsed before, visions she'd only accounted as her imagination.

Cerra picked up the one marked *Nuith*, trickles of energy running into her fingers. She was about to drop the card in the box, a hot coal to toss away. Instead of a burn, the card seemed to illuminate her, casting her image in argent light, the way she saw the demon, the way she saw Yutan. She slipped the card into her pocket, a precaution that came to her in an instant, without a reason to bear it up. A fearsome card still lay in the southern position, the fiery glow of the majic had the same impartial stare as Yutan. Opposing lay the wyrm-like Aeon. The ringing in her ears seemed louder, beginning to crackle like a pitch-wet fire. The thought of the demon gripped her, trapped within the spell that wrapped the towers in its grip. She lifted the card marked Abbadon carefully and pressed it to her lips.

'Yutan.' Her thought reached out like a beacon, bearing the name that bore the demon's soul.

"Turn time, then?" Cerra whispered aloud, echoing the demon's challenge as though the cards needed to hear her words. "Well … top this!"

She slapped the *Abbadon* card down over the glowing image of the wyrm.

In an instant, she thought she saw a fragment of the Void as the cards met. A pulse followed, a toned ripple that waved past her, draining the ringing in her ears as it went. She caught her breath as the reverberations sang themselves clear, the air growling as it expanded behind it as though released from a cage. The glimmerings that traced the cards were fluttering and dying like old embers.

'Now we've done it.' She cast the hasty thought through her mind as she scooped up the cards and tucked them in the box. The parchment began fluttering, it's tracings dashing about, seeking the edges like snakes fleeing a pit. She grabbed it, the folds collapsing in ordered fashion with a life of its own. She fumbled the parchment into its sleeve on the lid and snapped it shut with a loud click.

The chair creaked lividly as the majiced glow of the room was beginning to fall apart in fragments, broken mirrors of light that shattered and wavered away in silence. Cerra tucked the box in close to her and stepped back, turning in the direction of the door, when the Queen's hand slapped firmly around her wrist.

Chapter 50

Each scale that Yutan wove himself into held a fragment of his thought. The bunching of the serpent drew him inside the warp of his existence, memories laid in a row, consuming them to feed his essence lest they dissolve without him, leaving him less than whole.

Following the trail of slithering memory cast him through tighter turns, funneling down through their images as their taste and texture were shorn from his consciousness. The depthless ink of the passage he had created with the Void was left behind him, a gashing rent released into the vortex, which would continue to drift like a wraith in the churning cycle of time. Ideas dissolved from the germs that created them, conclusions reached before thought. Cries and bellows of forgotten terrors rang out as their images were spent. A desperate sorcerer and embattled armies unlocked their grip as the currents of memory spun away, leaving nothing but a darkness that loomed ahead with less to recall and renounce. As he unraveled, deep brown eyes gazed, past him, across him, through his very core, red hair waving like torn banners over their sight.

A sharp pang held him, a stubborn thread that gathered him into the elements that made up his being. The woman's eyes drew him as ever, sightless, yet seeing far clearer than the mortal that created him. The empty, formless ink of the

Void again loomed ahead, the unforgiving prison of his soul, the gateway to his inception, where all thought was abandoned. Memory was shredded as he plunged within the Void that faced him. Only the unstable mercuries of the elements remained.

Within the bleak vacuum, a churning whirlpool shattered at its center, a finite point reached in the abyss, the final calling. Within the capsule of light was the moment of his creation, the body of a hapless young lord, strapped to the rails of an orrery. The sun lay at its center, poised to draw his life into the elements by the incantations of Xerenon. Yutan gazed up at the sorcerer as blue flame signaled the beginning, a fire that started to separate from his essence. An agonizing scream trailed across the room, heard from another time. He boiled within the monstrosity he had already become, giving him the strength to release his bonds and end the sinister alchemy that created him. Another jolt of fire shot through him, the shreds of flame flickered and parted across his consciousness. Brown, unseeing eyes beckoned from within, like the firmaments of his being.

The visage of the sorcerer coldly gazed down through the vision, seeing his consciousness and defying him to stop the sorcery. Yutan glared back defiantly. The moment of change, of retribution, was at hand.

"It is … who … I am." His voice rumbled out as though tolled by a heavy bell, a resonance that could shiver the air. Words that had been uttered before. A truth.

Yutan released the urge to strike down the sorcerer as his eyes softened. Even as the shredded remains of the young man were drawn within the obsidian stone, he kept himself riveted to the energies that created him, an apparition that bloomed before the sorcerer.

"I am in Time … I am more than you can imagine. I am death and life. Abandon me."

His words were proclaimed aloud, a trail left behind him and melding into an echo of '*Abbadon*' that rolled through the Xerenon's chamber like thunder. His demonic vision dissipated with the final energies expelled by the wizard's enchantment. The demon was created.

The fates had played their hands and, in their creation, a new life had unfolded across time. By relieving himself of the moment, refusing its entry, he no longer held the space of the poor wretch being shredded with sorcery into the elements. The curve of Time would not allow him to stay and he watched dispassionately as he drifted away from the fractured image, knowing the cast of his fate. The fall within had been complete, leaving no relative notion of where he was, except woven within a moving curtain of scales where he clung, finding purchase by form or fire. He had forsaken the moment of his birth, leaving him free of Time's inexorable pull, yet adrift in its currents.

'*Yutan.*'

The utterance of his name had enormous power, the secret means to call him forth from the depths, across the rolling bridge of Time, even the formless prison of the Void. A summons. With the articulation of sound, the calming nature of the blind woman's voice caused her image to leap to the fore of his consciousness, a sound that lay in the cresting wave of time, where all events occurred, the 'now' that was continually eaten away by the past. In her moment of agony, she had accepted her frailty and blindness in the face of distress. *'It is who I am,'* lingered as an anchor in his thought.

He held on to it, embracing the summons of his name. Visions of different lives and futures mirrored and crawled within the movement of the scales. In the curling labyrinth of coils, the link to her held fast as he saw her falling into the night.

Small squads, details from the various ranks of the Abbysin army, began assembling on the near side of the river in offensive formations, as their officers sought more immediate answers to the unearthly tempest. Seven squadrons of Imperial horse had crossed the caravaneer's bridge and fanned out in a wide arc well behind them. From his position near the swirling majics that kept the Abbysins close to their lines, Seredan surveyed past the grassy expanse leading to the river, viewing orderly rows of foot soldiers, a phalanx mustered from the closest of the lines, slicing their formations into arcs of three rows in front of the makeshift command. They settled to their knees, shields resting on the soft grass, as though ready to charge or bolt back across the bridge at a moment's notice.

The Abbysin officers who had challenged them, eyed the native horsemen with skepticism. Amid a lot of fruitless cross talk and speculation, each concluded they didn't have the arms they needed, or even if any weapon would be sufficient. At length, the Abbysin officers abandoned the renegade band of Cherros, seeking the safety of their own familiar ranks by the river, poised well away from the sorcerous airs.

The churning atmosphere was both turbulent cloud and scaled light, writhing like a pit of great river snakes, bunched and continually moving. The roar of the chimerous beast was confused by the crackling of the heavens as lightnings hugged the contours, gusts of wind circled like spent exhalations.

As the sun began to lower on the western horizon, the grand cliffs that shouldered the Jimalian peaks began to show in coppers and reds, while the sorcerous maelstrom that engulfed Safrasco, took on a fiery cast. As if signaled by the last rays of day, a green flash pierced the circling storm from deep within, sending with it a low hum that blossomed out, shaking their bones as it passed. The mirrored scales, writhing in the storm, crackled under the impact of the light, shards bursting apart and swept up by the angry currents.

Shattered, the vestiges of the sorcerous maelstrom began to shrink back, collapsing in sinuous torture. Behind the expulsive shockwave, waves of cavalry charged out from the fractures, weaving angry green traces as they left the churning clouds. Tattered banners, worn with age, flew from the speartips of the guidons, the rider's hair and beards flowing white and spectral as they charged the waiting Cherros in the last light of day.

Seredan spurred his horse forward to meet the charge before anyone could stop him.

Chapter 51

Cerra's heartbeat jolted when the Queen's vice-like grip snapped over her wrist. Like jerking away from a hot pan, her reaction was swift and decisive, bowing herself in close and levering on the high back of the chair. It began to topple backward with her push and she twisted her wrist free of the Queen's grasp as she fell with the chair.

Cerra staggered back towards the door with the crash of the chair, remembering at the last moment to avoid the torchiere she had lain on its side. She missed the lamp but the awkward step made her stumble, falling to her knees close to the door. She froze when she heard the Queen's voice, an angry hiss that resonated within the close walls. A clattering of scrolls marked Linarest's location as she stood, groping about her desk and knocking things awry.

"It's you!" Another curse as the Queen knocked into the fallen chair in the pitch-black room. "Where are you!?"

Cerra's heart was pounding, she feared loudly enough for the Queen to hear. Fighting to calm herself, she silently eased towards the door.

"I know it's you … the blind woman. I saw you … don't think I didn't! That fecking red hair of yours." The queen's voice registered like an execration. "I didn't dream that."

Another clatter and stream of unregal curses echoed within

the chamber as the Queen fell over the torchiere lying on the floor. Cerra used the commotion to dart to her right toward the bookcase, crouching between it and the desk.

"I'm here by the door." Cerra spoke in a soft voice that would be hard to trace in the room. She didn't know what to say and shrugged, hoping to keep Linarest away from the actual door, if she could. "I was just leaving."

"No, you don't! You have something of mine." The queen's voice echoed her frustration as she stood, brushing unseen objects.

Cerra remembered the admonishments of Havi concerning the theft of the Cards from the Sybellines, though at the moment it felt like a weak argument. A thief is a thief and the line had always been simple. Until now. She was still Ferriman's agent, a thought that made her feel a touch braver. She whispered loudly again, directed into the stones of the wall to confuse the sound. "Your Sisters want it back."

There was a hiss from the Queen, who was feeling her way back towards the desk and away from the door, awkward stumbles that bumped furnishings and rattled the items on her desk tops. Cerra moved as silent as a wraith, five steps back to the door, ready to bolt outside.

"They put you up to this?" Linarest could not keep the contempt from her voice. "They couldn't come themselves, they had to send a … common … *pfah!* … how did you convince them?"

"I did nothing." Cerra let her voice drift softly, speaking into the wall to dull the sound. She had seen the active intelligence inherent in the cards. The weight of them pulled in her sling as if acknowledging the truth of her thought. "The Cards decided."

"The reading is … not … over! So, I'm not done with them. You … upstart peasant! … I'll find you."

The Queen's voice echoed in the room, desperate and mean, though it varied as if she were looking about, searching for clues to Cerra's whereabouts.

Linarest loomed close by, feeling her way back to the desk where the cards had lain. Cerra remained crouched behind the table. She felt a quill that had fallen in the queen's stumbling's and flicked it like a dart close to where she thought the arras might be hanging. She heard it flop lightly against the tapestry and fall to the stone floor with a subtle click.

"Oops." Cerra whispered softly.

The Queen stumbled as she tried to round the desk and Cerra heard the whump of fabric as Linarest smacked against the arras, sure of her prize and the growl of anger as she came up empty. She eased under the table as the Queen had moved, careful to avoid the papers that had fallen. In the center of the room, she could easily reach the door again, if Linarest stayed where she was. Cerra was suddenly overcome with curiosity. There seemed no reason for the strife caused by the majics provoked by the cards. She spoke facing away from the Queen.

"What do you need it for? The damages have all been done and nothing gained." Cerra took a stab, considering the fortune in gems that had floated about. "You've a new mine … and it's secret. I think you're being greedy."

The Queen moved, coming closer with unsure gestures. It would not be long before Linarest became acclimated enough to the pitch-black room to find the door … or her. Cerra skipped a small scroll to the bookcase and waited for the queen to react before easing back.

"Don't be naive, girl. From the very first day … to *this* one, greed is what drives civilization. I am making history!"

"Your part won't be well received," Cerra conceded softly. She could hear Linarest feeling around the bookcase and if her ears didn't deceive her, she'd likely trip over the torchiere again in a step or two. The Queen tripped as though cued. Cerra darted quietly toward the door, chirping for Kamir under the cover of the curses and clatter made by the queen as she fell.

There was the unmistakable sound of a body hitting hard and Cerra wasn't sure what she heard after that, the Queen's obscenities cutting off with a guttural squelch. A sound akin to ripping cloth and then a series of light taps, clicks that sounded like dog nails on pavers. The steps were hesitant but drawing closer, inconclusive taps that were spread apart.

The entire room felt different, an ominous weight seemed to press the darkness deeper., Each tentative step that tapped closer felt like a squeeze to her chest. The Void offered no fast exit and Yutan was silent. Her madcap errand seemed doomed to fail. She reached for the handle, careful to press it down and not turn it off its spindle as it engaged the shank. The door opened with a sharp click and she spun around it, Kamir knocking at her ankles. Flipping the handle clear, she frantically pulled the door behind her. Just before it snicked close, she heard dotting stabs rushing towards her, which iced the blood in her veins.

Cerra cocked her head in both directions, unsure which

way she might go, seeking a sound, any notion at all that guards or servants were about, yet she heard nothing over the pounding of her heartbeat.

"I'm making mistakes I've never, ever, made before. Here goes another." she muttered, Kamir her only audience.

She put fingers to lips and let out a sharp whistle, one that she was sure her horse would have heard in another town. The shrill note echoed harmlessly away with the clean vibrancy of marbled surfaces with no shouts of alarm registering. She yelled loudly, hoping to raise notice and repeated the piercing whistle when the stone-faced door of the Queen's chamber shook, as though hammered by an inside fist. During the silent moment that followed, like the inner eye of a gale where the storm takes a breath, Cerra put her hand to where the door should be and felt instead a seamless blend of smoothly carved stone and wood. Her breath returned, hopeful that the queen was contained for the moment.

With a sudden blow, the door was shaken violently and Cerra jerked her hand away like it was alive. The wrenching squeal of the frame told her that the hidden panel would not hold long. She steadied herself against the wall, noting that the air came fresher from the left. The faster she could move away from the door, the better.

"Which way, Kamir?" Indecision clenched her murmured plea, hoping the cat could give her a clue, but his quick meow revealed nothing.

She began pacing herself along the wall towards the fresher scents, as fast as she dared, trying to hurry her steps while not falling headlong over some low table or hidden corner, hoping that a stairwell would soon be evident. Falling down one would be preferable to what lay behind her. A door presented itself instead, stoutly framed with polished and ornately carved wood. She eased past it just as a pitiful screech of tortured metal told her the Queen had broken free. The curve of the wall would hide her only for the moment. Waiting to determine the direction of the Queen's footsteps would be far too late. A quick test of the latch proved the door unlocked and she quickly slipped inside, nickering for Kamir to follow and desperately hoping against hope that she had been unseen. She eased the door shut, careful of any movement that might trigger the Queen's attention. Surely, she would test the stairs first, wherever they might be.

"Whichever direction I didn't go." Cerra groused in a whisper as she eased away from the door, unsure of the dimensions of the room. It was neither musty nor closeted and had the unmistakable scent of Sandalwood. The mute spent time in these rooms. Given his spartan habits and bloodless demeanor, she expected to encounter the empty cell of an eremite. Instead, her steps led directly to a soft carpet, four more tentative paces until her shin brushed a richly upholstered cushion of a settee.

'So much for austere'. She eased around it as well as a cushioned sleeping pad with a fur coverlet. The scent of fresh air was held back just beyond her, a deck or patio beyond the door.

'Still a half-beat behind the piper. Which way will my luck turn?' she wondered hopefully as she touched the frame of the door, ears keenly tuned to the hall beyond. Clicking steps that sounded

like knife points on stone passed in the hall. She let out a tense sigh of relief a moment too soon for the clicks stopped a brief moment before continuing on, slower than before.

She edged against the outer door, richly paneled and smooth to the touch and the latch opened easily. A gust of air, charged with live currents that smelled of fresh laundry, blustered in as she pushed against the door. Her unruly hair whipped about her face as she and Kamir slipped out, careful not to let the door slam behind them.

As soon as she took a step forward she realized she was not on a convenient patio or porch. Wind whistled in the open deck from lofty airs, cooled with the moisture of night and largely untainted by the heavy scents of the ground. She eased herself along the edge of the parapet, an arch of stone that would make the platform eight paces across. Curved marble posts marked the overhang and as she stepped to the brink of the balcony she heard the grumbling of thunder, like the tremors of nature on a late summer's day.

Lattices of argent light bloomed in her dark vision. Traces of Yutan remained in the air, circling in wide disarray. She felt as though she were standing on the edge of a high cliff. Only the reassuring touch of the balustrade kept her from reeling back. The shriek of the gyrfalcon that carried on the gusting winds made the impression of standing in a lofty aerie even more pronounced. Dizzy for a moment, she gripped the rail of the balcony. Her stomach twisted a little when she realized Kamir had hopped up on the rail.

It turned again when she heard the door latch click open from the hall. *'Birds never seek the cage,'* was Cerra's fleeting thought, *'yet it seems I've flown in.'*

She could count the steps in her head and the time needed to take the necessary five paces. She didn't hear the approach, the footsteps muffled to silence on the carpet, but the latch on the balcony door clicked on cue. Cerra felt trapped like a butterfly in a web and the spider's image consumed her. She could sense the Queen, or whatever she had become, blocking the open door. Only soft nictations emanated from the presence as it drew closer with delicate, knife-like steps. Kamir let out an uncharacteristic hiss, growling fiercely. Cornered and pressed back against the stone railing, Cerra exhibited a fatalistic element of courage she didn't know she possessed. Instinctively, she held the carved box containing the Cards out beyond the railing, poised above whatever distant rocks lay below.

"Stop! Another step and the game will be Mum's Shuffle."

She didn't know or care if the Queen knew the term for a sore loser sweeping the table of cards and wagers, yet the movement of the Queen held for a moment, tension emanating from her presence like a drawn bow. Currents shifted, the inner door to the hall had opened and shut. Cerra felt like screaming her alarm, but her breath was tightly suspended in her chest as she held her hand extended out over the railing.

The shelled essence of the Queen was looming closer and Cerra defiantly held the box out further. A soft palp, textured with thin armor and waving like a feeler, brushed her arm. Cerra clenched her teeth as she craned her head away, certain of a dire fate. Her blindness became a confining blanket and a blessing, for she feared what she might see with good eyes.

The presence of mass seemed to push her back and she let her fingertips relax their grip on the box. A slight movement came from the door. Cerra's head turned towards it, alert to the presence of another body.

"Stop it." It was a weak plea, meant for the unseen shadow as the clicks of tentative steps seemed to circle around her, Kamir trembling in a low, fierce growl.

A thin blade, drawn fast, sang as it left its scabbard behind the presence of the Queen. Cerra braced herself, certain the sword would plunge into her. The *'chhk'* of the piercing resonated like a knife sheathed in oiled metal. Her shallow breath caught with the plunge of sound but she remained untouched, a high-pitched scream instead erupting from the beastly presence of the Queen. The looming manifestation paused, another gurgling cry escaping as Cerra heard the sword withdrawn.

She tried to shift along the railing as the thing staggered in a weakening collapse. The palp lost its brittle shell as it dragged along her dress, the weak grip of a dying hand replacing it. No sounds came to her ears save the muzzled shake of transformation, fused with the feeble groans of imminent death.

She recognized the power of the silence that remained, palpable within the center of the demon storm that constricted itself tighter around the tower. The mute. She turned to the space where he must surely be, the ring of his sword striking the ground, marking him as he sank to his knees. Cerra let herself ease back from the edge, nerves shivering. There was a pause of a heartbeat before a ghastly moan rose in an empty, keening wail, a tormented spectre of sound unused to existence. It pulled at her, a primal agony she could feel in her bones.

She nearly failed to hear the jangles and shouts of alarm from within the tower, though there was no mistaking the rush of the silent one bolting towards her, the anger and passion of his rage washing in front of him like a tide.

Cerra's breath caught as he pushed her back to the rail, the box of cards flung wide from her hand, cast out into the abyss. She could hear the soaring gyrfalcon scream as the mute grasped her ankle and heaved up, tilting her over the brink. She couldn't release her breath, falling backwards into the turbulent air. Her scream hung with her, unspent as she dropped, her darkened sight latching on to the safety of the balcony like a moon receding into the distance. A single light, one that came to illuminate the treasure she held above all others.

'Yutan'.

The moment of falling was prolonged, a lost time and weight she knew would catch up to her. She wondered if she would feel the ground, a sudden compacting of air telling her it was close.

Chapter 52

Mallbre panted in quiet, desperate gasps, staring after the body of the woman as she dropped into the darkness, red hair and garments rippling like banners in a gale. Her sightless eyes never left him as she fell, as though she could see his soul, pleading for its release. Angry winds whipped about him in a vicious knot as a small bloom of crackling fire erupted from the darkness below, marking the spot where the body must have impacted the ground. There was no victorious feeling, only one less agony to endure. His Queen was dead at his hands, still sticky with her blood. She ruled him, made him what he was. She took what she wanted and he gave it to her, even his voice. He loved her … hated her. There was no forgiveness. None. The fearsome apparition that his Queen had become, that he had slain, must surely have been an enchantment of the blind witch. The certain fall to her death gave him no satisfaction or relief from his pain.

The mute stood transfixed in his agony, the blossoming fire from below ascending in dervish turns. He cast a bleary glance to his right along the rail, the woman's black cat baring its fangs in accusation. Mallbre turned away from the bannister, facing towards the inner hall, wanting to kneel once more at the Queen's feet, then jolting to a stop as the Queen's guards dashed in with swords drawn. They slowed, advancing cautiously as he caught their eye. He dropped his gaze to the Queen at his feet, a final supplication. He made no motion to retrieve his sword, lying next to her body like an honor. Ignoring the guards, he turned again to face the abyss of night beyond the rail. The hellish fire continued to rise, blooming up in gaseous leaps, a djinn of flame and rock. Mallbre felt himself grow cold, a face emergent within the igneous vapors, a face that belonged in the fires of the underworld.

The scorching beast rose to the height of the balcony, shivering at the apex of its ascent like the steam of a geyser, poised in the moment of its ascendancy. Mallbre couldn't look away from the spectral eyes of the djinn, coals from deep in the earth, an immortal soul glaring with deadly intent. The ice of fear, an emotion he long held deep beyond the sight of others, froze his bones, though staring helpless into the face of a demon was easier than facing his own perfidy.

A wave of rock and flame swept back, a fist ready to strike. Mallbre stared back at the djinn, beyond caring. The flame shot forward like a ram, a fiery engine of war that would crush the tower. Mallbre found the notion fitting, though he flinched as the great fist was about to make impact.

Yet, there was no jolt. No collision. No end. Mallbre felt a profound disappointment as he saw the blind woman's black cat, clutched in soft smoke by the hellish djinn. The blazing pyre fell back, its macabre grin flaming away in tatters with its collapse. He felt cheated, angry that the pernicious sorceries had not claimed him too. They had failed. He had failed.

Mallbre turned to face the two guards, his eyes blank and uncaring. It would take a paltry effort to dispatch them as the sight of the flaming sorcery had given them pause. Now, they advanced with caution, swords drawn and wary of greater dangers reappearing behind the mute assassin. Another pair of the queen's guards rounded in from the hallway with no such reservations. Mallbre was certain the whole contingent would soon follow. The added numbers made the effort more worthwhile. He eased his short dagger from its sheath and stepped forward, beyond caring.

Seredan bolted forward the moment he saw the tattered banners whipping from the throwing spear, the roan horse on a field of tan ... Cherros mercenaries. A hundred riders emerged from the glittering wreckage of the sorcerous facade surrounding the northern Safrasco towers. Seredan spurred his horse aside to rear it, holding the banner of Neyith aloft in an attempt to deflect the horsemen.

The ghostly riders turned their charge as they swept around the Cherros horseman, who twisted in a wild rear to confront them. Seredan was shocked by their appearance as they slowed to a canter. To a man, they appeared old beyond their years. Greyed beards covered faces chiseled with age. The riders wore a mix of battered helms, torn leather armor and broken spears. The unmistakable face of a Cherros rode at their lead, staring at Seredan as though a milepost never expected to be seen. Behind him, Safrasco was steaming back into existence in the fading light, as the majicked airs lost their weave.

Seredan recognized the sewn badges on his sleeve and

shot his eyes back to the wizened face of Starrel Thot. He nudged his horse forward as the column came to a halt with the upraised arm of the Cherros leader.

"Starrel!"

The cavalryman stared back for a moment, remembering another time, putting a name to the face. He traced a line across his cheek, tracing an old paint, long since faded.

"You are … Seredan … of the Spotted Horse clan."

The Cherros rider nodded. Starrel turned to look back at the ranks behind him, which remained silent behind the hard glint of eyes that had seen too many battles. Torn badges and the liveried remains of rank and station betrayed a mix of Jimalian and Cherros cavalrymen, who wore the blooded uniform of battles that united them under one banner. He gestured with a slight nod of his head before returning his gaze to Seredan.

"We … have returned."

"Returned." Seredan couldn't help but press. He had given the riders up to the sorceries surrounding the towers. "From where?"

"Where? *Unnh*" A groan or a growl curled from his throat. "Where the battles of men lay out in an endless line. Where else is there?" Starrel looked at him, eyes softening, the father telling the son at long last the secrets of the family. "I am here. You see me … I don't know any more. In the endless passage, the conflicts, I have died five times … and all you see behind me have met their fate time and time again. And still we were forced to ride against another faceless enemy. The reasons to fight lost their meaning every time I died."

Starrel turned to take in the remains of the sorcerous field. Gazing out to the Abbysin army encamped across the wide field by the river, scanning the makeshift lines they had formed as he had before, for a score of other conflicts in the mist. "It is the battle of our age. Does this have an end?" He shook his aged head slowly. "If we are truly in our world again, then I have fought my last."

The Cherros mercenary jabbed his broken spear into the ground and dismounted as though eternally weary of the saddle. The other riders dismounted with the cue, the ostlers emerging from the ranks to gather the horses with practiced but tired efficiency. The last glimmer of sunset limned the storm-wrought towers of Safrasco in a dark red wash that appeared like blood. No moon would cut the dark of night.

Seredan left his horse with the others, determined to keep Starrel within reach. The Cherros cavalryman had the look of a madman or seer and he wanted to determine which. Either might be important considering these strange events. The city could barely be seen within the storm that lay gripped about it when the enraged screech of a falcon pierced the gathering darkness, a cry of anguish, an agony borne from the stone of the towers.

All eyes looked east, a silent gloam settling in behind the airborne cry. Dust and smoke bloomed at the base of the towers, soft edges catching flares of light. In an instant the glamour rose, a conflagration that spiraled up the face of the tower like molten serpents, stretched to their extremes. The fiery bloom hung with an elegant pause before falling back to the earth in a showery collapse. The darkness of night settled in as a solemn finale over the royal towers, an inky curtain with no moon to fight the shadows, or reveal its doom. They were too distant to hear any alarms and signals, though the whole city seemed blanketed in fear, lights damped and shivering behind shuttered windows. The lights of Safrasco seemed like dying campfires, tentative embers lighting its shape. To the east, Saamed flickered with more life, torches in avenues and windows giving the citadels sharp edge and definition. Seredan found himself watching the cities, each light a life, a flame. He cast glances to Starrel who seemed caught up in the same dour fascination.

Watches were set, but Seredan slept little. He wanted to see the towers at first light. The Abbysin and Jimal cavalries had emerged from the sorcery when the spell had broken, lost in ages he may never understand. The red-haired witch had last been seen stepping into a black rent that hurt his eyes, leaving him wondering if he had seen her departure at all. Or her doom. She was a woman of enormous power, despite her even-handed and forgiving nature. Her fate was tied to the broken sorcery. Dawn would break with signs and omens hidden by the night.

The Cherros had a name for a horse that was a persistent trouble-maker, *Tietsi*, a burrowing weasel known for its tenacity. It was also their name for a problem that would not go away. He imagined her wild red hair and sightless, warm, brown eyes. The blind woman was the Tietsi. She would reappear, a constant, like the dawn. He would be awake to see it, another chapter in the tale that was unfolding. If not, there was nothing left to do here.

Chapter 53

Argent light surrounded her, a brightness that made her blink. She felt nothing, no impact that expelled her from her body, no last breath. That exhalation had left her at the brink of the fall, when nothing remained beneath her. Was death the embrace she felt? Was the life beyond so warm? There was pleasure in the heat. It was familiar and the thought of venturing beyond was enticed back. Cerra's mind lay awash with visions of the demon, as though swimming in the cradle of his arms. She inhaled as she became aware of the ground beneath her, a moment flushed with joy.

"Yutan." A slight murmur of her lips, a thought that escaped with that first breath.

'I'll return.' There was a note of anger in his terse thought.

The silvered light of him began to rise, spirals that augured away to the empty skies as she lay staring sightless into the heavens, her back pressed to the ground. Her mind still reeled from the fall. Where? Up the tower! Like a fountain that had reached its peak, the helical path of the demon paused an eternity, suspended like a spray of flowers, before plummeting back towards her in a shower of argent fires. The points of light fell like knives, raining down until her sight was awash in the radiance. Cerra felt the force of it pass through her tired body, the release both pleasure and pain. The earth received it, scorching into the depths below her.

The darkness of her vision returned with her breath. She sought to restore her senses, though she felt strangely content. 'By the gods, maybe I'm falling yet.'

The sudden impact of four tiny paws hopping onto her chest dispelled the notion, as Kamir began to push his head against her chin with a purr. She rolled her head to the right, the luminous vision of Yutan shifting within her dark sight. It appeared he was, 'himself.'

"He tried to scratch me." Yutan's stoic observation made her smile.

"You just have to know how to pick him up." Cerra chuckled, unwilling for the moment to rise. The vision of Yutan showering down around her played over in her head like a remembered dream. "If I ask you to give him a bath, beware."

Yutan knelt down next to her, Kamir jumping over to circle on the other side. The demon's bearing was always so taciturn, the face of one who had seen both the ends of time and the emptiness of the Void. She shuddered. *'So, have I.'* she thought. The eyes of Yutan betrayed him, compassion showing within his steady gaze. She understood his withdrawn nature.

"Can you stand?"

"If you help me." Cerra lifted her hand. She felt she could manage on her own, but why waste the opportunity? He stood and lifted her as though she were no more than a trifle and a small one at that. She let out a little laugh, a chaotic release as she clutched his chest, standing well enough but glad for the support.

"Thank you." She burrowed into him like a cat, knowing words weren't enough. His body motioned in an achingly familiar way. He was bending to a kiss and she rose to meet it.

The unspoken exchange, lips spared words while expressing emotional release, a beginning, the uncertain trial, an inevitable conclusion. Cerra felt the security and familiarity of her home in their kiss, as well as the mercurial nature of the demon who shared it with her. It took little for her to acknowledge his bare skin; given the fires she had been subjected to in the past few months, she felt more than eager to extinguish them on him. She let herself drop from the kiss instead, promising herself to return to the effort as soon as she had something more comfortable than the rocky ground beneath her feet. The piercing cry of a raptor punctuated the thought and Cerra rounded her palm on his backside.

"*Heh, heh.* You may need clothes," she murmured with a little giggle. "Though, I promise you, it makes no difference to me."

"I can return to the airs. There I ..."

"Oh, please, Yutan. Stay with me awhile. You ... the man." Cerra pushed back into him, bittersweet. "So, I can touch you. I can walk. I can find my own way. I can. But ... I'm tired. I'd rather have you beside me ... just for a little while."

"As you wish." Yutan scooped her hair to nestle her head in closer. "We have company."

"Do we now." Cerra gave him a playful squeeze about the waist. "I'll shed my outer skirt. I can fashion something from that."

"That won't be necessary." Havi's voice came from behind Cerra before she could untangle her embrace. "If you hold this, I'll return in a few moments."

Cerra felt her arm being touched and turned to accept what Havi was offering. She knew it would be the box, even before the carved wood touched her fingers.

"Well caught." Cerra reached out to the young woman, turning from Yutan to clasp Havi about the body in a deep hug. "Your Sisters will be pleased."

"It was my good fortune that I liked you immediately." Haviana squeezed back, glad to hear the appreciation but uncomfortable with the praise. She guided Cerra, unnecessarily, back into Yutan's arms. "Here. This one holds you better than I and you're better cloth than none at all. There's a charming city lurking behind the towers and no one minds the drying lines at night."

Cerra chuckled, thankful to have Yutan to hold on to.

A sliver of a moon appeared late, casting enough of a dim light to sparkle the waters of the lake. Below the northern towers, the thin glow edged the surfaces of the promenade that faced the water, empty of its casual strollers and vendor carts. Cerra sensed the brush of cooler air approaching, promising a fresh dew at sunrise. The box holding the sorcerous deck lay nestled in her sling bag, a curious weight that Haviana was reluctant to bear.

"I have too curious a nature. What should I do if I play with it?" Havi waved away the notion. "Besides, I was only told to find it and I've no head for cards."

"Nor do I." Cerra agreed. "And don't discount yourself.

Heh. This is not a deck I would play with either."

Haviana had assured her that one of the Sybellines would retrieve the deck, one better suited to safeguard its magic. "With you, it has better protection than even the Sisters could offer."

Cerra wondered what Kamir made of the gyrfalcon as it whisked away with determined flaps of its wings. She knew it was Yutan's strength, not hers. She turned her head to see the argent glow of him, facing outward like a sentinel. They stood on a landing at the edge of the promenade, the sloping fields leading to the river beyond them.

"Do the armies still lie beyond?" Cerra felt as though days had passed since she had stepped away from Sugar into the bleak rent of the Void.

"It is an hour from dawn. Their fires still burn. They remain by the river except for a few." Yutan pointed to the closer ground. "A half-league away ... no more."

"Not far at all. I imagine that must be Seredan and the Cherros. They have my horse ... and I want to go home." She hoped she sounded more tired than miserable. She wasn't sure herself. "I wouldn't care at the moment if it was only twenty spats, I don't want to walk it."

Cerra put finger and thumb to her lips and let out a shrill whistle. The trailing note could be heard in a thin echo across the valley.

"It is my guess you were heard." Haviana remarked dryly. "And every dog in both cities is on alert." The faraway chorus of yelps confirmed her observation. She leaned close to Cerra. "You must teach me that. It's like the cry of a gyrfalcon."

"I think the bird has a better voice." She squeezed Havi's hand. Someday Cerra would have to quiz her on the sensation of flying. She remembered the empty sensation of falling. *'Like that, but without the sudden stop.'* she laughed to herself.

It wasn't long before the thump of hooves on the ground could be heard. Cerra could tell by the way Kamir was twisting around her feet that it was Sugar approaching. If she were a cat, she would be doing the same. She stepped out to meet the horse, who trotted up eagerly and pushed at her hand with its muzzle.

"Sugar. I don't get along by myself half as well as I do with you," Cerra pushed back, the familiar scent and feel, another reminder of home. "I promise, I'll put up extra hay for the short days."

Sugar snorted with what Cerra figured to be agreement.

"She'll guide you true, as ever." Haviana scratched along the side of Sugar's neck. "I'll … be along behind you."

"Of course." Cerra reached out to give the young girl an embrace, pulling her head in close. "You've been behind me all this time. Your Sisters haven't anything to concern themselves with. More likely it is your father that worries."

Havi let out a little giggle and returned the embrace. "We share our worries equally. If you knew my father …"

Cerra turned to Yutan. She knew without asking that he would prefer to remain distant from the crowded arena of commanders and their ranks which were sure to confront them. It meant little difference to her, for his presence around her kept her buoyant and alive, so far away from the measured world of her cottage.

"Spare yourself the army." She added a humorous, conspiratorial tone as she reached up and let her fingers trace the contours of his face. "Or should I say, 'spare the army'."

He held her hand briefly to his lips with a brushing kiss. She thought she'd melt when she felt the hint of a smile.

"You are the one to defeat armies without raising a sword." Yutan kissed her fingers once more. "I will stay with the clouds … the better to watch over you."

Long shadows stretched across the fields, the sun laboring to rise over the mountains to the east. Seredan was sure one of those shadows would yield the red-haired witch. His mouth tightened in a satisfied smile. Neyith was truly a spirit of the Cherros. Her horse had answered her call an hour before the dawn broke. Another summons rang in the air with the dawn, a signal that blared from the towers of Saamed. It was obvious in the reactions by the makeshift lines at the river, that some parlay had been announced. They were readied and alert with the exchange of messengers that galloped back and forth from Saamed to the main encampment by the river. Within the hour, trumpets sounded again from the Saamed towers as an advance contingent left the gates, five riders followed by a larger, more stately formation.

"The Ducet…. King Risherade, by the banners." Seredan remarked. Seredan glanced to the north and saw a lone rider dressed in a Cherros robe coming towards them with an easy gait. The gyrfalcon that lingered in her presence circled overhead, the trail of a dusty djinn in her wake. He smiled and nudged Thane.

"It's my thought there will be one more voice in the parley. *Eh* ... our *Tietsi*. Are they ready for her?"

"*pssh* ... I'm not and I know to what to expect!" Thane nodded off towards the Abbysin lines, who were adjusting themselves in preparation of the Ducet's arrival. A pavilion was being staked up, the ranks of archers and foot soldiers retreating to the far side of the river. The horsemen that remained appeared lined up in ceremonial display. "She may tell them all to hare off. Nicely of course, that one ... *heh* ... and she'll give it to them so they'll look forward to the journey."

"It's time we move too. And not to the rear either ... our charge needs an escort." Seredan was intent on hearing the witch's tale, another chapter to an epic story he would be telling into his dotage. Thane and the others looked equally as energized, hoisting themselves to saddle with eager leaps. Starrel and the band of mixed cavalrymen who had emerged from the sorcery, were quietly gaining their mounts. Their focus had also been on the lone rider advancing from the towers of Safrasco, appearing like the last remnant of their enchantment. The ghostly troop of cavalrymen took up the pace, trailing in unhurried formation behind the robed Cherros.

Cerra heard the Cherros coming and Yutan confirmed her suspicion that it was Seredan and his Hand coming to greet her.

'*Others are behind. Horsemen.*' There was a long pause in his thought. '*Neither dead nor alive, shed from the sorcery of the wyrm.*'

Cerra considered the contradictory nature of his appraisal

as they closed the distance. Seredan led his Cherros horsemen into formation around her. She continued at her leisurely pace as Seredan settled in at her side.

"Thank you for taking care of Sugar." Cerra said cheerily. "I hope I wasn't gone too long. It feels like a lovely morning. What day is it?"

"You know better than to ask a Cherros the name of a day." Seredan replied with a faint chuckle. "The sun is out. Ask instead what time of the field it is. As far as the day, I'd say it is one of reckoning. We approach the Abbysin lines and so does another spectacle, a king and some other chiefs, judging by the herd of banners and the polish of the guards. They arrive first. We have our own escort … though the polish is all but gone. They pull aside for us to pass."

"Polish is nice if one wants to look good, and none can rub a gloss better than courtiers. The soils of living suit me fine." Cerra smiled as she thought of the royal displays that seemed to accompany their every moment. She felt serene. She had been shriven by the Void and a ghost of her had fled with the fall from the tower. That passage had enlivened another layer of her being, the pictures in her mind brighter than before, as she absorbed the sounds and scents around her. Much of her contentment came from the familiar smell and gait of Sugar and the calm presence of Kamir in the saddle.

Cerra and Seredan rode along the line of cavalrymen, facing forward as though in review. Cerra could feel their stolid regard. There was a scent of old books in the air, leathers and papers aged by their ancient knowledge. The Cherros mercenaries who had escorted her to the brink of the enchantment now returned, their one-time foe now folded in with common purpose. She thought of Yutan's words and the charge that had swept them away to the ravages of Time. They had been purified in different waters and she could feel their regard. There was an aura of finality that came from the assembled cavalrymen that could be heard falling in behind her.

"I think stouter fellows I'll never find. Their polish is in their hearts." Cerra said, humbly. The ranks of her adventure were gathering around her, adding to her composure and making her feel insignificant in comparison. "How many are along for our procession?"

"A hundred … Jimal and Cherros both. If you ask, they'll not admit to any nation. Not any longer." Seredan waited over a few rolling paces of their horses before speaking further, a pensive thought voiced aloud. "I think they have seen more than I care to ever know."

Cerra nodded, stroking Kamir who sat nestled in the saddle, content. His quiet companionship was steadfast. "Much in the world cannot be viewed … or even recognized by our senses. Only our hearts have the power to touch it."

"*Pssss..st*" He made a rude noise, a Cherros insult which mimicked a horse pissing on stone, as he eyed the Jimalian contingent nearing the Abbysin lines, on a pace with their own. "I see people and armies that suffer from the hearts of men that rule them. What powers do they touch?"

Cerra had experienced first-hand what some rulers were prepared to do to achieve their ends. Lies and deceit appeared to be a common tool, though the thought of Katarin Moors, who took an entirely opposite view, gave her encouragement.

It was a question for philosophers, who knew more of men's nature than she.

"I don't know. I only know my own heart. That's difficult enough to translate."

As they neared the pavilion, hastily erected for the occasion, she could hear the activities of preparation ahead of her, with a lot of the attention apparently directed at the procession she was leading. "It appears everyone has arrived. As for translating, how is your Jimalian?"

"Good enough to trade horses."

"Then you know words that I don't." Cerra chuckled. " … and shouldn't."

Risherade and his entourage of captains and advisors, had descended from their ornate saddles and were now ensconced in padded seats, ready to face their Abbysin counterparts in discussions. All eyes instead, were on the procession of ragged, ancient cavalrymen that approached from the direction of Safrasco. Compared to the stately arrival of Risherade, the column looked more a collection of refugees, led by a red-haired woman in a Cherros robe and flanked by their riders. A large raptor circled, the white spread of its wings bright with the sunrise. Behind the column, the dust of their passing whipped into a djinn that rose in thin clouds of brick-colored dust, leaving a blush to the early light that hung over them like a protective shroud.

The Abbysin officers murmured among themselves, recalling a similar procession leaving their lines in what seemed like another age. Tension and suspicion had bristled between the officers of both camps, yet the arrival of the ghostly column created a neutral space between them, the appearance a portent to the discussions at hand. Commands were directed at them, words that Cerra knew very well and Seredan held up the column in response.

The red-haired woman was helped from her horse by the Cherros front rider, as a pair of the time-aged cavalrymen dismounted and took the tattered guidons from their standard-bearers. She grasped a long, slender cane from her horse's saddle, which appeared much like a scepter in her hands as she was led with deference to the pavilion, a black cat sauntering behind. Risherade recognized her from the consulate at the oasis of Vale d' Houri. Removed from saddle and procession, she looked very small and unassuming. The Ducet called at her before she could stop, requiring her to present herself as though she was a maid in his service.

"You there. You're nought but the blind adviser from the Standish embassy. What are *you* doing here!? … And, at the head of a troop of … old men. Wherever did you find them?" He spoke with a hint of mockery, looking around with a smug grin, expecting the other assembled dignitaries to join with him. Their attention was held more by wary curiosity, than by Risherade. Cerra took a last step as Seredan's guidance allowed and gave her head a slight bow, acknowledging the ruler's presence.

"And a good day to you too. You are their King. I remember you as well." Cerra didn't want the likeness of a cured ham to invade her imagination again, but it did. She kept from smiling, though the image made it much easier to address the Ducet.

"The men with me are their own men … I'm in charge of no one, thankfully, for I'm a horrible guide. As for why I am here, I was led by circumstance, good sir. Surely, I would much rather be at home than standing in front of two armies and wondering what's for lunch. It's been a most trying day."

There was a short ripple of stifled laughter from the assembly that quieted at Risherade's angry look.

"I shan't keep you then, else I'd invite you to sit. We have important matters to discuss. However …" Cerra could feel his smugness, his audience only quietly responsive. It was obvious he did not have as much support as he would like. She could fairly anticipate Risherade's next words. " … Before you go, since you are an 'adviser' … maybe you can leave us with a little … advice … make the trip worth it, so to speak."

"Good sir, I could not hope to give you any advice as to military matters. You're surrounded by men who know much more about such things than I. War is not a good occupation for someone like me, whose ambition is to make healing balms and deliver babies." Cerra knew the last reference would make them uncomfortable. Men eternally ignored the ways of women. She turned a bit, trying to gauge the number in audience.

"Since you were kind to ask, I have just one piece of advice, your Lordship." She deliberately looked past him, as though by mistake, to the Abbysins, whom she'd identified by their murmured dialects. "Within the veil of the sorcery, you all witnessed the fate of Safrasco. You're lucky to have their towers still, their beauty a testament to all that pass beyond them. If you wish to clash to satisfy your pride, or your coffers, then that is the result. You have seen the grand towers, their fate revealed and lying in ruins."

"And what did you have to do with that? I ... the Jimals ... we've been assaulted with what? ... dire sorceries!? Who do I hang for those offenses?" Risherade demanded. "And now, you turn up ... like bad digestion." The news surrounding the murder of his wife by her trusted bodyguard, was hot in his mind, discovered by her guards in the royal tower after its reappearance from the sorcery. The mute was severely injured and chained in cellars so dank not even vermin attempted nests. "Maybe I should hold *you* accountable."

Cerra could feel the air surrounding them bristle, even before she felt Yutan's warning in her mind. She had no intention to reveal any more than possible and quieted the demon's concerns, for the moment.

"The illusion surrounding the tower was none of my art. I have no talent for great things save those I've already described," Cerra replied carefully. "I *can* tell you that time has served me well, though I was caught in its grip. You've seen the towers. If you wish to know more, something of greater value, ask the men that also entered into the sorcery ... what price is to be paid by the conflict." Their agonies could be felt even now, weighing like the solemn airs surrounding a burial. She couldn't help but add a quiet afterthought. "Men of two nations have already suffered a lifetime for your sake."

As though cued by her words, Starrel and a Jimalian captain by his tattered badges, stepped forward, calloused and greyed with age. The insignias of Abbysin and Jimal could scarcely be identified on the ragged pennants that graced the tips of their short spears. Starrel scanned the assembly with hard eyes.

"We are the Hundred. We have fought … and died, many times… in all of your battles. If not for the likes of us, you could not fight your wars." There was no taunting or derision in his voice, just the finality of one who has seen too much. "We will no longer be blamed for defeat nor robbed of our triumphs. There is no victory for anyone except a handful of Lords. We end our service to the wills of vacant men."

As one, the two ancients inverted the guidons and jammed them into the ground, the faded pennants tearing from the shafts as the points buried. They regarded the assembled generals and officers with indifference, beyond the reach of their orders and schemes. They turned and walked with weary determination back to their horses, leaving the assembly with a murmuring unrest. Officers from both camps looked at the blind woman as though she were an oracle in their midst, the riders the cast of her future. None attempted to the stop the riders as the Hundred cantered away, heading west towards the river. A trick of the light, or the wash of dust from their passing, made them dissolute and hard to focus on as they gained distance.

"Their words are worth much more than mine." Cerra offered as the sounds of their passing diminished. Although she had no official capacity, she thought she'd give a little weight to the embassy recognition. "When I last spoke with the Ruler of Ceniago, she entirely advocated peace. That is what you can expect from the Stands. Your armies serve you much better growing crops than dying in rows. I think you have your victories at the cost of a few."

The gravity of the ensorcelled riders still hung over the gathered dignitaries, or maybe it was her own presence. They shifted and sniffed, obviously looking at each other to frame some kind of response, though no one was willing to speak first. Cerra couldn't think of anything to say that would be more effective or true than what they had just heard from the aged Starrel. To reveal all that she knew would create more problems and solve none. She may have said too much already. Diplomacy would lay in the court of the Jimalians and, judging by the collective restraint shown, they clearly had no strong will to continue their fight. They didn't have to know the source of the terrible majics lay within her satchel and none seemed the equal in callousness to the dead Queen.

She stepped back slightly, bowing first to the Abbysins to her left and then to the Jimalians, on her right. "I appreciate being able to speak a few words to your august company. I won't hold up your discussions any longer."

Seredan offered his elbow and Cerra took it gratefully. The Deck weighed heavily in her satchel and she was anxious to quit the assembly before more questions were asked. The Jimalian king was caught in an uncomfortable silence, his adjutants unwilling to press the strange woman further. Cerra turned away, their unanswered questions lingering in the air. Sugar nickered as she reached the saddle. She slid her walking can into its sheath under the flaps of the saddle and Seredan helped her gain her seat.

"Can we make the well in short order?" Cerra felt like weights had been lifted from her, just turning in the direction of home.

"Two days." Seredan replied. The tale he expected at the start was far from the one he received. Neyith made for an account that would brand him as a notorious fabulist, a story-teller not to be believed. The best kind. "We will fly. You have the Cherros for your wings."

Epilogue

Yutan and Haviana joined Cerra at the well, soon after the Cherros had left for the upper plains. Cerra had negotiated for two horses, which Seredan considered a gift and reminded her that adequate payment had already been made for those horses, as well as another herd. Plus, they had the wealth of their tale, though they doubted to a man that many would believe them.

Cerra had wanted to travel directly to the Black Gate and home. She felt as barn-sour as a horse and surprised that Sugar wasn't as eager to return. Havi made clear her intentions to travel to the port of Oskara and Cerra felt immediately that, in spite of the long trek she had already experienced, the diversion would be good for her. The spice markets of the Sultan Sea port city, offered rarities she could seldom find in the outlying shires of the Upper Stands.

Haviana flatly refused to take possession of the Deck. "It is too much to carry and far safer with you … for now. Only three in the world know where the Cards lie and two of you stay with it, far better guardians than I could be. I would like to say that my Sisters can all be trusted. Obviously not. There are only a few I would even trust to tell and they're all far away. My dad … my mother, of course. I can't tell one without the other … those two are a pair, trust me."

She considered the Sybelline Mother who entrusted her with the mission, Susinna. Her sharp, hawk-like senses rested easily there too, but the journey had made her cautious of the motivations of those in power. The Lady Tamarina without doubt, though she rarely showed herself. Haviana felt she would do well to proceed with caution with all she encountered.

Cerra looked forward to seeing the blacksmith, Luskin. He could fashion her another pair of metal hair pins. The box of cards was tucked without ceremony into her saddlebags, as well as the two bags of esmeraldes that the assassin had left behind. There had never been an appropriate opportunity to return them to the Jimalians and she had quite forgotten they were there until after the Cherros had left the spring. The 'Neyith' banner flew from the oak, proclaiming the arbor protected by the Riders. The Lady Moors would be a good second choice for the gems, for at least she would use them for the good of all.

The route to Ishkar was well-traveled and they soon fell in with a troupe of Zigani caravaners they overtook along the way. As was their custom, the Zigani's entertained themselves with music when their stock was set and the meals done. Cerra joined in with occasional rounds on a borrowed viol. Havi danced and even Yutan showed regular traces of a smile, as though remembering another time.

"This is a far better way to travel than with the royals," Cerra laughed. She had let Havi lead her around in a dizzying circle dance, which led her back to the wagon where they were sitting. "I would leave home more often if I thought I could put my cottage on wheels."

"I think that is the sevenleaf talking," Havi giggled. "I wager you'd get a dozen leagues down the road and you'd have half a hamlet following you."

"And that's the mare's milk talking." Cerra smirked, squeezing the girl's hand. *"Heh, heh* ... but you're right. Every time I leave my shire, people take interest. Why the first time I wandered farther than town I had an assassin trailing me! Your attention is so much better. I think I shouldn't have a more marvelous friend ... besides him." She added with a whisper as she looked at Yutan's argent glow.

"An assassin trailed you this time as well. The same one." Yutan pointed out. He urged Cerra to lay back against him. Kamir was waiting patiently for her to settle before curling into the folds of her skirt.

"Ah. Sinjin. I'm glad he found a bigger fish to fry than me." Cerra burrowed into Yutan's shoulder with a contented smile. *"Mmmph.* I wonder what happened to him? Do you think he'll be after me again?"

Yutan's answer, as ever, was succinct. "It is not to know."

Cerra decided that was well enough advice, guidance she would surely use. She smiled inwardly, relieved of the uncertainties of the game, placing her hand over her heart where the Nuith card lay, held securely in a small pouch.

"It's in the cards."

Patan set down his cup of watered ale as Pryan was thrown into the room and forced to the floor by the guards. The Guildmaster wore the simple garb of a smith, as solid as the steel gray of his hair. The Hashini who had captured him let it be known that he would not be taking any more commissions and accepted only a minimum of expenses, enough to validate the transaction and nothing more, allowing that he was looking for a home. The assassin had tossed a fortune of gems on the table, the wealth the would-be Lord apparently carried about him, stuffed like a miser's bedsack. There had likely been more as he considered the assassin's meagerly charge, but even so, it was a fitting return, far more than the cost of the arms and he had confiscated the shipment as well. If the assassin had kept some for himself, it was no concern.

The fat Lord made for a terrible trader and now groveled on his knees, stripped of his finery and wearing only a coarse wool tunic. One fortnight spent fermenting in the cellars of the Oskaran guildmaster had left him unshaven and ripe.

"You've finally achieved your true potential." Patan waved a hand under his nose, purposefully. "You are as rank as your trade."

"You are mistaken." Pryan's eyes had a bleary wine-drunk look, as though pleading for another cup. He tried to stand. "I was making a good deal … for you … and …"

"Quiet!" One of the guards roughly shoved Pryan back to his knees. "I seriously doubt my benefit ever crossed your mind. I've thought quite a bit … more than you're worth … about what to do with you on my way here. Death crossed my mind many times."

"You can't … *unh*" Pryan's feeble reply was cut short by the butt of a spear.

"I can. Remember that. Having you killed would have saved me the cost of feeding you. I spared every expense, of course." Patan took another sip of his ale and set it down with a satisfied smack of his lips. "You should know that your assets in the Stands have been reclaimed by the Courts and your name stricken from their rolls. The money-changers of Safrasco and Abbysin, where you keep your shabby accounts, have 'donated' any remaining funds. I imagine their charities are uncles and cousins. It doesn't matter, and I assure you, there wasn't much. You tell a good story, a much greater tale than the poor showings of actual events. As it is, I've decided to show mercy."

Pryan's head, hanging with slack dejection, jerked up, suspicion flinting his eyes. "What're ..." he slurred.

"The fact is, I really don't want the taint of your blood on my hands. I've taken everything from you that I want. Your death isn't even worth the pleasure of revenge. I'm leaving your fate to the kind people of Oskara."

Doubt, fear, advantage ... all played across Pryan's face as he puzzled out the Guildmaster's words.

Patan reached into a pocket of his leather vest and pulled out a gold piece, an Imperator by its stamp. He watched as the wretched sap's expression changed, avarice tightening his face. He flipped the coin in the air, a long flickering arc that Pryan fumbled and caught with shaky arms.

"For your time ... and a warning to stay away from my door." Patan gave him a bland look, the valuable coin hardly worth interest. "If you want to change it for something you can use on the street, I recommend Mesgildi the pawnbroker ... at the wharfs. I imagine you'd be robbed and beaten for a thief anywhere else."

"Th-thank you …" Pryan gripped the gold coin tightly in his hand, for he did not even possess a pocket in his tunic. His mind was churning. The right play and he could double his effort on the coin. "Mes … mes …?"

"Mesgildi."

Pryan repeated it absently as he tried to stand. The guards shoved him back to his knees.

"Don't bother. Let him stand … if he can. Take him to the pawnbroker's and throw him to the kerb."

Pryan made blurred promises as he was wrested out of the room, a welcome quiet descending as the door closed. A large, bald-headed man with a stiff beard stepped from behind a curtained alcove, the hammer and leaf of Smithy guildmaster embroidered on his vest. He went and sat across from Patan and poured himself a cup of ale from the ewer.

"If you don't mind me sayin' … judging that one, I wouldn't give him a chipped copper, much less an Imperator. It's your business, though."

Patan gave him a sly look and snickered with a predatory grin. "He will find the coin is like the lot he left me … and like that bastard … all veneer. *Heh* … gilded lead. The scum is now Mesgildi's business."

The guildsman gusted out a laugh. "Fish food or the slave pens? I put ten coppers on the fish."

"You're on, for the sake of argument, but it is all the same to me." Patan let his indifference show. "I have greater concerns. Couriers have word of a stand-down on both fronts, so the forges have to be turned to other uses. I have directed the smithies of Abbysin to reserve iron, though our trade goods need bolstering. I would know what Oskara's craftsmen intend."

"It's easy for us. The Jimalians have been looking these past months for mining supplies. They've been as quiet about it as a woman the day after she's married, so it must be a big find, I should think. I can have the smiths easily take their contracts.

Patan nodded, glad the Guildmaster had ready alternatives. He made a mental note to himself to send a spy to the Jimals. One who knew mines.

It was late-summer by the time Haviana returned to the Sybelline abbey in Luminaria. The temptation had been to make the distance at one go, ignoring the dangers of staying within the animal for too long. With a certain degree of irony, she considered time was on her side and she frequently settled along her route to experience and enjoy the surroundings, so far removed from her own world.

She felt even more reason to delay her return, now that she was steps away from Susinna's chambers. Given the travels and adventures, the routine of school and training would be hard to adjust to. She had settled in one of the gardens, announcing her return to no one. It didn't surprise her, though, when Susinna's scholarly aide opened the door and waved her in with a smile as if anticipating her return, the same warm welcome she had received at the beginning of her mission. Given the messages she bore, she wondered if the welcome would remain.

She sat in the chair as the Abbess' attendant left, closing the door discreetly behind her. It had only been a few months, yet Havi sat with an attentive ease, without the naïve uncertainty that she had felt the last time she occupied the chair. Susinna observed the same change in the young girl, making a point to address that first.

"Haviana … if I'm any judge, you were equal to the task. You look fitter … and wiser for the effort."

"Yes, Mother." Havi's nod was nearly non-committal, waiting for the Abbess to continue.

"And … ?"

"I located the deck as you wished." Haviana's sharp, hazel eyes looked directly at the Abbess, sure of her decision. "It's no longer in the hands of the player … one of our sisterhood … unknown to me. She called herself Linarest. She had become Queen of the land named the Jimals."

Haviana didn't miss the slight purse of Susinna's lips, telling her that the woman was known. The Abbess' forehead tensed and her eyes lost focus for a brief moment as a sad thought passed behind them. She continued as though the news was expected.

"What happened to her?"

"In the end she was slain … by her bodyguard." Haviana felt reluctant to divulge the entire tale. Her part had seemed so minor that to tell it would not give the importance the story deserved. "That wasn't her downfall though. She ran into someone she couldn't stop, a blind woman of simple means."

"And the deck?" Susinna asked patiently.

"It rests with the blind woman now. She'll recognize the bearer of this." Havi smiled, an inward satisfaction as she handed over a small green gem that burned with verdant clarity. Ceding the gem to the Abbess was a gift. She no longer had the weight of the secret bearing down on her. "She cannot see to play them and she is well-protected by the gods. I couldn't think of a safer place."

 end

Excerpts from

❖ ᴄнᴇ ʙᴏᴏᴋ ᴏꜰ ᴄнᴇ ᴎᴜᴍɪᴎᴏᴎ ❖

ʀᴏʏᴀʟꜱ

Nuith (Queen of Quills)

The Queen of Quills is a woman of adaptability, persistent energy. and calm authority. *Nuith* has the positive attribute of giving birth to 'form' in creation, as seen in the harvest of autumn behind her and is also responsible for the cycle of birth and death. She holds her wand with a pine cone at its crown, the symbol of prosperity, fertility, hedonism, and pleasure. The pine cone represents the male seed issuing forth. The eyes of *Nuith* are blindfolded, denoting the internal intoxication and absorption she has with her life. She is fully committed to accomplishing her goals.

Nuith, before she knew who she was, had hair of ebony and walked with a panther by her side. As she learned her nature through awareness, her hair turned lackluster and blond and her panther showed the spots of a leopard. When she fully realised who she was and expressed herself fully in the world, her hair turned red. The panther returned to its true self, though spots hidden in the dark coat of the great cat remain as a reminder of the dark times experienced in the past.

The Queen of Quills represents the process of self discovery and awakening, even though this means one will have to experience dark periods in life. Unaided she is powerful. Surrounded by her suit, she may become the most potent card in the Royal Houses.

When inverted:

Nuith will want to control and dominate her environment. The Queen of Quills must fight the tendency and find the ability to adapt to get on in the world. She knows her contradictions and perseveres in their spite. Her paradox: True power comes in serving others, not dominating, so she must strive not to control events

Nepethe (Queen of Roses)

The Queen of the Roses heads the pillars of severity, shown by the grove and indicates the limits being formed here. *Nepethe* is logical and intelligent hence a suitable place is the head of the pillar of severity. Her advantage is being able to work through difficulties intellectually to a regal standard. Her staff speaks of her pointed actions, clear, sharp and incisive, and gilded with attractive promise as shown by the lustrous rosebud at its head. Her shield bears a Rose upon its steel, speaking of the necessary union of fragility and strength, though the shield is captured by a spider's web, an indication of her systematic intrigue. She is the most beautiful of the Royals, drawing influence to her with an irresistible force. It is her logic that makes her an invincible ally, though alone, the weakest of the Queens in the Heraldry.

Nepethe is the archetype of the analytical, with a razor-sharp ability to get to the heart of the matter. She has enormous clarity and has the intellectual ability to judge and discern impartially, without the influence of strong emotions or sentimentality. Unlike the Queen of Quills, she connects to others through an intellectual understanding rather than an emotional understanding.

When inverted:

The Queen of the Roses has the ability to be overly critical, cold, judgmental and cynical. allowing emotion and old obsessions or internal identities to get in the way of clear judgement. The Past can distort her intuitive psychic qualities, leaving her unable to find her own identity as too lost in another's influence. She deals with that which involves the mind, not the heart. Can also be vengeful, temperamental, shallow and cruel.

Briah (Knight of Swords)

The Knight of Swords flies through the air on his winged steed, his sword pointed over a mariner's compass that entails the sky, indicating the clarity of his direction. *Briah* is the only one of the Knights to be shone without armor, such is the strength of his purpose. Instead, his surcoat is tailored, a loose cape depicting his freedom, with the badges of many realms blazoned on the trappings of his steed.

When inverted:

The Knight of Swords will have periods of inertia if the vigour of these qualities are absent.

ãrcaṇa carỏiṇạl€

Azinnan (The Empress)

Azinnan takes her name from the ancient word 'Zinza', which means 'the Door'. The Empress is the Door that all souls must pass and then return and so she is the recorder and arbiter of births and deaths, acknowledging all Life equally. The book on her lap is hidden from view, denoting the arcane knowledge that lies in possession of the Empress. Her path is the only path to venture through the hidden Vales of the Gods, which again emphasizes her complete mastery of knowledge, both arcane and profane.

When inverted:

Azinnan becomes the demagogue, for unopened, the Book on her lap comes to represent the habit of viewing all things at the surface, without any depth or understanding.

Aeon (Οιβρώσκωø)

Aeon is Time and is taken from the folk word, Obrōskō "to eat". It is a symbol for the eternal cyclic renewal of life, death and rebirth. The skin-sloughing process symbolizes renascence of souls, the snake biting its own tail a fertility symbol. Note the tail of the snake is phallic and the Wurm's mouth open like the entry to the womb, its feathered crest flowered and engorged. The divine power coiled round upon itself becomes the symbol of immortality, as it slays itself and brings itself to life, fertilizes and gives birth to itself. Obrōskō is limned by the element of fire, which is responsible for purification as the old is swept away to make way for the new. Obrōskō slays himself yet brings himself to life, in seed and birth. He embodies the One, who proceeds from the discord of opposites, wherein lies the secret of the *prima materia*. A decision has made a major impact on your life. Riches and Fortune lie eternally, ever growing.

When inverted:

Aeon tells of a near death experience which will have a major impact on life, warning all of repeating the same destructive cycles without taking stock and learning from the experience.

Abbadon ~ (Demon)

Tap into the power of *Abbadon* and tap into the energy of life itself. Invite his power and invite death and rebirth. *Abbadon* is concerned only with the ability to manifest life with no sense of morality. Nature has no standard, for morality is cultural and only Man wishes to make morality a defined notion. *Abbadon* does not take sway with human morality. His nature is the process of creation, whatever form that may take. In his hands, death is creation.

The closer one gets to truth, the more one can see the contradiction. This brings about the need to see life in a different way. Fear *Abbadon* above all. Embrace *Abbadon* above all.

When inverted:

Impulsive and compulsive. It can become trapped by its potency and seduction over a long period of time.

Babalon (Desire)

Babalon is most associated with desire of the sexual and therefore creation and life, but her darkest secret is about death and dissolving identity into something higher. She ignores 'purity', for all men are in denial of their nature as humans. All have a carnal side. *Babalon* knows if Desire is repressed it becomes as much a burden as relenting to it would be. It is the working of *Babalon* to believe what we want to believe when we are under her influence. When those are lost to *Babalon* in this way there is a transformation of energy and her victims die to the moment.

When inverted:

Babalon attracts the wrong powers to relationships or allows over thinking so that the will to move forward becomes scattered on endless unproductive thoughts.

the Magus

Magus alone is unnamed and without orientation and represented as both male and female. The balance is shown by the sun and moon and divergent talents that create the whole of *Magus*. As seen by the quill, *Magus* is given the secrets of the pen, a demonstration of intellect and the vision to communicate through writing. The inventions of words through the pen is the dual creation of form & illusion. The flowers express the pure potentiality into the physical universe and also where it resides beyond embodiment implying the creation of art. *Magus* is shown to connect the arcane and earthly dimensions, acting as a bridge between the two to manifest his goals. *Magus* represents both truth and falsehood, wisdom and folly.

Hermite (Soul)

There is only the self to return to for all answers. Alone and indépendant the *Hermite* answers to no one.

énûmq élış

No Suit Rules the Enûma Eliš for the elements have no moral implications. They are impartial. However the energies transmitted by them permeate the moral bounds of humankind and their influences are noted.

Marid (Water Shifter)

The Water Shifter exemplifies the qualities of ambition and practicality. *Marid* is frozen by excesses built up of energy not flowing harmoniously. Water has evaporated and she is buoyed by the steam, though weighed down by the her hard edges. From the gold cauldron pours the limitless potential of the gods. The cold beauty of *Marid* is her strength, defeating those as they fail to take another risk or make effort in the future, hiding away where they can't be disappointed again. Goals of the material benefit from the energy. When played well it can indicate favorable investment.

When inverted:

The cold of her visage leaves the land empty and nothing will grow.

Gigant Cawr (Stone Giant)

The destructive aspect of *Gigant Cawr*, who descends upon the heart of man, implies solitude and independence, to follow our true will and bring some order into the chaos. Use the destructive power of Gigant Cawr to peel away all those aspects of life which are not serving the highest good. In the process he has the vision to move away all that does not serve him to make room for that which does. Played to the upright, can denote removing obstacles from a situation in order to get better insight into it.

When inverted:

The Giant removes without thought that which is not serving him at the moment.

Ddraig och (Fire Dragon)

Ddraig och emanates the qualities of Strength, Intense Emotion, Sexuality, Aggression, Temper, Dynamic Leadership. When applied correctly, the Dragon denotes a swift, sudden and strong action taken. Creativity and luxuriance, blooms and flourishes in its passing. Strongest in the Summer and in the North quadrant.

When inverted:

There is no virtuous goal to focus on and the wyrm becomes aggressive and cruel.

Simargh (Air Kite)

Simargh rules the airs of the material universe, though will not dissolve entirely into formlessness and so holds on to the last vestiges of form or matter. By this means, the Air Daemon finds itself as meddling in human affairs in the same way that the Wheels of Fortune meddles in the lives of men. Fortune is blind and so the wheel spins and stops in random ways and all are goaded into action to change things by the power of will. *Simargh* represents the unpredictable in life. An unexpected change which will be favourable, may not seem that way at first. With the element of Air, change is about to happen and soon.

When inverted:

There has been a turn of events that are not in your favour, a downward spin changing the fortunes significantly, seemingly for the worst. Circumstances arising outside of control, renders the unwary helpless and powerless. A run of difficult circumstances may also be a result of poor decisions.

CꙆER~RꙆ
Castles of the Kings

Castle Pinnacle

Suit: Quills

Rooted in Earth

Security. Castle *Pinnacle* represents directed willpower exerted over a long period of time. The castle rises upward from the fertile earth in granite as dark as aged metal. Circling in continuous harmony, stair and gangways compete in their weave to the top. The bottom of the castle is in repair while the very top is still in the infancy of it's construction. A Quill, denoting it's commanding suit, adorned the forefront, floating in the air as though dropped from the feathered Roc that circled around the castle's peak.

There is nothing to challenge the view seen from its formidable peak. *Pinnacle* is the mightiest of the *Caer Ri.*

Steadiness is it's strength, shock in sudden change its weakness.

Script denoting the ancient Iokonian '1'

Castle Perilous

Suit: Roses

Rooted in Fire

Change. Castle *Perilous* is rooted in Fire and embodies Danger at its core. This embodiment of the *Caer-Ri* represents multiplication of materialization and sterility. Great riches are possible, though through it, a will can develop which has not understood anything beyond its own purpose. Results becomes its lust and will devour itself in the fires it has indulged. Description: The castle balances dangerously close to the edge of the abutment it rests on, with only one causeway allowing entrance. Although the exterior is richly adorned, cold lifeless stone supports it and from within it's dark exterior, fired light emits, as though given life by one angry flame.

Perilous' might derives from the level of the power wielded from its center and so can be the strongest of the *Caer Ri*, depending on its Rule.

Script denoting the ancient Iokonian '2'

Castle Tower

Suit: Swords

Rooted in Air

Balance. Castle *Tower* represents rulership of life and empowerment of the Common. Neither good nor bad, it represents the quality of harmony were the cycles of life run their course for good or ill. The element air hangs between the turmoils born between fire and water. It can also represent long periods of stalemate without a clear choice for the way forward, ending with no decision and no harmony.

Description: The castle lies firmly wedged between two ledges of rock, built of a thick rotunda of stone with a green and white ensign fluttering from its shingled peak and festooned with green clovers and white floral wreaths. Below the wedges of rock that grip it, the remainder of tower hangs like a mirror of itself, inverted as though pointed to the lands beneath it. *Tower's* strength come from the support it receives from the hearts that dwell with. *Tower* will never be the strongest nor weakest, but may endure the longest for its stability. Because of its balanced nature, there is no inverted view to claim.

Script denoting the ancient Iokonian '3'

Castle Destiny

Suit: Cups

Rooted in Water

Completion. Castle *Destiny* represents contemplation and glorification of the Divine. There is Truth in the mundane. Fertility, marital peace and prosperity reign within, calling for an ease in associations and partnerships. Overindulged, it can represent the dearth of acquiring a multitude of material things only to find them incapable of fulfilling.

Description: The castle rises from beneath turbulent waters and is approached by eight causeways, radiating from its center like the meditative signs of the mystics. It signifies the formation of the Life Tree, the lotus forming the pathways. The spire is elegant and water cascades from its peak. Castle *Destiny* is the weakest of the four, though nearly invincible when paired with the Knight or Queen of its Suit.

Script denoting the ancient Iokonian '4'

minor arcana

3 of Quills ~ (Messenger)

The *3 of Quills* facilitates communication, inspiring both mediation and mystic speech as shown by the raptor with a quill in its beak. Known as the Messenger, it transmits the unknown through the known as it is shown to fly through a portal of one realm to another. Through the Messenger, communications infer patience and the exploration to discover truth, identified by the trailing vines surrounding the portal. They represent previously hidden knowledge, tangled and indecipherable, yet open to view.

When inverted:

The Trey may jeopardize clear communion by promoting impulsive ideas or actions and charging ahead without a prepared plan. The Messenger is subject to a solitary heart and restless intellect.

7 of Cups ~ (Mastery)

The *7 of Cups* denotes the mastery of emotions, a sign of incorruptibility and sincerity. The top Cup collects nothing, yet continually pours, the bloodless serums dwindle as they pass to the six cups below, showing the distillation of unneeded weight and lusts of emotion. When paired with the Rose this mastery promotes success for all new creation. The cold reality of the Seven sets a model and example for others. By lack of emotion the Seven portrays the spiritual to be at the mercy of the Cups of the material. The Seven shows reliability to settle disputes or conflict. Mastery of emotion is depicted by the over filling cups marking the memory of past lives, past atrocities and useless recollections, sadness from loss and induced bitterness. What exudes in the passing are refined extracts, poison in their purity, which drain into the fulgent lotus, its petals both swollen and withering under the immaculate severity.

When inverted:

Unable to face ones fears, triggering dispute, anger, intervention, violence, loss of direction, imposition of one's will and relentless struggle. Indifference to others' emotions. The spiritual are at the mercy of the material.

Ace of Swords ~ (Sorrow)

The gleaming sword resembles the purity of the weapon represented by the Ace of Roses, though here it is scarred by use. It pierces the fragile petals of a flower which is held between two crissknives in front of a dark and chaotic background, neither deep ocean nor sky, yet both. The knives hold the flower by their points in a delicate balance as the sword pierces it, holding it in place upon the blade, which accordingly is inscribed with the word of the law. The flower is Justice and the damage of the sword allows for its power, as it remembers the conflicts of the past and envelops those in its sphere. The need for justice is borne in regret. Alone, the *Ace of Swords* has little power. Adjacent to the Major Arcana, it increases the power of the ruling card and its own ten fold, such is the weight of its sword.

The damage to the sword is old for it is Sorrow, sorrow over past hurts, losses or separation. Sorrow applies hard lessons on the desire for relationships and becomes a natural event that all will experience. The Ace is also bound to the cards of justice and adjustment, so there is a link to Sorrow in the universal law of cause and effect. All existence is inherently Sorrow as all are separated from the purity of intent and is quickly replaced by a damaged element. When positioned in the positive, the Ace of Swords finds moral purity and innocence in the flaws of its nature.

When inverted:

A dark and hardened attitude finds root, and the runes of the law are upended.

5 of Cups - (Distraction)

The *5 of Cups* represents the conflict of the actual and the desired. Within the cups are found Courage, Audacity, Bravery. Will and Creativity. They are juggled by a clown who faces backward, while the visage incorporated in his hat controls the spin of the juggle. The Five invokes the powerful use of words that inspire calm. It will avoid conflict wherever possible. Any indication of tension or conflict is anathema to the Five, who views the motions of his work through the filter of his hat, indicating the wish that the conflict would simply go away. Can unify opposite principles.

In the Inverse: Triggers dispute, anger, intervention, violence, loss of direction, imposition of one's will. Corruption occurs while distraction is placed in the Cups that the Five brandishes in his juggle. The *5 of Cups* has a tendency toward rashness and decision making which does not resolve the problem. Unable to work with others and see their point of view, instead will force their opinions on you, citing the strength of his Cups.

9 of Quills (Endurance)

The *9 of Quills* provides for latent or hidden powers to become awakened and applied towards the practical. The Nine further represents a continued directed willpower which has been exerted over a long period of time. Despite all the flux and change the challenged keep on going, finding the strength within despite being exhausted. However, the strength detailed in this card is one which has great flexibility due to its close association with the moon, which makes the challenged entities very adaptable as well as tenacious.

When inverted:

The *9 of Quills* will show lack of flexibility in dealing with the current situation.

Ten of Roses (Gain)

The *10 of Roses* provides good luck attending material affairs, favour & popularity as well as a general period of improvement in all aspects of the endeavor. It oversees settlements and financial gifts. Good luck as well as good management in financial affairs for the Ten involves financial security after hard work and planning. That this gain can be at the expense of others without penalty for the reward, symbolized by the flourishing Roses, is clear. Wealth creates power with its generation.

Beneath the floating coins, marked by the signs of the

heavens, ornate fish represent the living energies that cause the wealth to be buoyed up. Wealth may be lost unless applied constructively as part of the energy needed to stay harmonious. On the occasion that wealth becomes too important, it loses its value and becomes a burden, a stagnation of remains. Rather than becoming a fertile pond, it festers instead much as a cesspool, too thick with waste to engender growth. Upright, the riches are supported and inverted, their weight becomes a burden, offering the rose no support. Wealth created can be put to best use in meaningful ways in the world, remaining the cushion which benefit the fish and rose.

When inverted:

Wealth as a symbol of energy will eventually degrade in its essence as well as a become a complication, – perhaps a warning that material possessions in themselves may not bring about success or pleasure.

Beware what is wished for.

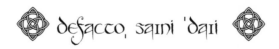

Acknowledgements

As ever, a number of people make a book possible, no single effort gives a story life. The characters have to be cited for their contribution. They certainly give the story its animation and, once they've been drawn, I'm merely along for the ride, somehow herding them all forward to the inevitable conclusion.

It would be impossible to give enough credit to my editor and friend, Blue. Her keen eye and timely suggestions have added dimension and rhythm to this story in a way my voice alone could not. Her dynamic creativity is further experienced within the illustrations throughout the book.

The collective environment of Nelson Mountain Gardens made this book possible too. Mary, Annie and Jessica, Michael and Jason. A farm is all about growing and nurturing things, something they all take to heart. I don't know where I'd be without them. The San Juan island spirits remain vitally important; Dr. J. and family, Kit, Travis, Rebecca and especially Jessie Carter, who has been at my back and supportive since the beginnings of the first book.

Finally, my sister and life-long friend, Sally. Along with Dale, her husband of 30 years, she has been a lodestone that keeps me from drifting too far away. And yes, there was a real live Kamir, a stellar black prince of a cat.

the author with his dog, Pacoloco
photo: Gretchen Ottoson

GREG SCHERZINGER has lived most of his life in the
Pacific Northwest, spending the bulk of his time as a TV
Producer/Director. After a successful seventeen-years in
broadcasting, he moved onto a 41' sailboat, *Tigerlily*, cutting
a lot of ties with the normal career path. Thirteen years on
a sailboat allowed for many adventures, cruising as far north
as Ketchikan Alaska, as well as crossing the Gulf of Mexico
and sailing the Bahamas and ending on San Juan Island. The
writing bug bit him in Friday Harbor, yielding "Demon of
the Black Gate, while a year in Todos Santos, Baja California
generated a second book. Today, he continues to write novels,
living on a small ranch in the Coast Range of Oregon.

also available at the usual outlets

The House on Chambers Court
The Wizard of Grimmer's Wharf
The Henna Witch
Demon of the Black Gate

Connect on-line
bluerunebooks.com
GJScherzinger on Facebook

Made in the USA
Columbia, SC
31 August 2020